PAYNE OF THE PAST

AMBER PAYNE — BOOK 4

JEFF BRACKETT

Payne of the Past
Copyright © 2022 by Jeff Brackett. All rights reserved.
First Print Edition: 2022

Cover and Formatting: Streetlight Graphics

No part of this book may be reproduced, scanned, or distributed in any printed or electronic form without permission. Please do not participate in or encourage piracy of copyrighted materials in violation of the author's rights. Thank you for respecting the hard work of this author.

This is a work of fiction. Names, characters, places, and incidents either are the product of the author's imagination or are used fictitiously, and any resemblance to locales, events, business establishments, or actual persons—living or dead—is entirely coincidental.

ALSO BY JEFF BRACKETT

THE HALF PAST MIDNIGHT SERIES

Half Past Midnight
The Road to Rejas
Year 12

THE AMBER PAYNE SERIES

Streets of Payne
Payne Before the Storm
Payne and Sacrifice

OTHER NOVELS BY THE AUTHOR

Chucklers, Volume 1: Laughter Is Contagious
Pangaea Exiles

SHORT STORIES BY THE AUTHOR

Apex (in the *Prehistoric Anthology vol.1*)
The Burning Land
Ghost Story

The most recent information on Jeff's publications can be found on his Amazon Author Page.

For advance information on new releases, sign up for his mailing list at https://sendfox.com/jlbrackett. Or to read his works as they are being written, you can support him on Patreon at https://www.patreon.com/jlbrackett.

DEDICATION

For Shamra,

We'll miss you, dear friend. You shared your light and brightened our lives. Our world is better for having had you in it.

DAY 01
TUESDAY

CHAPTER 01

Amber rushed in, powering forward on cybernetic legs, then dropped to her knees and slid beneath her opponent's blade. She jabbed with her stun blade and heard the satisfying curse as it delivered its charge. But Amber didn't escape unscathed. As she moved past, she felt a sharp jab in her left shoulder, and her arm spasmed. Abruptly numb and useless fingers dropped the left blade, but she swung back blindly with her right. The muscles on the left side of her neck tightened with the electrical charge she'd received, so she couldn't even turn her head to see where she struck. But she knew it was a good hit by the solid feel of the training blade hitting flesh.

"Dammit!"

Smiling at Scott's curse, Amber rolled to her right side and pushed to her feet. She turned just in time to see Scott fall, and she laughed at the sight of her friend grasping his jerking leg. Her last strike had connected with his thigh, and the training stun had caused him to lose control of the limb.

"Still having fun?" she asked him.

It was a standing joke with her team that Scott had a warped sense of fun, often rushing into situations that would cause others to pause, all in the name of entertainment. Scott's reply was decidedly nonverbal, though the extended finger he showed her communicated exactly how he felt about her joke. Before either of them could say any more, the door at the far end of the training room opened, and their new boss, Tinasha Gibbs, stepped into the gym.

Fem Gibbs was accompanied by a white-haired man carrying a narrow black case just under a meter in length. The white hair appeared to be unrelated to his age, for his face had a youthful vigor and a mischievous smile. Amber assumed the hair color was either a cosmetic affectation or simply a genetic predisposition to premature graying.

Amber stepped over to Scott and extended her left hand to help him to his feet. The two of them stood and faced Gibbs as she stopped at the edge of the sparring mat.

Gibbs looked them over for a few seconds before speaking. "You're both doing very well with your training. I've been told no one else here can even come close to you when it comes to rough-and-tumble blade work."

Amber narrowed her eyes. In the months she'd known the woman, Gibbs had never been one for compliments unless they were used as a prelude to an unpleasant surprise. "But?" she asked, waiting for the other shoe to drop.

"But you're both undisciplined. You've learned your skills on the street, and it shows. Your instructors tell me the two of you are nearly unparalleled when it comes to sparring, but they feel it's not your skill that makes you so good. It's your enhancements."

Scott shrugged. "So? You don't tell a strong man not to use his muscles or a smart man not to use his brain. It's just a part of who he is."

Gibbs nodded. "True. But neither of you seem to take the combat training seriously."

"It's hard to take an instructor seriously when I can beat him on the mat every time we spar. I mean, if that's the case, then who's really teaching who?"

Gibbs looked at Amber. "And you feel the same way?"

"To a certain extent." She tossed her stun blade to the mat. "You've had us training with your people for eight months. You told us your combat instructors could teach us to be better, but so far, Scott is the only one who can even touch me on the mat. No offense, but I think it's only natural that we should question what your people really have to offer us when it comes to fighting."

Gibbs shook her head. "You just love proving me wrong, don't you?"

The man beside Fem Gibbs touched her arm and stepped forward.

Amber noted with interest that the other woman fell silent at his touch. "I see you are no using pads or face shields. Are you having them available?"

Amber noted his accent and foreign speech patterns as she pointed to the door through which Gibbs and this mystery visitor had entered. "You passed through the locker room as you came in. They should have something for you in there."

His smile grew as he shook his head. "Apologies. I am not being clear in my meaning. I am asking if you have padding that *you* use for training."

Scott shook his head. "We find we don't have much use for it. The stun charges only last a few minutes, and we both find the pain to be a great motivator."

The man placed the case he carried on the mat and unlatched it. "I am to ask you to make an exception this one time." He pulled out two training blades. One was just a bit shorter than Scott's, perhaps sixty to sixty-five centimeters long. The other was about the length of a long knife, more like thirty or forty centimeters. They appeared to be of exceptional quality, even for a group with the deep pockets of the Fixers.

Amber began to feel a bit uneasy, as if she was being set up for some great joke. She glanced behind her at the observation gallery high on the back wall. Sure enough, the gallery was full. Her sparring sessions with Scott often drew several spectators from the other classes. As Gibbs had said, no one else here could touch either of them when it came to bladed combat. But never before had she seen the gallery so packed that there wasn't enough seating to accommodate all the spectators.

Yep. We're definitely being set up.

Before she could ask what was going on, though, Scott had already jumped in with his mouth running full speed. "You act like you expect to do something with those fancy toys."

Amber edged closer to him. "Scott?" she whispered. "You might want to think a minute here." But he ignored her.

"I do," the man said. "I expect to test you... possibly to teach you."

Scott grinned. He understood, as Amber did, that this was some kind of challenge. But Amber also saw that while the man before them might

3

be unknown to her and Scott, the audience in the gallery seemed quite familiar with him.

She looked from the mystery man to Gibbs. "Who is he?"

"This is your new instructor," she said. "Maestro Brent Harris. You should be honored. He's very particular about who he takes on."

"There is no need. There is no honor yet. I do not decide to accept them. Do not know yet whether or not they are worth my time."

Again, Amber noted the patois and accent, but she couldn't identify it. She didn't think it was Spanish or Esperanto, but it was definitely a Latin-based language. It was enough to tell her the man either came from one of the ethnic boroughs or another part of the world altogether.

Scott raised one cocky eyebrow at the man. "Maestro, is it? The problem, so far, is we haven't found any instructors here who are worthy of *our* time. What makes you so different?"

Maestro Harris pointed to the blades Scott and Amber had dropped on the mat. "Pick up your weapons, and we shall to see."

Gibbs backed off the mat, moving to the far wall. Amber exchanged a look with Scott. Despite her certainty that they were being set up, she had to admit to being curious about what this man had to offer that the previous instructors didn't. She and Scott turned to get their blades. As they stepped away, she sidled closer to her friend. "You do realize this is an ambush, right?"

He glanced back. "They sure seem to think so. That doesn't mean it'll work, though."

"True." She considered. "How much juice do you have left in the tank?"

Scott's adrenal pump gave him extra speed and strength while he tapped his internal reservoir. Once emptied, though, he crashed, and crashed hard.

"We haven't been going too long. I haven't gotten my warning yet. I'm guessing I should be good for another fifteen minutes or more."

"Then you take him first. If you win—"

"When I win."

She couldn't help but chuckle. "Then you can deactivate your pump and start refilling your reservoir."

Scott hefted the training blade he had retrieved. It was custom-made to the same length and weight as his own sword, but the edges were dulled, and the weapon delivered a stun charge when it touched someone. He waved it in a quick circle to reassure himself of his control then turned to face the maestro.

Amber picked up her own two batons, similarly matched to the flame blades she typically carried. She started to step away as Scott nodded to Harris.

"Let's play," Scott said, his smile almost vicious.

"What setting do you train at?" Harris asked.

"Seven."

Harris nodded. "Acceptable." He adjusted the dial on his blades.

Amber raised an eyebrow in surprise. On a scale of one, the equivalent of a bee sting, to ten—the incapacitating shock of a LEO's stun baton—seven was more than most people were willing to face on the training mat.

She started to step away from the men on the mat, but Maestro Harris stopped her.

"You are sure you are not wanting to get your pads?"

"No, thanks," Amber said. "It would take longer to put the pads on than the match will last."

The maestro gave a quick nod. "On this point, we are in agreement."

Once again, Amber started to leave. As she stepped off the mat, the maestro stopped her again.

"Fem Payne?"

She turned back with a raised eyebrow.

"You concede the match without even to try?"

She pointed to Scott. "He's got the first match."

"No," he said. "You both have first match."

Amber turned to face him fully. "You want to spar both of us?"

He smiled and pointed back to the mat. "Please, to humor me."

She considered him. The man was a bit shorter than Scott and carried himself with the balance and poise usually seen in top-level dancers, gymnasts, and yes… martial artists. She had to admit, his presence was a bit intimidating.

But she finally nodded and stepped back onto the mat. She faced him, observing the placement of his feet, his balance as he rose on his toes before sinking back down, as if anchoring himself to the mat. She watched the rise and fall of his chest as he breathed slowly.

Maestro Harris held both of his training blades in his left hand. He raised his right fist and touched the back of it to his forehead then opened his palm to touch his chest and bowed in a gesture she recognized as some sort of formal salute. Scott must have been familiar with it because he returned the gesture without hesitation. Rather than risk bumbling the salute, Amber simply bowed to the man and raised her batons.

The gym was suddenly filled with the hum of the maestro's stun batons powering up. Amber and Scott's batons answered. There was a split second of stillness, and then Scott shot forward. Harris parried Scott's blade aside and stepped to his left, away from Amber. The man just barely managed to avoid Scott's blade. But evade it, he did. Scott whipped around, pivoting on the ball of his right foot, keeping his blade aligned on the maestro, who skipped just out of range.

Amber was surprised when Scott missed the man. Harris hadn't moved unusually quickly, yet he managed to stay just outside the range of Scott's blade, almost as if by accident. She decided she needed to get into the fray. He was about four meters away, at her two o'clock. A confused-looking Scott was at her eleven. She watched for Scott to make his next move, and the second he shifted his weight, she jumped to the opposite side of the maestro, faster and higher than a normal human could, to trap the man between herself and Scott.

That was what she thought was going to happen, anyway. The reality was somewhat different.

Scott slid in, smooth as silk. Amber jumped to where she expected Harris to move. Logically, he should have shifted to either side or backed out of range of Scott's blade. Instead, he threw the shorter of his two training blades, striking Scott on the cheek. A level-seven stun charge to the head dropped her friend like a rock.

Even as Harris threw the smaller of his two weapons, he spun to meet Amber's attack, advancing to her left as she flew toward him. When she landed, he was beside her.

Amber started to pivot to face him, but his left hand, now empty, slammed into her bicep and shoved. Amber staggered slightly, stumbling for only a second. She knew immediately that he had her at a disadvantage, and rather than push a bad situation, she jumped up and back several meters away from him. She landed lightly on the balls of her feet and glanced past the maestro at Scott. The charge to his head had taken him out of the fight, and he lay unmoving on the mat.

Again, she jumped… up and over the maestro's head, hoping to keep the man guessing as to her next move. He watched impassively as she flew above, well out of his reach, and landed beside her fallen friend. A quick glance showed he was going to have a pretty wicked black eye but would otherwise be fine. Still, it was a reckless attack, and it angered her that the man would risk injuring her friend to make some sort of point.

She turned back to Harris, leaping forward as she wove her training blades in an interlacing figure-eight pattern. It wasn't terribly effective as an offense in and of itself. But it was nearly impossible for an opponent to break through, and her two-bladed attack had a slight advantage over the maestro's single remaining blade.

She advanced, forcing the man backward. Then he stopped, reached out, and tapped her blade with his own. It was a light parry and threw her blade off-center by the smallest amount, and only for a second. But it was enough to give him an opening.

Keeping his blade engaged with hers, Maestro Harris lunged at her, slightly to her left. Amber was concentrating on disengaging her blade from his, and his sudden move caught her by surprise. She tried to turn, only to find his free hand on her left arm once more, jamming it across her right. She had a moment of anger and panic as she realized he had used her own left arm to block her right, even as the pommel of his training blade came down on her hand. She felt the crack of breaking bones, and her left blade fell to the mat.

Knowing she was beaten, Amber still fought through her pain to at least get a single strike in. Calling on her enhanced nervous system, she inverted the blade she still grasped in her right hand and pivoted away, spinning backward with all the enhanced speed she could summon. She stabbed the blade behind her as she moved and was rewarded with the feel of the tip striking the man across his thigh, even as he slashed his blade across her abdomen. Amber convulsed as the stun charge forced the air from her body, and she fell to the mat, gasping as her lungs tried to remember how to work again.

She gagged, struggling to draw breath, and rolled to her side as the maestro limped toward her. He bent over to give her another of those infuriatingly calm smiles. "You are dead. Both of you."

She nodded but managed a feral grin of her own.

He furrowed his brows. "This amuses you?"

"No," she managed after a second. "Not that."

"What, then?"

Maestro Harris jerked rigid as a partially recovered Scott Pond jabbed the tip of his blade into the man's back. He held his weapon there for several seconds to maximize its effect.

Then Harris fell to the mat beside Amber, convulsing as he, too, suffered the aftereffects of a training charge. Cradling her broken hand to her chest, Amber managed a weak laugh.

"*That,*" she said. "That amuses me."

CHAPTER 02

It took a minute before Amber was able to stand again, and even then, it was only with Scott's help. He pulled her to her feet, and the two of them left Maestro Harris twitching on the mat. They limped out of the gym, silent but for the occasional groan or gasp of pain when one of them moved the wrong way.

Missy Hutson was waiting for them as they exited. She was a Fixer Amber had met on a few occasions during her training. She belonged to another team, but the two of them had struck up a quick friendship. Amber wondered if it was because of their shared stature, since Missy fell within a few scant centimeters of Amber's diminutive height. The look on the woman's face as she and Scott came through the door told Amber this wasn't a congratulatory visit.

"Let me guess," Amber said. "Gibbs?"

Tracy nodded. "I'm supposed to escort you both to her office right away."

Amber gently raised her broken left hand. "Can it wait? I'd really like to spend a few hours in a Doc Box."

Missy winced. "Sorry. She's pissed."

"Isn't she always?"

"True. But some days are more fun than others."

Amber turned to Scott. "Time to face the music."

"And you might want to hurry." Missy jerked her chin at the clear window on the door to the gymnasium. "Unless you want to have another go with Maestro Harris."

Amber looked over her shoulder to see the maestro beginning to struggle to his feet. "No, I definitely don't want that. Come on, Scott."

Pissed was an understatement for Gibbs's mood.

"What in the blue-fuggled hells do you think you're doing, pulling a sneak attack on Maestro Harris? Do you have any idea how hard we worked to get him to come and evaluate you two? The man traveled here from Novo Brasil because the rest of our instructors have given up on you!"

Scott shrugged. "To tell you the truth, we've pretty much given up on them too."

"With all due respect," Amber added, "so far, the instructors you've had us working with haven't been up to the skill level you said they would be."

Gibbs glared at her. "Still trying to prove me wrong?"

"No, Fem. But I think your bladed combat trainers here could use some improvement."

Scott chuckled. "I'll say this, though—this guy is the first person you've thrown our way who was worth our time."

"I am glad to be knowing I am worthy opponent."

The calm voice came from behind them. Amber closed her eyes with a sigh. She took a deep breath and turned slowly to find Maestro Harris standing in the doorway.

Amber inclined her head in a small bow. "Maestro."

He returned the gesture. "Fem Payne." Then he looked at Scott. "That was…" He looked past Scott to where Gibbs was still seated. "What is the word… *sorrateiro*?"

"Sneaky," Gibbs provided.

Harris nodded. "Yes. Sneaky. You cheating."

Scott shook his head. "There are no rules in a fight. And if there are no rules, there can be no cheating."

Harris narrowed his eyes a moment before suddenly grinning and turning his attention back to Gibbs. "*Obrigado*," he said. "Finally you bring me *guerreiros*." He and Gibbs exchanged a few more words in that unfamiliar language. Then Harris spun on his heel, leaving them alone with Gibbs.

Amber looked back at her new boss to find the woman grinning. "What's going on?" she asked.

"Maestro Harris has decided to train you. You begin tomorrow. Make sure all of you are in the gym by 09:00."

"All of us?"

Gibbs nodded. "He wants to train the entire team."

Amber frowned. "No offense, but how is he planning to train Jordie or Richard? Jordie's no fighter, and Richard's a mountain."

Gibbs shuffled through a few tablets, scanning the contents as she spoke. "I'm interested in finding that out myself. But if he says he can do it, then who am I to question him?" She waved her hand in a dismissive gesture. "Go take care of your hand. We're done for today."

Scott and Amber left her office. He walked her to the bank of Doc Boxes in the huge medical facility downstairs.

"You get the feeling we've just been set up?"

Amber shrugged, wincing slightly at the pain in her hand. "I get the feeling she expects the Maestro to tame us."

"Yeah." Then Scott grinned. "Ought to be fun, eh?"

The hand was still a little tender after only an hour in the Doc Box, but Amber was in a hurry to get home. The abbreviated session set and mostly healed the bones, and that was enough. She could live with the pain until she got a follow-up session in the morning. She would just need to be careful with it until then.

The *message waiting* indicator on her dash console caught her attention as she settled into the driver's seat. There were two messages. The first was from her best friend, Shamra.

"Hey, sweetie. It's been a month since I've seen your face. That means you're working too hard again. Come on, girl. You deserve a little happy too. We need another girls' night. Maybe drinks… dinner? Call me and we'll work out the details. Miss you!"

Amber smiled. It *had* been a while. She'd try to carve out some time this weekend. Saving the message with a reminder to call Shamra back, she looked at the second message in the queue. The detail box attached to the indicator showed it was from her old friend and former boss at Securi-Tech, Chief Jon Fischer.

Amber activated her navcomp, tapped the *HOME* icon, and engaged the pod's autopilot. Then she turned her attention to the message, hesitating only slightly before tapping the icon. Chief Fischer was something of a father figure to her, and he had fought against his superiors during the political blowback from her last case there—the case that had cost her the job she had loved up to that point, and her badge.

She had moved on, but he had stayed, and she wasn't quite sure how she felt about that. She couldn't blame him, but it was difficult to separate him as a person from the company for which she now felt such disdain. But the company was not the people who worked there. She still had friends at Securi-Tech—good people. She couldn't blame them for the actions of the board of directors. Fischer was still a good man.

The smiling face of her friend and mentor appeared on her dash screen. "Hello, Payne. I haven't heard from you in a while and wanted to check in." His expression was a little reserved. He knew she hadn't approved of his accepting a new contract with Securi-Tech, but he'd explained to her that they had made the offer too sweet to ignore. They needed someone with his expertise to run the investigative branch and had been willing to pay handsomely to keep him. So while it had stung a bit that he had stayed, she couldn't really blame him.

"Listen," the recording continued, "I was scanning the night sheets, and I came across a case I wanted to let you know about. I wouldn't bother you with it normally. I know how you feel about Securi-Tech, and I can't say that I blame you. But this case, it's something you might want to take a look at. Something you might take a personal interest in."

Fischer reached forward and did something out of range of his screen's vid pickup. He continued speaking as he worked. "I'm attaching the file for you to look at. If you're interested, meet me at the address in the file. I'm keeping it off the books until I hear from you, but I'm going in to interview the witness tomorrow. Once you read the case file, I think you might want to be there too." He looked directly at her from the screen once more. "I hope to see you tomorrow."

The screen blanked, and she saw the file-attachment indicator. Her finger hovered over the icon for several seconds before she reluctantly pulled it back. Nathan was cooking dinner tonight, and she knew herself well enough to realize that if she got pulled into a case file, she wouldn't be able to think about anything else. She would brood over it, which would make her a lousy dinner companion and would probably spoil her evening with the man who she was coming to realize she loved.

The thought made her smile. Neither of them had used the word yet. They were content to let the relationship coast along as it had for the last several months. But she relished the unspoken seriousness of lovers in the early stages of a life together, and she didn't want to screw it up.

That thought firmly in mind, she sent the attachment to her tablet and put thoughts of crime and mayhem out of her mind for the rest of her trip home.

"I'm home," Amber announced as she walked in. The scent of spices and cooking food wafted through the air.

"Dinner's almost ready," Nathan called from the kitchen.

Amber smiled. At eight months into their relationship, this was still one of the most anticipated times of her day. Odie came scampering through the house, tail wagging so hard his rear end had trouble moving in the same direction he was running. When he reached her, he stood on his hind legs, whining and begging for attention.

Amber dropped her pack on the floor and knelt to scoop him up, trying to avoid his licking tongue as she scratched him behind the ears. "There's my good boy!" She smiled as he squirmed.

"You okay?" Nathan asked as he walked in from the kitchen. His expression reflected his concern, and she knew he was worried about her hand. She had told him it was injured in the message she'd sent to let him know she was going to be late. But per their agreement, she hadn't given details.

"I'm fine. Just needed a little time in a Doc Box." She held up her left hand and wriggled her fingers to show him they were all right. She managed not to wince at the minor pain the action caused her.

"I don't suppose you could tell me what happened?"

"Just a training incident on the new job."

He frowned. "The job you can't tell me anything about."

She pressed her lips into a thin line and shrugged. "You know the deal."

He sighed. "Yeah. It doesn't mean I'm not going to worry though."

She knew that, but they had come to an understanding. Since he already knew she came from a law enforcement background, she promised not to lie to him about what she did or about the risks. But she also let him know that she wasn't going to be able to talk about a lot of it. He didn't even know the name of the group she now worked for. The Fixers were a clandestine organization, so that was the only way their relationship was going to work.

And she *really* wanted it to work. The new house was a step in that direction. With the newfound wealth Dem and Acamas had set her up with, a house she would never have dreamed of owning just a year ago was a simple thing for her to acquire. She had bought the home, making sure it had the amenities she wanted. It had three bedrooms, an office, a panic room, and a state-of-the-art kitchen.

That last had caused her some mental acrobatics, as she had grown up eating fast food or instant meals heated in a standard hot spot in a tiny kitchen. Nathan, on the other hand, was an amazing cook, practically a gourmet. It took her three months to admit to herself that he was the reason she'd insisted on such an upscale kitchen. She asked him to move in with her a few days later.

The only thing she really missed about her old apartment was having Shamra and her son, Davy, as next-door neighbors. But she made sure she had them over as often as schedules allowed and was determined to make sure their friendship didn't fall by the wayside.

She leaned in and kissed Nathan. "So, what smells so wonderful?"

"Spicy shrimp and tofu fried rice."

"Mmm. Sounds delish."

Nathan had been raised by his aunt, a nationally recognized gourmet chef in one of the fancier seafood restaurants in the city. As a result, he'd spent much of his childhood in the kitchen with her and had learned to cook at an early age. She imagined he could probably cook at any gourmet restaurant he wanted, but he seemed to prefer his little coffee-and-tea shop, where he sold custom blends of caffeinated beverages.

She had never appreciated fine cooking until she met Nathan Pedde. Now she was addicted.

She put Odie down and smiled. "Let me wash up, and I'll set the table."

"It's already set. The rice just needs a couple more minutes, and we'll be ready to eat. So hurry."

Going into the bedroom, she couldn't help but smile. She wasn't foolish enough to think they would always have perfect domestic bliss. But working in a dangerous field as she did, she had long ago learned to cherish the good times. And this was definitely one of the good times.

She hurriedly palmed open the upright weapons safe and stripped off her pistols and flame blades. She placed them in the safe, slid the duffel bag with her training gear inside, and locked the door before stepping into the restroom to clean up.

Nathan was setting the bowl of rice on the table when she came up behind him and wrapped her arms around his chest. "Mmm. It smells amazing."

He turned in her arms and leaned down for a kiss. The man was wonderful and understanding. He put up with her crazy hours and the uncertainty of her work.

"You're too good to me," she said.

Some of the guilt must have shown on her face because he frowned at her. "What's wrong?"

She shrugged. "I'm not used to having good things in my life. Not this good, anyway. I can't help wondering when you're finally going to say, 'that's enough,' and walk away."

"You really think so little of me?" he chided.

"No! It's me. I mean… I know the situation isn't perfect, and our relationship isn't going to be a normal one. My job isn't going to let it be normal."

He pulled her in tighter and kissed her on the forehead. "Who wants normal? Normal is overrated."

She smiled. "I just don't want you to think I don't appreciate how difficult it is for you. I don't want you to ever think I'm taking you for granted."

"I know you don't." He lifted her chin, bent down, and kissed her lips, and after a few seconds, the kiss went from loving to lustful. Then he pushed her back. "But if we don't stop now, we're going to have to reheat dinner. And shrimp doesn't reheat well."

She grinned. "We could skip dinner and go straight for dessert."

"And waste all the time I put into cooking?" He feigned shock. "How could you suggest such a thing?"

"Fine. But this dinner had better be outstanding if I'm going to put off my favorite dessert for it."

Nathan's grin turned cocky. "So I'm your favorite dessert, am I?"

She pursed her lips as if considering. "Maybe not. That tiramisu you made last night was pretty amazing." She waggled her hand in a seesaw manner. "It's pretty close."

"Then you're in luck. There's some left in the cooler. So if you're good and eat your dinner, you can have both of your favorite desserts afterward."

She pretended to think about it. "How about a counteroffer? We eat dinner, then I get to eat one of my favorite desserts… off of my other favorite dessert?"

"That's going to get pretty messy."

"Oh, I'm counting on it."

DAY 02
WEDNESDAY

CHAPTER 03

Amber had read Fischer's case file, and all the old feelings had returned. She stared at the stranger in the mirror. It had been six months, but she was finally beginning to get used to the hazel eyes staring back at her. Her old cyberoptic implants had been a source of insecurity since she'd first gotten them, and she'd fought a constant tug of war with her feelings about them for years. She hated the way people's attitudes changed as soon as they saw them. But she also loved the edge they gave her on the street. And over the years, she'd learned to take advantage of how they made people nervous, as if they feared she could see into their minds with them. Nevertheless, each time she looked in the mirror, the implants were a constant reminder that she was less than perfect... less than human.

It wasn't true, of course. Intellectually, she knew she was just as human as anyone else. In fact, if one were to measure a person's humanity as a flesh-to-cybernetics ratio, her legs would count against her much more than her eyes. But the legs *looked* normal. Her eyes hadn't. The flat metallic orbs staring out of her eye sockets had immediately set her apart from anyone else in the room.

They were a personal reminder of the rash behavior that had nearly cost Amber her life. And despite all the negatives those eyes had brought her, she had also invested much of her identity in them. She'd known what people saw when they looked at her. It had helped her to build the thick skin and the tough-as-nails attitude her peers knew and respected.

So it was a conflicted woman who stared back from that mirror now.

Stared through eyes that still didn't *feel* like her eyes. They were a vibrant mix of brown and green, like normal eyes… shone with moisture, like normal eyes… had irises that expanded and contracted in response to light like normal eyes. To the outside observer, they were indistinguishable from organics.

She admitted to herself, with more than a hint of guilt at the thought, that there was a part of her that worried her peers would no longer give her the respect they had accorded her. That insecure part of her feared that perhaps this was the day they saw past the shield of her eyes and realized she was bluffing her way through life—that her next case would be the one that demonstrated her utter incompetence. Without the shield of those eyes—those hated but necessary eyes—she would be revealed to the world as an incompetent wannabee.

Then she blinked. The woman in the mirror blinked back at her. And Amber shook herself.

That's about enough of that shyte. Time to put your big-girl panties on and get going.

She was wallowing in her insecurity, and if there was one thing she couldn't stand, it was self-pity.

Old eyes, old job, old life.

She reminded herself that the old eyes had also come with a hefty price tag. They had indentured her to Securi-Tech for an additional ten years on her contract. And since they had technically been the company's until she served out her time, Securi-Tech had the right to review anything she saw through them, either on recordings or in real time.

At least she didn't still have that hanging over her head. Acamas paying off Amber's contract had ended Securi-Tech's right to access, so she and her brother, Demophon, had shut off the transmitters in Amber's eyes, effectively blocking Securi-Tech or anyone else.

The new eyes were so much better than the old ones. Like her old eyes, they could record sight and sound at a blinked command and see into the infrared and ultraviolet spectrums. They could zoom in to view microscopically as well as out to view telescopically. All of the functions of the old eyes.

But the new eyes *looked* completely natural. That alone would be a huge improvement once she learned to drop the emotional baggage. She could also change their color, shifting from hazel to blue, green, brown, or any other color she wanted, natural or not. Even better, though, she could alter her retinal patterns. She could upload any retinal pattern and mimic it well enough to fool even the best biometric scanners.

That little option was completely illegal, but Gibbs had guided her to a specialist who had an arrangement with the Fixers. The question of legality was never brought up. The new eyes had cost her more than triple what her first pair had, and back in the day, she hadn't been able to afford even the old ones. Securi-Tech had paid for them. But once she decided to take the plunge, she hadn't even hesitated. Once again, money was no longer a consideration. Things were finally beginning to go her way.

Until last night, when she'd read the case file Fischer had sent her.

Realizing she was once again dropping into a fugue, she shook herself and got about the business of applying her makeup. It was something she was beginning to pay more attention to. Now that she had accepted the job with the Fixers, she had to blend in with the general populace. The eyes were part of it, and so was regular civilian makeup. And she hadn't slept well last night, so the makeup was doubly important.

As she applied it, a new mantra came to her. *New job, new eyes… new life.*

She had a feeling she was going to be leaning on those words a lot in the coming days.

CHAPTER 04

"Tiny!"

Richard chuckled. CC Miller was probably the only person in the city who could get away with calling him Tiny. Before meeting him, Richard had always been confident he would be the biggest guy in any room he entered. He'd had been gifted with genetics that allowed his body to easily convert food to muscle, and he had cultivated the advantage with hard work and weightlifting from a young age. But even with Richard's street banger augmentations and body mods, CC dwarfed him.

"Just living the dream, brother. Thought I'd get a little time on the weights before the day starts."

"What classes are they torturing you with this month?"

"LEO."

CC rolled his eyes. "That stuff was rough. *A* is legal in this industry but not in that one. Data theft is a higher priority rating than murder *unless* the victim is a C-level executive, in which case, the murder is higher. I don't know how whoever wrote those laws ever managed to get a decent night's sleep."

"No argument here." The truth was that unlike many other Fixers, Richard was already a fully certified LEO. He was qualified to work on cases rated up to Priority Two on his own and on P-1 cases if he had a P-1 rated partner.

CC's eyes flicked to the wall chrono. "You're not going to have time for much of a workout before your training. Not if you want to get a shower, anyway."

"Luckily, I got pulled into some special training with Amber and Scott. Something about a new combat specialist. You know anything about it?"

CC shook his head. "Sorry."

"No worries. But since it's in the gym, I figure I don't need to worry about getting cleaned up beforehand."

CC shrugged. "All right, then. I'll see you later."

Richard nodded to him as he headed toward the showers. Richard went to the weight wall and stepped onto the mag pad. He tied his earbud into the frequency marked on the wall before him and spoke as he reached down and lifted the weight bar with one hand. "Richard Kayani." He let go of the bar, and it hovered before him, hanging in the magnetic field projected from the ceiling. As it hovered, he read off the UIN inscribed on the bar.

He heard the lifeless voice of the weight room control system. "Universal identification number recognized."

Richard grabbed the bar, pulled it down to his waist, and held onto it as he spoke. "Set resistance to one hundred kilos."

"One hundred kilograms. Set."

The bar didn't suddenly drop in his grasp. The mag field held it in place for the moment. But when he began to curl his arms, the bar resisted his movement exactly as if he were lifting one hundred kilograms. He knocked out ten quick curls to warm up then called out, "Increase resistance to one-fifty."

"One hundred fifty kilograms in three, two, one, set."

The bar still didn't drop, but when he tried another curl, he could tell the resistance was increased. He did another ten curls then increased the resistance twice more. When he had finished a total of fifty curls, he stepped it up to two hundred fifty kilos.

"Set bar to neutral." The bar continued to hover, but now he could easily move it to whatever position he wanted, its weight evenly suspended between the upper and lower magnetic fields once again.

He dragged a heavy-duty weight bench into the field and lay on it beneath the bar. Pulling the bar down over his chest, he commanded, "Set resistance to one hundred kilos." Once more, he stepped through his routine, increasing the resistance in increments as he worked his way through a routine that, for him at least, was just enough to warm his muscles up. Ironically, this was how the big man relaxed.

He worked through the various muscle groups, allowing his mind to drift where it would. And after CC's comments, it naturally wandered over the path that had led him here.

When Richard was twenty-two, his sister had been kidnapped and his mother killed in a neighborhood raid. He'd taken the plunge after that, spending every credit he could scrape up to get the street banger enhancements he would need to protect his friends and family. It had taken him two months, but he'd found and rescued his sister and avenged their mother.

Vowing to do more to protect his people, he sold his skills as a bodyguard and organized his fellow bangers in Dineh Village into the neighborhood protection group known as the Night Watch. Strangely enough, that was how he'd ended up here with the Fixers. He'd been pulled in as a suspect on one of Amber's cases, but she had quickly vindicated him and had taken him under her wing, first using him as a skilled consultant, then paving the way for him to get his badge and a job as her partner at Securi-Tech.

The credit he'd pulled in there had helped him get better equipment for the Night Watch and had given him a career. Since then, he'd grown to genuinely admire Amber. She had proven herself to him and his people on several occasions. Her values would not be compromised. Even to the point of costing her a career she loved.

She might not know it, but his respect for her was such that he would follow that woman into hell. As far as he was concerned, she was as much family as his sister was. To him, she was Dineh.

Richard changed the angle of the bench and started his next set of exercises.

CHAPTER 05

Amber's tablet flashed a reminder as she drove to Fixer HQ. She needed to call Shamra back. She set her autopilot and scrolled through her contact list to her friend's call code.

"Amber!" Shamra turned on her video immediately, and Amber couldn't help but smile. The woman was eternally cheerful, and her smile was infectious.

"Hi, Sham. Sorry I haven't called lately. The training for the new job's been insane. It's like starting university-level classes and only getting a year to learn it all."

"Oh, I understand, sweetie. You don't have to explain. I just thought you could use a break."

"Most definitely. What did you have in mind?"

"Well, my sister offered to watch Davy this weekend. You want to go to dinner or something?"

The two of them chatted for the few minutes it took Amber to get to the general shipping facility that served as a front for the Fixer's local base of operations. In the end, they still hadn't decided what they wanted to do, and Amber had to qualify their plans with the understanding that she might end up busy on a new case. It depended on what she found out from Fischer.

"That's fine, girl. I know how your job goes. Just don't forget me. Consider me your happiness coordinator and keep me in mind if you can get some time."

"I will. Talk to you later?"

"Damn right you will. Love you, sweetie."

"Love you too. Discomm." As she said it, Amber noted that she had absolutely no problem saying the words to her friend. So why not Nathan?

It would take a dozen therapists a dozen years to untwist your messed-up melon, Amber. Don't try to figure it out in the five minutes it'll take you to get into the gym.

She grabbed her duffel bag and headed inside. A few minutes before 09:00, she wandered to the mat and found the rest of her team already waiting. The observation gallery was full again, a fact that hadn't gone unnoticed by Jordie.

"What's with the peanut gallery?" she asked.

"Probably here to watch us get our asses handed to us again," Scott said with a rueful grin.

Jordie's brow shot up. "This guy beat you?" She looked from Scott to Amber then back to Scott again. "Both of you?"

Scott nodded. "Both of us."

Jordie looked to Amber, who nodded. "At the same time."

"Whoa, whoa!" Richard said. "He took on both of you at the same time?"

Amber nodded again.

"And won?"

"Mostly."

"Mostly?" Jordie chimed in. "What does that mean?"

"It means if the weapons had been real, we would both be dead. But since they weren't, Scott was able to get him from behind while he was busy watching me twitch on the mat."

Richard whistled. "And this is your new trainer?" He grinned. "I wouldn't want to be in your shoes."

"As amusing as that might be," Jordie said, "I don't see why the big guy and I need to be here. This sort of training is your thing, not ours."

"What kind of mods does he have?" Richard asked.

Before Amber could tell him she had no idea, the door at the far end of the gym opened, and Maestro Harris strode across the room toward them. He carried only a small personal tablet.

"It's my understanding he wants to train all four of us," Amber said quietly.

Jordie looked from her to the man walking toward them. He moved with purpose, his expression all business. "Well, shyte," she muttered.

Maestro Harris stopped a few meters away from them. He looked at them for a few seconds before lowering himself into a cross-legged position on the mat. "Please to sit."

They did.

He glanced at the tablet another second before lifting it. "I am to reading about the four of you." He placed the tablet on the mat in front of him. "You have all followed very winding paths to get here. A LEO who lost her eyes, a street banger turned neighborhood protector, and a pair of thieves turned *legítimo* to bring justice to a friend's killers."

"*Legítimo?*" Jordie asked.

"Many apologies. My English is sometimes not so good. *Legítimo... honesto?*"

"He's saying you turned legit to get the Chosen Ones," Richard said.

Harris surveyed the group, nodding. "You have become an effective team."

He looked directly at Scott. "You hit me from behind, while I am distracted and after you are already out of the match."

Scott pursed his lips. "With respect, maestro, I wasn't out of the match, or I wouldn't have been *able* to hit you."

Maestro Harris stared at Scott for a moment before grinning. "Excellent answer." He turned to Amber. "I break your hand. You should have tried to get away. Instead, you attack. You hit me. Get a good strike at my leg." He beamed at her like a happy child. "It is a rare thing these days to have a student get good strike on me. And to do so under these... ah, what is the word? *Circunstâncias?*" He looked at her expectantly.

"Circumstances?" It was the only word that sounded like it might fit.

He smiled again. "Yes! This is the word. To strike me with these circumstances shows strong spirit, and I applaud this. For these things, I have agreed to teach your team."

He peered intently at the four of them. "But if this is to work, you must also to accept for me to teach you. Do you accept me?"

Richard, Jordie, and Scott all looked at Amber. Harris turned when they did. "You lead this team. This is *óbvio*. Do you accept me?"

Amber looked at the man for a moment. "Do you have any mods? Any cybernetics?"

"I do not know 'mods.' But I have no *cybernéticos*. This is important?"

"Yes. It means you beat Scott and me without any augmentations. How did you do that?"

"This is one of the things I will teach." The maestro grinned. "*If* you accept me as your maestro."

Amber looked at the others. Scott gave her a subtle nod, which she returned. Turning back to Maestro Harris, Amber stuck out her hand. "I think you have a deal."

CHAPTER 06

T HE REST OF THE MORNING wasn't what Amber had expected. She had imagined scenarios where the maestro took all four of them to the mat, humiliating them as he beat the sludge out of them. Instead, he spent the next hour explaining how he had beaten Scott and her.

"Most fighting is done without thought. No finesse, no real understanding. But if you accept it for what it is, a fight can be a thing of beauty. It is game of chess where opponents are to make each other bleed. And like chess, while many people can play, very few are masters."

"And you can make us masters?" Jordie scoffed.

"No. Only you can do this. But I can make you better players of chess. Good enough that perhaps one day you can become maestros."

"Even me?" Jordie asked.

"Yes. To fight properly is to take what nature has given you, understand your advantages and limitations, and learn how to use them on the chessboard." He waved a hand at her. "You are small woman. You think of yourself as weak?"

"Compared to who?" she joked.

Harris seemed to consider her words then nodded. He turned to Richard. "Will you please to help me demonstrate?"

Richard looked surprised but stood at the man's gesture. When Maestro Harris led him to the middle of the mat, the rest of them backed away. They watched as he did the little fist-to-forehead, palm-to-chest salute that Amber had noticed the day before. She leaned over to Scott.

"What's with the salute thing?" she whispered. "You seemed to know it yesterday. Does it tell you anything about him?"

"Not really. Just that his style is one of the old, old, *old* martial arts. Supposedly goes way back to the sixteenth or seventeenth century. But all those old styles have been mixed and changed over the centuries. It's impossible to tell what came from where anymore."

She nodded, turning her attention back to the mat, where Maestro Harris stood opposite Richard. Richard towered over the smaller man. Then again, Richard towered over most people. The only person she had ever met who was larger than her friend was the similarly augmented Fixer, CC Miller.

"This man is much larger than me, no?" Harris looked directly at Jordie as he spoke, as if this lesson was specifically for her.

She grinned. "That man is much larger than everyone."

He chuckled and turned back to Richard. "Please attempt to striking me."

Richard took a half-hearted swipe at the maestro.

"This is how you fight?" Harris said with a chuckle. "How is it you are still alive?"

Richard smiled, nodded, and took another punch at the man. Harris stepped aside the slightest bit and shook his head. "You maybe need new eyes like Fem Payne?"

Richard jabbed again, and again Harris slipped aside.

"Faster!" he said.

Richard obliged. He shot a jab-cross combo, moving faster than would be expected from a man his size. But still, Harris slipped just out of range.

"Again!"

Richard threw another jab. This time, Harris leaned a bit to the side, letting the fist slip by him, reached out with his own hand, and latched onto the massive arm. When Richard jerked the arm back, Maestro Harris jumped up and allowed Richard to pull him closer. Harris took advantage of his new position by jabbing a bladed hand into Richard's armpit. Then, as the big man pulled his arm back in pain, Harris released it, kicked out as he dropped, and slammed his elbow into the side of

Richard's thigh. Each strike was perfectly placed, hitting the meaty area between the posterior and anterior armor plates of the banger's SDA.

The double hit caused Richard to lean, and Harris slipped behind him, kicking the same point on his thigh before he jumped away. The entire exchange lasted seconds and ended with Richard dropping to one knee. As he fell, he spun on his good knee and faced Harris, hands raised to defend himself. But the Maestro was finished with his demonstration. He stood calmly out of Richard's reach and looked back at Jordie.

"This man is larger than me. He is stronger than me. He is…" The man seemed at a loss for the proper word and turned to Amber. "What was this word? Mode?"

"He has mods. Or you can call him augmented."

Harris smiled. "*Aumentado*! Yes!" Turning back to Jordie, he said, "He is aumeented. I am not. Yet our fight is over." He waved a hand at Richard. "I stand. He does not."

Harris approached Richard and held out a hand to help him back to his feet. Richard limped back to stand with the others as the maestro addressed them all again. "This is what I wish to teach. It is angles, distance, efficiency of motion. You will learn to analyzing the enemy's attack in a new way. Not as attack against which you counter but as angles you will either evade or alter to your own advantage."

He pointed to Amber and Scott. "You two will be especially good. Your speed will give you great advantage." He pointed to Richard. "You will benefit least. You are already big and strong, though. And you have the heart of a warrior. What I teach, you are not needing so much. But you *will* still learn."

Harris stepped forward to stand before Jordie. "You will never be the warrior that the others are. You have other talents." Amber saw a look of bitterness and a flash of anger cross the young woman's face.

"Still," Harris continued, "you have much potential. You may not become as formidable as your friends, but this does not mean you will not *be* formidable. You will improve beyond what you believe you are capable of. You will become like the snake—small, precise, deadly."

Jordie drew her lips into a thin line and nodded. "Then let's get started."

For two hours, Maestro Harris trained the four of them in new concepts of unarmed combat. Rather than viewing attacks as a series of techniques and counters, they learned to see them as vectors, ranges, and zones. They learned to think less about countering and more about evading—slipping outside the ranges and angles of attack and... shifting their weight on their hips to bring their torsos out of the line of attack without giving up ground.

Ironically enough, it was Scott who seemed to have the most trouble. "This footwork goes against everything I was taught. Every time I think I think I have it, muscle memory takes over, and I fall right back into my old way of moving."

"This is as expected." The maestro shrugged. "Those with much training must unlearn before they can learn."

As if to prove his point, Jordie picked up his instructions quickly. Of the four of them, she was by far the most improved at the end of their first training session.

When Maestro Harris gathered them together to close out their combat training for the day, Amber found herself grateful it was over. It wasn't so much that she was tired. Not physically, at least. The physical workout hadn't been too bad, since their new instructor spent as much time demonstrating and discussing the new concepts as he did drilling them. But mentally, she was exhausted. In fact, she didn't think she could take in another new idea and still retain what she had learned.

"You have done well for a first day," Harris told them when they stood before him. "Think on what I have shown you. We meet here again tomorrow." He drew himself up. "Now, do as I do."

He placed his fist, palm outward, on his forehead. "Fist to head reminds us to think before we strike." He turned the fist and placed it, palm inward, on his chest. "Fist to heart reminds us to feel empathy before causing harm."

Everyone began heading to the locker room, and Amber stepped up to walk beside the maestro. "What is that from?" she asked. "The salute, I mean."

Scott, who had been on the other side of Harris, chimed in. "I recognized some of it. It looks like something I learned from a Filipino knife fighter in the Glads."

Harris shrugged. "Is possible. It is said Primeiro Maestro, first master of our style, is from old Itália. This is some few centuries ago. Supposedly, he studies to fight on small island nation called Malta. There is trouble there, and he must to flee to other places with enemies always chasing."

"What kind of trouble?" Scott asked.

"Someone kill his teacher. Primeiro sees this happen… avenges teacher. This makes much dishonor to others and makes him target. It is complicated matter and not important for now. But in fleeing, he travels the world, studying at the feet of many martial *artistas*. He learns, taking various concepts and techniques from what he is learning, and spends some years taking some, throwing out some. Eventually, he creates *Punho Deslizantes*. You would call this *sliding fists*."

"And this is a Brazilian style of fighting?"

He seesawed his hand. "As I say, Primeiro Maestro is from Itália. You may know this by the title of *maestro*. This is Italiana word, yes?"

Amber shrugged, but the maestro continued as if the matter was settled.

"When Primeiro flees, he plucks pieces of fighting styles from all over the world. So the style has no single source." He stopped and held up a finger. "But he eventually settles in Old Brasil, living there for many years. There are perhaps fifty maestros around the world now, but most are still from Novo Brasil." He grinned. "So we claim it as our own."

"I'd love to hear the story of what happened with Primeiro's teacher," Scott said.

"Perhaps another day, after we have known one another better."

Amber smiled back. "Thank you, maestro."

He nodded, and they resumed walking toward the locker rooms. "Where do you go now?" he asked. "You have other training?"

She shook her head, calling up the time on her HUD. It was 11:19. "I'm taking the rest of the day off."

Harris frowned as they entered the locker room. "You do not train more today?" The man clearly disapproved of downtime. "If you have no more classes, I can give more time for your combat training."

"Thanks," she said, "but I can't. I'm consulting with an old friend on a case."

"Ah! Then this is another kind of work. This is good. I respect this."

She wasn't surprised. Training was everything with the Fixer organization—all day, every day. There was unarmed combat training, firearms training, legal training, history, geopolitical socio-economics, and various other instructions on the way the Fixer organization interacted with the modern world. Of course, once they got into it, Amber quickly learned why. In joining the Fixers, Amber and her team had entered a whole new world when it came to law enforcement.

LEOs took their name, and even the shape of their lion's head badges, from an old term that no longer applied—law enforcement officers. But LEOs were no longer *officers* at all. Not since the Security Forces Privatization Act.

The SFPA had been a rubber stamp intended to legalize private security forces for large corporations, something that had already been in existence for several decades. It granted those security forces legal carte blanche while policing their own campuses. But it also specified that such security forces were not to be accorded "any military rank, authority, or cooperation commensurate with that of any governmental legal, security, or military force." It was odd wording that had the unintentional side effect of eliminating the term "officer" from law enforcement vernacular.

But the SFPA had also given credence to the private security firms who had been contracting their services to those corporations for decades. In doing so, it fractured the already fragile cooperation between the old government police forces and their private counterparts and created a Gordian knot of law enforcement agencies, each one vying for superiority over the others. The tangle was so intricate that it often took legal specialists to determine who had jurisdiction over any given crime scene.

Economics was unraveling that knot, though, and government LEOs were slowly becoming a thing of the past. There was more profit in privatization, and more profit meant better equipment, training, and job opportunities. Amber had thought she understood all this from her time working for Securi-Tech. Then, on her last case with Securi-Tech, Amber and her team stumbled into the group known as the Fixers, a service so high above other LEO agencies that most of the world didn't even know they existed.

And Gibbs had made it abundantly clear that if Amber wished to become part of the group, she and her team would train for at least a year before being assigned a case. They were just over halfway through that year, and the training *was* fascinating. The Fixer organization had resources and weapons she hadn't even known existed. But she longed to be back in the field.

"A case?" Scott's voice was eager. "What kind of case?" Evidently, he wanted to get back into the field as much as she did.

"What?" Richard also chimed in. She kept forgetting about his hearing mods. "We have a case?"

They *all* wanted to be back in the field.

Amber shook her head. "Not really. I'm just consulting. Chief Fischer sent me a message last night. He has a case he thought I might be interested in. Organ jackers left a woman in the street without her eyes."

They all stopped in their tracks. She sighed, turning back to face them.

Maestro Harris stopped to watch.

Amber spread her hands. "And this is exactly why I didn't want to say anything. It's just a private consulting gig. No big deal."

"Same MO as your attackers?" Scott asked.

Harris looked on with dawning comprehension as Amber nodded, and silence fell over the group for several seconds.

Richard broke it first. "I'm coming with."

"Me too," Scott and Jordie chimed in at the same time.

Amber shook her head. "I already cleared the time off with Gibbs. You guys haven't."

They fell silent.

It was true. Despite the Fixer policy on not allowing rookies to take a case until they had a year of training under their belts, Gibbs had approved Amber's request. From her perspective, it wasn't a Fixer case, so it was unimportant.

"This is not problem," Maestro Harris said. "I will arrange with her. Is good chance for to integrate more with my students."

Amber blinked. "You want to come with us? On a case?"

"I thought it wasn't really a case," Richard said with a grin.

But she kept her eyes on the maestro, who nodded in answer to her question. His ever-present smile never faltered.

Finally, she sighed and looked back at the others. "Okay then. Just understand—I'll try not to, but I might get wound a little tight on this one. I don't know how it's going…" She shrugged, unable to continue past the lump in her throat.

Richard put a huge hand on her shoulder. "You've had my back more than once. I can put up with whatever you throw at me. At least for a little while."

"Hell." Jordie snorted. "If it wasn't for you, me and Scott would probably be training roaches to dance in a prison somewhere."

The corners of Amber's mouth turned up a bit at that. "Thanks, everyone. And I apologize in advance if I get tweaked over any of this."

"Meh." Scott jerked a thumb at Harris. "If you get too far out of line, we'll just get the maestro to slap you around a little."

CHAPTER 07

True to his word, Maestro Harris got approval for the entire team, and the five of them met Chief Fischer in the parking garage beneath Silver Crest Hospital. Fischer smiled tentatively as Amber exited the luxury van.

"I'd heard you came into some money." He waved a hand at her new vehicle. "I had no idea it was like this, though."

She shrugged and stepped up to give her old friend a hug. "How are you doing, Chief?"

He froze for a moment, and she remembered that the man wasn't big on public displays.

"I'm not your chief anymore, for one thing." He pushed her away and blinked in surprise. "Your eyes! You got new eyes!"

She smiled. "Money makes a lot of things more accessible than they were before."

"So I see." He looked up as the others piled out of the van. "And I see you kept the band together." Then his head cocked a bit as he saw Maestro Harris. "And gained a new member?"

Harris gave a slight bow in acknowledgment then looked at Amber with a slightly raised eyebrow, obviously waiting for her lead.

"This is Maestro Harris. He's the unarmed combat instructor for our new employer."

"The private security gig?"

Amber nodded.

Fischer stepped forward and offered Harris his hand. "It's a pleasure to meet you."

The maestro took the hand with a smile. "For me as well."

Amber could tell her former boss wanted to ask for more details. But she could also see that he was still a little unsure of how she might feel about his accepting the new contract with the company that had so royally screwed them over. She didn't harbor any ill will over it, but she also couldn't very well have him asking questions about her new job either. As much as it pained her to do so, she had to keep him at arm's length.

She started walking toward the entrance to the elevators, leaving the others, Chief Fischer included, to catch up. Before he could say anything more, Amber took charge of the conversation. "I read the files, and I understand why you thought I would be interested."

"You say that as if you aren't."

"Oh, I definitely am. But I need you to understand from the beginning, I won't work for Securi-Tech directly. They burned that bridge with me, and it's not going to be rebuilt by dangling a tasty morsel in front of my nose."

"That's not a problem," he said. "Securi-Tech won't touch this one. The victim has no credit, no rich family, and no corporate sponsors."

"So no one who can afford a LEO contract." Amber's voice was bitter.

"I'm afraid not."

"Then why are you here?" she asked her old friend.

"Officially? I'm following a hunch to see if there might be a connection between this case and an attack against the CFO of a local tech firm. But I already know there isn't."

Amber raised an eyebrow at her former boss. "And unofficially?"

He shrugged and grinned. "Can't a guy do an old friend a favor?"

Amber returned the grin. "Thanks, Chief."

"Not your chief anymore, remember?"

"Old habits. Speaking of old friends and favors…" She reached into her jacket and pulled out a card. "Besides the personal-security gig, I also started my own PI firm."

Fischer took the card with a tight smile. "Payne Security Consultants. So you did it after all."

When the legal fallout of her last case with Securi-Tech cost her the job she loved, Fischer had offhandedly suggested she open a private-investigation firm. A few weeks after settling into her new wealth, she'd decided the idea had merit, if for no other reason than as a cover for her work with the Fixers. So she'd created PSC, filed the legal documents, and printed up business cards.

"I did."

PSC was barely more than a name, a tax number, and a rarely used office building. She'd bought the building because it was in a poor neighborhood, so the price was low, yet the structure was still in excellent shape. Most importantly, though, it provided a cover if she needed to run investigations without leading back to the Fixers.

He slipped her card into a pocket, looking almost like a proud parent.

She grinned, shrugged, and resumed her walk to the elevators. "What floor is she on?"

"Seventeen."

The elevator doors slid open, and Amber stood still, waiting for Chief Fischer to lead the way. He glanced at her as if expecting her to say something, but she gestured for him to go first. "You're the one who knows where we're going."

He turned and led them down the hallway to the left. Two more turns and he stopped at a final corridor. Fischer turned to the group. "Before we get any closer to her room… Fem Payne, you read the file. Did the rest of your team?"

"No, sir, they haven't."

His expression hardened. "I'll stick with the highlights for now. Our victim's name is Tracy Pierce Malloy. She was on her way home from a huff house last night when someone black-bagged her and threw her into a van or cargo pod. They drugged her, slapped her around just enough to get her good and submissive, tied her up, and threw her onto a table of some kind."

Fischer hesitated a second. "Next thing she remembers is waking up strapped down." He looked at Amber again. "You sure you're okay?"

Amber realized she was grinding her teeth. "I'm fine." Addressing the rest of the group, she took over the synopsis. "They took her eyes, her liver, and both kidneys. Then they dumped her in a back alley to die."

"And she lived through all that?" Jordie asked.

"That's why we're at a hospital and not a morgue," Scott quipped.

Amber gave Scott and Jordie a pointed look as she continued. "Good Samaritan found her bleeding on the street and commed Emergency Services. ES recognized the handiwork as organ jacking and reported it to city LEOs. The city didn't have the resources to investigate, so they posted it to the night sheets for anyone else to snag if they wanted it." She waved a hand at Chief Fischer. "Luckily, the chief realized I might want it, so he grabbed it and sent the file to me."

She turned back to Fischer with a sigh. "For which I thank you, Chief. This one hits a little close to home."

Fischer's lips grew thin, and he nodded. "I can only imagine." He waved a hand toward the room. "Shall we?"

They entered the room to see a young woman lying in a bed with all sorts of monitors and lines attached to her. The steady beeping of the monitors was the only sound.

Amber couldn't tell whether or not the woman was conscious, since her eyes—or where they had once been—were hidden behind a heavy layer of gauze and bandages. The cinnamon skin tone of her face was marred by heavy bruising. It grew darker, more angry-looking the closer one looked, and Amber recalled that she had once looked just as bad. She had seen the pics in her own file.

She took a deep breath and stepped around to the left side of the woman's bed. "Fem Malloy?" she asked softly. "Are you awake?"

A slight jerk of the head told Amber she was, even before the woman nodded. "Yes," she croaked. "Who are you?"

"My name is Amber Payne. I'm an expert consultant brought in by Securi-Tech."

"Expert, huh?" Malloy's voice was bitter. "I doubt it. I don't think they make too many experts in getting your eyes ripped out of your head."

Amber sighed. "Well, I agree it's an elite club, but there are a few of us that pass the entrance exam."

Malloy cocked her head slightly in Amber's direction. "You?"

"I'm afraid so." She waited a moment to see if the woman in the hospital bed wanted to say any more. When she remained silent, Amber pushed forward with her interview. "If you're up for it, I'd like to ask you some questions about what happened. Is that okay?"

Fem Malloy licked dry lips and gave a barely perceptible nod. "Could I get something to drink?"

"Of course." Amber spotted a small cup of water on the bedside table. As she reached for it, she pointed to Richard. "Can you get some chairs in here?"

"Sure." He tapped Scott on the shoulder, and the two men left the room.

As Amber put the cup in Malloy's hand, the woman whispered, "Who were you talking to?"

"My partner," Amber said. "My entire team is here, five of us, plus my former boss from Securi-Tech. Is that all right?"

Malloy took a small sip and shrugged. "I guess." She handed the cup back to Amber.

"Good." Amber put the cup back on the nightstand before taking Malloy's left hand. The woman started at the touch but quickly grasped Amber's hand.

"We're here to get as much information from you as we can. The more you can tell us, the better our chances of catching the people who did this to you."

"Okay."

They were interrupted by Richard bringing in three chairs, two in one hand and one in the other. Scott followed with another pair. After a few seconds of everyone arranging seats around the bed, Amber sat beside the hospital bed and spoke. "Sorry for the interruption. Now, Tracy, are you ready?"

"I guess so."

"Let's start by you just telling us in your own words what happened. Take as long as you want, and you can stop anytime you need to take a break. We'll take it at your speed. Sound good?"

"Sure. Just…" Her voice broke. "Sorry. This is going to be a little hard."

"I understand." Amber squeezed the woman's hand. "I do."

Fem Malloy hesitated as if gathering her courage before starting. "First, I'm sorry if I'm not much help. Everything happened so fast, and I... it's all flashes." She drew her lips into a thin line. "And I was a little high. I remember going to Homer's. It's a huff house on Lockwood."

"You go there a lot?"

"Depends on what you call a lot. I go once or twice a week. My daughter left home about a year ago. We had a big fight, and she packed up her things and left."

"I'm sorry. How old is she?"

"Seventeen. Seventeen going on thirty. Thinks she knows everything. The group she was running with was bad news, and I tried to get her to see it. But she knew better, and one day... I guess she had enough of me fighting with her." Malloy fell silent for a few seconds. "Anyway, she left."

Amber saw the way her throat bobbed and knew the woman was working through some bad memories. She gave her a moment before prompting her. "I'm sorry, Tracy, but what about the huff house?"

"Ever since Lilah left, I've been going to Homer's... huff a little forget-me-not to take the edge off. Helps me hang on to her without going nuts."

"Forget-me-not?"

"It helps you deal with bad memories."

Amber made a note to look the drug up to see if it would affect Fem Malloy's testimony.

"So you were on your way home?"

"Yeah. I only live a few blocks away. No need for transport. But it ain't the best part of town. In retrospect, I guess something like this was bound to happen sooner or later."

"Hindsight always makes it easy to see what we should have done. We're not here to judge. We just want to catch the people who did this to you."

Malloy squeezed her hand once more. "Thanks. I had just gone past a service alley. I remember hearing footsteps and laughing. There was something about the laughter... it was ugly."

"Male or female?" Amber asked.

"Male. At least two of them. Maybe three." Fem Malloy cleared her throat. Her lips quivered, and she began to hyperventilate. Some of the indicators on the monitors edged out of the green and began flashing yellow. The monitor's steady beeping began to speed up, and Amber realized the woman was struggling with her emotions. She didn't want the medics to stop her questioning, so Amber spoke calmly.

"It's okay, Tracy. Take a deep breath. We're in no hurry here, okay?"

Malloy did as Amber suggested, inhaling deeply and holding it in a few seconds as she fought to keep her feelings under control. After several more breaths, the beeping slowed once more. Fem Malloy squeezed Amber's hand, and Amber realized her touch was a lifeline in Malloy's new dark reality. She added her other hand over Malloy's, holding the woman's one hand between her own.

"Better?" she asked.

Fem Malloy took one last breath and exhaled. "Yes. Sorry about that."

"There's no need to apologize. You never need to apologize for being human. I was scared shitless when it happened to me. Thought my life was over. But here I am."

"Thanks."

"You think you can go on?"

Malloy nodded. "Yes." She took one last calming breath and continued. "So I heard that nasty laughter. I started to turn toward them, but I was too slow." She gave a half shrug. "Like I said, I was high. They put a bag over my head so I couldn't see anything, then one of them slapped a popper on my neck."

She started breathing faster, and whether consciously or not, her grip on Amber's hand tightened almost painfully.

"Deep breaths, Tracy. Deep breaths."

Tracy Malloy struggled again to calm herself. "Next thing I knew, I was on a table. I was screaming. My back and my guts were on fire."

"From where they cut you?"

Her lips quivered as she nodded, and she stopped talking, obviously agitated once more. The monitors again gave their warning, and Amber saw a medic step through the door. Before he could interfere, Chief Fischer stood and walked the man back outside. She could see them arguing but chose to let Fischer handle that particular problem.

Amber patted the woman's hand. "I'm right here, Tracy. You're past it now."

Fem Malloy licked her lips and took another deep breath. "We were in a pod of some kind. I could feel us moving as they drove." She nodded. "I didn't know it at that point, but they sliced up my back and took my liver and my kidneys. Doctors told me they used some kind of self-cauterizing blade. Otherwise, I would have bled out. Then they rolled me on my back to take my eyes. That's what woke me up. I never felt pain like that before."

Amber's hand actually hurt where Tracy squeezed.

"They slapped some kind of cylinder over my right eye."

Amber remembered that cylinder. How the man had laughed as he'd pressed the button, and the vacuum had popped her eye from its socket. "*What's wrong, baby? Don'cha wanna party with us?*" To this day, she still had nightmares.

Amber blinked the memory away and concentrated on Malloy. The bandaged woman was sobbing quietly at that point, and Amber patted her hand. "It's okay. I know what that part was like."

Snot flowed freely from Malloy's nose. "I'm s-sorry."

"No! Don't be sorry. Be angry. Be pissed. Be ready to shove a red-hot poker up the ass of the person who did this to you. But never apologize. This was not your fault!"

Fem Malloy's lips drew into a determined line, and she wiped her nose with the back of her right hand. Jordie stepped up and tapped Amber's shoulder. Amber looked at what she held and extracted one of her hands from Tracy's grip.

"Here, Tracy. Jordie got you some tissues. Hold up your hand."

Amber handed her a tissue and let the woman gather herself once more. When she'd wiped her nose and calmed again, she gave an exhausted sigh. "Thank you… Jordie, you said?"

"Yes, fem," Jordie replied, "and you're welcome."

There were several seconds of silence as Tracy continued to calm herself. Finally, she asked Amber, "Why would anyone do this? Why take organs? Why take eyes? I mean, we have bioprinters, right? I've read about them. They can print organs now."

Amber sighed. "I used to ask the same question after they took my eyes. I've had a long time to research it."

"Yeah? Did you find any answers?"

"Bioprinters can print skin, bone, tendons, even most organs. But it's an expensive process. They have to draw stem cells from the host, stimulate them into the right kind of cells for the organ, integrate them with the proper suspension gel, and then—"

"That's it?" Malloy practically spat her bitterness. "Bioprinting is expensive, and people are cheap?"

"I'm afraid that's most of it. There's more when it comes to eyes. Despite all they can do with most organs, they still can't print eyes properly. It turns out there are more than one hundred million rods and six or seven million cones in the eyes. Between that and the neural interfaces to the brain… well, from what I read, they gave up on even *trying* to print eyes decades ago. But for the most part, yeah, people are cheaper than tech."

They fell into silence for several seconds as the bitter reality of the world in which they lived hammered home.

Finally, Amber cleared her throat. "Tracy? I'm sorry, but I have a few more questions. Are you okay to go on?"

Fem Malloy nodded, swallowing again before asking, "Could I have another drink?"

Amber grabbed the cup and put it in the woman's hand once more. When she'd had her fill, Tracy handed it back and sighed.

"Okay," she said. "What's next?"

"I know it's tough, Tracy. But when they took my eyes, I had a few seconds where I was able to see around me. I need you to think back. Tell me anything you can remember about those few seconds. The color of the vehicle's interior, what the men looked like, anything you might have seen through any windows. Anything at all."

"All I saw was the one guy's face."

The monitors began to beep quicker again.

"He smiled, and his teeth were bright white. His breath was all minty, like he'd just cleaned up for a date."

Tracy began to breathe faster again, obviously struggling to remain calm through a traumatic memory. And with her next words, Amber's blood froze in her veins.

"I'll never forget that damn scar," Malloy sobbed. "From his left temple through his nose."

CHAPTER 08

"It's Trev!" Amber paced rapidly back and forth in the lobby. "It's got to be him."

"Maybe," Fischer conceded. "We can't know for sure, though. And you have to approach the case as if it isn't. No preconceived ideas."

"Who's Trev?" Jordie asked.

Amber ignored her, still intent on her argument with Chief Fischer. "Oh, come on, Chief! What are the chances? An organ jacker with a scar on the left side of his face?"

Jordie tried again. "Boss? Who's Trev?"

Amber just waved a hand at her as if brushing away a buzzing insect. "Chief, do you know how long I looked for that sludge bucket?"

"I do, actually. I had to sign the waivers to give you access to the files."

She stopped pacing. "You did?"

Fischer nodded. "Do you really think the higher-ups would let a rookie detective investigate her own case? Even unofficially?"

"Oooh," Jordie said. "You think it's the same guy that took your eyes?"

"Of course I do!" Amber snapped. She shook her head. "Sorry. Yes, it's the same guy." She walked to one of the chairs in the room and sat. "I was out on medical leave for almost three weeks when I lost my eyes. Between the surgery to repair the damage and the company selecting and paying for the implantation of my cybernetics, it was more than a week before they got the DNA sequencing and the optical integration done. A few days more before my brain learned to interpret the signals from the cybernetics through my optic nerves so I could see again."

Everyone was silent as she told her story.

"When I got back to work, I was on desk duty, and I started looking through any files I could find that mentioned organ jacking—especially instances where they took the eyes." Her face contorted as she remembered. "It didn't take long for me to realize just how…" She swallowed then hardened her expression. "Just how lucky I was to be alive. Almost all of the case files I read ended with dead victims. Of the handful where the victim lived, only three got a look at their assailants. And one of them described a man with a scar on the left side of his face."

"The same guy that… that took your… that jacked your eyes?" Scott's voice was wary as if he was afraid of setting her off again.

"Of course it was. You think I would be freaking out right now if it wasn't?"

"Sorry."

Richard jumped in. "And how do you know his name?"

Amber hesitated before admitting, "I went through a phase of hunting down organ jackers. Any case that showed up on the sheets, I grabbed it. I was still on desk duty, but that didn't stop me from reading files. And after hours, I conducted my own investigations. I got a few leads on some local jackers. I tracked them down, did some things that probably weren't entirely legal."

"Probably?" Fischer said.

She shrugged. "I got to know a few of them pretty well before…" She stopped, staring at the floor. "They either ended up in cells or hospitals, or I convinced them to move on to greener pastures. But during my… discussions with them, I learned about a pair of jackers who matched the descriptions of the men who attacked me—a man with pretty blue eyes and a man with a nasty scar on the left side of his face. Dewey Trev and Carl Hartzman."

"Holy shyte!" Scott said. "You were the Reaper, weren't you?"

"No, she absolutely was not!" Fischer was vehement in his denial. "That individual was a criminal who we never caught. And because of Fem Payne's association with the subject matter on that case, she was thoroughly investigated and cleared of any connection to the case."

"Who is this Reaper?" Maestro Harris asked Scott in a low voice.

"He," Scott said, "or *she* was the boogeyman for organ jackers about ten or fifteen years back. Nobody ever found out who it was for sure, but they singlehandedly shut down the black-market organ trade in this city. It's only in the last few years that it's started to come back."

"And once again, whoever that individual was, it was *not* Fem Payne. Am I understood?" Fischer was very firm in his rebuke.

Amber continued, ignoring the sidebar conversation. "I've been looking for Trev ever since I found his name. But whoever this Reaper was, they evidently scared him out of the area."

"And what about the other guy? Carl Hartzman?" Richard asked.

Amber went poker-faced. "A report eventually came across my desk. A body matching his description showed up facedown in a ditch. I arranged to see the body at the morgue. It was him." She looked up. "I'm not going to pretend I was broken up over it, but I didn't kill him."

The rest of the group was silent, and she didn't know whether or not they believed her. In the midst of her emotional hurricane, she really didn't care.

"But if I'm being honest, if I had found him in time," her expression hardened, "I honestly don't know whether or not I would have."

The room was silent for several seconds until Richard decided to bring the conversation back to the case at hand. "I guess it's safe to assume we're taking the case. So, what now?"

Amber nodded. "Right." She turned to her former boss. "Chief, we'll take the case. Just don't let your bosses know you pushed it our way. I don't want those SOBs thinking they can come to me anytime they—no, scratch that. I don't want them thinking they can come to me *ever*. If they find out, make it clear to them that I'm doing this as a favor to *you*."

Fischer nodded. "Thank you."

"No need. We both know you're the one doing the favor here. Thanks." She faced her team. "We start hitting street cams in the area. See what we can find there. I'll contact Dem and Acamas to see if they can find any John Doe cases from the night sheets or Emergency Services that might have been organ jacking cases. Maybe there's a pattern or a localized area of operation."

"That won't work," Fischer said. "You're not a LEO anymore. You don't have access to the night sheets."

Amber grinned. "Chief, I've got access to a lot more than you would be comfortable knowing about. As a matter of fact, you might not want to know about the rest of our plans. Plausible deniability, you know?"

Fischer stared for a moment before shaking his head. "You always did like to dance in the gray." He pulled out his comm and looked at the chrono on it. "Well, I guess I should get back to HQ. Let me know how the case progresses."

"I will." Amber watched as Chief Fischer walked to the elevator. Once he was gone, she looked at Jordie. "You still have sources for good security and electronics?"

"Sure. What are you after?"

"You know the building I bought for Payne Security Consultants?"

"Yeah."

"We're going to need someplace to work the case from. It might as well be a resource we already have. I want you to set us up with a conference room like we had at Securi-Tech and add anything else you think might come in handy." She led them to the elevators.

"What's the budget for this?"

Amber palmed the elevator open. As they walked inside, she shrugged. "I'm still getting used to the idea of having more money than I know what to do with. You and Scott are more used to living that way, so I'll leave it up to you. Just try not to run my finances into the ground."

Scott cleared his throat. "Speaking of finances, does this mean you're hiring us?"

Amber was silent for a few seconds before she shook her head. "No. I'm offering the three of you partnerships in PSC. You interested?"

Scott grinned as the elevator doors opened, and they stepped out into the parking garage.

Richard spoke immediately. "I'm in."

"Don't answer too fast," Amber warned. "You don't even know the terms yet."

He shrugged. "I trust you."

Amber stopped as they reached the van. She faced the four of them, and her eyes rested on Maestro Harris. "Maestro, you've never worked with us before, and I don't know how deep you want to get in this case. You heard Chief Fischer mention how I like to dance in the gray. Do you understand what that means?"

Maestro Harris, who had been mostly silent throughout the morning, nodded. "I am thinking so. It is *dar um jeitinho*."

"Daroomjay cheen-oo?" Amber struggled with the pronunciation.

"Yes. It is the bending of rules to do what must be done."

"Sounds about right. And how do you feel about that? I'll admit, having you along could come in very handy on this case. Things are likely to get ugly. But I anticipate we might end up… sidestepping the law on this one. If you aren't okay with that, this might be a good time to walk away."

"And what is it you think we Fixers do? We step in when the law is… ahh." He pulled out his tablet, obviously irritated. "*Como você diz?*" he muttered as he tapped an icon on the screen before speaking directly into the tablet's mic. "*Inadequada.*"

The tablet immediately spoke for him. "Inadequate."

"Yes!" he said. "We are Fixers. We step in when the law is inadequate."

Amber nodded, looking at the faces around her. "Then let's get to work."

CHAPTER 09

As a physical business, Payne Security Consultants barely existed. It was born from a combination of Amber's realization that she might need a location to meet people who couldn't know about her association with the Fixers and the knowledge that she had more money now than she knew what to do with. She'd found a location with growth potential then had Acamas and Demophon file the legal forms to set it all up. That had been less than six months ago.

Other than a few walkthroughs, though, she'd never really spent any time in the building. Now she looked it over with a more critical eye. The building was small, built in an area that had gone through economically tough times. That meant there were several empty buildings in the area, which could come in handy for someone wanting to avoid drawing attention.

The building itself consisted of three floors and an underground parking garage. The ground floor opened into an atrium that also served as a lobby. She knew it was wasted space, but Amber liked the view as one walked through the front entrance. There was an ostentatiousness in being able to look from the first-floor lobby up to the walkways spanning the second and third.

There were sturdy faux-stone reception—or security—kiosks on the east and west walls, designed to funnel visitors through the middle of the building. The first floor consisted of the atrium, three conference rooms, and six offices. Upper floors opened to a view over the atrium, and each had two conference rooms and several more offices. She honestly hadn't spent enough time in the building to recall exactly how many offices there were.

The furnishings were Spartan—some low-budget desks, chairs, and outdated wall displays. Even the conference rooms had little more than basic tables, comm systems, and old-style projection systems for video calls.

It was in the largest of those conference rooms on the first floor that they all gathered. Amber tapped the embedded menu on the desk in front of her seat, and an old projector dropped from the ceiling.

"Wow." Jordie eyed the antiquated piece of equipment and sighed. "I can see my work's cut out for me."

"Give me a break. I just bought the place a few months ago, and I didn't really expect to use it much. In retrospect, I think I was mistaken." Amber tapped a few more icons as she spoke. "So if you can help get us set up here, I'd appreciate it. Concentrate on this room first. I—"

The images of Demophon and Acamas lit up on the far wall, distracting her for a second. She held up a finger to them, indicating they should wait while she finished with Jordie. "I'd like a holo setup like we had at Securi-Tech so Dem and Acamas can interact a bit more realistically."

"How about something more like what we have at The Glads?" Scott interjected.

Amber recalled the state-of-the-art systems they'd seen in the luxury suites of the underground fighting arena. The holo-projections had been so realistic she couldn't tell that T-bone was a hologram, and the sound system had targeted audio projectors that followed the hologram to make it seem as if the sound came from the same place. The result was such a realistic projection it was almost indistinguishable from a real person.

But she also recalled Scott mentioning that the equipment in each of those suites came with a multimillion-credit price tag.

Amber shook her head. "I doubt I can afford that."

"You keep underestimating how much money you have now. Besides, if you're serious about bringing us in as partners, then we'll split the cost. Between the four of us, it won't be bad at all."

Amber chewed her lip for a few seconds. "Hold that thought." She turned to the images on the wall. "Acamas, Dem, we have a case that's going to require we start working out of the offices here at PCS. We're looking at upgrading the holo setup to make things more tolerable." She pointed to Maestro Harris. "We also have a new associate who's going to be working with us for a while. Meet Maestro Brent Harris. He's our new combat-arts instructor."

Demophon nodded to Harris. "It's a pleasure to meet you."

Acamas nodded as well but remained silent.

"It is pleasurable for me also," Harris responded.

"Dem and Acamas are our cybersecurity specialists," Amber replied to the maestro's questioning look. "You won't find anyone better."

"Truly? But they are so young."

Younger than you know.

The brother-and-sister pair were AIs who had been "born" scant days before their father, T-bone, had been killed some eight months earlier. They claimed to have most of his memories, but because T-bone had been forced to radically alter their base kernel, their personalities were very different. As far as anyone was aware, they were the only two AIs in existence, and no one other than Amber, Richard, Scott, and Jordie knew what they really were. As far as the rest of the world was concerned, fully sentient and self-aware AIs were still an impossible dream.

Demophon chuckled at Maestro Harris's comment. "Cybersecurity is a profession for the young. The technology changes so fast, and we were born to it."

Amber nearly choked at his comment. She jumped back in to guide the conversation back to safer ground. "Acamas, we're going to be upgrading the systems here at PSC. Time to turn it into a real business."

Acamas nodded. Of the two AIs, she was by far the more serious and analytical. She had less of a sense of humor than her brother but was better with finances and systems analyses. "That sounds good. Which systems are you upgrading?"

Amber pointed to Jordie, who took over the conversation.

"I'm putting together a list," Jordie said. "But from what I've seen so far, it's going to be a full gut and rebuild. We'll prioritize the conference rooms so comms will be high end." Jordie tapped a button on her tablet. "I just sent you a file with some of the basics. We'll need pricing and availability ASAP. The idea is to get this rolling right away. Tonight if possible."

Acamas looked over the list and nodded. "You'll also need to rebuild your network infrastructure to accommodate the extra data streams from all the holo and sound emitters."

"Okay, whatever you think. The goal—"

"Guys?" Amber interrupted them. "You think you could take it to the other room? Sorry, but the rest of us need to discuss the case."

"Sure." Jordie pulled out an earbud and slipped it in place. She tapped a few commands on her tablet. "Acamas, can you hear me?"

Evidently, she could, because Jordie gave Amber a thumbs-up and left the room. Acamas disappeared from the screen.

"Okay," Amber said. "Dem, did you get a chance to look over the case file I sent you earlier?"

"I only had time to skim it."

Amber knew better. She had forwarded him the file—as well as the recording of her interview with Fem Tracy Malloy—from her van after leaving the hospital less than half an hour earlier. Nevertheless, she was certain he already knew the case more intimately than she did. And she'd been dwelling on it since the night before.

But the presence of Maestro Harris demanded discretion.

"Have you had time to form any first impressions?"

Demophon made a show of looking off-screen as if checking a monitor. "First impression, huh? How about, are you absolutely sure you want to take this one on? I mean, this has got to be pretty personal for you."

"I've thought it through. Stick to the case."

He shrugged. "It's your therapy bill." He looked off-screen again. "Fem Malloy mentioned the area around Homer's Huff House isn't really the safest part of town. If anything, she downplayed it. Sorting LEO databases by location indicates it's in the top ten percent for violent crimes in the city."

"Is that a recent uptick?" Scott asked.

"Yeah. It was already bad, but stats show it's been climbing steadily for the last year or so. It's gotten really bad in the last six months."

Amber almost hated to ask the next question, but she was determined to keep her emotions in check. "What about organ jacking? Has there been a significant increase?"

Dem looked off-screen again. "Yes and no. It's gone up over the last few years but not statistically higher than over the rest of the city."

"So it's going up all over the city?" she asked.

"Apparently so. Not a lot, but the numbers indicate an increase of about six percent over the last year."

"Hang on a second," Richard said. "You're basing that off the LEO databases, right?"

"Yes. Why?"

"Look for ambulance and morgue reports where they've picked up bodies missing organs." Richard turned to Amber. "I'll bet you tomorrow's breakfast we find a lot more unreported cases that way. Unregistered and homeless people don't get reported."

Amber remembered that Richard lived in Dineh Village, one of the poorer parts of town.

"The big guy's right," Demophon said. "The numbers more than quadruple when I add those in."

"Compare the annual stats from the last five years," Amber told him.

It took him only a moment. "Hardly any organ jackings until three years ago. In 2245 and 2246, organ jacking crimes were statistically insignificant. Less than a dozen were reported over those two years. Then in 2247, there were twenty-seven. In 2248, there were sixty-three. Then last year..." He whistled. "Last year, there were a hundred eighty-nine. So far this year, they've already got over two hundred."

Amber pursed her lips, speculating about what it meant. "They probed to see if it was safe to set up shop again. And when no one came after them, they got down to business."

They all fell silent for a few seconds before Richard cleared his throat. "So, now what? We know there's a crew of jackers back in town."

"More than one," Amber said.

"Why do you say that?"

"I got familiar with the way they work, remember? They keep their teams small... tight. The most I ever saw on a single team was five people. Most were two or three, and they usually only jacked one person a week." She shook her head. "Nearly two hundred victims last year, and on track for three hundred this year? That's too many for a single team. I'd guess we have five or six teams working the city now."

"No way!" Scott protested. "Someone would have noticed that many."

Richard shook his head. "Who? Municipal LEOs are so underfunded and understaffed that it's all they can do to patrol downtown. Private law enforcement companies only care about the contract. That's the reason homeless and unemployed people are always good targets. Nobody can afford to file contracts for them. It's been that way for centuries."

"So how do we find them?" Scott asked.

"I'll look for patterns in the times and locations of the crimes we've found," Dem said. "Since we aren't just going by the LEO information, we've got a lot more to track than anyone else. Maybe I can find something that way."

Amber nodded. "Do it. Anyone else?"

When no one said anything, she rapped her knuckles on the table. "All right. Let's call it for today. Do whatever you think you need to do to recharge. We all need to be fresh tomorrow. The condition for us being able to work this case is we have to continue our training with Maestro Harris."

Harris nodded in acknowledgment.

"So study the files this evening. Or go party with friends, or whatever you need to do to start fresh tomorrow. But we all meet back at Fixer HQ in the morning. We get in our morning session with the maestro, and then we start working the case."

They all nodded.

"Okay, I'll see you all tomorrow."

CHAPTER 10

Amber walked through the front door and dropped her duffel to the floor. She leaned back against the wall, trying to wrest her mind into some sort of calm before facing Nathan. She usually tried to keep from bringing the stress of her new job home with her. With this case, though, that was going to be impossible.

But if she'd wanted to have a moment to calm her mind, she shouldn't have dropped her duffel bag so carelessly. There was a sharp yip, and Odin came sliding around the corner from the kitchen, tiny claws skittering on the duraplas floor as he struggled to maintain traction. There wasn't going to be any respite to find her calm. But the eternally happy pup was the next-best thing.

Amber smiled wearily and knelt as Odin, or Odie, as she and Nathan usually called him, reached her and stood on his rear legs, whining for her attention. "Hello, Odie. Have you been a good boy?"

The little bundle of black fur yipped happily and licked her face when she picked him up.

"He's been good. He just missed you."

Amber looked up as Nathan entered the room. He slung a dish towel over his shoulder as she stood to greet him with a kiss.

He smiled. "Mmm. And so have I." He stepped back, looked at her intently, and frowned. "What's wrong?"

She briefly considered blowing the question off and pretending she was just tired. But that wasn't how she wanted their relationship to grow. She had told him from the beginning that she wouldn't be able to tell him everything she did but had promised to be as honest with him as she could, whenever she could.

"We've got a case," she said.

Nathan raised an eyebrow, silently inviting her to continue.

"It's going to be a tough one."

"Aren't they all?"

"This one hits on a personal level." She took a deep breath before getting to the hard part. "It's organ jackers."

Nathan's lips drew into a thin line. After a few seconds, he nodded. "What do you need from me?"

She smiled and touched his cheek. "Do you realize just how perfect that was? No false bravado. No trying to reassure me that everything will be okay. Just seeing what I need."

He shrugged. "We're eight months into this relationship. I learned on day two that you're more than capable of taking care of your own business." He chuckled. "Hells above, you can handle things that would bury me. There's no competition on shyte like this." He pulled her in close. "And since I have no idea what you're going through or what I can do to help, I figure the best thing for me to do is ask."

Amber leaned in and kissed him again. "Like I said, perfect." She put Odie back on the floor and picked up her duffel bag. "Let me put my gear away, and I'll tell you about it over dinner."

"Sure."

Five minutes later, they were seated at the table, starting the simple meal of pasta primavera. Amber knew by now that none of this was purchased in a store. When her man cooked, he cooked from scratch. He had a small roof garden where he grew his own herbs and vegetables, and she'd seen him make pasta by hand. As far as she was concerned, the man was a master of some arcane magic that produced food fit for gods. Usually, it was enough to wipe away the stress of the day.

Not tonight, though. Amber picked absently at her plate, barely tasting the food she put in her mouth.

"I'd be insulted if I didn't already know you had something important on your mind," Nathan said.

She looked up. "What do you mean?"

"If you can close your eyes and tell me what you've been eating, I'll eat my hat."

"You don't have a hat." Amber forced a smile. "But you're right. Sorry." She put her fork down.

Nathan followed suit, setting his fork beside his plate. "Okay, you already said there was more to the case. You also said it had to do with organ jackers. And it's obviously got you twisted up enough that you don't even know what you're eating. So let's talk about it."

Amber nodded but remained silent as she looked down at her plate. He patiently waited until she finally started talking, telling him about Fem Malloy and her attack. When she reached the part about Dewey Trev being one of the men who had taken her own eyes, Nathan let loose a stream of curses the likes of which Amber hadn't known her lover was capable.

"Look," she said, "I'm not going to pretend this isn't going to affect me. But I'm going to do my absolute best to work through the case in a professional manner." She lifted a shoulder. "Or as professional as I'm able. I'll have the whole team to help keep me on track and to keep an eye on me."

"But it's still going to mess with you. There's no way it won't. And you already have nightmares about this guy. I know—I've been there when you wake up screaming."

Amber nodded. "And I can't argue with any of that. But there's also no way I can leave this case for someone else."

He was silent for only a second before nodding. "I know. I'm still going to worry about you, though. So let me ask you the same thing I asked earlier. What do you need from me? How can I help?"

She smiled. "Just bear with me. I'm liable to turn into a horrible bitch during the course of this thing, and I don't want to make you regret moving in with me."

He smiled. "Not possible."

"That's sweet of you to say, but—"

"No, seriously. I mean, have you seen the kitchen in this place? Buddha himself couldn't convince me to leave."

Amber reached across the table and grasped his hand. "Thank you."

DAY 03
THURSDAY

CHAPTER 11

There were some changes in their training session the next morning. Maestro Harris insisted they all train with live shock blades, though he had them reduce the setting to their mildest of shocks. Each touch stung but wouldn't incapacitate. Still, it served as a great incentive to avoid getting hit.

They also had a few extra trainees. Harris had arranged for CC Miller, the only other Fixer in the same weight class as Richard, to train with them. He had also brought in Missy Hutson as a partner for Jordie. Other than Amber, Missy was one of the only other Fixers short enough to be a match for Jordie. And Harris was adamant about wanting Scott and Amber to train together as much as possible. Their speed enhancements eliminated nearly anyone else as a viable partner for either of them.

"Angle one!"

At the maestro's command, Amber sliced down at Scott's left collarbone. She saw Scott set his frame and slap his training blade against hers, knocking it off target.

"No, no, no!" Maestro Harris shouted. "You do not simply to parry. You must also to pivot and change zones. This removes you from your opponent's line of attack while keeping them in yours. You cannot always to count on changing the angle of your opponent's attack. So you change where you are in relationship to this angle."

The maestro tapped Scott on the shoulder, signaling him to move out of the way. "Observe." He took Scott's place before Amber and raised his practice blade.

Harris nodded to Amber. "Angle one. Strike."

Amber swung her blade.

Harris slapped her blade aside with his own. "This is what you did, Mr. Pond. Correct?"

Scott's lips drew into a thin line, frustration evident on his face. "Yes. And it worked."

"This is true. It worked against Fem Payne. However, would it work against Mr. Kayani?"

Scott looked at the hulking body of Richard Kayani and suddenly appeared much less sure of himself.

Harris signaled Richard to stand beside Amber then turned to face Scott. "Would you to use this kind of defense against this man?"

Scott reluctantly shook his head.

"Why?"

Scott sighed. "Because he would power through the parry like it wasn't even there."

"Correct. Now, observe." Maestro Harris moved to stand before Richard and nodded. "Strike with full power. Angle one. Strike!"

Richard swung with a growl, power evident in his strike. As soon as Richard began his move, Maestro Harris slipped slightly to his right, shifted his weight onto his right hip, and pivoted as he struck. Richard tried to keep up with his moving target, but with his momentum already committed, he was off balance. He bent at the waist as his blade hit the mat with a resounding thunk. Maestro Harris's blade, on the other hand, rested lightly on the back of Richard's neck. Luckily for Richard, the maestro was the only one with his training blade powered off.

Harris lifted his blade and tapped Richard lightly on his shoulder. The larger man stood up.

"Please to step back," Harris said. Richard moved back into line across from CC Miller.

"Now," the maestro continued, "analyze my counter. Tell me quickly, strengths and weaknesses."

"You waited until your opponent was committed," Scott said. "Then you removed yourself from his angle of attack while adjusting your own position and angle."

Harris smiled. "Yes! Those are the strengths. What are weaknesses?"

"You were exposed to his left hand. If he had been quick enough, he could have hit you with his free hand."

"Excellent! How I can keep this from happening?"

Amber bit her lower lip. When no one else volunteered, she cleared her throat.

Harris inclined his head at her. "Yes?"

"If you can pull it off, you could shift to your opponent's right side instead of his left. It would be hard to get under his blade, but if you can get to his two o'clock without being hit, then his right arm will block his left. It's like what you did to me the first time we sparred."

Harris grinned like a child with a new toy. "Excellent!"

"But getting past his attack would be risky," Amber reiterated.

"Not so much as you would think." And the maestro proceeded to demonstrate a high circular strike that could be used as a parry. Amber recognized it as the same strike he had used against her the first time he had beaten her. The rest of their training session consisted of them practicing that technique.

When their time was up, they all gathered around Maestro Harris.

"Mr. Pond," he said, "you did surprisingly well."

Scott feigned hurt feelings. "Surprisingly?"

Harris smiled before turning to Amber. "I assume we have more workings on your case?"

Amber nodded. "We do. Will you be joining us again?"

"I have notified Fem Gibbs that I plan to work as a member of your team. You should consider me your subordinate in all matters other than your training. Make use of my skills as you see fit."

"Wait a second," Missy said. "You guys have a case? But you haven't finished your training yet."

"It's not a Fixer case," Amber reassured her. "It's something personal. And I cleared it through Gibbs."

"You need any help?"

Amber started to tell her no, but Missy kept going.

"I know you guys don't have a chemist on your team, and I'm the best in the division."

Amber stopped, intrigued. "Chemist?"

"Sure. Drugs, explosives, whatever. You name it, and I can probably make it."

That was, indeed, something that might come in handy. A throat cleared behind her. Amber turned to stare into the sternum of CC Miller. She looked up. "Let me guess—you want in too?"

Miller answered in his pleasant alto. "If there's room. I think anyone would rather work an active case than spend every day training and waiting on an assignment."

Amber supposed that was true. It certainly was for her. She pointed at Missy. "She's a chemist. What do you bring to the table?"

Miller blinked, apparently taken aback. Then he stepped back and waved his hands down at his body as if to say, "Isn't it obvious?"

Amber chuckled. "Yeah, I guess that was a stupid question." She turned to Maestro Harris. "Do you think you can get them cleared to work with us?"

Harris hesitated before answering. "I am believing so. But I would recommend we keep this from becoming common knowledge. If others learn you offer a case, then I am thinking you will get many, many requests to join you."

Amber nodded. "That's true." Turning to the others, she made sure everyone was paying attention. "Not a word about the case leaves this room. No one else should even know we *have* a case. You don't mention it to anyone other than the people in this room and Fem Gibbs. Clear?"

There were nods all around.

"Good. Then let's get cleaned up and meet at PSC in an hour."

"PSC?" Missy asked.

"I'll send you and Miller the address. Assuming Gibbs clears you, I'll see you there."

CHAPTER 12

The PSC conference room was a mess when Amber walked in. There were piles of boxes and packing materials scattered all over the floor and table surface. She heard cursing from beneath the table and bent down to see Jordie working on a bundle of wiring.

"You got here fast," Amber said.

"I rode my uni."

Last year, Jordie had fallen in love with Richard's single-wheeled power cycle. A few months ago, she'd bought one of her own. Amber had ridden on the back of Richard's a few times and had to admit to a certain thrill in the wildness of the ride. But she had no desire to have one of her own.

"I needed to put a few finishing touches on the new holo system." Jordie connected a few final wires and groaned as she climbed out from beneath the table. She stood and wiped her hands on her pants.

"You got it installed already? How did you manage that?"

"I slept here last night while Acamas worked behind the scenes to expedite some of the hardware. She woke me when it got here, and I did a quick install. It's not completely done, but it's better than what you had."

"Still, that's a lot to get done in one night."

Jordie shrugged. "Like I said, it's not complete. But we can use it. At least, we can after I finish installing the control interface."

"That's awesome, Jordie. We have about twenty minutes before the others are due here. Is that long enough?"

"It should be."

Amber smiled at her friend's confidence. "Then I'll try to keep out of your way." She looked at the trash all over the room.

"Oh, yeah," Jordie said. "I made a bit of a mess."

"A bit?" Amber snorted but began gathering the boxes and piling them in the back corner of the room. "There isn't anything in this I need to worry about keeping, is there? No manuals, data chips, or anything like that?"

"No. It's all ready for the compactors. Which reminds me, we're going to need to buy some cleaning bots. If this place is going to be a legit consulting firm, you're going to have to run it like one."

Amber sighed. "I suppose. But I really don't need the distraction of running a business while we're working with the Fixers."

"It doesn't need to be a distraction. Set it up where your rates—"

"Our rates," Amber corrected. "Partners, remember?"

"Okay," Jordie conceded. "Where *our* rates are high enough that we only get the most elite clientele. That should weed out most of them and keep the cases interesting."

Amber was shaking her head before Jordie had even finished. "That's something I told myself I would never do. Part of the reason LEO firms go bad is they worry more about the bottom line than the people they're supposed to help. Hells above, we're even seeing that on this case! The main reason we're ahead of the curve here is because we're digging into records no one else cares about. We're seeing firsthand what happens to the people who can't afford to contract with the private LEO companies." She shook her head. "No. I didn't leave Securi-Tech just to turn into another version of the same problem."

"Technically, you didn't leave Securi-Tech at all. They fired you." Jordie raised her hands to fend off Amber's retort. "Don't get me wrong—I'm glad it all worked out the way it did. And I get what you're saying. I just mean there are ways to set us up where there's a legitimate income source *and* something we can all be proud of."

"We?" Amber grinned.

Jordie shrugged. "Partners, remember?" She returned Amber's smile before picking up a control panel. "Now, here's how the new system works. The easiest way to use Hecter is through voice commands."

"Hecter?"

"It's the acronym for holographic entertainment and communications transmitter. *H, E, C, T,* and they added the *E* and the *R* from the end of transmitter to spell Hecter.'"

Amber blinked. "You've got to be kidding me."

"I think someone thought they were being clever."

"*I* think someone had too much time on their hands."

Jordie smiled. "Can't argue there. Anyway, Hecter answers to his name. Turn the system on with this button"—she showed Amber the button on the panel—"and call out his name. He's like your typical Chasm unit but a lot more robust." She handed the panel to Amber. "I recommend you set voice recognition and just use verbal commands all the time, but the panel gives you a silent option if you want it."

There were all sorts of icons and menus to adjust sound and visual outputs as well as some blank ones that weren't yet programmed. She carefully avoided them all. Instead, she pressed the power icon. "Hecter." Amber made sure to speak clearly.

"Yes, Fem Payne. How can I help you?"

She was surprised at how lifelike the voice sounded. She turned to Jordie. "Does he have a contact database loaded yet?"

Before Jordie could answer, Hecter spoke. "I have a contact database of fifty-seven entries. My records indicate it was uploaded at 02:23 by Fem Jordan Dyer."

Jordie smiled. "I loaded the ones I know. We can always add more as needed."

"Are Dem and Acamas in there?"

"I have a contact entry for Acamas Delos. I have no entry for a Dem. However, there is an entry for Demophon Delos. Are these the entries to which you refer?"

Amber looked at Jordie. "Delos?"

"It means 'from the bone' in French. There was a field for a last name, and I thought they needed a link to T-bone."

Amber smiled. "I like it." Speaking again to the system, she said, "Yes, Hecter. Acamas and Demophon. And append the Demophon entry with an alternate name of Dem."

"Done. Would you like me to open a line of communications with them?"

"Yes."

"Initiating calls."

A second later, two holographic figures appeared at the end of the conference table. Dem looked around the room. "Incoming resolution on this end still needs some work." He looked off-screen in the manner he and Acamas both used in front of outsiders. T-bone had done the same thing when he needed to keep up the fiction that he was a human cybersurfer. "Coverage through the building isn't complete yet either. Is anyone else around?"

Amber shook her head. "Just me and Jordie at the moment."

Dem looked at the image of his sister. "I thought you were going to spec out a top-of-the-line system."

"It's not complete," Acamas retorted. "This is the bare minimum until the rest of the equipment is installed."

Demophon nodded. "What else is going in?"

"Twelve more holo emitters for this room, with more scheduled to populate throughout the building. We'll concentrate on the conference rooms first, but we're going to cover the entire building with enough holo and sound emitters for us to have a holographic presence in any room, hallway, or lobby. We're also putting in a top-level security system so we can see and hear anywhere in the building."

Amber couldn't help but worry again at the cost of the setup. She knew she was wealthy now, at least by most standards. But a system to cover seven conference rooms plus the rest of the building was going to come with a pretty sizeable price tag. "Hold on a second. Just how much are we talking about?"

Acamas pursed her lips as if thinking. "Roughly seventy million credits for the whole building."

Amber swallowed.

"Don't worry." Jordie chuckled. "It splits four ways, remember?"

Amber sighed. "Numbers this big make my head hurt."

The conversation was interrupted as Richard walked in. She noticed he was wearing a fancy long duster similar to Scott's favorite garb. Richard had commented on Scott's coat when he and Amber had arrested him and Jordie, identifying the maker as Lori Kidd, one of the best designers of custom tactical clothing.

Amber sighed. *Money is changing us all.*

Richard was followed by Scott, Missy, Maestro Harris, and CC Miller.

Amber nodded at them. "Have a seat, everyone. Hutson and Miller"—Amber waved a hand—"meet Acamas and Demophon. They're our cybersecurity specialists. The best in the business."

There were informal nods and "pleased to meet you"s as they all acknowledged one another. Amber didn't let the conversation go any further.

She addressed the two newcomers to the team. "Did anyone tell you what we're doing here?"

Hutson nodded. "Scott told us on the ride over. Organ jackers." She looked uncomfortable as she added, "And it looks like it is related to whoever took your eyes ten or twelve years ago."

"Fourteen," Amber said. "But yeah. So I won't lie—this case has personal baggage for me. I'll do my best to keep it to a minimum, but if you can't handle the idea of me in a bad mood, you might want to reconsider joining us."

"You mean this is you in a *good* mood?" Scott joked.

Amber took the jibe with a smile. "Funny." She looked at the slightly pixelated hologram of Demophon. "Dem, were you able to find any patterns after we spoke last night?"

"Some. Comparing notes on various med center reports, I can say for certain that there are at least five teams of jackers in town, probably a few more. But I've been able to spot patterns for five. One team in particular seems pretty sloppy."

Amber pulled out her tablet to take notes. "How so?"

Dem made a show of working on something off-screen, and a picture popped up on the wall. "They're exceptionally brutal, and they hunt the same areas of the city often enough that they're starting to draw attention."

Amber winced at the picture. The body was mutilated, and there was so much blood that it was difficult to determine exactly what she was looking at.

"This is what was left of Judite Freitas. She's the latest casualty in the area."

Maestro Harris leaned forward.

Amber noticed. "You have something to add, Maestro?"

"This woman was from my country, I think." He looked from the picture to Amber. "The name tells me this. It is being common name there."

Dem nodded. "A large percentage of the neighborhood is from Novo Brasil. I'm unsure whether or not that has anything to do with choosing the area as a hunting ground, but it looks like there have been seventeen similar killings in the immediate surroundings. Fifteen of them have been immigrants from Novo Brasil."

A list of names popped up beside the picture: Ana Ferreira, Noêmia Santiago, Otávio Magro—Amber's reading was interrupted by Scott's voice.

"Hey, guys?" He turned his head sideways, squinting at the projection as if the new perspective might let him see more detail. "Where's the head?"

"What was left of it was found two days ago in a malfunctioning flash can at a nearby park," Dem said. "Residents of an apartment complex across the street complained about the smell. When a repair crew came out to fix it, they found the partially charred head blocking some of the incinerator nozzles. The eyes had been removed, and the left side of the face was burned off. The damage was extensive, but the flash can malfunctioned before it could completely destroy the… evidence." He put a picture of the remains on the wall.

"That's disgusting!" Missy said.

"Yes," Dem agreed. "But it's also what I mean about the team getting sloppy. When the med center reported the death to Fem Freitas's husband, he refused to cooperate in any investigation. The follow-up report has a notation indicating he acted like he feared some kind of reprisal."

"So they're threatening the locals?" Scott asked.

Dem nodded. "That seems a reasonable conclusion. But scaring one person doesn't guarantee none of them will talk."

Amber took a deep breath as she thought. "What part of town did they find her in?"

Dem projected a map of the city onto the wall. A red circle pulsed in the southwest quadrant. "From what I can tell, this team works mostly in Sixth Ward."

"Which means they won't take kindly to LEOs poking around," Richard said.

"Technically, we're not LEOs anymore," Amber said. "We're PIs."

"They won't care. Strangers walk in and start asking about organ jackers in their neighborhood. As far as they're concerned, we're LEOs."

They were all silent for a few seconds until Scott asked, "How about a reporter?"

Amber looked up. "You think she'd do it? I mean, I never really came through on our last deal. I got fired before I could give her that exclusive on the Conley case."

"She'll do it for her baby brother."

"If you think she'll go for it, then sure. You might want to plan on going with her, though. It's a rough neighborhood."

"Perhaps I should go as well," Harris said. "It is being possible that someone from Fem Freitas's home country could setting her husband to ease."

Amber considered for a moment.

Scott nodded at Amber. "We already know the maestro can handle himself. Between the two of us, Colleen'll be about as safe as she can be."

"Fine," Amber said. "Do it."

Scott left the table, pulling out his comm bud.

"What about the rest of us?" Richard asked.

"I want you, Jordie, and CC to work with Dem on narrowing down possible locations for some of the other jacker teams." She pointed to Missy. "You got me thinking when you mentioned your background in chemistry. If you don't mind, I have an idea, but I don't know if it's possible. I'd like to pick your brain and see what you think."

Missy nodded. "Sure."

"Acamas? Would you mind staying with us? You're one of the best researchers I know, and I have a feeling that's going to come in handy too."

"Sure."

Amber watched Richard and the others leave the conference room. Once the door was closed, she turned back to Missy and Acamas. "Let's talk about fear."

That night, Amber tossed restlessly in bed. Beside her, Nathan snored lightly, and she was jealous of the ease with which he slept. This case robbed her of that ability. But she had learned several mental exercises over the years to help her fight her anxiety, and eventually, she found her way into sleep. Still, her rest was far from uneventful. There were simply too many nightmares… too many memories. As she wandered the corridors of sleep, those memories pounced.

CHAPTER 13

– FRIDAY, MARCH 26, 2236 –

FOURTEEN YEARS EARLIER

AMBER HAD FOUND THE PLACE after days of painstaking comparisons of housing records versus power-consumption archives. Those searches had gained her a list of more than three dozen discrepancies, and she'd been inspecting them for weeks. She checked at least four addresses each night, and this place was the third on her list for tonight.

The first was occupied by a band of homeless families—men, women, and kids who had the good fortune to have someone in their midst who knew how to bypass corporate power access lockouts. The second was being used as a temporary clinic for a street doc. Amber had no quarrel with either of those.

But this third address...

It was registered as abandoned, of course. There didn't appear to be anyone in the building, and from the outside, it looked completely uninhabited. The walls were dingy and tagged with the logos of three different street gangs, and the grass in the little plot of a yard was heavily overgrown. All of these things were expected.

But the windows sparked a mental alarm. First of all, they were all intact. Every single one. Most abandoned buildings had at least a few windows that were broken or shot full of holes. Not only were these windows whole, but they were also painted over with flat black paint… from the inside. Someone didn't want anyone to see what was going on inside.

Amber slipped into the narrow alley to the side of the building and examined one of the windows closely. It was about half a meter over her head and painted over like the others she had seen. She noted a darker area in the upper corner too. She blinked through the menu on her new eyes, still a little clumsy with the interface, but quickly found how to set her eyes to infrared and zoomed in on the spot that had caught her attention. There was a cooler area there, a device with small leads going from it to random spots on the glass.

Vibration sensor.

Someone *really* didn't want anyone looking inside. Amber smiled. She was prepared for that. She switched her eyes back to the default setting, reached into her vest, and pulled out a small screwdriver-shaped tool with a blunt end. Securi-Tech's surveillance department had all sorts of handy little gadgets. This was a Hi-Temp, Lo-Profile Penetration tool—HiTLoPP for short. She reached up and placed it gently against the high-density plas-screen window and pressed the button on top. Within seconds, the tool melted a hole one and a half centimeters in diameter through the window. And melting it hadn't caused the slightest vibration.

She blew on the end of the HiTLoPP to cool it down before slipping it back into her vest and pulling out an optics fiber cam. She linked the lead wire of the cam to her tablet and threaded the other end through the hole in the window.

Inside, the storeroom was dark except for dozens of flickering LEDs. The lights hinted at active equipment, though, so she changed the fiber cam setting to low light. On the screen of her tablet, revealed in pixelated green hues, she saw what appeared to be quite a bit of medical equipment.

Somehow, I doubt medical equipment would have been left in an abandoned building. It was enough to warrant a closer look.

Amber went around back and scanned the setup. There was a private parking pad and a fence. No windows, a single back door, a power generator, and a chiller-heater unit. After a second's thought, she went to the generator and scanned the setup. She found the leads running power into the building and slapped a wireless power shunt over the cable. Another standard LEO tool… one she would have to remember to disconnect and take with her before she left.

The lock on the back of the building further convinced her she was on the right track. It was a high-end, state-of-the-art security lock, well beyond the price range of most common citizens. Again, not something likely to be left on an abandoned building. State-of-the-art or not, the lock was no match for the lock popper she'd snuck out of Securi-Tech. Of course, it was completely illegal for her to use the device without a case number to attach it to, but Amber wasn't going to let a minor technicality stop her. She popped the lock and slipped inside.

The plan was to sneak in, take some video of the setup, and set up a few button cams. Then she would get back outside to stake the place out.

That was the plan.

When she slipped inside, the room was pitch-black. Blinking LEDs around the large room were the only source of light. There was a satisfying irony in the fact that, if not for the low-light setting on the new cybereyes, she wouldn't be able to see in the room. She liked the idea of using her new eyes to go after the people who had taken her old ones. There was a kind of karmic symmetry to the whole scenario.

As she looked around, she saw something her probe hadn't been able to show her from the window. There, in the back of the room, was an area cordoned off by long and heavy blackout curtains. Now she was virtually certain she was in the right place. Someone *really* hadn't wanted the light from their work to give away their presence.

Amber had done her research. Over the last few weeks, she'd become something of an expert on the way organ jackers worked, and she knew the nature of their business didn't allow for them to work in a low-light environment. They had to be able to see the subtle shades of red that enabled them to sort healthy tissue from unhealthy, so blacked-out lab areas were a common feature for them.

The back wall had a bank of ten restaurant-quality food chillers, and her bile rose when she examined the contents of the first one. She probably wouldn't have recognized the containers of meat within had it not been for the labels.

Kidney – healthy female – AB positive – harvested March 10, 2236.

Liver – healthy female – AB positive – harvested March 10, 2236.

Kidney – healthy male – O negative – harvested March 6, 2236.

Spleen – healthy male – B positive – harvested March 3, 2236.

This was definitely an organ jacker chop shop. The chiller probably held more than a hundred such containers. And it was one of ten such chillers. Amber held up her tablet and set it to Record. The med techs told her that her new eyes would automatically do that, but she'd paid a street doc to disable the feature for the moment. The eyes were new enough that she could claim technical difficulties without drawing any suspicion, and she didn't want anyone to see what she was doing for the time being.

After getting plenty of video of the building, she pulled a small case out of her vest and opened it. Within it, a dozen miniature button cams were nestled in foam-padded insets. Looking around the large storeroom, she tried to decide where to place them for maximum coverage. She would need a few inside the curtained work area in the back, so she hurried to get them placed.

She'd only planted two more when she heard the beep of the lock and dove for the shadows behind the chillers.

So much for her plan.

She tucked herself into the darkness and activated the monitor on her tablet. She set the ambient light to its lowest setting, so the glow from her screen wouldn't give her away, and relied on the low-light setting on her eyes to help her make out details. On her tablet, she watched the feed from the button cam she'd placed to cover the entrance. Three men came into view.

They were all dressed identically—dark bodysuits, complete with head coverings, masks, and goggles. The suits had strategically placed flat plates woven into the fabric that indicated high-level body armor. Over the armor, they all sported black tactical vests festooned with all sorts of weapons and tools. Each of them wore a pair of packs, a large one on their backs and a smaller one in front.

As soon as the third person got inside, he locked the door behind him and pulled off his goggles. "Lights."

Amber squeezed her eyes tight against the expected flare of lights. It was an old trick whose origins were lost in the past—close your eyes and count to ten when going suddenly from low light to bright, and you mitigated the blindness that could otherwise incapacitate you.

She listened to the men as she mentally counted to ten.

One.

"Rufio, make sure the door is locked."

Two.

"I just did! You think I don't—"

Three.

"—know how to lock a freak—"

Four.

"—in' door?"

Five.

"Well, you damn near fuggled up the—"

Six.

"—hit tonight. What in the—"

Seven.

"—nine hells were you thinking—"

Eight.

"—hittin' the guy in the face—"

Nine.

"—like that? You could'a damaged—"

Ten.

"—the eyes. Then where would we be?"

Amber cracked her eyelids just the tiniest bit, gritting her teeth to keep her fury in check. There would be time for that later. *For now though…*

The light in the storeroom surprised her. Instead of the brightness she'd expected, she saw they had tied faint green LEDs into the lighting system. *Smart*, she thought. She'd recently had cause to learn a lot about the human eye and knew low-level green lighting helped preserve one's night vision and still allowed the eyes to see better detail than the more common red.

Amber suddenly realized she likely didn't even need to do the whole count-to-ten thing. Her new optics would probably just reset automatically. Despite having had them for a week, she still had a lot to learn about them.

"Rufio, Taylor, both of you shut up and take your packs into the lab." It was the first time she had heard that third voice, and she looked at the screen as they bickered.

The two who had been arguing fell into a sullen silence as they began slipping off their backpacks and walked to the hanging curtains.

Guess we know who's in charge.

He was taller than the others and broader in the shoulders. She couldn't be sure in the green light, but she thought he had muscular augments beneath his shirt. *Probably a street banger.* She would have to be extra cautious with him.

Rufio and the other man-child pulled the curtains aside and slid their packs onto the metal table within.

Amber switched her monitor to the cams she had placed inside the curtained work area. The screen flickered over to that view just in time for her to see Rufio bump his shoulder into his companion as he passed him. The other man shoved back, and a second later, they were pushing one another like pre-pube bullies with an overabundance of testosterone.

"Stop it, you fuggled morons! One more time, and I'll crack your heads together."

On her tablet, she saw the men begin unloading their packs, sliding several padded bags and jars onto the worktable. Rage flared as she recognized some of the contents—especially the two jars with miniature vacuum pumps attached to their tops. Amber was intimately familiar with those devices.

The last thing she had ever seen with her natural eyes was chambers just like them being shoved over her eyes as jackers activated the vacuum pump. The agony of her eyes being sucked from their sockets without the benefit of anesthesia… it was the nightmare that wrenched her from restless sleep every single night. And while these men might not be the actual pair who had maimed her, Amber's fists still clenched in fury as she watched them. She was going to stop them tonight, and they would never again subject another person to the kind of terror she'd suffered.

Amber slipped her coat off and placed it on the floor beside her. This little project of hers was completely illegal. Unlawful use of company equipment on a personal investigation was bad enough. What she was thinking about doing now was far worse. But the whole organ jacker problem in the city had become epidemic over the last few years. She had no idea why most LEO agencies glossed it over—there was probably just not enough profit in it. But now it was personal, and she wasn't about to ignore the problem.

Still, there was that whole *illegal* thing. And since she was a LEO, whatever she did had to remain anonymous. So Amber pulled her mask up and turned on the integrated vox unit. She lifted the cover on the controller strapped to her arm and slid the vox augmenter as far into the bass range as it would go. Between the black body armor, mask, and vox, no one would ever be able to identify her. For that matter, they wouldn't even be able to tell her gender.

All she had to do was not get caught.

She lifted the tablet and tapped the command to activate the power shunt. The building went black. Every light, even the LEDs on the chillers and other equipment, went out. Between the power outage and the fact that they had so thoroughly blacked out their windows, Amber found that her low-light setting was suddenly almost useless. She switched to infrared.

The expected cursing sounded from behind the blackout curtains. "Taylor, go find the power reset and get us some light."

Amber dropped her tablet onto her coat and stalked toward the curtained lab area just as someone, presumably Taylor, stepped out.

"Hello, Taylor." The words coming from her vox unit were so deep they didn't even sound human.

"What th—"

Amber's stun baton across his nose interrupted the question. Blood sprayed, and Amber spun, swinging the baton again, hitting him this time at the base of his skull. The jacker dropped without another word.

She knew the other two would have heard her, so she didn't give them any time to figure out what was going on. She stepped to her left, ducked low, and slid through the curtain. At the rustle of curtains, the larger of the two men—the leader whose name she still didn't know—spun, hand cannon already drawn. He fired blindly, and Amber was thankful she'd had the foresight to duck before coming through.

She swung up, slamming her baton into his gun hand with as much force and speed as she could summon from her enhanced reflexes. The man grunted and dropped the pistol.

If this were a lawful LEO operation, Amber would take the opportunity to identify herself and give them the chance to surrender. But she wasn't a LEO at the moment. She bumped up against the workbench. It was less visible in her IR setting, showing as a pale blue. But there were all sorts of warm red-and-orange shapes on top of it. She looked down and realized what they were, and with a snarl of disgust, she gripped the edge of the bench and dumped it over.

Rufio screamed like a frightened child, which made Amber chuckle wickedly. With the vox unit engaged, it sounded like a cross between laughter and a low, demonic growl. Amber liked the sound, and it gave her an idea. The vox settings would need a bit of tweaking, though. She ducked and slipped back out of the curtains.

She heard the two men scrambling to figure out what was going on.

"Taylor? Is that you, man?" Rufio's voice held a note of barely restrained panic. He was going to be easy. "You better not be messing with me! I'll slice you up and leave you twitching."

"Shut up!" the large banger growled. "There's someone else in here."

Apparently, the big guy wasn't as easily spooked.

It took only seconds for Amber to add a bit of echo to the vox. She doubled the volume level for good measure and crawled back to peek through the curtain. She stepped up behind Rufio and pushed. Hard.

Once more, Rufio screamed. He stumbled, firing a single wild shot that caused both Amber and Rufio's as-yet-unnamed partner to duck.

"Buddha's balls, you fuggled moron! Holster that cannon before I shove it up your bunghole!"

Amber smiled and stepped to her right. Her left foot landed on something soft and wet. She looked down at the warm red glow on the floor and recalled the bags from the workbench. "Ew!" But once again, the vox transformed the sound into that heavy, echoing growl.

"What the hells *is* that?" The smaller man, Rufio, spun toward her, gun hand shaking as he stared blindly into the dark. He sounded terrified. "Lugus? That ain't no someone. That's a some*thing!*"

So the big guy is Lugus. Amber added that bit of information to her mental file cabinet. *Lugus and Rufio.*

Amber chuckled, and the sound came out as insane, demonic, echoing laughter, nearly deafening in its volume.

Rufio's whine sounded like a tiny teakettle letting off steam. It was irritating and pitiful, and Lugus appeared to share that opinion. He grabbed the man in front of him and slammed a massive fist into his face. Rufio dropped, unconscious and finally—blissfully—silent.

Amber realized that, whether purposefully or by accident, Lugus had silenced everyone in the room except her. She watched as Lugus held onto Rufio's gun hand and stripped the weapon from it before letting his partner fall to the floor.

She nodded in grudging respect. Lugus was not going to be as easy as Taylor. She stepped quietly to her left then right as she laughed again, relishing the maniacal sound and the way it made the big banger swivel his head as he tried to pinpoint its source. But Amber kept moving around, silent in the ink-black darkness. And when he looked like he was zeroing in on her location, Amber backed out of the curtained area.

This time, she must have made some sort of noise, because Lugus flung the curtain aside and stepped into the storeroom after her. "All right," he said. "Enough with the games. Come here, and I'll give you something to laugh about."

He was still blind, though. The windows he and his partners had painted over worked against him now. But in Amber's IR vision, he still glowed bright red. She stepped back and ducked again. "Welcome to the first circle of Hell, Lugus."

He swung his gun in her direction and pulled the trigger. He fired to her left by more than two meters and half a meter over her head. But it still made her flinch.

She cranked the volume up even more. "You think you can kill me with a little hand cannon? I am *death*!" The last, growling word echoed wildly off the walls, and she winced at the ringing in her own ears.

Lugus was muttering quietly, speaking so low that Amber couldn't make it out. Was he talking to someone else? Was there a fourth person? She scanned the warehouse, searching for any other heat signature, but saw nothing. No one.

He was evidently nervous enough that he was talking to himself. Amber decided it was time to stop playing with him. Desperate people took desperate chances, and she didn't need this man acting unpredictably. Plus she needed to take him down quickly before all the noise attracted attention from outside. She drew her stun baton and flicked it on.

That was nearly her undoing.

Stun batons made a slight humming noise when powered up, and the sound was enough for Lugus to home in on. He aimed and fired even as Amber dove away. But scrambling that quickly didn't allow for moving silently, and Lugus rushed forward, firing blindly, barely missing her each time. Ironically, his blindness was both her salvation and her downfall. For while he missed her with every shot, he tripped and fell over her as he rushed forward.

His hand cannon went skittering across the floor, but he grabbed instinctively at her. Before Amber could scramble away, he latched onto her leg and yanked her back into his grasp. Amber whoofed, the vox once more translating it into the demonic growl as she swung her baton. She connected, but Lugus growled back and grabbed her arm. He stood, never releasing his grip, and hauled her up with him.

"Heh." Lugus panted. "Not so scary now, are you, little man?" He grabbed her baton and wrenched it from her grasp, twisting her wrist in a direction it was never meant to twist. He jammed the stun stick into her shoulder, and her right arm went numb from shoulder to fingertips. He flung the baton away and shifted his grip to Amber's lapels.

Then he paused. "What in the nine hells?"

She felt his hands slip inside her vest and grab a breast.

"A woman?"

She slammed her forehead into his nose and brought up her left fist. Before she could strike, though, she gasped in pain as his grip on her breast tightened cruelly. She screamed, and the vox intensified the volume in the banger's ears to a deafening level.

He almost dropped her, apparently remembering their situation at the last second. He grabbed her arm and jerked her back toward him, swinging wildly at where he expected her head to be. Amber still had a slight advantage in being able to see the strike coming and managed to duck most of it. Nevertheless, even a glancing blow from that massive fist was enough to make her vision swim.

His hand shifted, fumbling for a second as he found her throat, and he squeezed. "No more noise."

She swung a left hook, but subdermal armor protected his jaw, and she figured she hurt her hand more than his face. He lifted her, then slammed her down on the bare plascrete floor, never loosening his grip on her throat.

Adrenaline flooded her body, and her mind played the trick where everything slowed around her. Her thoughts went crystal clear, and she felt each heartbeat, heard every breath, and sensed the slow-motion trickle of sweat running under her arm. She called it battle brain, and ever since she'd had her reflexes tweaked, it happened more easily with her. Amber's breath left her chest as she hit the floor. Her heart pounded and vision blurred as the banger tightened his grip. Mind racing, Amber felt something in her vest poking into her side. Realization struck, and she slipped her hand up and pulled the tool out. She flipped the power on and jabbed it into the man's eye.

The HiTLoPP was made for rapidly cutting through high-density materials like plas-screen. The human eye stood no chance at all. Lugus screamed and dropped her, finally giving way to the panic that had overcome Rufio only minutes earlier. She rolled away, coughing and gasping for air, as Lugus clawed at his face before he staggered and dropped to his knees beside her. Then he quit screaming and fell forward.

Amber knew she wouldn't have much time before someone called the LEOs over all the noise, so she fought her way back to her knees. She rolled Lugus over and wasn't surprised to find the man dead. He had fallen forward onto the HiTLoPP and driven it through his eye and into his brain. She hadn't intended to kill him, but she couldn't say she was sorry either.

She yanked the tool from his eye socket and staggered back to where she had left her coat and tablet. With shaking hands, she called up the menu and deactivated the power shunt. The green lighting came back on, and Amber hurried to gather her things. She found her baton and staggered back over to Taylor. Making sure the stunner was set to maximum, she jabbed it into the side of his head. It wouldn't kill him, but it would keep him unconscious for the next few hours. And the headache he would have when he finally came to would likely make him *wish* he was dead.

She gave Rufio the same treatment before retrieving the button cams she had set up. She thought back over her time in the storeroom, making sure she hadn't left anything else in the building before leaving through the back door again. She made sure to leave the door slightly ajar so LEOs would be able to enter without a warrant.

Finally, she disconnected the power shunt, dropped it into her pocket, and walked around the back corner of the building to leave the parking area. She slipped her coat back on, making sure the hood covered her face as she entered the darkened alley where she had knelt beneath the window.

A silhouette jumped from around the corner ahead of her. Amber blinked as he raised an arm, and she instinctively ducked. There was a flash accompanied by the deafening boom of a hand cannon, and the window over her head exploded, showering her with plas-screen shards.

Amber jumped up and ran back down the alley with all the haste her enhanced speed and reflexes afforded her. She rounded the corner of the building and pressed herself to the back wall, drawing her stun stick.

So Lugus *had* been talking to someone else after all. *Now what?*

She took slow, calming breaths, baton at the ready, hoping to get the drop on whoever might come around the corner after her, fighting back the sudden fear of the situation. A stun baton against a hand cannon was never a fun situation. She'd barely survived a similar encounter just minutes earlier, and she'd had the advantage of seeing where her opponent couldn't. Now, with streetlights and moonlight illuminating the night, she was going to need more than her stun baton.

But it was all she had. She gripped it tighter, waiting… waiting…

Amber waited almost a full minute, but no one came. She ducked and peeked around the corner. Nothing. Was he going around the building to get another angle on her? Had he gone in the front entrance? There was no way for her to know, and those two possibilities meant he could conceivably emerge from either of two different places. She needed to move.

Amber scanned her surroundings. The parking lot suddenly seemed to be a huge, wide-open killing field surrounded by a standard two-meter-high fence. It wasn't particularly tall, but neither was she. Still, she had scaled higher obstacles during her training.

If she moved quickly, she might be able to get over the fence and lose herself among the buildings on the other side. Of course, she could just as easily run directly into the shooter's sights.

And sitting on your ass worrying about it gives them more time to get the drop on you. There's no time.

Taking her inner voice's advice to heart, Amber sprinted across the parking lot and, when she reached the fence, jumped and reached for the top of it. She nearly sobbed with relief as her fingers locked onto the upper ledge, and she pulled herself up and over. She sprinted for the next building, turned another corner, and kept going. She didn't slow until she neared the next street.

It took only a moment to regain her bearings, and Amber found the direction she wanted to go. She forced herself to walk slowly, not wanting to attract the attention of anyone who might be nearby, turning repeatedly to see if anyone was following. After several minutes, she figured she'd gotten away and began to breathe a little easier.

She checked the settings on her vox and adjusted it back to something closer to normal. Closer, but still obviously digitally enhanced. She didn't want her real voice on the record. Pulling the scrubbed burner comm from her pocket, she placed the call.

"Central Dispatch." The man who answered sounded bored.

Amber spoke quickly, knowing the call was being recorded. She rattled off the address as she walked down the street. "There are three organ jackers inside—two unconscious, one dead. There's a live one in the area, too, so have your people take precautions. You'll also find several chiller units full of human organs."

"Wait, what?" The man was suddenly a lot less bored. "Who is this?"

"I left the back door open for you."

Amber disconnected. Still walking, she pried open the comm casing as her street contact had shown her and pulled the UIN chip from the circuit board within. She approached a pod parked in the street. Stopping beside the vehicle, she reached into the pocket of her coat and fished out a battery-powered electromagnet she carried for just this purpose. She knelt as if adjusting her shoe and attached the magnet over the chip beneath the frame of the pod. Once it was secure, she stood and continued her walk away from the organ jackers' storeroom.

The magnet would degrade the chip until the battery died or the pod hit a bump strong enough to knock it from the frame. At that point, it would likely be in the middle of traffic, and the chip would be further damaged, if not totally destroyed, by more pods driving over it in the street. Between the magnetic degradation and the probable road damage, it was unlikely any information would be extracted from the chip if it were ever even found. Her source had assured her that no one could track his chips, even without her taking extra precautions, but Amber believed in being thorough.

Sirens approached from overhead, and Amber resisted the urge to look up as drones zipped past. No use adding her face to the list of people in the area. She kept walking. Three kilometers more and she reached the spot in the darkened alley where she had parked the rental pod. She punched the nine-digit lock code into the side panel and slid inside. She'd paid for the rental with untraceable credit chits and had worn gloves any time she was in it, so there should be nothing to trace back to her when she returned it in a few days.

More sirens announced a Metro squad pod approaching, so Amber ducked down until they passed. Then she started the engine and drove slowly away.

DAY 04
FRIDAY

CHAPTER 14

Amber awoke strapped to a table, completely immobilized. The ceiling was lost in darkness behind the dazzling lights hanging overhead.

A man stood over her, his face barely visible with the brilliant radiance behind his head. He leaned over her and sneered. "Good! Our little donor is awake." He slapped her face lightly, just hard enough to emphasize her helplessness. "You cost me an O positive out there, little one. That body would'a paid for new upgrades for me an' my friend here."

She sensed movement behind her but was unable to move her head far enough to see clearly.

"I think it's only fair you should pay some of what you cost us."

Rough hands seized her head, and the second banger leaned over her, inverted to her view. She struggled to no avail, and he chuckled. "What's wrong, baby? Don'cha wanna party with us?"

They laughed, and she looked frantically from one face to the other. Then the first one placed a clear cylinder over her right eye and pressed something on top of it. She heard a whirring noise and felt a vacuum form. Her vision distorted, and she screamed as an intense throbbing agony shot from her eye to the back of her head. There was a moment of relief as the pressure eased then searing torture when the eye popped from its socket.

She bolted upright in the bed, a ragged scream trying to force its way out. All that escaped her throat, though, was a pitiful mewling whimper. Heart pounding in her chest, skin sheened in a cold sweat, she gasped as she struggled to sort nightmare from reality.

"Amber? Amber!" Nathan's voice pulled her back. "It's okay, babe. It's just the nightmare again."

It had been several weeks since she'd awakened like this. Until a few years ago, it was how she'd awakened nearly every morning. Having Nathan and Odie in her life had helped immeasurably. But of course, there was no way she could hide the nightmares from the man who shared her bed. And her current case brought it all back to the forefront of her mind.

She gulped and patted Nathan's hand. "I'm sorry. Go back to sleep."

He pulled her back, but she knew sleep was out of the question for her. "Don't worry about me. I need to get an early start anyway." Amber slipped out of bed and into the bathroom before he could argue. She ordered the bathroom to configure itself for a hot shower and stripped. Standing in front of the mirror, she performed the ritual that had gotten her through the last several years. She closed her eyes and forced herself to review the occurrence that had cost her her eyes. She recited the bangers' descriptions in her mind, committing their faces to memory once more.

The first banger had deep blue eyes—pretty eyes, completely out of place in an otherwise unremarkable face. The second had a jagged scar running from his left temple to a ragged split in his nostril.

When she finally had her heartbeat and breathing back under control, she stepped into the hot shower.

Having ignored her instructions to go back to sleep, Nathan had a hot breakfast waiting for her when she got out.

"I didn't know how long you would take in the shower," he said, "so it's just a quick omelet."

She chuckled. "Just an omelet? This is fine dining compared to what I would have been eating this time last year."

He smiled. "I do recall you mentioning a lot of sticky rolls and cho-caffeine when I first met you."

He slid the plate in front of her and handed her a fork.

"Aren't you going to eat with me?"

"I'll eat later." He slipped up behind her and began massaging her shoulders. "Right now, I have something more important to do."

Amber moaned in pleasure. "I'll give you just five years to stop."

"Deal." But despite his words, he stopped massaging, leaned in, and kissed the side of her neck.

She pouted. "Why'd you stop?"

"Because you don't seem to be able to eat while I'm rubbing your shoulders. And you need to eat. Go on—I didn't make that thing just to have you let it get cold."

She sighed but cut into the cheesy omelet, moaning again at the taste of fresh peppers, onions, and tomatoes. Between the shower, the massage, the omelet, and the thought of how much she cared for Nathan, the memories of Dewey Trev and Carl Hartzman were, at least for the moment, pushed to the back of her mind, where they belonged.

CHAPTER 15

She took her time on the drive to PSC, arriving only a little earlier than she had planned. The rest of her team was already there, and she made a mental note to start getting in earlier. Amber liked to get in before her team. She felt it set the right example as the team lead.

Everyone was gathered in the parking garage beneath the PSC building. The suggestion had surprised Amber, but it had come from Maestro Harris himself. One of the conditions Gibbs had insisted on before agreeing to allow Amber to pursue the case was that her combat training with Harris was to remain a priority. The stipulation had been expanded to anyone who joined her.

But as Harris pointed out, said training didn't have to take place in the gym at Fixer HQ. He said the parking garage beneath the building was perfectly satisfactory as far as he was concerned. And it would save them time if they didn't have to travel from their homes to HQ then back to PSC. It seemed even Maestro Harris was eager to work on an actual case.

So they met in the parking garage at 07:00, and the maestro worked with them, demonstrating blade techniques and how they translated into similar unarmed techniques. The session was light, in deference to the unforgiving plascrete surface of the garage. But he still managed to work them into a mild sweat before declaring them finished for the morning.

They gathered their training blades and headed for the elevators. Richard and CC took one car, the two behemoths barely fitting inside, while the rest of them took the second. Amber happened to inhale just as the doors slid closed, and she was struck by the rather fragrant aroma of five sweaty people in close proximity.

"Jordie," she said as the elevator rose. "While you and Acamas are working on building upgrades, would you see about getting us a locker room with showers?"

"I was just thinking the same thing," Jordie answered. "And how about a real training area too? We could strip the offices from the third floor and convert the whole level. We could even extend the floor over the atrium area to give us more floor space."

"As long as we still have enough room on the other two floors to run the business."

The elevator doors slid open, and Amber led the way to the main conference room. "Get some drawings to me, and we'll see if it's feasible. But we need a locker room and some showers at the bare minimum."

"I'll have them to you by the end of the day."

Richard and CC joined them as they approached the conference room. Amber heard him whisper to Jordie as he fell in beside them. "What are you doing by the end of the day?"

"Plans for a locker room and showers."

"Oh! That's a great idea."

Amber pushed open the doors to the conference room, speaking as she walked in. "Hecter?"

"Yes, fem?"

"Please call Dem and Acamas for me."

"Of course, fem."

Within seconds, the two holograms appeared at the end of the table. Amber was startled to note the difference in the resolution from the pixelated mess they had been just the day before. He and Acamas looked quite real, and they appeared seated in holographic chairs, with holographic screens and keyboards before them. It reminded her of the way their father, T-bone, had often joined her team in their war room at Securi-Tech. The memory caused her throat to tighten.

Demophon looked around with a nod of approval. "This is *much* better!"

"Glad you approve," Amber said. "You guys look better from this end too."

"They sound better too," Missy said. "It sounds like his voice is really coming from his projection." She looked at Jordie. "How'd you manage that?"

Jordie pointed to the dozens of small protrusions around the top of the room. "Audio projectors are tied to the hologram emitters. They're programmed and balanced to make it seem that the sound comes from wherever the holograms appear."

"Nice."

Amber cleared her throat to halt the conversation. "If you don't mind?" She looked at Scott. "Did you talk to your sister?"

Scott nodded. "She jumped at the chance. As a matter of fact, she wants to start this morning as soon as we can. She's between stories and in a hurry to get something to her supervisor. I'm supposed to meet with her as soon as I can get free here."

"Then consider yourself free. You and Maestro Harris both. Get us a lead. But you're not to move against anyone, no matter what you find. You're just fact-finding. Am I clear?"

Scott nodded. "Got it, Boss." He stood, patted the maestro on the shoulder, and tapped the comm bud in his ear as the two of them left the conference table. "Hey, sis?" Scott said as they walked out. "We're on. Meet us at—"

The door closed on the rest of his conversation, and Amber looked at Demophon. "Were you able to find locations for any other jacker teams?"

Dem's lips drew into a tight line as he shrugged. "Not exactly. But I think I've narrowed down a hunting area for one." The hologram looked offscreen, appeared to tap out some commands, and a city map appeared on the wall. A red circle pulsed in the south-central part of the map. "Whoever they are, they're more subtle than the first team. But in their own way, they might be even more ruthless."

"What do you mean?" Jordie asked.

A text box popped up on the wall beside the map, even as the map zoomed in on the circled area.

"The circle covers an area of just under ten square kilometers. Approximately three million people live there." He tapped on the screen again, and hundreds of small green dots popped into being, scattered around the map area. "Three years ago, more than fifteen thousand people were reported to the local authorities as missing persons. It's unfortunate but normal." Dem tapped again, and more dots appeared, yellow this time. "Two years ago, the number increased to eighteen thousand." With a final tap, even more dots appeared. These were red. "Last year, it jumped to twenty thousand."

Amber narrowed her eyes. "How does that correlate to population increases in the area?"

"Population density in that section of the city has actually been going down."

Amber leaned back in her chair. "So the uptick in missing person reports is even more disproportionate."

"It gets worse." Dem tapped his screen again, and even more dots appeared.

"What's this?"

"After Richard demonstrated how low-income citizens tend to not report on official channels, it occurred to me that there might be another way to track missing-person stats. I checked payment records for local utility accounts in the area then searched for locations where service for two or more services have been discontinued without a forwarding address. Then I—"

"You don't have to explain your process. I believe you." Amber stood and walked closer to the map on the wall. "So we'll assume you're right. This is another hunting area. Why do you say they're more ruthless?"

"Each one of these dots represents a place where a family lived. Then, for no apparent reason, they disappeared. And in each case, not a single man, woman, or child who lived there has ever been seen again."

"Buddha's balls!" Missy looked embarrassed to have said it loudly enough for the others to hear. "Sorry. But they're taking entire families?"

"They're organ jackers," Amber spat. "Morality isn't one of their strong suits." She turned back to Dem. "What else?"

"Unfortunately, I don't have much else. At least, not yet."

Amber chewed her bottom lip, thinking. "All right. Then what about the team that took Freitas?"

"That one's easier. Like I said, they're pretty sloppy. Lucky for us, they're also more predictable. They hit like clockwork every three days. Records indicate they usually hit between midnight and 03:00. As for where, they always hit in or around one of the densely populated highrise apartment buildings in the area. I guess they figure there's enough turnover that fewer people will notice if someone disappears there. Interesting point, though." Demophon looked a little puzzled. "From what I can tell, they've hit more than fifty families in the last year, and never once have they taken anyone above the third floor."

"They want a fast escape route," Jordie said. When Amber raised an eyebrow at her, she shrugged. "Environment was always a consideration for jobs back when Scott and I ran on the other side of the law."

"Uh-huh," Amber deadpanned before turning her attention back to Dem. "Can you narrow it down any more than one of several high-rise complexes somewhere within a twenty- or thirty-block area?"

"Based on their records, my best guess is they'll hit tonight somewhere in this highlighted area."

"Tonight?" Amber turned around to look at the map again. A yellow rectangular area pulsed. Behind her, she heard Richard sigh.

"That's still an awfully big area to cover."

"Only at first glance." It was the first time Acamas had spoken since the conference call had begun. "It's twenty-two city blocks. But one of those blocks is a musical conservatory and its school. About thirty percent of the rest are businesses, soup kitchens, temples, and eateries. And the green section in the middle is a small park."

Amber nodded. "I assume this means you've narrowed it down a little more than your brother?"

Acamas smiled. "Of course." She tapped her screen, and three areas within the yellow rectangle turned red. "Eliminating all the nonresidential areas means there's a better than eighty percent chance the hit will go down in one of these three sectors."

Studying the map, Amber nodded. "Good work, guys." She turned to Jordie. "I assume you still have a lot of equipment from your days on the other side of the law?"

Jordie gave an impish grin. "Sure. What did you have in mind?"

"We need to be able to see and hear inside buildings in those sectors."

Acamas spoke up. "I think Dem and I can help with that. All the apartment buildings have internal security cams. Baby bro and I can break into the feeds and handle the visual surveillance."

"Hey!" Dem protested. "Who are you calling 'baby bro'? I was born before you were!"

"Maybe so, but you still act like a baby." Acamas calmly turned her attention back to Amber.

Amber nodded. "Good. What else?"

"I can set up wireless overrides to shunt the feeds directly to our surveillance systems," Jordie said.

"Can you make them portable?"

"Shouldn't be a problem. The trick is going to be getting the overrides installed. Acamas, how many buildings are we talking about?"

"There are twenty-three buildings that fit our search parameters. What kind of coverage will your transmitters give you?"

Jordie shrugged. "It depends on the layout of the hallways. I suggest omnidirectional pickups with—"

"Guys?" Amber could see a conversation full of tech-speak coming—a conversation she would barely understand. When they looked her way, she told them, "This is another one where I don't really need all the details. Just tell me two things. Can you do it? And can you get it all set up by tonight?"

"Yes and yes." Jordie sounded confident. "I'll need some help with the footwork and installations, but Missy and I should be able to get it done with time to spare."

Amber shook her head. "Can you take Richard and CC instead? I need Missy to help me out with something else."

"Fine with me." Jordie looked across the table at the big banger. "You guys okay helping me?"

Both of the big bangers shrugged.

"Just show us what to do," CC said.

"Good," Amber said. "Take it to conference room three. I need to talk to Missy and the Wonder Twins about something."

CC, who had been in the process of getting up, stopped with a quizzical look. "Wonder Twins?"

Richard tapped him on the shoulder. "Don't ask. It'll just end up being an ancient reference to some thousand-year-old entertainment vids."

"Don't exaggerate," Amber snorted. "They were less than three hundred years ago."

CC looked at her, then at Richard, then back at her.

"What?" Amber said.

"Nothing."

Richard chuckled and slapped the bigger man on the back. "Come on," he said. "You get used to it."

The two men left the table, accompanied by Jordie, who was busily tapping on her tablet, apparently oblivious to the banter between them.

As the door closed, Amber looked at Missy. "Were you able to work anything out on our little project?"

Missy nodded. "Acamas and I found a combination of items that should get the effect you're after. There's a gas called carbogen. It's a mixture of CO_2 and oxygen that tricks the body into thinking you're suffocating. That triggers subliminal anxiety, which quickly ramps up into fear then terror. The trouble is the target needs to be exposed for several seconds before the gas begins to take effect."

"How long?" Amber asked.

"It varies from person to person, and there are a tonne of other variables that—"

"Just an estimate," Amber snapped.

"Best case, fifteen seconds. Realistically, more like twenty or thirty."

"Shyte." Amber shook her head. Twenty seconds was a long time when a person was fighting for their life. "I'll take what I can get, of course, but I'd like something that works faster."

Missy smiled. "Which is where Acamas comes in."

Amber looked at the black-haired hologram. "You have something?"

Acamas gave her a quick nod while tapping on her screen. A schematic appeared on the wall where the map had been. "This is a subaural sound wave projector. That's the fancy name for a speaker that projects sound below the hearing threshold of normal human perception. We can use them to blast subsonic waves at around a frequency of nineteen hertz. People can't hear it, but it's like the audio version of Missy's gas."

"I call it the fear frequency," Missy chimed in.

Acamas ignored the interruption. "It causes discomfort, dizziness, anxiety, and fear. It also has the advantage of causing blurred vision, if aimed directly at the face of your target, by actually vibrating their eyeballs. A final side effect is it can cause some materials to vibrate."

Amber walked back to her seat. As she sat, she asked, "How big is it?"

"It's a speaker," Dem said, jumping into the conversation. "It can be as big or as small as you need it to be. Small speakers aren't as powerful. Big ones aren't as portable. What do you have in mind?"

Amber thought for a few seconds before calling up a blank screen on her tablet. She began to sketch. "I'll send you a list, but I'm thinking of something like this." She tapped the tablet and projected her drawing to the wall screen.

The others studied it for a few seconds, and Dem was the first to speak. "How fast do you want all this?"

"Within the hour."

He shook his head. "Not possible, Boss. Especially the drone setup. That's custom work."

"Then how fast can you get it?"

"How much do you want to spend?" Dem countered.

"You guys keep telling me I need to stop worrying about money. Spend whatever it takes. I'll send you my account number."

"Then I can probably get it delivered here within four or five hours."

"Offer a twenty-five percent bonus if they can do it in two. Ten percent for three hours."

Dem nodded. "That should speed things up."

Amber turned to Missy. "How quickly can you get me that gas and a delivery system?"

"Gas grenades are simple. But I recommend something less blatant. If you put them on their guard with something obvious, they'll be harder to scare. It needs to be subtle." It was Missy's turn to type notes. A moment later, she grunted and nodded. Then she turned her tablet around so that Amber could see the screen.

Amber nodded. "Can you make it?"

"Assuming you have the body armor."

"I do." Since joining the Fixers, Amber and her team had all been issued new state-of-the-art body armor from the Fixer armory. She had taken advantage of her new finances and had ordered a second suit so she always had a spare. It was probably paranoia, but she had the funds. Why not use them? "But I still want the gas grenades too."

Missy nodded. "I can do that."

"Can we get them in the same time frame as the speakers?"

Missy grinned. "We have everything we need at Fixer HQ."

"Go, then. I want to have it all by tonight if possible."

Missy nodded then looked up as if she'd just remembered something. "Amber?"

"What?"

"I rode here with Scott."

Amber sighed. "And he just left with Harris." She pulled out her tablet and created temporary activation codes then sent them to Missy's tablet. "Take my pod. Those codes should be good for twelve hours. If you need longer, comm me, and I'll extend the time."

Missy blinked. "You're going to let me drive your fancy luxury pod?"

"Just don't wreck it."

"Schwanky!"

"You sure you can get it done by tonight?"

"Where's the armor?"

"Spare suit's in the back of the pod."

"Then I can do it."

Amber nodded. "Go."

Missy scooped up her tablet and hurried out the door.

When it closed behind her, Demophon spoke. "I can't help but notice you've sent everyone else out of the building. Do you have plans?"

Amber nodded. "I haven't slept very well the last few nights. I'm going up to my office to take a nap."

"Anything I can do?"

"No. It's just this case… it's bringing up old memories—things I thought I'd managed to leave behind."

"Memories about your eyes?"

She sighed. "And what happened after."

Dem was silent as if waiting to see if she wanted to elaborate.

She didn't. Amber left the conference room without another word.

CHAPTER 16

Scott sucked absently on a piece of frozen fruit as he leaned back against the heavily armored half-track. The vehicle had become his de facto work van ever since Jordie had bought her uni six months earlier. Like Richard, Jordie found the freedom of zipping through the streets on the single-wheeled death machines to be invigorating, almost addictive, and she seldom drove anything else now.

So Scott took to driving the old paramilitary van. Familiar as an old pair of boots, he, Jordie, and Kitty had operated out of it for years, up until a job had gone bad on them last year… a job that had gotten Kitty killed. A job that had eventually thrust him and Jordie into this new life with Amber, Richard, and now the Fixers.

So much had changed in the last year. And though this new path had cost him an irreplaceable friend in Kitty Cope, he couldn't help but be grateful for the way it had all played out. He and Jordie had gone from working as common—if extremely talented—street criminals to doing a short stint as cooperative witnesses and civilian consultants for Securi-Tech to doing an even shorter stint as private security consultants for Micronics. And now they were partners with the same LEOs who had first arrested them. He counted them as close friends and knew Jordie felt the same.

"Life is crazy," he muttered.

"Of course." Sitting on the hood to Scott's right, Harris said it absently, as if it were a basic tenet of life.

And when Scott thought about it, he supposed it probably was.

Harris pointed to the cup in his hand. "What these are called?"

Scott looked at the cup of fruit. "Watermelon. Frozen watermelon balls." Scott furrowed his brow. "You never had watermelon before?"

"Water. Melon. Yes, we have this. Is the word I am learning, not the food. At home is called *melancia*."

Scott scanned the street once more, watching for his sister. When he didn't see her, he turned back to his companion. "Maestro? If you don't mind me asking, why don't you use a translation app?"

Harris nodded over his cup of watermelon balls, never looking up from the snack. "I do sometime. But I rather to learn on myself. The brain is not needing updates or license agreement. Also, it cannot be used to track me from cyberspace."

Scott chuckled at the maestro's simple and pragmatic way of looking at something most people took for granted.

"I believe your sister is coming to behind you."

Rather than turning, Scott glanced at the storefront window in front of him. Sure enough, he saw Coleen's reflection as she approached from across the street. She wore casual attire and carried a small case—nothing that made her stand out in the crowd. So it intrigued Scott that Harris would know who she was. "What makes you think that's my sister?"

"You say she is reporter. This woman's hair is shaved on one side to fit a reporter recorder." Harris furrowed his brow at that before grinning. "This is correct way to say it? Reporter recorder?"

Scott smiled back. "We just call them reporter's rigs, but 'reporter recorder' is a good description. I like it." Seeing in the reflection that his sister was within earshot, he said, "Hello, Fem Thompson."

"Sludge," she said. "I'm never going to be able to get the drop on you, am I?"

He turned and smiled at her. "Not likely." He stuck his hand out, and she shook it. Looking over at Harris, Scott said, "Maestro Harris, I'd like to introduce you to an acquaintance of mine. This is Fem Colleen Thompson, reporter for the Multi-Corp News Network."

The maestro looked somewhat puzzled at the introduction but nodded and took the hand she offered. "It is pleasureful."

After shaking his hand, Colleen slapped her hand on the side of the half-track. "Still driving this old thing?"

"She's saved my glutes too many times for me to even consider dumping her." He palmed the lock panel on the side, and the cargo door slid open. "Shall we take this inside?"

Colleen stepped in. Scott and Harris followed.

Once they were all seated and the door was closed, Maestro Harris asked Scott, "Why do you do the hand shaking with each other? I thought you were brother and sister."

"We are. But not many people know it." Scott shrugged. "Jordie and I have a pretty colorful past, and my reputation could have kept Colleen from getting a decent job. So we got her a new background."

Colleen looked at Maestro Harris. "And forgive me for being blunt, but who exactly are you? And how do *you* know we're related?"

Scott jumped in before Harris could answer. "My fault, sis. I let it slip, but you can trust the maestro."

"Maestro?" Colleen's brows rose.

"Sorry," Scott replied. "This is Maestro Brent Harris. He's working with me, Jordie, and the others."

"The others being Payne and her partner?"

"Actually, Jordie and I are her partners too now. Amber has a startup consulting company, and she invited us in."

Colleen sat back on the bench and raised an eyebrow. "Really? So you guys are staying legit?"

"That's the plan."

Colleen grinned broadly, leaned over, and hugged her brother. "It's about time!"

Then she hugged Harris. "And I don't know who in the nine hells you are, but if you're helping keep my baby brother on the straight and narrow, then thank you."

Harris smiled in return. "You are welcome."

Scott chuckled at Harris's bemused expression. Then he pulled his tablet from within his jacket. "Now, I think we should probably get back to the task at hand." He thumbed the tablet on and pulled up a screen. "Did you read through the files I sent?"

Colleen nodded. "You really think there's a team of organ jackers working the streets again?"

"From what we can tell, there's several." He gave her a short version of what Dem had reported.

Colleen pursed her lips as she absorbed what Scott told her, then she asked what, for her, was the most important question. "I've got an exclusive on this?"

Scott chuckled. "Yes. But we need your help to be able to investigate. The neighborhood we're heading for... the people don't trust LEOs."

"But you figure a reporter can gain their trust."

"We hope so."

"Okay, I'm the reporter. Who are you?"

Scott shrugged. "Fellow reporters?"

She shook her head. "Nope. Sorry, but you'll never pass for reporters."

"What, then?"

Almost tentatively, Harris raised a hand. "I can also be witness. We are thinking this victim is from Novo Brasil. This is also my country."

Colleen nodded. "Good. We can use that." She looked at Scott. "You're my assistant and security. MCNN sometimes hires security when reporters go into rough areas, so it's not implausible."

"Okay." Scott clapped his hands together. "Do you have everything you need?"

She patted the case at her feet. "Got my rig in here."

Scott grinned. "Your reporter recorder?"

"My what?"

Scott smiled and moved to the driver's seat. "Never mind. Let's get on the road."

CHAPTER 17

SCOTT PULLED UP TO THE address Dem had provided. The building across the parking lot was run-down, with most of the ballistic windows on the bottom two floors covered by splashes of paint or worse. Neon gang tags decorated the walls, and a few men and women sat on benches outside. The group didn't look like bangers, but they watched Scott, Colleen, and Harris suspiciously as they piled out of the half-track. When Colleen slipped the rig over her head, some of the hostility left their faces, but it was obvious they were still curious.

Scott spoke to his sister softly. "You okay with this?"

She didn't even look at him as she stepped forward. "This isn't even close to being the worst place I've gone for a story." She pulled her tablet out and glanced at it. "The Freitas place is on the second floor." She spoke loudly enough for the group on the bench to hear, and Scott realized she did it intentionally to let them know why she was there.

Scott waved Maestro Harris forward then took up the rear of their little procession. They'd hardly taken three steps before the largest of the men stood. He wore a threadbare blue tunic with black trousers. Another man wearing a green shirt and a yellow cap pulled at his arm, but the larger man shook him off.

He didn't appear to be augmented in any obvious manner, and his clothes were plain and unarmored. But Maestro Harris wasn't augmented either. And Harris had beaten Scott and Amber at the same time without breaking a sweat.

Scott moved in front of Colleen and slipped his hand inside his duster to rest on the butt of a flechette pistol.

"I hear you say Freitas," Blue Shirt said. "You are here about Judite?"

Even as Colleen put a hand on his shoulder, Scott noted the man had an accent similar to Maestro Harris's, further reminding him of just how dangerous this new man could be. But Colleen's hand on his shoulder was insistent, and he let her step back in front again. She put a hand on his chest as she reclaimed her point position.

Blue Shirt's eyes followed the exchange, noting where Scott's hand had disappeared. The man made a point of keeping his own hands spread and visible. Scott was now established as the muscle, and Blue Shirt was making sure he didn't provoke him.

But Colleen's hand on his chest and Scott's reaction also made it clear she was the one in charge. So while Blue Shirt made no threatening gestures, he also turned his attention back to Colleen.

"Yes," Colleen said. "I'm here to look into the death of Judite Freitas. Do you know anything about it?"

The man spat and nodded. "You will know too when you go into the building."

"How do you mean?"

"They warn everyone to stay quiet. They threaten to come for anyone who talks to LEOs."

The man who had tried to keep him from talking to them shook his head. He said something in a rapid-fire tangle of words and syllables Scott had no chance of comprehending. He knew by now that the language was Portuguese, but that did nothing for his understanding of it.

Harris stepped closer to Scott and Colleen. He spoke quietly so that only they would hear him. "The man with the hat warns the bigger man to keep quiet or they will to find him on the street without head like Judite. Big man says we are not LEO, and message says nothing about reporter."

The man in the cap spoke again, but the first man ignored him.

"He says the ghosts will take him. That he was warned."

"Ghosts?" Colleen asked.

Harris just shrugged. "I just tell you what they say."

"Would you ask them?"

Harris stepped forward and spoke to the men in their native tongue. They seemed surprised but answered quickly.

Harris nodded and turned back to Colleen and Scott. "The ones who kill Judite. They call themselves ghosts."

Blue Shirt nodded at Harris's translation. "They kill others too. Not just Judite."

Colleen nodded. "Tell me about them."

"They warn us not to say anything."

"Would you be willing to let me interview you?" Colleen asked him. "Off the record?"

At that, the rest of the group stood and walked away, leaving their talkative companion on his own. They clearly had no intention of being recorded in any way. Even the leader of the group looked like he regretted having said anything.

"No. But when you enter building, you will receive message on your tablet. It comes as advertisement but is warning from the ghosts. Maybe you track where it comes from. Find them."

Colleen nodded.

"When you find them. You tell the world about them. Tell them about Judite and the others." With that, the man turned and followed his friends.

"Well, that wasn't ominous at all," Colleen said.

Scott nodded and tapped his earbud. "Call Demophon."

Dem answered on the second chime. "Go for Demophon."

"Dem, it's Scott. We're about to go into a building here, and we've been assured we're going to get a message from the jackers as soon as we're within range of the building projectors."

"What kind of message?"

"A warning. It's got the locals scared to talk to us. Is there any chance you can intercept and track it? If we're lucky, it might give us a lead on their location."

"Hold tight for a second. Let me link to your comm..." There was a moment of silence as Dem did something in the background. "Got it. Now, do you just want me to track on yours, or do you want me to watch everyone in your group? If you want me to track everyone, I either need the universal ID numbers to their comms or have them call me and I can link that way. Either way works."

"I'll have them call you. It'll be easier than trying to walk us through how to find the UINs."

"Probably a good idea," Dem agreed. "I'll be waiting for the calls. Discomm."

"Discomm." Scott sent Dem's contact information to his sister and Maestro Harris. "Call Demophon before we go in. He can link to our comms and might be able to trace the ad."

"Really?" Colleen asked. "Is he that good?"

Scott shrugged. "We'll find out. But it doesn't hurt to try, right?"

She nodded and called the number. Within seconds, her conversation was finished, and Harris followed suit. Seconds later, they all received text messages.

Linked. You can go in now.
  -Dem

Colleen raised an eyebrow and looked at Scott.

He raised one shoulder. "It's your show. I'm just the muscle, remember?"

She snorted before walking away, leading the way to the building. Scott and Harris hurried to catch up.

"How close do you think we need—" His earbud chimed receipt of a message before he could finish his question. "Never mind." He pulled his tablet from within his duster and thumbed the screen on. Rather than activating their own tablets, Colleen and Harris grouped up beside Scott and watched his screen.

A grisly half-burned and charred head—no doubt the missing head of Judite Freitas—appeared on Scott's screen. In the background, a digitally disguised voice spoke in Portuguese, its robotic monologue droning, void of any emotion.

"It says they kill Judite," Harris translated. "If you don't want same, you stay quiet. Ghosts are watching. Ghosts are listening. Ghosts live among you."

The message ended, and Colleen looked at her brother. "You're sure this is organ jackers?"

"We're pretty sure. Each victim had their eyes, kidneys, livers, and various other organs missing. Whoever did it chopped up the bodies to make it look like they'd been run through a giant fan, but all the reports mention missing organs."

Colleen grunted. "Okay, let's go see Mr. Freitas then."

The inside of the building was no more inviting than the outside. The walls were tagged similarly to the outside, garbage lay in occasional piles in the hallway, and the air smelled of a mix of inhalant drugs and urine.

"Isn't this a lovely place," Scott muttered.

Colleen stopped and turned to face her brother. "Just because you're rich and legit now, don't forget where you came from. A lot of these people can barely afford even this. And as I recall, your way of making ends meet wasn't exactly honest work. Not for several years."

Scott raised his hands. "You're right. Sorry. But this is exactly why I took the route I did. It was the fastest way to get out of places like this."

The elevator appeared to be out of order, though there was no sign to confirm it. But nothing happened when they pressed the button, either. Scott took a quick look around to make sure they were alone in the hallway before leading them up the stairs. They found the Freitas apartment halfway down the hall on the second floor. Colleen knocked.

A moment later, someone called through the door, "Sim?"

Maestro Harris tapped Colleen on the shoulder and stepped forward. He called out something in Portuguese, and there was a brief exchange before they heard the whine of several locks disengaging. When the door swung open, the tall, gaunt man inside stepped back quickly. He was balding but bearded, with a touch of gray at the chin. More importantly, though, he aimed a pair of flechette pistols at them.

Scott slowly raised his hands and moved forward to put himself between the man—presumably Mr. Freitas—and Colleen, shielding his sister from the pistols. "We're not looking for trouble. We just want to ask you some questions."

At the same time, Harris spoke again. Once more, it was rapid-fire Portuguese. Of course, Scott had no idea what was being said, but after a moment of conversation, the man lowered the pistols and gestured them inside.

Scott shot a questioning look at Harris, who just nodded. He must have felt it was safe enough because he stepped into the apartment without hesitation. Scott looked around the room then followed Harris inside. Colleen walked in after him.

"Sorry for the poor greeting. I worry that those who kill my Judite are come for me."

Colleen stepped back to the front. "That's what I would like to talk to you about, Mr. Freitas." She tapped the rig on her head. "Do you mind if I ask you some questions about your wife's murder?"

The man hesitated a moment before shaking his head. "Ghosts will kill me."

"We can protect you," Colleen said.

"How? You will hide me somewhere? What happens when you leave? You give your story then leave. And I am still here. They will kill me." He shook his head again. "No. You cannot protect me. And I will not talk."

Scott looked around the apartment. It was sparsely furnished, and it was apparent that Mr. Freitas owned very little. He looked back at the bald man. "What if we can move you somewhere else? Somewhere the ghosts can't find you?"

Colleen stepped closer to him. "I can't get that authorized," she whispered.

"You don't have to. I'm rich and legit now, remember? And despite what you said, I haven't forgotten where I came from. As you pointed out, I lived in a place like this for years before I hooked up with Jordie and Kitty." He looked around again. "I can't fix the whole world, but I can help this guy fix his."

Scott turned to Harris. "Tell him if he agrees to answer Colleen's questions and lets her interview him, and he tells her everything he knows about the killings and the ghosts, I'll move him to a safe place away from here. I'll get him a new identity and a place where no one will know who he is. Make sure he understands he will be safe."

Harris raised an eyebrow but turned to Freitas. They conversed again, and Freitas seemed to be waffling. But he shook his head. "No. This is generous offer. But I don't know you. I don't know if what you say is truth. You say these thing. But maybe you say them, get your story, then leave. If that happen, they kill me. They kill me bad."

Scott blew an exasperated breath. "What if I move you now? How much stuff do you have?"

Freitas waved his hand around. "Furniture, bed, clothes." He shrugged. "All my things."

"Those are nothing. I can get you new clothes and a fully furnished apartment. What do you have that can't be replaced?"

That shocked the man. "You are serious?"

"I am."

Freitas seemed to think then walked into a back room. When he came back out, he carried a large box. He looked sad as he put the box on the floor. "This. All I have of my life with Judite is here."

Scott swallowed, understanding the man's sadness. To be able to fit all one's memories of a life with the person you loved into a single box—it put a person's priorities in perspective. "You're sure?"

Freitas nodded again.

"Then let's go." Scott tapped his earbud as they left. "Call Demophon," he commanded.

The response was nearly immediate. "Dem here."

"Dem, how fast can you build someone a new identity?"

DAY 05
SATURDAY

CHAPTER 18

Amber's dream, or memory if one preferred, from the night before bled over into her restless nap. She awoke exhausted and needed two cups of her newest addiction just to motivate her to get out the door. But the memories of the Reaper also inspired her.

The group of jackers she'd brought down that night had been the origin of the Reaper. It was Rufio's fault. He'd come up with the name and raved like a lunatic to anyone who would listen:

He was like some kind of Grim Reaper—a Reaper who waltzed through the three of us like we were children.

The Reaper was a demon four meters tall with a deafening voice from the bowels of hell.

The Reaper killed Lugus, burning his eyes from his skull with beams that shot from his own.

Slugs melted and ran down the Reaper's skin like raindrops.

His exaggerations had given the Reaper a reputation, and she'd built on it. Each team of organ jackers she brought down afterward only added to the urban legend. But the reality was she'd been a LEO conducting highly illegal raids. And she had done some things during those raids she wasn't proud of. So the fact that she had been the Reaper fourteen years ago was something she'd never admitted aloud.

The memories had also given her some ideas, though. So she sat here now, well after midnight, in the back of a Fixer surveillance van, riding stim poppers and adjusting the settings on her vox unit.

Missy and Jordie monitored a bank of display screens, watching the hallways of twenty-three apartment complexes where Jordie, Richard, and CC had spent several hours posing as maintenance workers. During their inspections of those twenty-three buildings, they'd managed to plant the more than two hundred fifty wireless transmitters that now streamed the buildings' security feeds to the surveillance vehicles.

Normally, watching for unusual activity on so many cams would have been nearly impossible for such a small team, but at 02:37, most of the feeds were empty, and any activity at all was unusual. Besides, Amber knew their effort was superfluous since Dem and Acamas were scanning the same feeds at speeds faster than any human was able. But CC, Missy, and Maestro Harris didn't know that, so the facade had to be maintained.

Between Dem's analysis and the information Scott had brought back from Judite's husband, they had settled on three locations as most likely to be hit. So they split into three vehicles, with one group to cover each of the three target areas. Amber, Missy, and Jordie were in one van. They were hidden in an alley in the middle of the centermost of the three areas. As the fastest of the team, Amber wanted to give herself the best chance to reach any sector they were surveilling.

Richard and CC occupied another van. As with the elevators, any standard vehicle got very crowded, very quickly with anything more than the two of them in it. Richard's enhanced hearing gave them a slight advantage when it came to listening for trouble, and anyone who saw the two of them together would give the behemoths a wide berth.

Scott and Maestro Harris were in Scott's half-track. It amused Amber that the two of them were getting along so well considering the first day Harris had met them. But they seemed to hold a mutual respect for one another, and Amber pitied anyone who ever challenged the pair.

All of them were linked into a private comm network constantly monitored and updated by Dem and Acamas. It had all been set up on the fly, but it was adequate for what they needed.

If they needed it at all.

Amber was beginning to fear they might have miscalculated—that nothing was going to happen. Her team had been in place for a few hours, having set up well before Acamas and Dem's target window of midnight to 03:00. But that window was closing, and there was still no hint of any activity. She knew better than to cling to any real expectations on that front, but it was still frustrating to sit and watch the minutes tick past with nothing to show for it.

She needn't have worried. At 02:42, Dem's voice came over the speakers in the van. "I think we have a winner. Check feed eighty-four."

Amber stood and moved to watch over Jordie's shoulder as the younger woman toggled up the right feed. When she stopped, they all watched as four men entered the front of an apartment building.

"You don't think they live there?" Missy said. "They could just be coming home from a late shift or a party or something."

Jordie shook her head. "When was the last time you came home from a party in a group like that, and none of you said a word to anyone else?"

They watched the screen as the men walked with purposeful strides directly and swiftly to the elevator and pressed the button to go upstairs.

"Someone get me that location," Amber said, and she heard Missy typing at her station. "Are there cams in the elevators?"

"No." Jordie consulted a quick schematic on the wall behind her monitor before tapping out a command. "But there are in the hallways. We'll pick them up again when it opens back up." Her monitor split into four views, and they watched for a few seconds until the elevator door opened on the third floor. Jordie tapped the view, and it filled the screen. Looking up at the schematic once more, she grunted and tapped her second monitor before typing in another feed number. Another view showed the group approaching down the hallway away from the open elevator.

Scott's voice on the speakers reminded Amber that the rest of the team was also watching. "Looks like they jammed the elevator doors," he said.

Amber looked behind the four interlopers and noted that the doors remained open. She knew the door alarm would start buzzing any second, but before it did, the four stopped at an apartment door. One of them pulled a small device from within his jacket and knelt. Just as the elevator began buzzing, the door gave way to the man's manipulations, and the four of them slipped inside.

Amber pressed her earbud in place. "Somebody get me that address."

"Sending the map to your HUD," Jordie said. "But they're over in Richard and CC's area. You'll need to hustle."

Amber popped open the side door on the van. "On my way." She switched to the night-vision setting on her eyes, overlaid it with the map Jordie had sent to her heads-up, and launched herself into the darkness.

"We're right behind you," Jordie said, and Amber could hear her moving around in the van as she hurried up to the driver's seat.

Amber cut across a small neighborhood park and leapt over some children's playground equipment. Her legs pumped faster than the swiftest unaugmented human had ever run. She could easily maintain speeds of over forty kph for extended periods. At the moment, she was probably pushing at least double that. But she still had her limits, and as badly as Amber wanted to make this confrontation face-to-face, she wasn't going to ignore any advantage she could find. "Jordie, do we have any drones in the area?"

"There are two. I've already got them zeroing in on the building. Four more are coming in pairs of two at three and six minutes."

"That's not going to be fast enough," Richard's voice chimed in. "They're already dragging a man and a woman out of the apartment. These bungholes don't mess around."

Amber cursed. "Richard, how close are you?" She could hear skidding tires in the background as he answered.

"We're about forty seconds out."

Amber glanced at the chrono display on her HUD. "You're going to beat me by about fifteen. Keep them from getting out of the building. Understood?"

"Roger that, Boss. They won't get past us."

Amber turned right at the next corner and poured on the speed. She ran up the street toward her goal. It was a straight shot from where she was, and she activated telescopic mode on her eyes. She saw the front doors open, and several people stepped outside just as Richard's van popped over the curb and tore across the grassy yard toward them. The bangers drew pistols and fired round after round into the van before retreating back into the building.

"They're going back upstairs," Missy reported. "Wait a second… they're not getting out at the same floor." Amber could hear the van in the background as Missy spoke. That told her Jordie was the one driving.

Amber slowed as she approached Richard's van and stopped beside his door. She slapped it, and he jerked inside.

"Holy happy Buddha!" he shouted. "You scared the sludge out of me!"

"Good. Get your glutes out of there, and let's get after them."

She ran forward to the building's entrance and pulled on the door. It didn't budge. "Dammit! Jordie, the door into the building is locked. Can you override it?"

"Not from here."

"How far out are you?"

"About a minute."

Amber hesitated only a second before drawing her pistol and firing at the lock. The lock held, her flechettes ricocheted, and Richard shouted from behind her.

"Whoa, whoa, whoa!" he screamed. "You trying to kill us?"

"They're getting away!"

"Well, that isn't going to get us any closer to them. Let me and CC take care of this."

She stepped back, holstering her pistol as she did.

Richard grabbed the handle on the left door. CC grabbed the right. "On three," Richard said. "One... two... three!"

The two behemoths yanked... and the handles came off the doors, leaving the barrier intact.

"Sturdy doors," Richard muttered. He looked at CC. "We're going to have to knock them down."

CC shrugged. "On three?"

Richard placed his shoulder against the doors and nodded again. "One..." He pulled back about half a meter from the door. "Two... three!"

He and CC slammed into the door with all the weight and strength the two men had at their disposal. Amber could feel the ground tremble as they hit. Still, the doors held. But the doorframe didn't. The entire structure—doors, doorframe, and the surrounding observation windows, as well as a portion of the supporting wall—fell into the lobby with a deafening rumble.

Amber ran past her companions toward the elevator the jackers had used. "Come on!" She hit the button to call the elevator back as she tapped her earbud. "Missy, what floor?"

There was a moment's silence before Missy's flat voice replied, "Forget it. They got away."

Amber froze. "What?"

"They went to the roof. Drones caught sight of them just as they rode zip lines to the next building. They had a cargo pod waiting. I tried to follow them with the drones, but I lost them."

Amber kicked the elevator door over and over. "Of all the sludge-fuggled, shyte-coated—"

Demophon interrupted her. "If you're about done, I'm tracking them on traffic cams."

That stopped her. "You have them?"

"I do. And if you're finished pummeling the poor defenseless door, you can get on the road to go after them."

Amber turned and rushed back out of the building. "Jordie, where are…?" She stopped as Jordie pulled up in front of her. Scott and Harris were right behind.

Amber ran around to climb in the pod's side door, and Jordie took off, even as Amber reached for her safety harness.

"Dem," Jordie shouted. "Give me a map and show me where we're going!"

He must have done it because she shouted back at Amber, "ETA is two minutes. Hang on for a hard right."

The van lurched and skidded before Amber could brace herself, and she barely kept her seat as inertia tried its best to toss her against the door.

Amber strapped herself to the seat. "Acamas, are you there?" she yelled into the comms.

"I am."

"Can you see about getting a repair crew on the door to that apartment building right away?"

"I can. And for the elevator door as well?"

Amber sighed. "Yes. Elevator door too."

CHAPTER 19

The van skidded to a stop as Amber was testing her breather. "You're sure this will filter out the carbonite stuff?"

"Carbogen," Missy corrected. "And yes, I'm sure. Keep the seal on your mask, and you'll be fine."

"And if I lose the seal?"

Missy grimaced. "Then you'll have the same symptoms as the rest of them. Even then, though, you'll have the advantage of knowing what's happening, so you should still be able to work through it."

Amber nodded as she adjusted the settings on her vox unit. Jordie had helped her tie the controls into the HUD menu on her new eyes, so adjustments were done quite literally with the blink of an eye. Missy had integrated both vox and breather into her armor's helmet, so when she slipped it on, everything popped up as an option on her HUD.

"Everybody ready?"

The deep, demonic voice issuing from the vox caused Missy to step back. "Holy shyte!"

Amber chuckled, and *that* sound made Missy step back farther.

"Okay, you need to stop that shyte right now!"

Amber blinked the vox unit off. "Sorry. Just testing it out."

"Well, it's freaking the nine hells out of me."

Richard opened the side door on the cargo pod and peered inside. "Was that you?"

Amber nodded. "Testing the rig out."

"Well, it sounded pretty gnarly." He nodded approvingly. "The vocals, combined with the gas and speakers, is going to loosen the bowels of anyone you go after."

"That's the idea." Amber looked through the windshield to the next intersection as she finished suiting up. Demophon had tracked the jackers to a building just around the corner and had stopped them out of sight. "Anything on the drones?"

"Not a thing," Jordie responded. "The whole building is completely dark. You sure this is the place, Dem?"

Amber replied before Dem could. "Zoom in on the windows. Are they blacked out?"

There was a short pause as Jordie manipulated the cams on the drones. "Yeah. Looks like it."

"Any of them broken?"

After another short pause, she said, "No."

"Then it's probably the right place."

Jordie swiveled in her seat to face her. "I don't follow."

"SOP for organ jackers is to keep anyone from getting a look inside their chop shops. They always have all the windows intact, and they're always blacked out."

Dem sounded a little peeved as he added, "And there's the minor detail of me having tracked them here on the traffic cams."

Amber checked the seals and filters on her helmet one last time, issuing orders as she spoke. "Okay, if we're going to save the people they took, we need to move fast. Jordie, move the drones into position. Missy, let her know where you want them, then start the sound projectors. Let's soften them up."

Satisfied that the helmet would protect her from the fear frequency and the gas, Amber checked the new plates and mail inlays on her recently modified armor. "So here's the plan." Satisfied with her rig, she looked up at the rest of her team. "I go in. The rest of you wait outside. After I've made my appearance and scared the shyte out of them, I'll let one of them get out. I want you to let that first man escape."

CC looked confused. "Why?"

"Because he'll spread the word. We already know there are multiple organ jacker teams, so we need to convince their community, such as it is, that the Reaper is back. Let the first person go. If anyone else gets past me, take them down."

Her team fell silent, looking somewhat unsure. CC was the first to voice concern. "You sure you don't want anyone else inside with you?"

Amber shook her head impatiently. "Multiple teams means multiple hits like this one. I'm setting us up for the long game here, and in order for it to work, we have to make them think the Reaper is back. And the Reaper worked alone."

"But after that first one gets out, there's no need for you to—"

"I'll be fine," she snapped. Amber looked at the faces around her. "Look, with the exception of Maestro Harris, is there a single one of you who thinks you can beat me on the training floor?"

"Training isn't the same as the real deal," CC protested.

"And do you remember the first time you met me?"

The behemoth frowned at the reminder.

"I dropped two of your team and had one of their pistols in your ear before you could stop me." She took a calming breath, struggling to keep her temper in check.

"I stand corrected," he said.

"I understand that you're all worried about me," she said.

"Not really," Richard interrupted. "We know you can handle yourself. That's not the question. But there are two victims in there, and they don't have your fancy souped-up reflexes or your cybernetics. They're just stuck in a chop shop with people who are going to kill them."

"I know that! I know it better than any of you!" Amber snapped. "So I'm going in pumping carbo-whatsis gas—"

"Carbogen!" Missy sounded exasperated as she turned from her console.

"Whatever! I go in, pumping gas. The drones will be pumping in the fear frequency soon—"

"Already going," Missy corrected again.

Amber slipped her helmet back on. "By the time I show up in this getup…" She activated the vox unit again. "With this voice…" She clicked it back off. "They'll be too busy pissing themselves to put up much of a fight. But if it makes you feel better, you'll be able to see and hear everything through my feed."

Amber didn't wait to see if she had convinced them. It didn't matter. And at the moment, she didn't care. "So as much as I'd love to sit and discuss the pros and cons of this, it's like you just said. There are two people in that building with jackers who are planning to cut them up and sell the parts. The longer we debate, the greater the chance is that they don't live to see daylight again. So this is what we're doing. Either get on board or stay in the fuggled van!"

They all fell silent until Jordie asked, "When do we go?"

"Kidnap victims! Remember?" Amber snapped. "I'm going now. Let me know on the comms when the rest of you are in position."

Amber knew her team was concerned about the op and the victims. And despite Richard's protestations to the contrary, they were probably worried about her state of mind. But they didn't have time for a debate.

She had warned them from the beginning. This case was personal on a level they couldn't relate to. She sped off before anyone else could argue.

Orienting herself for a second, she called up a map on her HUD. "Where's my entrance, Dem?"

"The back door is the most discreet. Vid feed from the drones shows the lock looks like one of the models Jordie tagged as susceptible to her new toy."

Amber grunted acknowledgment, mentally going through the inventory of new gear and gadgets she carried in various pockets and pouches on her recently modified body armor. The suit was heavier than what she was used to wearing, but if everything worked as planned, the added weight would be more than worth it. She ran down the alley toward the chop shop. "Dem, load images of the kidnap victims onto my HUD."

Demophon didn't bother answering, but the images popped up on the right of her main field of vision. She glanced at them then blinked them into the background, keeping them quickly accessible on the top layer of her menu. "Thanks."

She drew up to her target within seconds and slid to a stop in a narrow alcove to the side of the building. Amber looked up to see the drones hovering above the roof. She also saw a tiny reflective lens of a security cam as the light from a streetlamp scintillated off it.

Shyte!

She reported into her comm. "They have cams on the walls. They've probably already seen me."

"Plan B," Jordie said quickly. "You were moving too fast for them to have a defense set up yet. Go in hard and fast. We're right behind you."

Amber heard the screech of tires as the van raced up the street. She nodded and ran to the back of the building. She slapped Jordie's new toy, as Demophon had called it, onto the wall beside the keypad and reported into her comm. "Skeleton key is in place."

"On it" was Jordie's clipped reply.

Amber waited for what seemed like several minutes, though her HUD showed it was just over three seconds. She activated the carbogen pump on her back, set her vox unit, and checked her weapons. Then a soft beep sounded as Jordie told her, "Go, go, go!"

She yanked the door open, ducked, and dove into chaos.

CHAPTER 20

"BUDDHA'S BLUE-FUGGLED HAIRY BALLS!" Richard cursed.

Amber was letting her emotions get the better of her. She'd warned them, but in the few years he'd worked with her, he'd never really seen her so close to losing control. If she kept reacting this way, it was going to get her killed. And that was something he absolutely would not allow to happen.

"Dem," he said as he did a fast check of his armor. "Set me up a secondary channel on comms. Switch everyone except Amber to it and give us a fast toggle. Route Amber's comm through it, incoming only. I want us to be able to hear her without our chatter distracting her."

Demophon's response was immediate. There was a beep in Richard's ear at the same time as Dem's confirmation of "Done."

Jordie, on the other hand, chuckled softly. "Distract her? Don't you mean you don't want her to know what we're doing?"

"Right now, I think that's the same thing." He grabbed his helmet and slipped it on, still issuing instructions as he stepped out of the van. "CC, Scott, and Maestro Harris, I need you to join me at the back of the building. Jordie, you and Missy stay in the surveillance van and keep us apprised of the operation."

He started to run toward the chop shop but stopped when he saw Scott's half-track parked behind his van. "Jordie, do you have your flex-pad?"

She pulled a long, thin tube from a custom-made pocket in her sleeve. "Always."

"Good. I want you to do your remote thing with the half-track. We probably won't need it, but it might be a good idea to have it ready to ram the front door if anyone you don't recognize tries to get out that way."

She began to unroll the tube into a thin sheet and tapped her thumb on the lower-right corner. The flexible material hardened to a fully rigid console. "No problem. I'll have it in place in ninety seconds."

"Thanks." Richard looked at the others. "Everyone tested their breathers and armor?"

After a round of nods, he took a deep breath. "Amber told us this one was likely to trigger her. I think it's safe to say she was right. So it's up to us to watch her back, whether she wants it or not."

"She's not gonna be happy about it," Scott said.

"Let me worry about that. I'd rather have her pissed off than dead."

Everyone nodded their agreement.

Richard checked his chrono. Amber had just over a minute's lead time. And she was much faster than the rest of them. "Scott, open up your adrenal pump and get into position. We'll be right behind you."

Scott Pond reached into a pocket on his duster and pulled out a red popper ampule. He slapped it against his neck, and Richard heard the faint snick of the injection needle as it punctured the packaging. The needle delivered its payload, and Scott's eyes began to dilate. Then he stretched his neck, dropped the now-empty popper, and tore down the street at a speed that rivaled Amber's.

Richard looked at CC and Harris. "Let's go."

The three of them followed Scott, running as quickly as they could.

Amber yanked the door open, ducked, and dove to the right, rolling out of the doorway faster than most people could move. The quiet *brrrtt* of a flechette pistol on full auto and the answering tings on the door behind her spoke to the wisdom of her decision.

There was a metal cabinet on casters to her right. She rolled it away from the wall and took cover behind it. Protected for the moment, Amber pulled two padded canisters from her belt, pressed the triggers, and arced them high over the cabinet to either side of the room. The padding on them would keep the high dispersal units from clanging as they landed and emptied their contents into the room. She tossed two more of the carbogen grenades into the back corners of the room to her right and left.

She peeked from behind her cover. The man with the flechette pistol was running toward her, looking eerie in the dim green light. She looked up and saw emerald LED fixtures all over the ceiling... aimed... and fired. Lights exploded as she shot them out, showering the floor in a cascade of glass and plastic. Gambling that the shooter would be distracted by the crash and hail of debris, Amber jumped to the top of the cabinet she crouched behind, spotted her target, and leapt straight at him.

To the man's credit, he didn't panic. He kept his head well enough to spot her and fire a stream of flechettes that hit her center mass. Even if she'd been wearing normal body armor, it wouldn't have done enough damage to stop her. It would have felt like she'd been hit with a hammer, though. But the plate inserts and the Wyvern mesh of her new armor absorbed the hits and dispersed the kinetic energy of the flechettes as if they were nothing.

She landed in front of him, slipped to one side as she grabbed his pistol, ducked under his arm, and twisted the pistol. The move trapped his finger in the trigger guard, and he screamed as the finger snapped. She wrenched the pistol away and tossed it across the floor.

"Cooper?" The shout to her right was panicky, and Amber didn't know whether it was the effect of the gas, the fear frequency, or just the fact that he was in a mostly dark room with his screaming companion.

Probably a combination of the above.

But the voice caught her attention in time to warn her of the other man's movement. She slipped to the side, spinning the still-screaming Cooper in front of her just as the deafening boom of a heavy-caliber hand cannon echoed throughout the confines of the room. Cooper went suddenly quiet and slumped.

At the same time, voices in her ear began chattering as her team wanted to know what was happening, what the shot was, whether she was okay. But she didn't have time to answer them. She had the vox on, and answering would require her to scroll through a menu on her HUD, switch from vox to comms, answer them, then switch back to vox. She grunted instead, and the vox translated the sound into a deep, deafening, terrifying growl. She would need to reconfigure the interface later.

Assuming there is a later.

She reacted to the hand cannon with what had become one of her most common moves in a firefight—she dropped the body in her arms and jumped. Cybernetic legs gave her an uncommon advantage, letting her move quicker and jump higher than most humans. It almost always took opponents by surprise. The shooter tonight was no different.

In the low light of the chop shop, it would have looked to him as if Amber had disappeared. Even as Amber fell from above, the man spun in place, trying to figure out where she had gone. She landed to his left, kicked out at his gun hand, and felt the satisfying crunch of finger bones as his hand cannon went flying.

The banger didn't panic. With his good hand, he reached for another pistol. Amber saw it was a flechette pistol, knew the danger to her was almost nonexistent in her new rig, and decided to let him draw it. She calculated quickly. It had been about thirty or forty seconds since she'd tossed those first carbogen canisters. The drones had been pumping in the fear frequency for a few minutes before that. And now she was standing right in front of the man, pumping more gas and fear frequency directly at him. It was time for the coup de grâce.

At full volume, she shouted in the vox's terrifying bass, "Did you think the Reaper was gone?"

He screamed and squeezed the trigger, emptying the full stream of flechettes into her chest at point-blank range. Amber laughed. The man dropped his pistol and ran.

Now she scrolled through her menu, switched to comms, and reminded her team, "One is coming out. Let him go. Any others are fair game."

She switched back to vox and spun to look around. Nothing else moved in this room, but a door on the back wall showed where the other jackers had to be.

"Dammit!"

She thought quickly. That door meant the gas she'd tossed wouldn't have spread to the other jackers. And she didn't have any more canisters.

The fear frequency would still be affecting them, but she had no idea how well that would work on its own.

She toggled back to comms again as she examined the door. "Guys, the last two jackers are in another room with a closed door, so they won't have been exposed to the gas."

"You need help getting through the door?" Jordie asked.

"No. But I need you to concentrate the drones on the front half of the building." She looked up and counted windows. "The back half has four windows. Reposition the drones to cover everything forward of them. Then max out the speakers."

"On it," Jordie said. "Give me ten seconds."

Amber took a calming breath as she mentally prepared herself for what she knew was coming. "Wish I had it to give."

She toggled back to vox, cranked up the mini fear-freq projectors on her armor to their highest level, and kicked at the door where it hinged. It was a metal door, and even with her cybernetics, it held for three kicks. On the third kick, the door caved inward, hanging on by one twisted lower hinge. Light flooded in from the doorway—no low-light green LEDs in here. Normal, bright-white light poured into her room.

She hesitated, knowing the element of surprise was gone and the people on the other side of the door had heard her mow through their companions. They would be ready for her.

This is a really bad idea.

But she didn't see any other way. She dove through, rolled, and immediately felt the impact of flechettes on her armor. A single line of firey pain under her left arm told her that one lucky shot had found an opening between the plates and her ballistic mail. She grunted but kept her feet and managed to jump. In midair, she scanned the room from above. There were four people to her right.

One of the kidnap victims, the woman, was strapped to a metal table beneath a device composed of multiple blades and tubes that looked like something from a slasher vid. Amber had never seen anything like it.

Beside it, one of the jackers held the other victim, pulling back on a black hood over the man's head. He kept a choke hold on the hood, pulling the man close to his chest as a human shield. His other hand gripped a flechette pistol, firing a steady stream of projectiles as he spoke into an old-style boom mic strapped to his head.

Amber ignored him for the moment. Flechettes weren't going to do more than minor damage. But her eyes widened when she saw the last jacker. He stood apart from the others, his weapon tracking Amber as she flew through the air above them. The slug thrower he held was more serious than his partner's little flechette gun. This was a large-caliber hand cannon.

Buddha's balls.

The blast hit her center mass, its kinetic force more than enough to alter her trajectory. The air left her lungs in a loud *whoof* as she flew head over heels through the air. If not for the Wyvern mail, Amber knew it would have ended her. She landed in a heap, coughing and groaning, and the vox tried to compensate with horrible deep-bass barking. That was the only good thing about this situation. No matter what sound she uttered, the vox made her sound like a snarling monster.

Move, Amber, move!

She struggled to her knees, and another sledgehammer hit her just below the shoulder. Her arm went numb, and she yelled in anger and pain, the vox nearly deafening in the room. She turned to look at the man.

Amber rolled slowly to her side, trying to keep the strongest plates of her armor toward him. The man hesitated as if unsure of himself. His eyes widened, and Amber realized the subaudial prodding from the drones was starting to affect him. She embraced the groan that fighting to her feet elicited, knowing that when it translated through her vox, it would add to his fear. She got a foot beneath her and fought to stand, making sure as she did so that her shoulder-mounted audio projectors pointed in his direction. She didn't know how much of an effect they would have at this distance, but she would take any help she could get at this point.

It only occurred to her as the jacker raised his pistol that not everyone reacted the same way to fear. Sure, most people ran when given the option. But flight was only half of the "fight or flight" equation, and this guy was leaning heavily into the fight side.

Battle brain kicked in, and everything slowed.

Amber fought to regain her feet. Ten meters away, the jacker shifted his pistol, and she knew she wasn't going to make it before he fired again. All she could think to do was to try to take the shot on her reinforced chest plate. But he was aiming too high, going for the head shot. As she looked directly down the barrel of his hand cannon, she knew there was no way her helmet would stop what was coming.

Her vision narrowed, focusing on the giant well of blackness in the man's hand… the barrel of the hand cannon from which her death was about to emerge.

Fuggle me.

CHAPTER 21

The hand cannon fired, and something slammed into her shoulder. Even as Amber flew sideways, she heard more shots. There were screams around the room and more than a little confusion as she tried to come to grips with the idea that she wasn't dead—wasn't really even hurt. But something massive pinned her to the floor, and her mask had been shoved half off her face, blinding her for the moment. She gasped for air, shoving against the weight on her.

The weight moved, and she suddenly understood it was a person. Someone was smothering her. She screamed. The sound seemed far away, and she realized she had subconsciously expected the deafening sound of the vox unit. But with her helmet mostly off her face, the vox wasn't picking up her voice. The weight on top of her groaned and moved again.

Amber shoved and yelled as she struggled with her one good arm to wriggle herself free from the crushing weight. Two seconds felt like several minutes as she finally dragged herself out and rolled to her feet. Her right hand went to the stun baton at her waist, and a flick of her wrist telescoped it to full length. She winced as she tried to move her left hand, realizing the arm was currently out of commission. She swept her right hand up, baton and all, to knock the obstructing mask the rest of the way off her face. Then she thumbed on the power button as she raised her stun baton.

She was already swinging the weapon when her eyes made sense of what was happening. Richard lay on the floor, struggling to rise. She pulled her strike and looked around the room. Heart pounding, breathing quick and shallow, Amber struggled to wrap her head around what was happening around her.

A masked figure she recognized as Maestro Harris was releasing the restraints on the screaming woman who had been strapped to the table. Behind them, CC dropped the limp form of the jacker who had been using the woman's companion as a shield to the floor. CC held up his right hand, and a long, serrated spike retracted into the metallic glove he wore. A spreading pool of blood trickled onto the floor from a matching hole in the jacker's chest.

Amber gaped in confusion as she saw Harris speaking softly to the woman as he placed a breather over her face.

Scott, also wearing a breather, had disarmed the shooter so intent on ending her. In typical Scott Pond fashion, he had done so quite literally. The man's arm, still holding the hand cannon, lay on the ground before him, severed just below the elbow. He screamed louder than the woman on the table had, curling in on himself as he cradled his bleeding stump to his belly, sobbing between whines of fear and agony. Scott slammed the pommel of his sword into the back of the man's head, mercifully silencing the jacker.

Richard lay on the floor to Amber's right. His groans brought her attention back to him. He had shoved her away from the shots that would have killed her, but it looked like he hadn't escaped unscathed.

"Richard?" she said. "Richard!"

He struggled to his knees, another muffled groan escaping through his mask. "Buddha's balls. That hurt!" He rolled to his back, cradling his right side. "Holy shyte!"

She dropped to her knees beside him and saw a dent in his heavy armor. If it had done that to him, a direct hit would definitely have ended her. He hissed as she prodded.

"Stop it!" He pulled away. "That hurts!"

"How bad is it?" Amber worried that there could be some sort of permanent damage. She'd lost Kevin, her first partner. And T-bone just last year. She couldn't stand it if she lost someone else close to her. She panicked at the thought. "Don't you dare die on me, you hear me? Don't you dare!"

Richard just looked at her. "It's not that bad. Put your damn mask back on. You're overreacting. And turn off your carbogen pump." Then he reached up and tapped his earbud. "Missy? I think you can turn off the fear frequency. We're clear in here."

Amber recognized the symptoms in her reaction and reached down to grab her helmet. Then she scrolled through the menu in her HUD to shut off the gas convertor strapped to her back. Almost immediately, the tightness in her chest started to ease, and her heart began to slow back to a normal rhythm.

"Better?" Richard asked.

"Yeah. Sorry."

"You sure you're better?"

"Yes. Why?"

"Good." He groaned as he muscled himself back to his feet and took a deep breath. He let it out then faced Amber. "Then what in the nine hells did you think you were doing?" he shouted. "There was no fuggled reason in the world for you to run in here alone like that!"

Amber blinked, unused to her partner yelling at her. She stood and started to yell back at him, but he held up a hand.

"No! You don't get to talk yet. I'm not finished." The big man began to pace back and forth in front of her. "I get that this case is personal for you. You warned us, and you're sure as shyte running true to your word. But that doesn't mean you get to run into the freaking hornet's nest while the rest of us sit on our damn thumbs and watch you commit suicide."

Scott and Maestro Harris stood across the room, as frozen in place by Richard's outburst as she was. He didn't let that stop him.

"Yeah, sure, you have the souped-up speed and reflexes and the super legs and eyes and shyte. But the rest of us don't exactly come to the party empty-handed. And we depend on each other." He looked genuinely pained. "And we depend on you, damn it! Do you know how fuggled over we would be if you got yourself killed doing something this stupid? How would we explain it to Gibbs? Better yet, how would we explain it to Nathan?"

That one hit home, and the indignation that had been building within her fell away. She sagged...and nodded. "You're right."

Richard froze. "What?"

"You're right." She shrugged. "I told you this was going to mess with me. I guess I didn't realize how much." She looked up at him then at Scott and Harris. "I'm sorry. It was a bad decision on my part. I got hung up on bringing the Reaper back to life and the fact that he worked alone."

"Well, we let the first guy out like you said, so that part of the rumor is intact."

She waved her hand at the unconscious one-armed man Scott was bandaging. "But this one knows there were more of us now." She pointed to where Maestro Harris spoke quietly to the rescued victims. "And they know. It's going to get out."

Richard shook his head. "See? That's part of your problem. You don't give the rest of us enough credit. You always think you have to carry it all on your shoulders."

Amber wasn't sure if she should be offended by that but decided she'd already pushed her attitude as far as she should for the moment. So she stopped, gathered her emotions, and asked as calmly as she could manage, "Does that mean you have a plan?"

The big man nodded to where Harris was deep in conversation with the man and woman they had just rescued. "The maestro is convincing these two that it's in everyone's best interest to forget anything happened here tonight. No one but us saw them leave the building, and it's still early enough that we can get them back home before anyone even knows they were gone. And a generous donation from PSC will convince them to keep it that way."

Amber nodded. "That's good as far as it goes. But what about Stumpy over there?" She pointed to Scott's former opponent and current patient.

Richard chuckled at the nickname. "*Stumpy* is about to discover that the Fixers have a very private and very restricted detention facility where he will very likely live out the rest of his days."

"They do?"

"Maestro told us about it while we were waiting in back. They also have a cleaning crew that will be here in less than twenty minutes to sanitize this location."

Amber blinked in surprise.

"Yeah. Amazing what you can find out if you talk things out before you run into a situation without knowing all your resources."

"Okay, okay. I messed up," Amber said. "Don't push it." She looked around at her team again, realizing that they weren't just avoiding her attention. They were working without her, working on a plan they all knew. All but her. The realization made her swallow. She'd treated them like shyte. Yet here they were, cleaning up her mess… saving her ass.

And she felt half a meter tall.

"I don't deserve you guys," she muttered.

"No, you don't," Richard replied.

She kept forgetting about his audial implants. The realization was yet another reminder that she took her team for granted. With a sigh, she looked up to find him grinning back at her.

"But you're stuck with us," he said softly.

And for the first time since she'd lost her eyes fourteen years ago, Amber felt the wet trail of tears on her cheeks.

Richard looked as startled as she felt. "Buddha's fat and hairys," he hissed. "Stop that shyte right now!"

They laughed together.

"Sorry. The new eyes have all the upgrades."

"This is an upgrade?" Her friend was clearly dubious.

Her smile grew wider. "You have no idea."

Amber was surprised when Gibbs walked in with the Fixer cleaning crew. She walked straight to Gibbs. "I didn't think you cared about a job that wasn't a Fixer case."

"When it starts drawing on Fixer resources, I think I need to take a closer look, don't you?"

Amber sighed. "Yes, fem. What can I do for you, then?"

Gibbs looked around the room as her people took Stumpy into custody and loaded the dead jackers into body bags. Missy and Jordie had already taken the kidnap victims, Gail and Clemente Araújo, back to their apartment. "Walk me through it," she said.

And Amber spent the next half hour explaining the case and answering questions. When she was finished, she expected Gibbs to ream her. To her surprise, though, the older woman simply nodded. "All things considered, it looks like you and your team have done as well as can be expected."

The surprise must have shown on Amber's face. Gibbs smiled. "What? Would you rather I rant and scream?"

"No, fem. I just thought… I mean, we have two bodies and—"

"And a jacker with a missing arm." Gibbs raised a single eyebrow. "'Stumpy,' I think you called him?"

Amber swallowed. How had she known that?

Gibbs smiled. "Maestro Harris reported it without understanding it wasn't really the man's name. As you might have guessed by now, English isn't the maestro's primary language. This sometimes causes some interesting misunderstandings."

"Yes, I've noticed." Amber began to relax a little as she realized her boss wasn't about to blow a gasket. "Then you're not going to…?" She wasn't sure how to finish the sentence, and Gibbs saved her the trouble of trying.

"No. If there isn't anything here to link your operation to us, then I don't see any reason to interfere." She looked on as the cleanup crew rolled out another of the refrigeration units full of human organs. Another pair of men unbolted the contraption of scalpels and lasers from the floor. "Though I admit," she mused as she watched them, "this thing intrigues me." She held up a hand to stop the men from removing it as she walked over to get a closer look. Amber followed close behind.

"Have you ever seen anything like this?" Gibbs asked her.

"Only in a horror vid."

"I have," one of the cleanup techs said. "My grandpa was a butcher back in the day. They had something similar for cutting up pigs in the shop. It wasn't exactly like this, but close enough that you can see the resemblance."

Amber's lips tightened into a thin line. "They're turning organ jacking into an assembly-line process."

"It certainly looks that way," Gibbs agreed. She waved the men on, and they carried the monstrosity out of the chop shop.

"We can't let that stand," Amber said.

"Not true," Gibbs replied. "As disgusting as it may be, a ring of organ jackers in the city doesn't rise to the level of a Fixer case."

"So we do nothing?"

"No," Gibbs said. "The *Fixers* do nothing. *You*, however, are free to do whatever you wish."

Amber realized this was as far as Gibbs could go. She couldn't involve the Fixers, but she could release Amber and her team to take care of the problem.

"Just remember, this is your operation. Your case. *We*,"—she waved a hand to indicate herself and the cleanup crew—"don't exist."

"And Stumpy?"

Gibbs shook her head. "Never heard of him."

"I have to admit, fem, I'm not sure I'm completely comfortable with that. I mean, I know we operate somewhat outside the law, but this—"

Gibbs interrupted before Amber could finish. "Is there any doubt in your mind... any doubt whatsoever, that these people kidnapped two innocents?"

"No, fem."

"Any doubt they were about to kill those innocents and sell their organs on the black market?"

"No, fem."

"Do you have recorded evidence to that effect?"

Amber thought about the feeds from the building security cams, the drones, and her eyes. It could all be provided as evidence. "Yes, fem, I do."

"Do you believe you or your team did anything wrong in your apprehension of the organ jackers?"

"No, fem."

"And do you remember the purpose of the Fixers?"

Amber nodded. "To step in whenever the law can't."

"Or, for whatever reason, won't," Gibbs said. "I would think you, of all people, know how un*just* the justice system can be."

She did. She knew firsthand that in this day and age, law enforcement worked for the highest bidder, which usually meant big corporations and their shareholders. And the gods themselves couldn't protect someone who placed anything before company profit. That was how she'd lost her job at Securi-Tech.

"I understand," she conceded. But it still didn't sit right with her.

It wasn't until Gibbs and the cleanup crew were gone that Amber realized what it was about the argument that bothered her so much. Gibbs's words sounded an awful lot like the excuse Conley had used to justify her attempt to overthrow the government last year.

CHAPTER 22

THE SUN WAS RISING AS Amber and her team pulled into the parking garage at PSC. To everyone's immense relief, Gibbs had told them all to take a day off from training, so they each found a couch or corner to curl up in at the office. In Richard's case, he simply climbed into the surveillance van and crashed on the floor.

As she fell onto the couch in her office on the second floor, Amber had a final, exhausted thought. *I need to have Jordie add some bunk rooms to the new floor plans.*

She awoke to the mouthwatering aroma of her favorite blend of coffee, Nice and Naughty, and for a few seconds thought she was back at home. But the ache in her neck quickly disabused her of that notion. Her bed had never been quite so uncomfortable. She called up the chrono on her HUD before bothering to move, still debating whether her favorite coffee was enough reason to expend the energy. It was 10:08. She'd barely had four hours of sleep.

Then she heard voices laughing, Richard and… *Nathan?* What was Nathan doing here? The smell of spices and cooking food answered that question. Nathan was doing what he did best.

Well, second best.

With a low groan, she started to sit up, hissing at the pain shooting through her left arm and chest as she tried to leverage herself up. Shifting position to take any stress off that arm, she made yet another mental note for the floor plans. *We need a Doc Box too.*

Everyone kept telling her to quit worrying about money, but at the rate she was burning through it, she had her doubts.

She followed her nose down the hallway to the lunchroom to find her lover had set up a portable two-burner cookstove on which he was making breakfast.

"Good morning, Boss," Richard greeted her as she walked in.

"You're way too chipper for someone who got as little sleep as I know you did." She turned to Nathan and leaned into his shoulder.

He kissed the top of her head. "I hear you had a rough night."

"We did, but who told you?" She gave Richard an accusatory glare.

Richard put his hands up as if warding her off. "Don't look at me."

"Your boss commed me," Nathan said.

"Gibbs?"

Nathan nodded. "Seems to be a really nice lady."

Amber and Richard both snorted.

He looked from one to the other. "Did I say something funny?"

That, of course, prompted a round of real laughter. Richard's laughter wound down into a groan as he wrapped a hand around his aching ribs. Amber winced in sympathy.

"You need to go into HQ for some time in the Doc Box?"

"Maybe later. What about you? How's the arm?"

Amber felt Nathan tense, and she cursed under her breath.

"Something I should know about?" he asked.

She glared daggers at Richard before leaning back and smiling innocently at Nathan. "Just bruised my shoulder pretty bad last night. It's not a big deal."

The look Nathan gave her told her he didn't believe her for a second. "Mmm-hmm." He stared for a moment before shaking his head. "Okay. I get it. One of those things you can't talk about." He turned away from her and walked back to the stove. "Then can I at least make you something for breakfast?"

He made omelets that most people would never have known were the result of masterful manipulation of freeze-dried eggs and soy meat. The only reason Amber knew was she'd been the lucky recipient of his cooking for so long. But she recognized the veggies as fresh, straight from the garden at home.

The aroma must have carried throughout the building because Nathan had no sooner finished cooking for Amber and Richard than the others began drifting into the lunchroom. Short minutes later, they were all laughing and relaxing over a late breakfast, even Maestro Harris. Once Nathan finished cooking, he pulled up a chair and sat next to Amber, smiling at the easy banter.

He'd met Richard, Scott, and Jordie, but CC, Missy, and Harris were new faces for him. They all joked easily, and he quickly fell into the lighthearted conversation, though he was mostly quiet, content to share this rare glimpse into Amber's work life.

Amber smiled to herself at this momentary respite as she watched her friends enjoying themselves. But of course, it couldn't last, and the banter wound down as the last of the food disappeared and her team realized that, as much as they might like Nathan, they couldn't speak freely about the case around him. After one too many awkward pauses in the conversation, Amber squeezed Nathan's hand.

"Thanks for the pick-me-up this morning, but we have to get back to work." She addressed the rest of them. "Main conference room in five."

And that was the signal for everyone to push away from the table. They all thanked Nathan for the meal and discreetly left him and Amber alone in the lunchroom. He gave her a wry half smile. "I guess that's my cue to pack it up and head home." Amber leaned in and gave him a deep kiss. When she pulled back, he grinned. "I don't suppose you can take the day off? We could go home and continue…"

But she was already shaking her head. "I wish I could, but we have bad guys to catch. Consider that a down payment on what I owe you."

"Any idea when you'll be able to pay the rest?"

"You mean, will I be home tonight?" She grimaced. "I don't know yet. Probably not though."

He sighed. "Then I'll expect you when I see you."

"I'm sorry, Nathan."

He lifted a shoulder in resignation. "Don't be. You've been up front about your work. Or as up front as you can be." He leaned in and kissed her once more. "I knew what I was getting into."

"I don't deserve you."

"Nope," he agreed with a smile. "You don't. And I'll be sure you make it up to me another time. Now, go clean up the streets." He looked around at the dirty dishes they'd left scattered about. "I'll clean up in here."

She kissed him once more and went to meet her team in the conference room. Conversation in the room faded as she entered. Someone had already tied in Acamas and Demophon, and they all looked at her expectantly as she took her seat.

She looked around the conference table and took a deep breath before starting. "I owe you all an apology for the way I acted last night. I could say I warned you that the case was going to mess with me, but it's still no excuse. So… I'm sorry."

The others looked at her, then at one another in silence. Finally, Richard cleared his throat. "I think we said everything that needed to be said last night… or rather, early this morning. Just try not to do it again, would you?"

She nodded, grateful that it wasn't going to be a bigger deal and determined to not let her obsession get away from her again. "Thanks." She looked up at Acamas and Demophon. "I think it's safe to say we took one team of jackers off the board. Where are we on finding any others?"

Taking that as his cue, Dem tapped a screen on his side of the comm link and, with a flourish, flung a now-familiar map onto the conference room wall. Amber noted that the area from last night was grayed out. She assumed that was to mark it as having been cleared, but before she could ask, Dem launched into his presentation. "I can tell you where six more teams are, or rather, where their comm links are, anyway."

Amber's eyes went wide, and the others in the room shifted in surprise. "Six? How can you know that?"

Demophon grinned. "You want the long answer or the short one?"

"Short." Then she saw his disappointed expression. "But I'll want the full details in a written report so I can review it later."

Issuing a melodramatic sigh, he drew out a long "Fine." He tapped his screen and flung another display onto the wall. This time, it was a vid file, and she was hit with a serious case of déjà vu as she recognized the scene. It was a clip from her feed from the fight at the chop shop. It was a little disorienting as the view looked down at the floor and seemed to spin. She recalled diving through the door and rolling before she jumped into the air.

The view followed her recollection, and the point of view from the vid feed went airborne then panned right. She saw the first victim, the woman, strapped to the horror of a butcher's table. To the side was the first organ jacker. He held a black hood tightly over the other victim's head, pulling him back as a shield, firing his flechette pistol at Amber as she flew through the air.

The video continued to pan farther right and froze on the second jacker just as he fired the first shot from his hand cannon. Amber swallowed as she saw that immense barrel aimed in her direction again but was shaken out of her thoughts when Dem spoke.

"Did you see it?" he asked.

Amber's thoughts were on the barrel of the jacker's weapon, and reliving that moment left her with exactly zero patience for games. But her lack of patience was what had caused the friction between her and her friends last night... *This morning,* she reminded herself.

She bit back a sharp comment, trying to think of a more diplomatic way of telling Dem to get on with it.

Luckily, CC spoke before she could. "The comm set," he said.

Dem grinned and pointed at CC. "Give the man a cee-gar." Then he furrowed his brow. "Whatever a cee-gar is."

For the first time since the meeting started, Acamas spoke. "An old method of inhaling tobacco smoke. Similar to cigarettes but stronger."

"Doesn't matter," Dem said with a negligent wave. "What matters is that I caught this on Amber's feed last night and was quick enough"—he tapped his forehead—"and smart enough to catch the call and trace it."

He tapped his screen, and the video disappeared. Once again, the map appeared. "I was able to trace the call through four satellite routers, seventeen comm towers, and forty-three scrambled CAP nodes." He looked directly at CC as he clarified, "Those are cyberspace access points, for our less tech-savvy people."

CC showed Dem a single finger. "I know what a CAP is."

Dem ignored him and turned back to Amber. "Your boy really didn't want his comms traced."

"But you were able to do it?"

"That *is* what you pay me for."

Amber refrained from mentioning that no one paid him—or his sister for that matter—anything at all. But she was impressed at how seamlessly he wove the lie into his persona. Three people in the conference room didn't know the true nature of the two AIs, and he accounted for the fact, intertwining the human background into their conversation with absolutely no hesitation.

Once again, he tapped a screen, and numbers began to appear on the map. Dem continued his presentation. "Your boy called number one on the map." The large *1* began to pulse.

"Did you get an address?"

"Sorry. The pulse was too fast. All I was able to get was an area serviced by a small group of transmission towers. But he's somewhere in this area."

A large circle appeared on the map, the pulsing one in the center.

"I slapped spiders in the router that serviced the towers and in each of the CAP nodes attached to them. Less than two minutes later, another burst went from area one to numbers two through six."

The other numbers began to pulse, and Amber absently noted that one of them was in her old neighborhood. She wondered if there was any significance, considering her own experience. The thought briefly led her to hopes of finding Dewey Trev, the remaining man of the pair who had taken her own eyes. But she quickly realized there could be no correlation between the two. Where she had lived and where she had been ambushed while on patrol more than a decade in the past were in completely different sectors of the city.

"The call was another pulsed transmission that lasted less than two seconds then disconnected."

"An alert," Jordie said.

Dem shrugged. "Seems likely."

"This seems to be indicating your… organ jackers?" Maestro Harris looked at Amber for confirmation of the term. At her nod, he continued. "Are being more organized than those in Novo Brasil. This is normal here?"

"No," Amber said. "But an alert network, combined with that horror vid of a butcher's table, does point to a change in methodology."

"And maybe a change in management?"

Richard's question caught her by surprise. She'd never considered organ jackers as an organization before now. Past experience had taught her to expect a bunch of individually run teams who carved out hunting areas by force and intimidation. But the morning's events didn't fit past experience.

"Maybe," she conceded. "Too early to tell, but it's a definite possibility."

"Conley?" Scott asked.

Amber shook her head. "Come on, people. It's way too early to start jumping to conclusions. Let's just concentrate on the problem in front of us and not start chasing ghosts." She looked at Dem. "What did the message say?"

He shook his head. "Your boy at the chop shop routed through sixty-four different devices to place his call. Whoever or whatever was on the other end routed through more than two hundred. The message was encrypted and less than five seconds long. Nobody could have gotten it without the encryption keys."

Amber's heart sank.

Then Acamas spoke for the first time. "I might be able to help." She was tapping absently at her screens, not even looking at them until the silence in the room made her look up. Everyone, even her brother, was staring at her. She raised a hand to her face. "Do I have something on me?"

"You said you might be able to hack a file your brother tells us is unhackable?" Amber said.

"I didn't say I could hack it. I said I could help." It was her turn to throw a diagram onto the wall. Amber was barely able to interpret what she was seeing as a global comm network schematic. The only reason she knew what she was looking at was she had seen her old partner, Kevin Glass, work with them in the past.

Acamas tapped her screen again, and red lines progressed from device to device as she spoke. "Like Dem said, they routed through two hundred thirty-six different devices—satellites, routing stations, CAPs—all to deliver a four-and-a-half-second transmission. But what my brother sees as an obstacle, I see as an opportunity." She tapped again, and the global diagram rotated and zoomed. One of the nexus points on the diagram began to blink. "This is a Caracom communications satellite. Caracom is in the process of being bought out by Ferris Cheng Datanet, and they've been dragging their feet on cutting their assets over to the new owners. That includes their comm satellites." Another tap, and a list of satellite specs scrolled down the wall. "This is one of the satellites that the comm burst routed through. It's a Watch Tower 2 system, and—"

"Acamas?" Amber interrupted. "While this is all very fascinating, is there any chance you'll be getting to the part where you can help us?"

Acamas simply raised an eyebrow. Of the pair of AI siblings, Demophon was normally the more boisterous and invariably took over any conversation in which he was a participant. Acamas, on the other hand, was generally content to take on the role of bystander and observer. On the few occasions that she did enter a conversation, it was usually to correct someone's error or misunderstanding or to impart a serious piece of information someone else had overlooked. And she evidently took the implication that she would waste time with unimportant information as something of an affront. Amber filed that away for future consideration and shook her head.

"Never mind. You have the floor."

Acamas nodded in acknowledgment and continued. "The Watch Tower 2 satellites use a series of Cobalt Digital routers for communications traffic."

Jordie tapped a finger quickly on the conference table. "And Cobalt Digital just released an emergency security patch two days ago!" She was grinning.

"Precisely." Acamas tapped her screen again, and the view on their wall changed back to Dem's city map. With another tap, the view zoomed in on the *3*. "I was able to use the exploit to simulate the handshake used when a comm unit connects to the satellite and backdoored into the hand unit owned by one Danyael Antonov. By comparing the time stamp on the satellite transmission logs to the time stamp of files received on the unit, I was able to get a copy of the file sent in the burst transmission."

Amber grinned. "What does it say?"

"I don't have any idea. The encryption is top-shelf. Give us a day or two, and I could probably hack it, but I think you can probably get it faster on your own."

"What?"

Acamas tapped her screen, and the wall display shifted to a still shot from the earlier replay of Amber's attack. At the next tap, the picture zoomed in on the man hiding behind the male victim… the man speaking into a boom mic. "It seems to me that anyone on that communications network would have the encryption key on their comm. Otherwise—"

"Otherwise they wouldn't know what the message says." Amber reached for her comm as she spoke. "That's good work, Acamas."

She punched in the comm code from memory, and the voice on the other end answered immediately. Her boss sounded more terse than usual. "Gibbs here."

Amber explained what they were after and why, summing it all up in seconds.

"I'll have our techs make a clone of the comm and have it waiting for you in the med bay."

Surprised, Amber asked, "The med bay?"

"According to your team's reports, you and Richard both suffered injuries during your extracurricular activities. Since you have to come here anyway, I want you both to spend an hour or so in a Doc Box."

Amber self-consciously shifted her left arm and barely held back a wince at the pain. "Sounds like a good idea. Thanks."

"Well, I can't have any of my agents working at a subpar level."

Before Amber could say anything more, Gibbs cut her off with a brusque "Discomm," and the line went dead.

Amber stood. "Richard, you're with me. We'll be gone a couple of hours." She looked at the holographic projections of the AIs. "Dem, keep crunching data for more leads. We can't assume anything we get will lead anywhere." She pointed at his sister. "Acamas, you said you could crack the encryption in a few days. Might as well get started just in case." Turning to the others, she continued. "Rest up as much as you can while we're gone. Whether we get a break on the comm signal or not, we've all got some very late nights ahead of us."

CHAPTER 23

Her shoulder injury was more severe than she had known. As soon as she stripped to get into the Doc Box, she thought that might be the case. A quick look in the mirror made her doubly glad that she hadn't gone home with Nathan. Besides being painful, the mottled bruising on her left breast and shoulder was disturbing to see. The hand cannon had done a number on her.

The Doc Box diagnosed her injury as a level-seven bruised pectoralis major and a torn coracohumeral ligament. Amber didn't know what it all meant exactly, but it took the Box more than two hours to repair the damage, and the relief she felt when she emerged made her realize just how much pain she'd been carrying. The bruising was gone as well.

Richard was sitting in the waiting area, reading something on a tablet in the main room. His session in the Box had been completed before hers. He looked up as she entered. "You okay? You were in there a lot longer than I expected."

Amber gave a dismissive wave of her hand. "There was some ligament damage." She pointed to his tablet. "Anything new?"

"Yeah." He raised his pad. "Gibbs sent us a message. You'll have a copy in your inbox, too, but the gist of it is that her people can't get us a clone of the comm unit after all. They gathered the comms from the jackers last night, and all of them have built-in biometric security. If anyone but the owner tries to access them, it wipes them. From what they can tell, it takes DNA and voice recognition of an individualized passphrase."

"So we use the one from the guy in holding. Make him activate it."

"Unfortunately, that's the one they tried to crack this morning. They wiped it when they tried to clone it."

Amber cursed. "And the others?"

"Well, they aren't wiped, but their owners aren't going to be able to help us, since they're all... you know..."

"Dead," Amber finished with a sigh.

"Yeah."

"Did you let Dem and Acamas know?"

"I did." Richard grabbed his jacket, slipped his tablet into an inner pocket, and stood.

Amber led the way down a long hallway.

Richard looked puzzled as he hurried to catch up. "Where are we going?"

"I want to leave through the freight bays. Less chance of running into anyone and getting pulled into any conversations or explanations." As they walked down the empty corridor, she picked up the conversation again. "So, what else?"

The big man pulled out his tablet again and began reading as they walked. "Dem sent us his latest. Says he found patterns showing hunting grounds for three more jacker teams but needs more time to ascertain more. He's got the usual stats, facts, and figures. I don't know what they all mean, but I'm sure they're important to someone."

Amber smiled.

"The only other bit of news," Richard continued, "is that he found out several victims of the one he labeled *Team 3* had all frequented the same dance club, Club Karma."

Her eyebrows went up, and she grunted. "Huh."

Her partner looked up at her. "What?"

"I've been there. Used to go quite a bit, actually."

"Yeah?"

She nodded. "It's just a couple of klicks from my old apartment. Shamra used to drag me there whenever she thought I was working too much."

"Shamra? Davy's mom?"

Amber realized Richard had never met Shamra. None of her team had. But Richard, at least, had met Davy back when the boy was dog-sitting Odie. So had Jordie and Scott, if she remembered correctly.

"Yeah," she answered. "Sham's quite the dancer. Used to teach."

"Huh." Richard went back to reading. "There's not much more other than Dem's recommendation that we interview all the victims' known associates and family to find out if they had been to the club on or near the night they'd been killed. He sent a list." Richard thumbed his tablet closed and slipped it back into his jacket. "And the rest of our people have already started working on it. That's about it."

Amber thought for a short while as they walked. She couldn't find fault with anything Dem had suggested. After a few turns down intersecting hallways, she pulled out her tablet. She skimmed her messages, scrolled to the one Richard had referenced, and tapped out an acknowledgment. She sent another message letting the rest of the team know she and Richard were about to head to the first name on the list.

Jordie replied that she and CC had already interviewed the first two, and Scott and Maestro Harris had met with the third and were currently with the fourth.

Amber smiled ruefully. So much for her team getting some rest. She tapped out a quick response.

> *Amber: Good work, everyone. Color-code the list as you finish so we don't step on each other's toes. Red = complete. Green = in progress.*

> *Demophon: I'll make the list dynamic and adjust it now.*

A few seconds went by before he updated them.

> *Demophon: List is now live and color-coded. Click here to access it. Message me to let me know when you complete an interview and claim another name, and I'll update as needed.*

The *click here* line was a coded link, and when Amber tapped it, she saw another version of the previous list. The first three names were highlighted in red and appended with notes on who had conducted the interviews. The fourth name was green, with *S. Pond – B. Harris* beside it. The fifth name was highlighted in blue, with her name and Richard's beside it. She assumed blue signified that someone had claimed the name and everyone else should go to the next available. She nodded approval, but something tugged at the back of her mind.

She looked up at Richard. "Do you mind driving? I want to go over my notes."

"Drive your fancy new pod? Hells no, I don't mind."

She nodded absently, looking again at the list of names and addresses as they walked through the big shipping bay.

"Something wrong?" Richard asked.

"I don't know." Still looking at the list, she asked him, "You know how sometimes you get something tugging at the corner of your mind, but the more you try to figure it out, the harder it is to put your finger on what's bothering you?"

"Like that, huh?"

"Like that."

They got to her pod, and she climbed into the right-hand seat. "Controls are already slaved to that side," she told Richard, and he reached in to slide the seat all the way back. Most vehicles were too small for the huge street banger to sit in comfortably, but she'd had the seat controls in her new pod customized, anticipating times when he would drive.

He sighed contentedly as he sat and extended the driving console to within comfortable reach. "This is nice!"

Amber, studying her tablet, barely heard him. She mentally went over several questions she would ask during the interviews. *What was your relationship to the deceased? When did you last see them? Do you know when they last went to Club Karma?*

She tried to anticipate possible answers and follow-ups, imagining how the first interview would go, trying to figure out what her mind was trying to bring to her attention. They were only a few kliks down the road when it came to her, and it was almost anticlimactic—a simple oversight on the list. She dialed Dem's comm code on the dash controls.

Dem answered immediately. "What's up, Boss?"

"Dem, is there any reason you didn't put Club Karma's staff on our interview list?"

There was a split second of silence, followed by a quick curse. "Dammit! Anyone else in the pod with you?"

She knew he would only ask if he was going to reference his and his sister's existence as AIs. "Just me and Richard. You're safe."

"Okay. I'm sorry about that, Boss. Dad told us he often missed things that required creative thinking. We try to be better at it, but an AI is still an AI."

Amber knew that when Dem or Acamas used the phrase "Dad told us," what they really meant was they had accessed T-bone's recorded memories. She assumed they phrased it that way to spare her as much pain as possible. They would know from those same memories that he had done something similar when he'd changed his persona from K2 to T-bone. She appreciated the effort.

"Don't worry about it," she told him. "Just add them to the list and mark me and Richard as investigating." She noted with approval that Richard rerouted the navcomp for Club Karma as soon as she said that.

"Consider it done," Dem said.

"As a matter of fact…" Amber said, thinking.

After a few seconds, Dem prodded her. "You still there?" He knew she was, of course. But it brought Amber back out of her thoughts.

"I'm here. I just need to contact the rest of the team. That's it for now."

"You sure?"

"I'm sure. Discomm."

"Discomm."

The line went dead, and she synced her tablet to the dash screen. She spoke to Richard as she typed. "Do you dance, big guy?"

He chuckled. "I'm afraid not. You planning to spend some time at Club Karma?"

"I'm thinking about it."

"I'll post outside, keep an eye on people going in and out. But you should take Nathan. You guys could use some fun." Then Richard's forehead wrinkled. "Does Nathan dance?"

Her mouth pursed into a moue of uncertainty. "I honestly don't know. But I know someone who most definitely does." Amber tapped her earbud and spoke a command. "And she's been begging for a girl's night."

Shamra jumped at the prospect of a night at the club and promised to call back after she firmed up arrangements with her sister to watch Davy. In the meantime, Amber sent her message out to the group.

Amber: Join us at Club Karma as soon as you finish the interviews you're working on. I hope to stay for some dancing if any of you are up for it. We'll call it surveillance. Anyone interested?

Jordie: Hells yeah! I'm in.

Scott: You don't want to see what I call dancing. Better count me out.

Harris: I am good dancer.

CC: I'm more stomp, stomp, smash, than step, step, twirl. Maybe Scott and I should keep watch outside.

Amber: Suit yourselves. You can join Richard. What about you, Missy?

Missy: Sounds like fun.

Amber: All right. Everyone finish up your interviews, then meet me and Richard at the club. We're going to interview the staff there and then keep our eyes open for anything unusual.

She looked over at Richard. "What's our ETA?"

He glanced at the dash console. "Twenty-six minutes to Club Karma."

CHAPTER 24

Amber leaned toward the console on her side. "Guess we should let them know we're coming." She tapped an icon and asked Demophon to send her a list of all known employees and owners of the club as well as their contact information. She started with a call to the owner, Joani Loveless.

"This is Joani." The voice on the other end of the line was cheerful.

Amber tapped a command on the dashboard and activated video mode. The image of a middle-aged woman with just a touch of wrinkling around the eyes tilted her head a bit. Her expression was businesslike but showed a hint of puzzlement when she failed to recognize Amber.

"I'm sorry," Fem Loveless said, no longer cheerful, "but how did you get this calling code? This is a private line."

"Fem Loveless, my name is Amber Payne, and I'm a private investigator working on a case that may have a connection to Club Karma. Would you be available this evening to discuss the matter? I'd be happy to meet you at the club, or if you prefer, I can have one of my associates meet you at a more convenient location."

Loveless shook her head and held up a hand. "Out of the question. I don't have time for—"

Amber interrupted before the woman could get too worked up. "I understand you're very busy, fem. But there have been several murders in the area, and Club Karma appears to be the only link between them. Now, I would prefer to keep things quiet while we investigate. It's better for you, and it's better for my investigation. But if you don't want to cooperate, we can set up shop outside your club and interview your customers before they get inside. You know—so we don't disrupt your busy schedule."

"You can't do that!"

"I'm afraid we can. I can make sure everyone going in understands that twenty-seven people in the last year have been abducted and killed shortly after leaving your club and that we're investigating possible links between Club Karma and those murders. I can hand out flyers with details and requests to contact us if anyone has any relevant information."

"If you do, I'll have my attorneys—"

"And I can have the story on the media feeds for the next news cycle."

"What story? So far, all I've heard are wild allegations and the threat of some PI. Nobody will believe a word."

"Possibly," Amber said. "Then again, lots of folks believe lizard people live in the catacombs and ancient sewer systems beneath the city."

Loveless snorted. "Sure. Idiots with no education, no job, and nothing but time on their hands."

"So, you get a lot of the highly educated upper-echelon elites in Club Karma, do you?" Amber smiled sweetly as she saw the woman think through the possible loss of revenue.

"I can be there tomorrow afternoon."

Amber shook her head. "I'll be there in a few hours. It can be inside, speaking to you quietly, or it can be outside, speaking to anyone who passes by. Which do you prefer?"

"I can't possibly be there today. I have several meetings scheduled with vendors and investors."

Amber's first instinct was to tell her she would have to reschedule, but she clapped her mouth closed before letting her temper get away from her again. There was no reason to believe anything was going to happen that night. Dem's information indicated there were still a couple of days before the jackers would hit again.

"How about this, then—you contact all your employees and arrange to have them come into the club for us to interview. It shouldn't take but a few hours. Then you can come in either tonight or tomorrow morning, whatever works best for you."

Loveless frowned at Amber a moment before relenting. "Fine. I'll make the calls."

"And," Amber said quickly, forestalling the other woman's disconnect, "*you* will also meet with us tomorrow before Karma opens."

The other woman looked like she wanted to argue but finally just sighed. "Anything else?"

"No, fem. Thank you for your coopera—"

Loveless disconnected the line, cutting Amber off.

"Well, that was rude." She smiled at Richard.

He shrugged. "Some people just don't appreciate a good bullying session."

"I know! I mean, it's an art form. Right?"

He shook his head in mock sympathy before getting serious again. "What would you have done if she hadn't agreed? It's not like you can force her anymore. We're not LEOs."

Amber knew he was right. After nearly twenty years as a LEO, she was comfortable with that life. But since Securi-Tech had fired her, and without sponsorship from another LEO corporation, her license had lapsed. She hadn't been too worried about it, since joining the Fixers made her LEO badge superfluous.

But this case wasn't a Fixer case, so she wasn't protected under their umbrella. And without Securi-Tech's backing, she wasn't covered by the Security Forces Privatization Act either. For the purposes of this case, she was working as a private investigator, the lowest tier of law enforcement, barely more than a private citizen.

She was going to have to study what was and wasn't legal for her in this new capacity before she got herself into a jam. "That's something I'm going to have to get used to."

"All of us will."

She narrowed her eyes, thinking, before she tapped her dash console again. "Or maybe…"

Demophon answered immediately. "Yes, fem?"

"First, do you have that list of Karma employees?"

"You bet."

"Monitor the comm for Fem Loveless. If she doesn't start contacting her employees within the next half hour, let me know."

"You got it. And what do we do if she doesn't?" Dem asked.

Amber considered various options, both legal and... less legal. After a moment, she simply sighed and told him, "Then we'll have to add those names to our list of people to interview, and the next couple of days are going to suck."

"Luckily, that won't be a problem. She just made the first call."

"Thank Buddha," Amber said. "I didn't want to have to decide whether or not to break any privacy laws over this."

"How's that?" Richard asked.

"I was considering having Dem send messages from her account to bring them in for a mandatory meeting."

Her partner's right eyebrow rose as he stared at her. "Didn't I just say...?"

"I know, I know." Amber turned away from Richard's accusatory stare. "Dem, make sure all of us have all the information on the Club Karma disappearances available on our tablets. If we have to break into group interviews, I want everyone to have what they need."

"You got it," Dem said. Amber's tablet chimed receipt of a file even as he spoke.

"Thanks, Dem."

"No worries. Now, you said that was first. What's second?"

"Could you send me a quick report on what's required to make PSC a fully licensed law enforcement firm where we'll be covered under SFPA?"

Dem shrugged. "That one's easy. You just need enough funding to push through the certifications, a board of directors with a net worth of three billion credits, and at least four licensed investigators, one of whom needs to be P-1 rated."

"Three billion?"

"I said it was easy. I didn't say anything about it being cheap. The law is supposed to provide financial stability to ensure payroll for your agents and quarterly renewals of your certs, mainly for the renewal fees."

Richard snorted. "Gotta make sure the corporate licensing boards get their cut."

Demophon nodded in agreement.

"How much do the fees run?" Amber asked.

"Twenty-five thousand credits per licensed detective."

Richard whistled. "Sooo… expensive."

Dem shrugged on the screen. "That's part of the reason LEO corporations concentrate so much on clients who can afford to pay top credit."

Amber considered. "Can I afford to do all that?"

"On your own? Barely. But didn't you recently decide to take on some partners?"

Amber's eyes lit up as she remembered. There were some serious possibilities to that.

"And if you wouldn't mind two more partners, I *guarantee* you can afford it."

She looked up at the smile on Dem's face. "You and Acamas?"

The screen flickered and split to show Acamas beside her brother. "I like this idea," Acamas said. "Dem and I obviously can't do much footwork, but we already help out with cybersecurity and investigating. And as of about three seconds ago, we're both fully certified LEOs."

Amber gave a rueful chuckle. "You are, are you?"

Both AIs held holographic badges up to the screen. "Technically, we're on record as having passed our exams three years ago."

"Even though you weren't born until last year?" Amber shook her head at the screen. "Well, we'll just pretend those badges are real for now. I assume this is all leading somewhere?"

"A proposal," Acamas said. "We join PSC as investing partners and fully licensed LEOs. We'll handle keeping company certifications up to date, bookkeeping, and project management. That gives you six multibillionaires for your board of directors with more than enough financial clout to lift PSC out of the dirt."

Amber's mouth curved into a smile as she thought. "Draw up the agreements. I want to present it to the others ASAP."

Her tablet immediately chimed receipt of the files.

Dem spread his hands. "Partnership-agreement boilerplates and a proposal for incorporation are in your mailbox."

Amber looked over at Richard. "What do you think? Are you interested in being a LEO in your own firm?"

The banger grinned. "Hells yeah! And if I know Jordie and Scott, they're gonna jump at the idea too. Send me the forms. I'll thumb the agreements right now."

"Hang on a second," Dem cautioned. "It's not quite as simple as just taking your thumbprint."

"No," Acamas jumped in. "You have to hash out ownership percentages, operational and financial responsibilities…"

"Split it evenly," Amber interrupted. "Fill in the blanks, and we'll adjust it as needed."

"Not a good idea," Acamas said. "Someone needs to run the show. Someone needs to maintain a controlling interest. But not so much interest that the others can't overrule her if needed."

"Her?" Amber immediately saw where the conversation was headed. She started to protest, but Richard laid a hand on her arm.

"Her." He nodded. "It's your name on the building… you that pulled us all together. You already lead the team. So make it official. Take control."

"And what if I have another…" She considered how to describe her anger-management issues of the night before. "Lapse in judgment like I had last night?"

"Like Acamas said, the rest of us keep enough percentage to override you if we agree that you're too big a pain in the ass." He grinned, but Amber could see the wisdom in the suggestion.

She looked back at the screen, where Acamas and Dem waited. "What do you suggest?"

Acamas was already prepared with numbers. "Demophon and I each take five percent. The two of us are already richer than the rest of you, so it's not like we need the credits. You keep thirty percent, with Richard, Jordie, and Scott each getting twenty percent."

Richard nodded before Amber could say anything. "Sounds fair to me."

"Corporate buy-in will be commensurate with ownership percentages."

Amber swallowed. If she did this, it was going to be a big step for her, a huge responsibility.

"If we do this—"

"If?" Richard said. "Of course we're doing this!"

"If"—she held up a finger to forestall anything else he might have to say—"we do this, how quickly could we make it happen? The incorporation, the contracts, certifications, the whole deal."

"Normal lead time for articles of incorporation is three months," Acamas said. "But it moves much quicker when enough credit is used to grease the wheels. LEO certs depend on the individual applicants. Since you and Richard already passed your certification exams for your employment with Securi-Tech, we can pull them up and update your paperwork right away." She bit her lower lip as she stared at her console. "But Jordan Dyer and Scott Pond are another matter."

"How so?"

"After Securi-Tech fired you last year, they also negated your arrangement with Scott and Jordie."

"What?"

"All those cold cases you linked to their DNA but agreed not to put into the system in exchange for their help? Securi-Tech turned around and put them into the system."

"Fuggle me!" Amber cursed. "Those fuggled-faced, bung-slurping—"

Acamas raised a finger to interrupt Amber's tirade. "The good news is that none of the crimes in the cold-case files were Securi-Tech contracts, so they didn't bother informing the corporations Scott and Jordie had hit."

Richard chuckled. "No profit in it."

Acamas nodded.

Amber sighed and rubbed the back of her neck. "But an application for LEO certification involves a thorough background check."

It was Richard's turn to curse. "And the background check would reveal the cold cases."

Acamas nodded. "There are a few ways around that, though. We can go into the system ourselves and expunge their records…"

Amber pursed her lips, thinking. "I'm not wild about starting the company off with an illegal act."

"I understand, but let me point out that nearly all major corporations do exactly this for any key personnel they want to hire. They simply bribe people in the position to access legal records and have them do it. The bribery is illegal, but we would bypass that by hacking into the system and doing it directly."

"So bribery is illegal, but hacking isn't?"

"I didn't say the hacking isn't illegal. But at least it's a victimless crime."

Amber considered that before waving Acamas on. "But you said there are other ways?"

Acamas tapped absently at her console. Amber knew the action was a simulation designed to put her at ease. Acamas had no need of a console. When it came down to it, she *wasn't* using a console. While cybersurfers might "surf" the seas of cyberspace, Acamas and her brother were more akin to fish who lived within it. Their appearance onscreen was nothing more than a fictional interface designed to allow them to interact with humanity. Still, it was a fiction they all embraced, humans and AIs alike.

Acamas continued her pretense as she spoke. "They could simply throw themselves on the mercy of the courts—ask the court to consider their work with law enforcement over the last year and plead extenuating circumstances."

Amber snorted. "Without Securi-Tech backing them? Fat chance of that working. Any other options?"

"They could offer restitution to the companies involved."

Richard whistled. "I bet that's expensive."

"Possibly," Acamas agreed. "Especially since the type of work Jordie and Scott did was data crime. I mean, how do you put a monetary value on delaying a product release date or leaking a file to a competitor?"

"They could just throw any ridiculous price tag out there and claim it as 'damages due to unrealized financial income,'" Demophon added.

Acamas raised a finger again. "But we *could* contact these companies privately through a series of shell companies and make simultaneous generous offers with an ironclad contract that guarantees they won't pursue legal action on those cold cases. The contracts would include clauses specifically absolving anyone involved in those cases. We can probably get them to accept if there's a large enough write-off amount attached. After all, as far as they're concerned, it's free credit for not pursuing something they're already not pursuing."

"They'll know something's going on," Amber said.

Acamas shrugged. "Undoubtedly. But they won't know what. All they'll know is that something involved with their cold case has come to light with another company. They might even assume someone is hiring a person or persons involved in the commission of those crimes. But we can work it so that there's no way they'll know who's paying for their cooperation or who was involved in the crimes. It'll just be a blanket contract where they agree to drop anything to do with those cases."

Amber thought about it for a moment. "Getting back to Richard's comment, then, just how much are we likely to be talking about?"

"We'll have to talk to Scott and Jordie to confirm what past jobs they've pulled. But based on the ones Securi-Tech wrote off, and assuming there aren't too many others, I would assume we're talking about forty to fifty million credits."

"What!"

"It might be overkill, but we want to make the offers enticing enough that they'll accept quickly, without too much investigation."

"Not that I'm arguing, but why is it so important to do it quickly?" Amber asked.

"Because if we give them time to discuss it too much, word will get out that there are several such offers out to various companies. They'll figure anyone who can make multiple offers of that size has deep pockets, and they'll want to start negotiating for a bigger slice of the pie. But if we push all the agreements through at the same time, before they have time to realize others are getting similar deals…"

Amber nodded understanding. "Then we keep them all in the dark. As far as each one is concerned, it's just a single request, nothing all that unusual. So they thumb the agreements, collect the credits, and we keep the payout more manageable."

Richard glanced at her sideways. "You call fifty million credits manageable?"

She waggled her hand in a seesaw motion, and he snorted.

"The PSC partnership we're talking about can absorb it," Acamas said. "Especially with me and Dem helping out. So we pay off the wronged parties, they drop all charges…"

Amber nodded. "And the end result is basically the same as expunging Scott and Jordie's records."

"Yes. Then, with documentation of their help in the resolution of recent cases—letters of recommendation from you, Richard, Demophon, me, and perhaps even Chief Fischer—they could take certification exams and apply for probationary LEO certification right away."

"And Payne Security becomes a fully legit law enforcement corporation."

Acamas smiled and spread her hands as if presenting Amber a fine gift. "Exactly. With the proper amount of grease, we could be fully legit within a week."

After a moment of thought, Amber nodded. "Send me a write-up of my options—possible pros and cons, costs, anything you can think of that I should consider. I'll look it over and make a decision in the morning."

Amber's tablet chimed as it received a new message. "Done," Acamas said.

"Thanks. Next order of business… I need a list of which employees are at Club Karma right now."

"Already done," Dem said. "According to the schedule, there should be a dozen people there—bartenders, floor managers, and the night manager." Amber's tablet chimed again. "I just sent you their files."

She glanced at the files as Dem continued.

"There are also some part-timers. Twelve wait staff, eight floor walkers, and a five-piece band scheduled to arrive at 15:30 so they're in place when the doors open to the public at 17:00 hours."

"Thanks. And not just for the help on Club Karma." She looked at the AIs on the screen. "I've been thinking of PSC as a private investigation firm. It would have taken me days to flesh out even a rudimentary idea on incorporating. You guys did it in a couple of minutes. You showed me that we can be a lot more than I dreamed possible."

Dem grinned. "It was your idea. We just showed you how to make it a reality."

"Well, thanks."

Acamas shrugged off the thanks. "It's what we do."

Amber checked the time and saw they had just over four hours before Karma's doors opened. And since she had given Fem Loveless a reprieve, they weren't in any hurry to get to the club. "For now, I think I'll take Richard to get a late lunch, then we'll head over to the club. That should give the others time to finish their interviews."

Richard perked up at the promise of a free lunch.

Amber grinned and shook her head. The man was a giant walking stomach. "But let me know if there are any Karma employees that Fem Loveless fails to call in. We'll have to send someone out to interview them one-on-one."

"Will do," Dem said. "Anything else?"

"That'll do for now. Discomm."

"Discomm, Boss."

The line had barely gone dead when Richard chimed in. "Did you say lunch?"

CHAPTER 25

She and Richard took their time with a relaxed meal. The way their work went, chances like this were rare during an active investigation, and they knew better than to pass it up. Besides, Fem Loveless might need the time to strong-arm her employees into coming for interviews.

Even with the extended lunch, though, they still made it to Club Karma more than three hours before the doors opened to the public. Amber was happy to find Fem Loveless had been true to her word and the employees inside were waiting for them.

The shift manager greeted them within minutes of their entrance. Amber guessed his boss hadn't given the man too many details, though. He strode confidently across the empty dance floor to meet them, walking in the manner of someone used to handling himself in a scrap, but he directed his attention to Richard, evidently assuming the big man was the lead investigator. Amber held back a smile as he shook Richard's hand.

He was fairly tall, though not nearly as tall as her partner. Not many people were. He dressed casually—heavy work pants, a short-sleeved shirt, and black gloves. Interestingly enough, he showed no hesitation when he shook Richard's hand. Most people held back a second or two before surrendering their digits to the giant street banger's tender mercies. But this man extended his hand before he'd even stopped moving.

"I'm Anthony Staton," he said. "The boss lady said to expect some PIs this afternoon, and we've been instructed to cooperate with you any way we can."

Richard glanced at Amber. It was fairly common for people to assume

Richard was the person in charge if they didn't know better, and the two of them had learned to roll with it. Richard's look was his way of asking if he should correct Staton's misunderstanding. Amber gave her partner a subtle shake of the head, letting him know she wanted to observe a little longer.

"I'm Richard Kayani." Richard released the other man's hand, allowing the misapprehension to continue for the moment.

"It's a pleasure to meet you, Mr. Kayani. I like the jacket. It's a Lori Kidd, isn't it?"

Richard nodded. It was made of the best ballistic armor fabric, inlaid with interlocking compression mail, and had more adjustable pockets, sheaths, and holsters than he would ever need. "It is. Thanks. And thanks for agreeing to meet with us," he said, looking around at the inside of the club. "This is quite the place you have."

Mr. Staton followed Richard's gaze and smiled with pride. "Yes, it is. Best booze, drugs, and dancing in the city. We have four dance floors, each one with its own synchronized light show and audio projectors. We have prerecorded classics, professional sound mixers who make an art form of mixing music on the fly, and even a live band on the top floor."

Amber studied Staton as he continued to extol Club Karma's virtues. His confidence with Richard intrigued her. Richard was an obviously augmented street banger, at least a head taller than most men and bulging with subdermal armor and muscular augmentation. His arms were bigger around than a fat man's thighs, with none of the associated jiggle, and shaking hands with him was like sticking your hand into an oversized vise.

But Staton's manner reminded her of the easy exchanges she'd seen between Richard and CC Miller, the only person she had personally seen who was larger than her partner. Anthony Staton, this ordinary-looking night manager, carried himself with that same easy confidence, and it intrigued her. It spoke to some knowledge, some secret he had that made him think he could control the room even when someone like Richard stood in front of him.

Curious, Amber switched her eyes to infrared and scanned him. It took only a second to see that the man's arms were slightly cooler than the rest of his body. Cybernetics. And they were top of the line. She looked closer. No scar or seam showed where metal joined flesh, and there was no subtle coating designed to make the arms look like skin. As far as she could tell, his arms really had live skin over them. She had heard of such mods but had also heard they involved temperamental and expensive procedures. That drew her attention back to his gloves. Whatever his augmentation, the hands were likely the delivery system.

She came to that conclusion just before he turned his attention to her. "I'm sorry," he said. "I can go on and on about Karma. I might not own her, but I've put a lot of blood, sweat, and tears into making her what she is."

He offered his hand to Amber even as he looked over to Richard again. "And who might this lovely lady be?"

Amber answered before the man could dig his hole any deeper. "This lovely lady is Amber Payne." She placed a business card in his extended hand. "Senior partner and lead investigator for Payne Security Consultants."

Staton blinked, looking less than confident for the first time since she had seen him. He glanced at the card then back at her. "Well, I certainly stepped in the sludge, didn't I?"

Amber stared for a second longer then chuckled. "No worse than a lot of other people before you."

Staton returned her smile. "And you're more than happy to allow them to step in it while you observe, aren't you?"

Amber spread her hands.

He stood straighter and cleared his throat. "Will you allow me to start this over, then? My name is Anthony Staton, night manager of Club Karma and sludge skipper extraordinaire." He extended his hand to her again.

Amber looked at it then back up at him. "Is it safe to shake that thing? I won't receive an injection or a shock or something, will I?"

Staton pulled his hand back, slack-jawed. Then he laughed. "Now I see why you're the lead investigator. How did you know?"

She shook her head. "Trade secret."

"Fair enough. But the boss said to cooperate fully. So in the interest of full disclosure…" He stripped off his left glove and held up his hand. The palm was dotted with several tiny black cylinders. He flexed his thumb, and sharp metal spikes snicked out, locking into place with about a centimeter of shiny metal protruding from each cylinder. "They're sharp enough to punch through the gloves and deliver enough amperage to drop even the biggest street banger." He looked over at Richard. "Though you would be the biggest test I've ever put them through."

Richard raised his eyebrows. "How about we just skip that particular test? I've had a taste of something similar, and I'm not in any hurry to relive the experience."

Staton smiled and relaxed his thumb. He looked back at Amber as he slipped his glove back on. "So, what can I do for you, Fem Payne?"

She pulled out her tablet and thumbed it to life. "We're investigating a series of murders in the area. We're pretty sure there's a team of organ jackers working this part of town, and it looks like they're picking off customers from Club Karma."

"Organ jackers." He spat the words like a curse. "Nasty business." Staton's eyes narrowed, and he took her tablet, watching as picture after picture scrolled slowly past. He thumbed the screen on one of the headshots. "I recognize her. Used to be a regular here. I haven't seen her in months."

Amber reached across and tapped the information icon attached to the picture. "Stefanie Buswell turned up in a city morgue. She was a Jane Doe for three weeks before someone identified her."

Staton looked grim. "How many?"

"There are twenty-seven we know of so far. That's just in this area. Our case has shown similar hunting grounds for organ jackers all over the city. We're still trying to figure out details on the other groups. But the ones in this part of town all have one thing in common."

"Karma?" He seemed almost sad as he said it.

Amber nodded.

"Okay. What do you need from me?"

"First, access to any vid coverage you have that might show any of these people."

Staton shook his head. "You're welcome to what we have, but we don't keep more than a week of backups. There's just too much data. The only exception is the troublemaker feeds."

"And those are…?"

"If there's a fight or complaint or any other kind of trouble in the club, we make sure to mark the time and save feeds from the event in long-term storage. It lets us prove what they did and how we reacted. It prevents lawsuits against us and protects patrons who might file a grievance."

Amber nodded. "Then can we get copies of whatever you have? I have a cybersecurity team that can run your footage through facial recognition. We might get lucky."

"Of course. What else?"

"We need to talk to everyone who works here. I know you have people who aren't working tonight, but Fem Loveless is making arrangements for them to come in. For now, my partner and I want to talk to everyone who is here. We can do it individually or as a group presentation. Whichever works better for you."

"Actually, she already made the calls, and they've been coming in over the last hour. As for talking to everyone, how long do you need if we do it as a group?"

"At a guess, maybe an hour. It depends on how many questions and discussions there are."

"Let's do that, then. We can use the conference room on the second floor." He glanced at the chrono on the wall. "Let's do it quickly, though. We still have to get ready for tonight's crowd."

"We'll also need to meet with your part-timers and the band members. I was informed they should be here by 15:30?"

"You were informed correctly," Staton quipped. "Lucky for you, I anticipated you needing to speak to them and called them too. The last one got here about twenty minutes ago." He turned to lead them back across the empty dance floor.

Amber grinned. "I like a man who anticipates my needs."

Staton looked over his shoulder and waggled his eyebrows. He gave a mock leer. "Oh, you do, do you?"

She snorted. "Not like that. I'm already with someone."

"So? It wouldn't be my first poly experience."

Amber shook her head. "Men are such horn dogs."

Staton shrugged and continued toward the back of the building. As he walked, he tapped an earbud and started issuing orders to someone.

Amber followed, activating her own comm. "Dem, you there?" She spoke low so no one but Richard would be able to hear her.

"Here, Boss. What'cha need?"

"Let the rest of the team know we're here. And do me a favor—monitor my feed, would you? You might catch something during these interviews that I miss. I want you to watch pupil dilation, audit speech patterns, temperature changes—anything that might indicate someone is lying. Keep the channel open and let me know through my comm bud if you notice something. Got it?"

"Got it. I appreciate the trust."

"Don't sweat it. Your dad used to do it all the time."

"I know. But so did Securi-Tech."

Amber shook her head. "The difference is, I trust you."

CHAPTER 26

It took only minutes for Staton to secure the building and gather his people in the conference room. Amber linked her tablet to the display on the wall and began a rotating slide show that scrolled through each of the twenty-seven faces on her missing-persons list for the area.

"My name is Amber Payne, and my team and I are investigating the deaths of several people in this area." She waved back at the parade of faces scrolling on the screen behind her. "Each of these people has three things in common." She held up her index finger. "They were murdered." She held up her next finger. "They had various organs removed." And she finished with a third finger. "And they all frequented this nightclub."

Some of the Karma employees stirred and muttered among themselves.

"No one is accusing any of you of anything. We just need help with our investigation." She moved to the side of the display, making sure she wasn't obstructing anyone's view. "So the first thing I need is for anyone who recognizes any of these faces to raise their hand. Look closely. If you even *think* you recognize one of them, sing out, and I'll freeze the screen for you."

They all watched as the next few faces scrolled past, then one of the men slowly raised his hand.

Amber froze the screen on the headshot of a young woman in her mid to late twenties. "You know her?" she asked.

"Yeah. She's a regular at the bar. Venom Frenzy."

"Excuse me?"

"That's her drink. Always gets two or three Venom Frenzies. I'm the second-floor bartender, so I remember people by their drinks more than their names."

Another man nodded. "Yeah, I remember her. Always sat with the same woman."

"Always?"

"Yeah. I wait tables. Saw her and her girlfriend a lot whenever I worked the second floor."

"Anyone else?" Amber asked.

When none of the others said anything, she spoke to the waiter and bartender. "When we finish here, I'd like to speak to you in private."

They nodded, and she restarted the scrolling faces. Two faces further into the slides, the waiter raised his hand again.

"This one too?" Amber asked him.

The man looked sad as he nodded. "That's the girlfriend."

Twenty minutes later, they had cycled through the faces several times and asked quick questions of the employees. Most of the wait staff and bartenders recognized at least one victim. In one instance, three bouncers recognized a man.

Amber and Richard released those who hadn't recognized anyone after taking note of their names and Amber recording their faces with her eyes. Staton gave them quick instructions on last-minute duties before they left the room. Amber received a message from Demophon as Staton walked back over to her. Looking back at the number of people who they needed to question, he shook his head.

"Fem Payne, I know we're supposed to cooperate, but there's less than two hours until we open the doors, and most of my staff is still in here, waiting for you to question them. They all still have things to do before we open." He looked worried. "There's no way you're going to get them all questioned and released in time."

But Amber smiled. "We wouldn't if it was just the two of us." She nodded to Richard, who walked to the door. He opened it to reveal the rest of the PSC crew waiting just outside. "But we have help."

Jordie led the others into the room, with CC ducking his head as he entered last.

Staton's eyes widened. "How did they get in here? I locked up! We have a state-of-the-art security system. How did they get past the rest of my people?"

The muttering in the room told Amber that the rest of the Club Karma employees were just as concerned.

"I don't guess the 'trade secrets' thing would work again?" Amber said, but she could see in Staton's eyes that it wouldn't. His expression had already moved away from confused and concerned and was quickly approaching angry.

"Mr. Staton, every person on my team is a specialist in at least one area. Some are obvious." She gestured to CC's giant frame. "And some are more like your hands—subtle but very effective." She took his elbow and guided him to Jordie. "This is Jordan Dyer. You'll be hard-pressed to find any person in the world who knows more about security systems and how to bypass them. She got in five minutes ago."

"Pleased to meet you." Jordie extended a hand.

Staton ignored it. In truth, Amber wasn't sure he even noticed it. For the first time since she'd seen him, the man looked completely flustered. "That explains how you got in the door. How did you get past my people?"

Jordie laughed. "You have a storeroom two doors down from here. We just ducked inside until they passed."

"Anthony?" Amber pulled his attention back to her. "We have enough people now to get your interviews done. If you could help me prioritize them, we can get through the ones with time-sensitive duties first."

He swallowed again. "Okay. But after this is all done, we need to have a discussion about this. I need to know if my security is flawed."

"It's not," Jordie reassured him. "But no system is perfect either. If you like, I can make some suggestions on possible improvements when we're done here."

Staton nodded. "I would appreciate it." He looked past Jordie for the first time, looking over the rest of Amber's team. His eyes lingered on Scott, no doubt noting the long duster he wore. He looked back at Amber. "Fem Payne. I don't think I fully appreciated just how… effective you and your team might be until just now. You should all know that you're welcome here anytime in the future. No cover, free food, and first drink or pharmaceutical is on the house. I think the place will be much safer when any of you are here."

She bowed her head in acknowledgment. "Thank you. But for now, how about we get these interviews going?"

Short minutes later, Staton had divided Club Karma's staff into priority and nonpriority interviews. He also found various rooms for them to make the discussions more private. Amber and her team got to work.

The conversations all started the same way. A picture of whoever they had recognized, followed by a series of questions. "You said you recognized this person. When did you last see them? Did they normally come alone or with a group? Did you know anyone else in their group? Did you happen to notice anyone taking an unusual interest in them? Anyone watching them? Arguing with them? Following them?"

Most of the staff didn't know anything beyond the fact that one person or another was a regular at the club. They might know what kind of drinks or drugs they used in the club or maybe that they liked to dance to a certain kind of music. But there wasn't too much that could help Amber's team other than the fact that they confirmed the people as regulars at the club.

Things got interesting when Amber and Richard interviewed the bouncers who had booted one Remi Presas out of the club one night a few weeks back. Mr. Presas had been enough of a nuisance that he'd drawn complaints from other patrons the night he'd been evicted. Three women had complained about his aggressive sexual advances before the bouncers had asked him to leave. He'd been pretty baked and seemed to think he could take on three obviously tricked-out bouncers. The bouncer chuckled at the memory.

Amber narrowed her eyes. "Did you have to rough him up?"

He grinned back. "No, fem. There was no need. He went to grab Sammy and nearly tripped over his own feet."

"Sammy is one of the other bouncers here?"

"Yes, fem. Sorry." He shrugged. "Honestly, sometimes the hardest thing about this job is making sure the crispies don't hurt themselves before we get them off the premises."

"Crispies?"

"Too baked to be of any use to us."

Amber's mouth twitched, but she held back her smile. "So would you have the incident on your troublemaker feeds?"

The big man across the table from them nodded. "Probably. I mean, we reported it to cyber, so they should have it flagged and stored."

"Do you remember when this was?"

"Pretty sure it was a Friday night. Maybe a month or so back?" He narrowed his eyes as if digging through files in his head. "Sorry, I don't remember for sure."

"Okay. That gives us a target, anyway. Thanks."

Amber let the man go with a business card and a request to contact her if he remembered anything else, just as she had all the others. When he left the room, she asked Richard to handle the next interview on his own. She stood aside as the next bouncer walked in the door and slipped out after he passed.

Staton was still in the conference room where they had shown the slideshow. She signaled him with a nod, and he left the group he'd been talking with to join her.

"Did you find something?" he asked.

"Maybe. One of the victims caused some trouble here last month and had to be escorted off the property."

He rubbed his hands together. "So they're probably on vid!"

"That's my hope. Can we check them here?"

Staton nodded. "Let's go to my office."

She followed him and watched as he tapped the top of his desk to activate the display. He slid a few piles of folders out of the way so they could see the display that took up the part of his desk directly in front of his chair. "Sorry about the mess," he muttered and began calling out commands to his computer interface. He called it Cobie, and Amber listened as he had Cobie call up the club's security program. He turned to Amber. "When was the incident?"

"Your bouncer says it was a Friday night, about a month ago."

Staton called up a couple of links. "Cobie, call up trouble files from Friday night, three and four weeks back."

"You can scratch off the one from three weeks ago," Amber said. "Our guy was already dead before then."

He nodded. "Cobie, cancel the link to file one." He glanced at the display top of his desk. "Looks like there were only three incidents that night. This one is from the third-floor dining area." He ran the feed, and the two of them watched as a woman in a barely-there dress sat at a table with two men in cheap corporate power suits. The software highlighted her in yellow to show she was the person flagged for the files.

"Skip this one," Amber said. "Our victim was male."

"Next one is from the first-story dance floor." Staton tapped the screen, and a new feed showed up. "Nope. Another woman."

He tapped, and they watched the screen change again. This time, a man sat at a table with another man and two women. Amber watched the man highlighted in yellow as the four of them sat and talked for a moment. His back was to the cam feed, so they couldn't see his face.

"You have another angle on him?"

"I have *every* angle. Each floor has twelve cams around the dance floor and ten around the dining area. We also have two in each elevator and three at each entrance into the building." Staton spoke another command, and the view switched. "Whenever we flag an incident as trouble, we save all footage from every cam in the building to make sure we get any incidental occurrences that could impact a legal claim."

The subject's face was now visible. "Can you zoom in?"

"Cobie, freeze feed and magnify sector two." The screen zoomed in. "Repeat command," Staton called out, and the view zoomed in even closer.

Amber watched as the highlighted man froze in the act of shoving the table away and lunging for the man seated across from him. She shook her head. "That's not him either."

"You sure?"

Amber pulled out her tablet and called up the face. "Remi Presas." She laid the tablet on his desk display beside the face of the man on screen.

Staton compared the two and sighed. "Okay, let's go back another week."

That night had five incidents flagged. The first was a woman stripping on the fourth-floor dance arena. The second was a man urinating on a table at the edge of the second-floor dining area.

Amber frowned. "Ew! You get some real winners in here, don't you?"

"I'm afraid so. We try to keep people from overindulging, but what's not enough for one person is way too much for another. Short of running blood tests before letting anyone order something, there's no way for us to tell who's had too much until they get out of hand."

He had Cobie bring up the next feed.

Amber leaned in eagerly. "That's him!"

Staton froze the feed. "Third floor, high-top tables near the bar." He tapped the screen several times and stood. As he walked from behind his desk, he spoke to his computer again. "Cobie, transfer feed to wall screen and magnify. Split the screen and show all tagged views." The wall lit up with a large display split into four smaller screens showing three different angles of the incident as well as an overview from a ceiling cam. Amber joined Staton where he stood in front of the display. "Continue feed," Staton commanded.

They watched Remi Presas drawing angry comments from several people as he walked across the dance floor, sloshing drinks on anyone unlucky enough to be in his path.

"I don't suppose you have audio?" Amber asked.

"We do, but it's pretty much useless. Between the music and all the other people talking and yelling, it's damn near impossible to sort any one conversation from the background noise. And lip-reading software isn't reliable enough to hold up under a legal microscope."

Amber nodded. She'd had her own experiences with lip-reading from a vid feed. But she wondered if Richard might have any luck. "Can we get a copy of it with the audio to take back with us? I have someone who might be able to sort it out."

Staton gave a rueful smile. "Of course you do." He called out a command to freeze the feeds again. "What angles do you want?"

"The whole file."

"All of it? Not just the views showing your victim? That's going to be high-resolution footage from over a hundred cams. It's a lot of data."

"Everything. Like you said, we might get an incidental occurrence that links to the case."

"You have a high-capacity portable drive with you?"

Amber tapped her earbud and opened the team channel. "Payne for Jordie."

After a few seconds, Jordie's voice came back. "Jordie here. What'cha need?"

"You have any of your high-capacity data chips on you?"

"Always. How many do you need?"

"Not sure. Hang on." She turned her attention to Staton. "How big is the file?"

Staton shook his head and glanced at the screen again. "A chip isn't going to be big enough. You're looking at a little over a petabyte."

Amber tapped her earbud again. "Call it two petabytes."

"No worries. That'll hardly make a dent in one of my chips."

"Can you bring one to Staton's office? Fourth floor, northeast corner."

"I'll let CC know and head up there."

"Thanks. Discomm."

"Discomm."

Amber turned back to find Staton shaking his head. "What?"

"You carry data chips that can hold more than a petabyte of data?"

"Jordie has some custom chips. They come in handy sometimes." She wasn't going to explain that Jordie acquired those chips from Kitty Cope, her now-deceased cybersurfing partner. Or that Kitty had once upon a time used them for data theft and Jordie's aforementioned skill with security systems was mainly in bypassing those systems so Kitty could get into corporate networks to commit said data theft. Information like that might prove less than helpful when she was trying to maintain a professional image as an investigator.

To keep him from asking more on the subject, Amber jutted her chin at the screen. "While we're waiting on Jordie, I'd like to see the rest of the footage."

Staton sighed and called out to Cobie. Together, he and Amber watched as the now-deceased Remi Presas sloshed a few more people, generating more cursing and quite a few shoves as he staggered to a table where two young women sat chatting. He stumbled into the table, set the now half-empty glasses before the women, and started talking. From their expressions, the drinks were unexpected and his presence unwanted. After what appeared to be a quickly escalating argument, one woman shoved Mr. Presas away.

Presas refused to take the hint and leaned back in, whereupon the second woman threw the drink in his face. While he was wiping some sort of frozen slush from his eyes, the two women got up and hurried away. The screen remained focused on Presas, who seemed befuddled that the table before him was empty. Meanwhile, the two women left the screen.

"Can you follow them?"

"Sure. Cobie, rewind all feeds ten seconds and freeze." When the two women were sitting once more at their table, Staton reached out and tapped the image of each woman. "Cobie, highlight the two subjects I just tagged. Open a second display, sync time stamps, and follow their movements. Confirm."

"Confirmed."

Amber was surprised to hear a female voice reply. For some reason, she'd expected Cobie to have a male persona, like Hecter.

Jordie walked in as the second display opened, showing an angle focused primarily on the women. They were now highlighted like Presas. The second woman threw her drink once more, and they both slipped out of their seats and hurried to the bar. There was a lot of pointing and shouting, and the bartender tapped his ear, obviously activating a comm unit. Moments later, a pair of bouncers arrived. They listened to the two women, who pointed across the dance floor to where Presas was pushing his obviously inebriated and quite unwanted attention on yet another woman.

"I see you found Remi Presas," Jordie said. Amber wasn't surprised that she recognized the man at first glimpse. Jordie's eidetic memory made such things simple, if a little freaky for the rest of the team.

They watched the screen in silence as a third bouncer joined the other two, and they all converged on Presas just as the woman slapped him.

"Guy had a way with the ladies," Staton said. He furrowed his brow as a thought occurred to him. "You don't think that's what got him killed, do you?"

Amber shook her head. "Not directly. Not unless one of these women is secretly part of an organ jacker team. And they don't look the part—believe me."

He turned to her. "You sound like you've had some personal experience on that front."

"I'm afraid so." Amber didn't care to elaborate, and after an awkward silence, Jordie cleared her throat.

"Here's the data chip you wanted."

"Thanks. Hang on while this plays out."

They watched the bouncers carefully, but firmly, take Presas by the arms. He struggled for a moment, trying to shove one of the men. He might as well have tried shoving the wall, as all he succeeded in doing was pushing himself backward and tripping over a second bouncer's feet. If not for the men holding his arms, he would have fallen on his ass.

The three bouncers maintained an impressive level of professionalism, and they walked him to the elevators. Cobie switched views to inside the lift without being told, and they watched as Presas puked on the leg of one of the bouncers.

"No wonder they remembered him," she said.

"Like you said, we get some real winners."

They continued to watch as the bouncers walked the inebriated man through the first-floor crowd and out the door. The cam over the door outside showed him as he staggered through the crowd waiting to get inside. The last Amber saw of him, he was meandering safely away from the club.

"Your guys are good," Amber said. "Very professional. A lot of bouncers would have taken vomit down the leg personally. I've seen instances where bouncers sent someone to a street doc for less."

"Not here. That's bad for business. If my people get out of line, they don't stay employed for long."

Amber thought over what she'd seen for a second. Finally accepting that she wasn't about to solve the case with a eureka moment, she turned to Jordie. "Do me a favor and work with Mr. Staton to transfer all the feeds from this incident report. I want every feed from every cam on every floor."

"Got it."

"Also, the door feeds, elevator feed, and any other feed they have in the system. I want it all."

Jordie nodded, walked around to Staton's desk, and opened a hidden tray that Amber hadn't even known was there. Jordie took the data chip and slid it into the port concealed within. She looked up at Staton. "You want to watch me to make sure I don't tamper where I shouldn't?"

The man snorted. "Something tells me I wouldn't know what you were doing even if you did, so why bother? Copy anything you think might help."

"She'll behave," Amber said. "My people don't stay employed long if they get out of line either."

CHAPTER 27

Amber's team finished all their interviews with nearly an hour to spare. She spoke to Staton as they gathered up their equipment. "Thank you for your help, Mr. Staton. This could have taken a lot longer without it."

"Then it was in my best interest, and you don't owe me any thanks."

She smiled. "I have to admit, it was much more pleasant than I anticipated. Your owner was less than happy with my call today. I was afraid she was going to be representative of everyone associated with Club Karma."

Staton laughed. "Fem Loveless takes a pretty hands-off approach to the place. I usually only see her at our quarterly profit-and-loss meetings. As long as we don't drop into the red, she's happy to let me run things without her. I can't remember the last time she stepped inside Karma."

"Well, she's going to be here tomorrow."

"She is?" He seemed shocked.

"I sort of strong-armed her into it. Hope that doesn't cause you any trouble."

"So do I. I'll call in an extra cleaning crew and make sure we stay extra clean. Thanks for the heads-up."

She nodded.

"And I meant what I said about you and your people having a free pass here. Give me a list of everyone's names, and I'll leave them at the door."

"Funny you should mention that." Amber grinned. "Some of us were thinking we might drop in tonight."

Staton nodded. "Good. Like I said, give me a list of names, and you're all welcome."

"And what about if we bring friends?"

"Well, I can't afford to comp fifty people. How about every name gets a plus-one?"

"More than fair." Amber smiled and shook his hand. "See you tonight."

She commed Nathan, but he had to cover a shift at Caffeine-Nation, the coffee-and-tea specialty shop he owned. One of his employees had gotten sick, and rather than shuffle his other employees' schedules, he elected to take Odie in and work the shift himself.

"I can probably get Rita to come in if you really want," he offered, but Amber could hear the reluctance in his voice.

"That's okay. Sham's going to meet me at the club. We'll just make it a girls' night."

"You sure?"

"You bet. But don't let Odie get into the snack foods," she joked.

He groaned. "Don't remind me."

The last time Nathan had taken the little guy into the shop, Odie had found that the lower rack of nuts and sweets was right at his level. He cleaned out a good portion of them before Nathan realized it, and the resulting mess was disgusting. Not only were there torn and chewed wrappers and food bits scattered about, but it turned out Odie's stomach wasn't up to digesting some of the sweet and fatty goodness designed for human consumption. For the next hour, poor Odie had it coming out of both ends, and Nathan had been terrified the goofy dog had poisoned himself.

Nathan sighed before ending with, "All right. Have fun."

There was a split second of awkwardness before she replied. "I will. See you tonight."

"Sounds good." She could hear the smile as he said it. It would have to do for now. "Discomm, baby."

"Discomm," she replied. She didn't know why relationships had to be so hard—why *feelings* had to be so hard. As she tapped her comm unit off, she looked up to see Richard grinning at her.

He batted his eyes at her. "Ah. Young love."

"Get stuffed," she told him, even though she knew he was right. She just couldn't bring herself to admit it. Not to herself and especially not out loud. Of course, she wanted to tell Nathan she loved him. But the words wouldn't come. What if he didn't feel the same way? No. There was too much doubt. Too much angst. Too much uncertainty.

Nathan made her feel like a prepube little girl, completely lost in the swirl of emotions. She hated it. And she loved it. So why couldn't she say it? Maybe it was because she'd spent so many years pushing people away. Or maybe there was just something inside her so broken, so twisted, that she wouldn't ever be able to let her guard down enough to fully let someone else in.

I am so messed up it's going to take an army of therapists to unwind me.

She sighed. Then, as she always did when her thoughts meandered down that particular rabbit hole, she shoved them back into their box for later.

She tapped her earbud again. "Call Shamra."

A night out with Sham was always fun. Her friend had an infectious laugh and an unmatched optimism that never failed to bring Amber out of whatever funk she might find herself in. This evening was no exception.

And her dancing was outstanding. While Amber—and truthfully, most of the rest of Club Karma's patrons—were content to stomp or sway to the beat, Shamra was art personified.

Amber knew her friend had once been a serious dancer and had been offered a job with a traveling troupe in her younger days. But the offer had come shortly after she'd learned she was pregnant, and she had wanted the idyllic husband-and-wife scenario.

So she turned down the offer, electing to teach dance in underprivileged communities instead. It didn't pay as well, but it allowed her to continue doing what she loved. And her husband earned enough for them both.

Less than two years after little Davy was born, Big Davy took ill. It was an aggressive cancer that tore through his system. He went from having a slightly upset stomach to taking his last breath in less than three months, and Shamra was devastated. She'd told Amber later on that if not for the fact that she had a toddler to take care of, she might have ended it back then.

But she did have a child, and that drove her to push through her pain. She knew her dance lessons weren't bringing in enough credits to pay the bills, so she found something else she was good at... headhunting. She started an online employment agency, matching clients to jobs. She located people that she thought would fit a posted job and hired them herself. She then presented them to a prospective employer, and if the employer liked what they saw, they subcontracted the person. This allowed them to get an employee without being tied to a long-term contract with an unknown.

The standard length on subcontracted employees was ninety days. If the employer didn't like Shamra's candidate, they dropped them at the end of the term, and Shamra still held the contract. If the employer wanted to keep the candidate, they bought the contract from Shamra and paid her a finder's bonus. Sham had turned it into a nice little business, and it more than paid her bills now.

But dance still held a special place in her heart, and she and Amber had met at one club or another many times over the years. Tonight was different, though. On their previous nights out, it had just been her and Amber. And while Amber enjoyed relaxing at a nightclub well enough, she was more of a sway-to-the-beat person than an actual dancer.

To her amazement, though, Maestro Harris was excellent. He and Shamra quickly found they were kindred spirits on the dance floor, and everyone around them recognized their talent, quickly clearing out of their way. No matter what the music, the two of them dominated the floor, integrating the beat and style into movement that left everyone else in awe.

Sham and Harris finally surrendered the floor, laughing as they made their way back to the table where Amber and Missy sat. It made Amber smile to see her friend enjoying herself so much, though she wasn't quite sure how to feel about the idea that it was Maestro Harris who was integral to that happiness.

"You two were amazing!" Missy told them. "Where did you learn to dance, Maestro? Is it something from your sliding fist thing—your Punho Dezi-whatsis training?"

"Punho Deslizantes," Harris corrected automatically. "And no. Dancing movement is *contra* to fighting movement." He lifted his glass, drinking deeply before continuing. "I find over many years that training to fight is most times keeping people from knowing how to dancing. Feet move differently from one skill to another."

Amber listened, interpreting the man's broken English. "It's probably like you told Scott," she ventured. "You have to unlearn the footwork from one to master the other."

The maestro's smile broadened. "Just so! But I don't want to be limited in how I am moving, so I learn to dancing when I am young. It is a skill I am thinking helps me."

"Well, it is definitely helping me," Shamra said. "I haven't had such a good dance partner in ages."

"Hey!" Amber pouted as if her feeling were hurt.

"Sorry, sweetie. You're a lot of fun, but you can hardly call what you do out there dancing." Sham reached over and rested her hand on Harris's arm. "Not like Brent, anyway."

Brent? Amber looked at her friend's hand on the Maestro's arm and raised an eyebrow. Was Shamra interested in the man? Well, that could certainly complicate Amber's social interactions with the two of them.

To make matters worse, Harris laid his own hand over Shamra's. There was a definite connection forming between the two of them.

The group sat and laughed for a while, eating the complimentary food and generally enjoying themselves. Anthony Staton came by to see them, making sure they were having a good time as he walked the floor.

After some time, Harris stood and extended his hand to Shamra. "Do you care for dancing again?"

Sham took his hand and joined him. "I thought you'd never ask."

They left Amber and Missy at the table with barely a nod.

Missy looked at Amber. "You don't think there's anything going on there, do you?"

Amber shrugged. "Not my business." She caught a waiter's eye and raised her almost-empty glass. The waiter nodded and headed off to get her a refill.

"I guess not." Missy slammed back the last of her own drink and stood, bouncing up and down in time with the heavy bass beat from the sound system. "You want to dance?"

"Not right now. I think I'm going to have a last drink and call it a night. Too many late nights in a row."

"Ha! Speak for yourself." Missy turned and pranced onto the floor. She grabbed a man who was swaying to the beat and placed his hands on her hips as she led him deeper into the throng.

The waiter brought Amber her drink, and she sat and watched her friends enjoy themselves. After a while, she checked her chrono. She was tired, and 22:00 hours was late enough. She decided it was time to get home. Swallowing the dregs of her drink, she started to push away from the table when the waiter showed up with a frosted mug of some purple drink and a small box. He placed them both on the table in front of her.

"No, thanks," she said. "I didn't order anything else."

"Guy at the bar sent it over. Said it was a present."

She looked past him to the bar. "Which guy?"

The waiter turned, scanning the area before he finally shrugged. "He's not there now."

Alarm bells began going off in her mind as she looked at the box.

The waiter must have seen something in her expression because he started to look concerned. "Is something wrong?"

"No." She shook her head despite the gut feeling that her night was about to take an abrupt turn for the worse. She smiled up at the young man. "No, everything's fine."

"All right. Just let me know if you need anything else."

"I will. Thanks." She waited until he walked away to open the tiny box. Inside was an earbud and a note.

Put the comm in, or I kill someone close to you in thirty seconds.

CHAPTER 28

Amber looked around, checking to see who might be watching her. There had to be someone, or they wouldn't know if she did what they told her. A hand on her shoulder startled her.

"Don't turn around," the voice said in her ear. "There are two of us, and if you fight me, people start dying. Nod if you understand."

She nodded. The voice was deep and harsh. The grip on her shoulder was firm and confident. She had no way of knowing, but she imagined a big man. Perhaps even a street banger.

"Good. Now, by my chrono, you have about fifteen seconds left before my partner starts cutting someone. So you can either put that earbud in, or someone's death is going to be on your hands."

Amber did as she was told, placing her own earbud on the table and seating the new one in her ear. As she pushed it in, she heard a click. Her heart sank as the man confirmed her fear.

"Now, you probably heard a click when you put it in, didn't you?"

Still staring ahead, Amber nodded.

"Good. That was the activation switch on a microburst explosive in the bud. If we see you try to take it out, it goes boom, and you lose a little bit of your skull. Now, it's a small charge, so it might be fatal, or it might not. But I guarantee you'll lose the ear and end up with some serious brain damage. Trust me—I've seen it. Am I understood?"

Once more, she nodded.

"Say it."

"I understand."

"Good."

Her mind raced as she tried to think of a way out of her situation, but there were too many unknowns at the moment. She needed to learn more.

"Now, I'm going to fade back a little bit and let you take a call. My boss has some questions for you, and I suggest you answer them to his satisfaction."

She heard a chair slide back, but the hand remained on her shoulder. "Don't turn around, answer the questions, and you just might survive this. You decide to get froggy, my buddy presses a button, and you're done. Try to take the bud out, you're done. Cause us any trouble at all, and you're done."

Amber nodded again. "I understand."

"Good."

The hand left her shoulder, and after several seconds, she was tempted to turn and see if he was still there. She was starting to think maybe the whole thing was a prank when the earbud chimed in her ear. She jumped, images of gray matter and blood flashing through her imagination as she felt her heart pound in her chest. She reached up and tapped the earbud.

"Who is this?" She didn't figure there was any reason for pleasantries.

"This is the person with his finger on the button." The voice was electronically modulated, much as hers had been when she used the Reaper's vox. "So sit still, keep quiet, and don't speak again unless I ask something."

Amber clapped her lips tightly closed.

"Good. Now, tell me who you are."

"My name is Amber Payne."

"It's a pleasure to meet you, Amber. Why are you asking questions about Remi Presas?"

"Presas was one of several people killed shortly after having been seen at this club." She kept her answer short, unwilling to give away more than she had to. At the very least, she figured she would draw the conversation out long enough to figure out how to get the damned bomb out of her ear.

Surreptitiously, she used the zoom function on her eyes to scan the room, looking for some clue as to who was watching her. The man behind her had said there were two of them. She could only hope it was true, and there were *only* two people in the club. But for all she knew, there could be three, four, or more.

Her speculation paused when the voice spoke again. "And you're a LEO?"

"I'm a PI," she said. "I'm working on contract."

That didn't seem to be what he'd expected because there was a short pause. After a second, he continued. "Who hired you?"

This was where things could get tricky. Technically, no one had hired her. But that wasn't likely to fly with her inquisitor. At best, it would cause them to wonder why anyone would take a case for free. At worst, they would suspect she had a personal interest. Worse yet, if the person speaking to her was connected to the organ jacker network Dem was tracking down—and she didn't see how they wouldn't be—they might connect her activity to whoever had taken out the team the previous night. With the timing, they had to be considering that possibility already.

"I was subcontracted by Securi-Tech Corporation." It wasn't too far from the truth.

"Why?"

"I used to work there. It was a case they didn't want—not enough profit in it for them. But they knew I recently started up my own PI firm. It was just an old friend throwing me a bone."

"And how did you come to associate these deaths with Club Karma?"

With the idea that the longer she talked, the longer she lived, Amber went through an abbreviated version of how an anonymous someone had sent her a list of twenty-seven names, all of whom had died within a day of having been at the club. The story was close enough to the truth that it should hold up to scrutiny. Especially under the current circumstances.

"Who sent you the list?"

"A freelancer I use sometimes for cyber work."

"Give me a name."

"I don't know his real name." She swallowed. "He goes by the alias of T-bone."

I'm sorry, old friend.

"How do I find him?"

"I wish I knew. He was a contractor who helped me out on a few cases I worked when I was a LEO. I've used him for years, and I've never had a face-to-face with him."

"How do you get in contact with him?"

"He gave me a secure comm code to use when I need him."

"Send it to me."

"I don't have it memorized! It's encrypted into a soft-key on my tablet. I press it, and he calls me within an hour."

The voice cursed. "That's unfortunate. You see…" He stopped before finishing his sentence then demanded, "Who's that?"

Just as he asked, Shamra sat down at the table beside her. She carried two drinks on napkins and placed one in front of Amber. "Hi, sweetie! Whoo! I think I might have had a little too much to drink."

The voice in Amber's ear growled. "Get rid of her."

"Where's Maes… Brent?"

Shamra looked around. "I'm not sure. Now, where did that man go?" As she turned, she sloshed her drink onto the table. "Oh, crap nuggets! I'm so sorry, sweetie." She grabbed the napkin from under her glass and wiped at the spill. It wasn't a large amount, and it ran across the table away from them, but Amber grabbed her napkin automatically. That was when she saw the writing on it.

Dem picked up encrypted transmission inside the club. Traced it to you. Trouble?

Beneath that were two words.

YES and *NO*.

Amber placed a finger on the *YES* question before speaking. Then she continued as if talking about the spill. "Don't worry about it. No harm done."

As if spotting it for the first time, Sham picked up Amber's discarded personal earbud. "Oh no. I didn't get any on your earbud, did I?" She handed it to Amber. "You really shouldn't leave it laying out on the table like that. Put it in your ear right now before I spill the rest of this drink."

Amber took the bud and quickly stuffed it in her left ear. She now had the microbomb-slash-earbud in her right ear and her personal bud in her left.

In her right ear, the voice repeated. "Get rid of her. Right now. Unless you want her to be the first casualty of the night."

Amber took Sham's hand in her own. "Sham, I think you've had enough. Why don't you go find Brent and get him to take you home?"

"Oh no, sweetie. I think I'm gonna just sit here with you for a bit."

"I'm not really good company tonight. Why don't you—"

"It's okay, Amber. That's what friends are for."

"Shamra, get out of here!" Amber shoved her friend as if it was the start of a fight, knocking her to the floor. "I don't need your sanctimonious crap right now. I just want to be alone!"

She looked up to see Richard holding one of the bouncers back and speaking into the man's ear.

When did Richard get here?

Whatever he said to the bouncer worked, and the man hurried away. Richard looked in her direction and nodded at her before turning away.

"What in the hells is wrong with you?" Sham yelled as she staggered to her feet. "You don't have to be a bitch about it!"

"Just leave me alone, dammit!" Amber hoped Shamra knew it was an act. But it hurt her to say nevertheless. Hoping to give her a final hint, she sighed. "You can't help me, Sham."

"Well, fine!" With a huff, Shamra straightened her shoulders and flounced away, leaving Amber alone.

As she watched her friend walk away, Dem's voice spoke in her left ear. "You there, Amber?"

She couldn't answer without giving herself away to the voice in her other ear, so she said, "All right, I got rid of her like you said. Now what?"

She was disoriented for a second as she suddenly had two people speaking directly into different ears. It took her a second to sort them out in her head.

"I get it," Dem said. "Talking to someone on another earbud?"

At the same time, her mystery voice commended her on her performance. "That was well done. Wouldn't want to start the festivities too soon, would we?"

"No need to harm anyone at all," she said. "So, what do I have to do to get this bomb out of my ear?"

"Oh, holy shyte." Dem's response left no doubt that he understood the situation. "I'm patching the rest of the team in so they can hear you. We'll come up with something. Just keep them talking, Boss."

"Just be patient," the other voice said. "I have a few more questions. Then it'll all be over."

Amber knew right then that the man had no intention of letting her go. He was going to kill her. "Well, shyte." She said it aloud, knowing both her callers would hear her. "You're going to kill me anyway, aren't you?"

She heard him chuckle. All the while, Demophon was cursing in her other ear.

"Fuggle, fuggle, fuggle!" he said.

Vox Man sighed. "I'm afraid so. No hard feelings. You just stumbled into something you weren't supposed to."

"I get it," Amber said. "Before you do, though, let me ask a favor."

There was a pause. "You're not really in any position to be asking favors. But out of curiosity, what do you want?"

"Let me get outside before you do it. No need traumatizing the public, right?"

There was hardly a pause before the voice replied, "That sounds reasonable."

"And one other thing." Amber stared across the dance floor at a man watching her in the mirror behind the bar—a man who had chuckled at the same time as the voice in her ear.

"What's that?" The man at the bar spoke in sync with her earbud.

"You should know that I can see you."

He was good. He didn't flinch, didn't turn to look at her directly. If not for the telescopic vision provided by her cybernetics, she wouldn't have been able to see his mouth move at all.

"I doubt that." But his voice held hesitation, and he looked troubled.

"Blue shirt, flared sleeves, staring at me in the mirror so you don't give yourself away by watching me directly. You see, there are a few things you should know about me." She raised her drink to the man across the room, almost relieved to know this was going to be over in a few moments one way or another. She saw her team moving into position. Whether or not they would be able to save her was almost secondary. She knew the man wasn't getting out of Club Karma under his own steam.

He finally turned to look at her directly, grudgingly raising his drink in acknowledgment. No longer making any pretense of looking away from her, he spoke into his comm. "Touché." He took a sip and put his glass down on the bar. "So, what is it I should know?"

"Two things actually." She took a long drink before continuing. "I was injured in the line of duty when I worked for Securi-Tech."

"So that part at least was true? Good to know."

"Oh, nearly all of what I told you was true. All except why I took the case."

"Really? Care to enlighten me?"

She shrugged. "Sure. It keeps your finger off the trigger for a few more seconds, right?"

He laughed. "I like you, Fem Payne. I wish we'd met under different circumstances."

"Yeah, that's the story of my life. Always in the wrong place at the wrong time."

"So why *did* you take the case?"

"Funny story. It's actually related to how I was injured. See, when I was a young rookie, I got cocky. I chased down some guys who got the drop on me. Turned out they were organ jackers."

The man froze.

"They took my eyes, and I got some bargain-basement cybernetics. As a matter of fact, I just recently had them replaced with these." She tapped the real-looking but still artificial orbs with a fingernail. No one would have been able to do that with organics. "They're the latest model with all sorts of options... including telescopic vision."

His mouth tightened as she continued.

"And yes, I know the reason you went all still at the mention of organ jackers." Her smile went cold as she told him, "I know what you do." She put her glass down. "*That's* why I took this case. See, for me, this one's personal."

His smile gone, the man raised a small device in his hand. It was about the size of an activation fob for a rental pod. "I still have this. I suggest we step outside if you still want to keep this private."

Amber nodded. "Sure. But don't you want to hear the other thing about me?"

With her telescopic vision, she could see his eyes narrow even from across the room. "What is it?"

"You familiar with the Glads?"

"The street-fighting competitions?"

"The very ones. It turns out one of my partners holds a few titles in the bladed-weapons division there." Mentally changing gears, she spoke again. "Scott? Do it."

CHAPTER 29

THE MAN AT THE BAR looked puzzled for a second. He hadn't noticed Scott and Richard working their way behind the bar—hadn't seen them tap the bartender on the arm and whisper in his ear. Nor had he seen Anthony Staton calmly nod to the bartender, confirming that he was to cooperate.

And at Amber's words, the man's attention was focused on her, not the men behind the bar. He didn't see Scott's blade whip out—a blade so sharp that it took his brain almost two seconds to register the sudden agony of losing his hand.

Richard, standing beside Scott, reached across the bar and slammed a meaty fist down on the man's head, knocking him unconscious before he could scream. Then Richard grabbed the man as he slumped and dragged him across the bar to the back. The man was out of sight before any but a few noticed anything out of the ordinary. Scott casually grabbed the severed hand off the bar, and Amber couldn't help thinking with a bit of nervous laughter, *And another Stumpy for his collection.* He pulled out a rag to wipe the blood off the bar before more than one or two people even saw what had happened.

Two bouncers stepped in to calm them before things could get out of hand as Richard dragged the man toward the elevators in the back. It all happened so fast, and so few people saw what happened that the cleanup was in progress before an outcry had any chance of disrupting the night. It was almost comical to see Maestro Harris following behind Richard with a mop and bucket, swabbing the trail of blood as Richard dragged the unconscious man away.

Amber sat back and pulled the microbomb out of her ear, wincing as she did so, half expecting the thing to go off. It didn't, and she nearly cried with relief.

"Amber?" She looked up to see Shamra watching her. "You okay, sweetie?"

Amber did cry then. The stress of having to hold it together while a maniac made her stick a bomb in her ear then forced her to insult and argue with her best friend and finally confirmed that he was going to kill her anyway—it was too much. She stood and pulled Shamra into a tight hug. "I'm so sorry," she told her. "I had to get you away from me in case—"

"I know, honey. I know." Sham hugged Amber back. "I was just so scared I was going to blow it, bringing you that note and acting like I was drunk." She smiled cautiously. "I'm really not much of an actor, but Brent told me it should be me since whoever it was might know they worked with you and get suspicious."

Amber hugged her again. "I was just so scared I was going to get you hurt, and—"

"You would never…"

Then Shamra suddenly shoved Amber aside. Amber tripped over her seat, hitting her elbow on the floor as she landed. The action was so unexpected, so out of character, that Amber just lay there, mind reeling in confusion. She thought for a second that maybe Shamra was angry after all and the shove was revenge for when Amber had pushed her away earlier.

But the look on her friend's face immediately told Amber something was wrong. And there was a man there, one hand on her shoulder, the other braced on her stomach. It looked like he was trying to hold her up, and Shamra looked like she was in pain.

Then, to add to Amber's confusion, Sham reached up and dug her fingernails into the face of the man holding her up. He yelled and jerked away, but Shamra dug a thumb into his eye. Amber couldn't understand what was wrong with her friend.

He tried to pull his arm back from where he was holding Shamra up, but she grabbed his arm and held on with more strength than Amber would have thought she had. But it only lasted a second. Her strength seemed to leave her abruptly, and the man yanked his arm free.

Then there was blood. Blood on his hand, blood on Shamra's fancy dress… blood on the man's knife.

Amber growled, scrambling to her feet even as the man turned to face her. She kicked out, using her cybernetic legs to full advantage. His knee popped, and he screamed. He grabbed a woman beside him, trying to keep his balance, but she shoved him away. Amber kicked again, aiming higher this time. The elbow of his knife hand collapsed into an angle it wasn't designed for, and the knife skittered across the floor.

She kicked yet again, and ribs broke as he flew backward, only stopping when he crashed into another table. The people seated there scrambled to get out of the way as Amber stalked her prey. "You're a dead man!" she snarled, pulling on all the fear and anger of the last several minutes.

He tried to get to his feet, but a broken knee and elbow slowed him down.

"Amber!"

She recognized Jordie's voice but didn't turn. "What?"

"We'll take it from here."

Amber just shook her head.

"You're not in the right frame of mind to take this on. We need him for questioning."

Amber looked up, noticing the crowd that had formed around her. Several of them had tablets aimed her way, and she knew they were filming the fight for social media. The thought didn't faze her in the slightest. The man had stabbed her best friend, and he was going to pay.

"You can question what's left of him after I finish. *If* there's anything left."

"That's not how we do things. You pulled me and Scott onto the right path. I'm not about to watch you go down the wrong one."

"Tell me he doesn't deserve it!" she shouted.

"That's not for us to decide. Now, get your ass back there. Sham needs you."

Shamra.

She watched the man get to his feet and try to hobble away on one good leg. She kicked once more, knocking him down again. Then she deliberately stomped on his good foot, watching the bones shatter as he screamed. He wasn't going anywhere.

She hurried back to her table and knelt beside her friend. Blood bubbled from Shamra's mouth, but she was conscious. "Get a medic over here!" Amber shouted.

She tried to staunch the blood, applying pressure as she'd been trained. But there was so much of it. She'd never seen so much blood, and she knew the blade had done serious damage somewhere deep inside her friend.

She looked around and found Anthony Staton standing beside her. "Please tell me you have a Doc Box here?" She practically begged him to say yes, but he shook his head.

"We called EMS. They'll be here in a couple of minutes."

Amber looked at her friend and sobbed. "Hey, Sham. You hear that? Just hang on a couple of minutes, and Emergency Services will be here to patch you up."

Shamra struggled to focus on Amber and smiled sadly. She closed her eyes, and Amber slapped her cheeks. "Hey, don't you go to sleep on me, girl. Stay with me just a little longer."

Shamra opened her eyes again, and when she spoke, blood bubbled from her mouth. "Wish… I could. Too… tired. Close my… eyes for… a… min…"

When her eyes closed this time, Sham looked sad. Then her face relaxed, and Amber knew she was at peace. Shamra was gone, and no matter how soon EMS got here, no matter what they did, she wasn't coming back.

Amber held her close, not caring about her tears or the blood on her face and clothing. After a moment, her mind came back to her. Fury burned through her, pushing away her grief as she stood.

She walked back to the attacker, now cuffed and immobile.

"Amber?" Jordie was beside her again. "What are you doing?"

She kept silent as she walked up beside the man and raised her foot over his head.

She heard Staton speak from behind. "Fem Payne, I'll be the first to agree that this man deserves a swift kick to the head, but I have to remind you that everything in here is being recorded. What you do now will affect your future."

She put her foot down slowly.

"Sorry, bud," Jordie said, "but you don't really understand. She's got cybernetic legs that can kick a hole through a plascrete wall. She's not about to give the guy a love tap. This is more of a sledgehammer-and-watermelon situation."

Anthony Staton stepped in front of her. "Fem Payne, this isn't something you come back from." He placed a comforting hand on her shoulder. "I didn't know the woman, but she seemed a good person. Is this what she would want?"

"I don't know. You want to ask her? Oh, wait, you can't! This sludge rimmer just killed her!"

From where he lay on the floor, the man laughed. "Wasn't her I was going for. She just got between you and my blade."

Amber remembered Shamra shoving her aside. She must have seen the man over Amber's shoulder, shoved her, and taken the knife meant for Amber. She raised her foot again. Before she could decide whether or not she was going to follow through with it, she felt the sharp pain of several tiny punctures in her shoulder as Staton flexed his thumb. There was intense agony as the synapses in her body overloaded.

Then there was blackness.

The pain throughout her body was the first thing she was aware of. It felt like she'd had the most intense workout of her life, and every muscle had been overtaxed to the point of tearing. She tried to sit up, groaning as her body protested.

"Welcome back."

Hands on her arm steadied her, and she looked over to find Anthony Staton helping her sit up. "You stunned me." She didn't say it in an accusing manner. It was a statement of fact, said as much for her own benefit as his.

He acknowledged it in the same tone. "I did."

She thought about it for a moment before nodding. "Thank you."

Staton stepped back and sank into a plush chair across from the couch she sat on. He made a steeple of his hands and released a deep sigh. "Couldn't have you splatting some guy's melon across the floor."

"He deserved it." She remembered holding Shamra as her life slipped away. But the fury she'd felt in the moment was replaced by an agonizing sadness now. Tears fell again, and it occurred to her that she'd cried three times in the last few days, and two of those three times had torn her up inside. Maybe it wasn't as much of an upgrade as she'd hoped.

But intellectually, she knew better. The tears weren't the issue. It was the circumstances that caused them.

Staton brought her back to the now when he said, "Oh, no doubt. He definitely deserved it. But doing something like that in front of a house full of customers..." He spread his hands. "It's bad for business."

She wilted, unable to look the man in the eye. "She's dead?" She made it a question, as if unable to concede the fact.

"I'm sorry." Staton sighed. "She seemed like a good person. Do you need to call anyone? Husband? Wife?"

That brought a shock to her. *Davy.* "How long was I out?"

"Less than ten minutes." He had to have noticed the change in her attitude. His voice took on a concerned tone. "Why? What's wrong?"

Amber ignored him and tapped her right ear, remembering as she did so that she had placed her earbud in her left ear when she'd had the other bud—bomb—in her right. She switched it back to its proper place on her right and tapped. "Dem? You there?"

"Here, Boss. You okay?"

"Just wonderful," she snarled. "Dem, I need you to find Davy. Sham said her sister's watching him tonight. Find her name, comm code, address... send it all to me ten minutes ago!"

"On it." The line went dead.

"Fuggle me," Staton said. "She had a kid?"

"Yes. He's eleven." She ran fingers through her hair and exhaled. "And I have to go tell him his mom is dead."

Amber washed the blood off as much as possible, and a jacket covered the crimson stains in her clothes. The talk with Davy went about as well as could be expected. He was already in bed when Amber arrived, and Shamra's sister, Izabela, answered the door. Izabela—or Iza, as she preferred—looked puzzled to find Amber and not Shamra there.

Amber haltingly explained what had happened, keeping herself together with a strength of will she didn't think she had left. But when Auntie Iza woke her husband and Davy to come meet with Amber in the den, her strength was at its end.

When Davy began crying, she completely lost it, and seconds later, she and Davy, as well as Iza and her husband, were all holding one another, consoling each other in their mutual loss. Half an hour later, Amber left.

She was walking to her pod when the door popped open again, and Davy called to her. "Fem Payne?"

She closed her eyes without turning. "Yes, Davy?" She took a deep breath and turned to face the young boy.

"You got the man who did it, right?"

"We did."

With his face red and tearstained, his lips trembled, and he swallowed, clearly hesitant about something.

She walked back to him and knelt. "What is it, Davy?"

"I want to ask something. Something bad." Tears began to trickle down once more, but the boy seemed determined to staunch them. He rubbed the sleeves of his pajama top across his face angrily, struggling to get himself under control.

"You can ask me anything, Davy. I won't judge you."

He sniffed, nodded again, then took a shaky breath before finally screwing up the courage to ask her. "Did you kill him?"

Oh, Buddha's balls. She wasn't sure how to answer. She understood the heart of an eleven-year-old boy wanting vengeance against the man who had killed his mother. Hells above, she'd come so close to doing that very thing in the midst of her rage. But seeing that desire in such a young boy nearly broke her heart. What could she tell him to make him understand the need to temper one's emotions in such a situation? Especially considering her own actions?

"No, I didn't. I wanted to, but some very good friends stopped me."

"Why?"

"They reminded me that killing someone isn't the way to get justice."

"But you saw him do it!"

"I did. But I don't think he was the one who made the decisions. He wasn't the boss."

"And you want to get to the boss."

Amber nodded. The boy was smart. She'd always known it, but the way he immediately understood this *very* adult situation? Yeah, wicked smart.

"Okay. Then you get him. Promise?"

"I promise."

He wrapped his arms around her and squeezed again. When he turned to go back inside, Shamra's sister was standing there. It was obvious she'd heard the conversation, and she stepped outside after Davy passed. She stood in silence for a few seconds, staring at Amber. Finally, she sighed. "Sham told me about you. She said you were her best friend, someone who carried the weight of the world on your shoulders."

Amber didn't know what to say, so she kept silent.

"She also told me you were honest to a fault. Said that's partly what got you in trouble and cost you your job."

"There was more to it."

She could see the woman grinding her teeth as the emotions of the last hour pulled at her. "I don't care. Sham vouched for you, and that's enough for now. Just don't make promises you can't keep to that little boy. He's…" She took a ragged breath as she stalled to get herself back under control. "He just lost his mother, and he doesn't know how the world works. He can't understand that the good guys don't always win."

Amber shook her head. "Maybe not. But this time, they will. I was already going after them. It was already personal for me. But Shamra was out with me and my team. They liked her."

"So?"

"Now it's personal for them too. And my team would march through all nine hells for one of their own. So I promise you, we're going to find the people responsible for this. And we're going to take down every single one of them, from the bung licker we got tonight to whoever's at the top of their organization. Every fuggled one of them!"

DAY 06
SUNDAY

CHAPTER 30

Nathan was waiting up for Amber when she got home. Richard had already called and told him about Shamra. So at home, when she had finally let herself go, Nathan hadn't said much. He mostly just held her as she sobbed, and that was all she needed at the moment.

She awoke in their bed. Nathan had carried her into the bedroom and covered her without waking her. That told her how exhausted she'd been. Extreme emotions always took a heavier toll than a physical workout.

But her body ached with the physical exertions of the previous night as well. She stumbled out of the bed to the bathroom, stripping for her shower as she went. Nathan hadn't bothered to try to get her clothes off. He probably didn't want to do anything that might wake her.

She showered, reveling in the stinging hot spray as it massaged her aching muscles. She recalled Staton stunning her, making every muscle in her body seize up. Rather than getting angry, she smiled sadly. She would have to apologize to him.

Been doing a lot of that lately.

It was true. As if this case hadn't been personal enough…

Tears started once more as she recalled Shamra's face when her eyes closed for the last time.

No! You don't get to cry anymore. No more crying until we get the bungfuggled shyte eaters responsible for Shamra's…

But she couldn't even think the word. Instead, she ground her teeth, mentally fanning the flames of her anger. She had work to do.

"Chasm, water off. Dryer on, hot air."

The Computerized Home and Apartment Service Module obeyed flawlessly. Vents opened in the wall around her, and warm air blasted her, blowing the droplets from her skin.

Nathan was in the bedroom when she stepped back in. She was naked, and he would normally say something complimentary or possibly even lewd. He usually managed both at the same time. But her expression must have warned him off. Or more likely, he was just sensitive enough to know better.

"I brought you something to eat." He pointed to a tray on the bed.

"No time." She walked to the closet and grabbed a bra and panties from the cubby next to her clothes. "I have to get to work."

He was silent, and when she looked at him, she could see he didn't agree. He simply knew better than to argue.

She sighed. "I could really use some coffee, though."

"On the tray." He was still reserved, biting his tongue.

"I'm sorry. Could you put it in a bento box for me?"

"Sure." He picked up the tray and headed for the kitchen, handing off the mug as he passed her.

Nathan opened the door to leave the bedroom, and Odie rocketed past his feet. The four-legged black ball of fur ran straight to Amber and pawed lightly at her feet as she dressed. He knew she was off too, and he whimpered at her quietly until she sighed and leaned over to pet him. "Sorry, little guy. Mommy's a bit of a bitch this morning."

He whined and licked her hand before pressing his head into her leg in a manner that showed the unconditional love that bonded dogs and their humans. After a few calming moments, Amber stopped petting him and scooped him up. She carried him into the kitchen to find Nathan had already put her breakfast in one of his little compartmented bento boxes and had loaded several others into a tote box.

"What's this?"

He lifted a shoulder. "I know you well enough to understand that I might not see you until this is over. It was already under your skin. But after last night…"

She was surprised to see the emotion in his eyes and then remembered that he had known Shamra too. He'd met her several times when she and Davy had helped her move into the new house and in the months after, when they had come over for dinners and game nights. But in her pain, Amber had forgotten that Shamra and Davy were his friends too. He might not have known them as long as she had, but that didn't make his loss any less important.

She walked to her man and pulled him tight. "I'm sorry."

"What for?"

"For being so inconsiderate."

He squeezed her back. "There's nothing to apologize for. She was like a sister to you. I know that. But yeah, I liked her too. And Davy…" His voice cracked, and Nathan took a moment before continuing. "Richard told me he's with family. Are they good people?"

Amber nodded. "I don't really know them, but Sham always talked about her sister like…" And it was her turn for her voice to crack. "She always spoke highly of her. And after meeting her last night…" She recalled Izabela's words, how her concern was for Davy and making sure Amber didn't disappoint the boy. "Yeah. She seems like good people."

Nathan nodded and stayed silent. Amber realized he'd never spoken of his own parents, only of the aunt who'd raised him. She wasn't going to ask him about it, but she suddenly thought—no, somehow, she *knew*—that he'd been through something similar growing up. He related to Davy's plight in a way she hadn't considered.

Taking a deep breath, she pushed away from him and reached for the tote of lunch boxes. She looked inside and chuckled. "There's no way I can eat all these."

"You know me. I cook when I'm nervous. Or upset. Or angry. Last night, I was all of the above." He forced a smile. "I'm not a LEO… not a detective or a street banger or a fighter of any kind. But I can cook. So if I can help by feeding you guys while you're hunting down the animals responsible for orphaning that little boy, then that's what I'll do. That's my contribution."

She stood on her toes and kissed her man—her kindhearted, emotional teddy bear of a man. "I love you." The words were out before she could think about it. There was a split second of panic before she realized how good it felt to say them.

Nathan stood there, looking stunned. Then a huge grin split his face. "I guess we're there, huh? Well, I love you too, woman." The next kiss was long and tender, but they both knew there wasn't time for more. It was Nathan who pushed back this time. "I'll bring more food later this afternoon."

"You don't have to—"

"I told you, it's my contribution. Now, get out of here before I get all emotional."

She smiled, allowing herself to feel a little bit of positivity for the first time since last night. There was a pang of guilt at the realization. Then she heard Shamra's voice in her head. *Drink it in, sweetie. You deserve a little happy!*

In the garage, she nearly stumbled through her tears. She'd promised herself there wouldn't be any more of them until after she was done with the case. But she figured Sham wouldn't mind it just one more time.

The rest of the team was already in the main conference room when she arrived at PSC. They looked up as she walked in carrying the bento boxes, and Richard hurried over to take the big tote out of her hands.

"What's this?"

"Nathan cooks when he's upset. He's bringing more for lunch."

Everyone grabbed a box, but the conversation was minimal, and she could tell they were all walking on eggshells around her, even Maestro Harris. Richard finally broke the silence. "How are you doing, Amber?"

She sighed. "As well as can be expected right now. I'm sorry I broke down last night. It was just…"

Her voice cracked, and she bit the inside of her lip to keep more tears at bay. She was seriously beginning to think getting that option might have been a mistake.

"I'm okay now." She thought about what she'd said then shook her head. "You know what? Strike that. I'm pissed!" She slammed her hand down on the table before her. "That woman never did a damn thing to hurt anyone! She was one of the best people I've ever known, and I promised her son last night that I'm not going to stop until I get every last bastard that had anything to do with her death."

She looked at the faces around the table. "None of you really knew

Shamra before last night, but a few of you met Davy back at my old apartment. He was the kid that took care of Odie for me before I moved."

She saw Richard and Jordie nod their heads at the reminder. "That boy is a gods-be-damned orphan as of last night! And I intend…" Amber realized she was starting to get worked up, so she stopped and worked to calm herself. When she had her emotions back under control, she continued, "I intend to keep my promise to Davy." She looked at her people. "But I can't do it alone. I know that now. This isn't just a case anymore. This is a fuggled-all war, and I need help."

They all nodded, every last one of them. Then Richard cleared his throat. "Before you got here, we were all talking about something like that."

"We might not have known her before last night, but we all liked her," Jordie continued. "She was one of those people that lit up the room. You could see it right away."

"She was most excellent dancer," Maestro Harris said with a rueful smile. "She is not deserving this death. This is not Fixer case, but we will use Fixer way. We will do that which is necessary."

"*Dar um jeitinho?*" Jordie asked, and Amber vaguely recalled hearing the maestro equating the phrase to her habit of "dancing in the gray."

"Just so," Harris affirmed. "*Dar um jeitinho.*"

Amber swallowed. "I think we just agreed to do whatever it takes to bring these people down, legal or otherwise. Does anyone have an objection to that? Because if you do, now might be a good time to leave. Plausible deniability can be your friend."

None of them moved for several seconds until Missy opened her bento box. "I don't know about the rest of you, but I'm hungry." She opened the box, still talking. "And after yesterday's breakfast, I know your boy can cook."

Amber watched as the others followed suit, and she understood that this was their way of letting her know the matter was settled. They were in. Every one of them.

She nodded, grateful that no one was making a big deal out of the decision. She didn't need any more emotional stress.

CC Miller reached into his box and pulled out some of Nathan's spicy chicken and waffles. He sandwiched the chicken between two waffles and took a huge bite.

Amber shook her head. "One of these days, you're going to choke to death on a chicken bone."

He shrugged. "Then at least I'll die with a decent meal in my stomach."

Everyone ate in relative silence, none of them wanting to start the conversation that would inevitably reopen last night's wounds. But soon enough, they were stuffed, and the business of tracking down the organ jackers had to start.

Amber cleared her throat and called out, "Hecter?"

"Yes, fem?"

"Contact Dem and Acamas. Tie them into the conference room here."

"Of course, fem."

The two AIs appeared almost immediately. "Good morning, everyone." As usual, it was Dem who spoke for them. But his persona, too, was more somber than usual as he looked at them around the table. "Looks like everyone has eaten. Are we ready to get to work?"

"We are," Amber said. "Let's start with reports on what happened last night. And I guess I might as well start."

She spent the next few minutes explaining what happened from the time the waiter brought her the rigged earbud to the moment when Shamra stepped in front of the blade meant for her. At that point, her throat seemed to swell shut, and she leaned back in her chair.

Dem took over. "All right, I can fill in a few blanks." He turned his attention to the rest of the team. "I was monitoring your location last night when I detected some encrypted comm signals going in and out of Club Karma."

"What made these stand out?" Amber asked. "Everybody and their dog uses encrypted comms."

Acamas spoke. "A couple of things. First, you asked me to try and crack the code on the signal from the night before last. I haven't quite got it yet, but I'm familiar enough with it that when Dem told me he had similar activity from Karma, I took him seriously. I compared the streams with what I saw in the one from the jackers you took down at the chop shop and saw the coding was close enough to be concerned."

"Also," Dem jumped in, "do you remember the spiders I left in the CAPs after that first transmission burst we traced?"

"After the chop-shop fiasco?"

Dem nodded. "The comms last night routed through one of them."

Everyone at the table stirred at that.

"That's pretty damning evidence," Amber said.

"We thought so too. It was concerning enough that we tried to call you."

Acamas took over again. "Needless to say, we got a little worried when we couldn't get through. We climbed into Karma's security system, spotted you on the cams, and saw you already talking to someone."

"Funny thing was," Dem said, "even though you were clearly talking to someone, your comm wasn't showing any activity. We zoomed in and saw your earbud on the table. Karma's security system has top-notch cams, by the way. If you're ever worried about security here, you might consider something similar."

"I'll keep that in mind." Amber's tone was dry, and Demophon shrugged.

"Anyway, when Acamas told me she was pretty sure it was the same encryption, I contacted the rest of the team. Richard took over from there."

Amber looked at Richard.

He shrugged. "Me, Scott, and CC were watching from the van outside... basic surveillance."

"By which you mean you were recording everyone going in and out while eating, drinking, and gambling."

He shrugged. "You guys were dancing."

"Fair enough."

"Dem told us what was going on, and we went inside. I asked Maestro Harris if he had eyes on you. He did, and he confirmed what Dem said about you talking to someone. He said you looked angry. We sent..." He sighed. "I'm sorry, Amber. I had him send Shamra over with a note to see if we could figure out what was going on. I thought there would be less chance of her drawing attention than one of your business partners. If I hadn't sent her..."

Amber shook her head. "Don't. It's not your fault. It's nobody's fault except for the sphincters who…" She cleared her throat and moved on. "I guess we all know what happened from there." Another deep breath. "That was good work. All of you. You figured out what was going on and worked the problem." She looked at Dem and Acamas. "I don't suppose you were able to track the transmissions?"

Acamas shook her head. "It was a series of short bursts. These guys know what they're doing. Or whoever programmed their comm systems does. From what I can tell, it looks like they speak, and the system does a speech-to-text conversion, encrypts and compresses it, and then sends the encrypted signal in a short-burst transmission. The receiver extracts, decrypts, listens, then replies the same way. They could conceivably have a five-minute conversation that takes place with only a few seconds of transmission time. The only real drawback is the delay in the conversation while the comms do their thing."

"So it's secure but slow," Jordie said.

"Only on either end," Acamas clarified. "The signal compression means the transmission only spends a fraction of the time in cyberspace that a regular comm signal does. That's what makes it so hard to trace."

"Okay. So enough of what we don't have. What *do* we have?"

"Something nobody has mentioned yet," Scott said.

Everyone looked at him expectantly.

"How did they know about us? How did they know we were going to be there?" He looked at Amber. "And how did they know we'd been asking about Remi Presas?"

"Holy shyte." Amber leaned back in her chair. "They have someone on the inside at Karma!"

Jordie shook her head. "Not necessarily. Dem and Acamas just told us they were able to hack into the club's security system. It's possible someone else did the same thing."

"Actually," Acamas said, "considering Amber's conversation with them, that's probably more likely. And I don't think they got very far into the system at that."

"Why?" Richard asked.

"You guys were there for hours. You interviewed the employees regarding twenty-seven different victims. Yet the only one they asked about was Presas."

Amber clenched her fist. "The only one we got footage on. You think they tied into the trouble files?"

"Maybe," Acamas said.

"Or maybe they're hacked into the cams in the boss's office," Dem said. "Or into his computer system. When you think about it, there are several ways someone with eyes or ears in Staton's office would know about Presas."

Amber thought quickly. "Can you get into his office and check for tracks? Electronic fingerprints or whatever you 'leets do?"

Dem hesitated.

"What?" she asked.

"This sorta goes back to that conversation we had yesterday about legalities."

Shyte.

Amber considered for only a second. "Okay. You remember the thing in that conversation I told you I didn't want to do?"

"Yes."

"Do it. I want the paperwork pushed through. I don't care how you do it or how much it costs. I want us covered, and I want it yesterday."

CHAPTER 31

D EM AND HIS SISTER EXCHANGED a smile, and Amber sighed.
"Let me guess. You already did it?"

"Not exactly," Acamas said. "But we have everything ready. It's pretty much just a matter of sending out a few preprogrammed code strings."

"I'm that predictable?"

"No. But we like to prepare for contingencies. If you hadn't asked for it, we wouldn't have needed it. Of course, after last night, we figured you might want to accelerate the process." As she spoke, Acamas tapped on her console.

Amber's tablet chimed receipt of a message. Around the table, Scott, Jordie, and Richard glanced down as their tablets did the same. Amber opened the message, scanned it, and pressed her thumb to the lower right corner.

She looked up to see Richard do the same. But Jordie and Scott were looking in astonishment at their tablets.

Jordie looked up at her. "I know we talked about a partnership, but this is…"

Scott interrupted. "Payne Security Consultants is a legit LEO corp now?"

"It is once you thumb those contracts," Amber said. "There will be some details we need to discuss later, but the short answer is yes. Those contracts make us a fully legal security corporation under the SFPA, with all the rights and obligations that entails."

"Just like that?" Jordie tilted her head. "I thought it would take more time."

"I'm expediting the process." Amber sighed. "Look, I was planning to do it all by the book... safe and slow. But after..." She stopped and cleared her throat. "Let's just say I'm more inclined to take a risk and get it done right now. What happened last night forced me to reconsider how I want to move forward, and I didn't talk it over with you two. I'm sorry.

"But us trying to work this case as PIs isn't cutting it. We don't have enough legal clout to get things done without having to coax people into cooperating. Even then, there are too many things a LEO can do that a PI can't. The only way to cut through the crap is if we're fully licensed and certified. And the only way for that to happen is to kick our partnership up a notch. So as soon as you two thumb your contracts, you'll be licensed LEOs and twenty percent partners in a full-blown security corporation."

Jordie thumbed with a smile.

"We get badges?" Scott pressed his thumb to the screen too. "Real legit badges?"

Demophon chuckled. "They started printing as soon as you thumbed your contracts. They should be on the printers upstairs in a few minutes."

"And this is legal?"

Dem seesawed his hand. "Let's call it ninety percent legal."

"Here's the thing," Amber said. "You get your badges now. We need to move on this case, and we can't afford the hassle of working without the authority the SFPA grants. But I'm still going to require that you study and pass the certification exam after this is all over. Understood?"

"Won't that be a little awkward," Jordie asked, "having us take an exam to get badges we already have?"

"It will be in-house. Dem can set it up." She turned to Demophon, who nodded. "I just want to make sure you have the knowledge to back up the authority you get with the badge."

Jordie nodded. "No worries."

"Good. Any other questions?" She looked around the table. "I know I didn't include you three"—she waved a hand at Harris, CC, and Missy—"but the rest of us worked together before Gibbs recruited us. We were a team then and were already planning a partnership with PSC. This just takes that partnership a little further."

Harris nodded. "This is also to helping capture your organ jackers. I see no problem with this. *Dar um jeitinho.*"

Amber smiled. "I'm beginning to think that should be our motto." She looked at Dem. "So now that we're all legitimate and legal…"

Richard coughed.

"*Mostly* legitimate and legal," she amended. "Can you find anything in Club Karma's computers or security system to show how those two sphincter parasites found out about us? I want to know if it was a hack or if the jackers have someone on the inside."

"Already working on it," Dem said.

"Good. What else do we have?"

"The Stumpys," Missy said.

"That's right. Maestro?" Amber asked. "You told me the Fixers have their own prison. Is it safe to assume that's where last night's jackers went?"

Harris nodded.

"Is it nearby?"

"Of course. It is being beneath the building."

"Under HQ?" Amber didn't know why that surprised her. She had no misconception that she knew everything going on within the Fixer organization. Yet the idea of a prison beneath the building where she trained most days was still a surprise. "That must have been an interesting construction project. A whole prison beneath a building disguised as a shipping firm?"

"Is only fifty cells. Not big. All Fixer locations have these."

It made sense. The people and organizations that Fixers went after usually couldn't be allowed back into the general population. And one thing Amber's training with them had taught her was that Fixers operated at a much higher level of authority than LEOs. Hells above, they operated at a higher level of authority than most LEOs were even aware of. Yet they had top-level government and corporate support and the funding that came with it. They bridged the gap between power monoliths, with knowledge and funding at the topmost levels.

Amber remembered old entertainment vids about clandestine agencies that governments used to have and suddenly realized that this was exactly what the Fixer organization was. With that startling revelation, she also knew what role she filled. Amber and her group were the modern equivalents of old-time government spies.

Amber Payne, superspy.

She almost laughed at the ridiculous, yet somehow apropos, thought.

But as Gibbs had repeatedly pointed out, this wasn't a Fixer case. So she wasn't working in the capacity of super spy. She didn't care. She was completely comfortable in her old role of LEO.

"All right. Maestro, could you take me to this prison? I'd like…" She stopped midsentence. It would be too personal for her, and she couldn't afford to get emotional again. "Strike that. It would probably be better if you took someone else."

Harris nodded. "I am thinking this to be wise."

"I'll go," Scott said. "If Stumpy Two sees the guy who gave him his new nickname, he might get rattled enough to let something slip."

"Fine," Amber said. "I want to know who called in the orders. Get me something."

Scott nodded as he and Harris left the table.

"And don't forget to grab your badge off the printer upstairs," Demophon called after them.

"Hang on, guys!" Missy stopped them before they left the room.

"Something else?" Amber asked her.

"I have some things I ordered from R and D at Fixer HQ. Better sound projectors, carbogen convertors, and some thicker-walled high-pressure gas cylinders that I should be able to use to make better gas grenades. They should hold more gas and disperse it faster. If they're headed that way, it makes sense to hitch a ride."

"How are you getting Fixer resources when this isn't a Fixer case?"

"I sold the idea to Gibbs as R and D on a new tool. Told her how you were using it, and we decided this is good field testing. If it all pans out, the Fixer organization gets new toys for the armory, and we get access to the lab and shops at HQ."

"Well, I'm not going to look a gift cow in the mouth."

"Um," Missy looked confused. "You what?"

Amber shook her head. "Just a saying from the old west days. Back when cowboys—"

"Just add it to the list of Amber-isms," Richard interrupted. He pointed a finger at Amber. "I keep telling you, you watch way too many of those old vids."

She pointedly ignored her friend and spoke again to Missy. "How long until you can deliver the new equipment?"

"If they pass my inspections and testing, a few hours. Then a few more to fit them to everyone's armor."

The comment intruded into Amber's train of thought. "*Everyone's* armor?"

"I told her to do it," Richard said. "We all need to be able to go into any given situation. You and I talked about us working better as a team, remember?"

She did remember, though she didn't recall anything about having anyone else take on the risks of breaching a chop shop. Then again, doing it herself hadn't gone too well either. She nodded at Missy. "Go ahead. If it gets us more tools to use against these bastards, I'm all for it."

Looking at Richard, she said, "And you and I can discuss how those tools will be used later."

Richard looked unconcerned as he nodded.

Missy hurriedly grabbed her tablet and caught up to Scott and Harris. "Let's go. I want out of here if Mom and Dad are gonna fight."

The door closed behind them as Amber looked at Richard. "Are we going to fight?"

He snorted. "Hells no. You're too smart not to listen to reason, so we'll have a reasonable discussion on the merits of my idea. Besides, I know better than to fight you. As I recall, you were in trouble with HR at Securi-Tech when I first met you. Something about unnecessary and excessive violence against street bangers. I don't want to find out what you did to get that reprimand."

Across the table, CC Miller snorted.

Amber slowly turned her full attention to the behemoth. "Something funny?"

"Just the idea of you rolling Richard in a fight…" He stopped when he saw that neither Richard nor Amber was smiling. "You're serious."

Richard nodded. "How many times do you need to be reminded about how she beat you and two more Fixers last year?"

"Yeah, but that was just a trick."

"Sure. If having cybernetic legs, enhanced speed and reflexes, and knowing how to use them all to her advantage is just a trick. You went down in the fight that day pretty early, so you didn't see her going against the Storm Bringers. I suggest you call up the footage from the archives and watch it before you dismiss her."

Amber appreciated her partner backing her up. He always had her back, and the acknowledgment just drove home the fact that she needed to be more open to whatever he had to say later when they discussed the carbogen situation. Then she narrowed her eyes, looking from Richard to CC and back. "Did you two just play me?"

CC cleared his throat. "Gotta go." He stood, grabbed another of the bento boxes, and headed toward the door. "Thank Nathan for me, would you? The chicken is amazing!"

CHAPTER 32

Amber looked around the room. Richard, Jordie, Dem, and Acamas were the only ones left with her, and she realized everyone there knew about the AIs. They could all speak freely.

She sighed. "Are you guys about to gang up on me?"

"No," Jordie said. "We just want to make sure you remember what happened when you breached the chop shop by yourself. You can't keep doing stuff like that."

"You're good," Richard said. "I wasn't blowing smoke up CC's ass when I said what I did. But you aren't invincible. I've seen you shot, stabbed, and beat all to hell, trying to keep the rest of us in less dangerous roles. You need to stop it."

Acamas stepped in. "We understand why you do it. We have Dad's memories, and they include Kevin's."

Demophon nodded. "You lost both of them, and it left a mark."

"How could it not?" Amber said. "They died working for me."

"No," he replied. "They died working *with* you."

"Do you think the rest of us don't know what it's like to lose someone?" Jordie's voice was sympathetic, but her expression was firm. "Scott and I first met you after losing our best friend when a job went sideways. You think we don't wonder if we could have done something different? Something that might have kept her alive?"

"It's just the nature of this line of work," Richard said. "It's dangerous, and we're all probably just a little bit crazy to be in the field at all.

But for whatever reason, here we are—a bit nuts but good at what we do."

"You can't spend all your time trying to keep us from getting hurt," Jordie said.

"And we can't spend all our time trying to keep you from doing something stupid and getting yourself killed," Richard finished. "So let's be the damned team we need to be and catch these fuggled organ jackers."

They were right, and she knew it. She tended to take the most dangerous tasks for herself, even when someone else on the team was better suited for them. "Okay. You've made your point. I'll try to ease up." Looking at Richard, she leaned forward and placed her elbows on the table. "So, what's this about rigging up everyone's armor?"

"Well, the Reaper is supposed to be some giant, right?"

"That's just urban myth," she said.

"Maybe," Richard conceded. "But if they're expecting a giant, why not give them a giant?" He jerked a thumb at himself.

She automatically started to shake her head but stopped. That was what they were talking about. So she forced herself to stop and think the idea through. After only a second's consideration, she had to admit it had merit.

Richard better fit the image people expected when they talked about the Reaper. He was larger than life, heavily muscled, and impressive as all nine hells when wearing his Fixer armor. And even if his armor failed—which would require a *lot* of battering—Richard's SDA provided another layer of protection. Truth be told, Richard was probably safer walking into the middle of a situation than any of the rest of them, with the possible exception of CC.

But it wasn't in Amber's nature to leave a dangerous operation on the shoulders of her friends. If she was going to concede the point position to her partner, she was damn well going to find as many tasks as possible for the rest of them to support him and take some of the risk off her friend's shoulders.

"All right," she finally said. She was embarrassed to see the relief on all their faces. They really had been worried about her and apparently hadn't fully expected her to concede. "You're right. You make a better

Reaper than I do. But if you're going to lead the way, we need better planning—better backup tasks for the rest of us."

"Oh, so *now* you want a full team to back up the Reaper?" He said it with a raised eyebrow.

"Yeah, yeah. Don't push it." She looked at Dem. "Do you have leads on any more of the jacker teams?"

"Not enough to go on."

She was disappointed, and it must have shown.

"But not to worry," he continued. "I might have something better."

She cocked her head at him but remained silent.

"The spider that reported the encrypted transmissions last night also narrowed down the origin to a single CAP node. I was able to get into it and compare the transmission logs to our sequence of events. It comes down to a single name."

Amber's jaw dropped. "You got their records? You know, you probably should have led with that."

But Dem was shaking his head. "I already checked it. The records are fake. Name, billing history, address—all bogus. It's a spoof account."

"Then what *do* you have?"

"That transmission node serves fewer than six hundred customers. And while we might not know exactly which one the message came from, six hundred spiders is easy enough for a couple of AIs to manage."

Jordie guffawed. "You tapped the stream of every customer on the node?"

Dem smiled. "The next time they send one of those transmissions from that location, I'll be able to tell you exactly where they are."

"What makes you so sure they'll call from the same location?" Richard said. "What if they call from somewhere else? Don't calls route through different nodes if they're on the move?"

Acamas nodded. "They do. And we have no way of knowing when they communicate from different areas. But the fact that we have two communications from the same area, and both of them appear to be giving orders rather than receiving them, indicates they have someplace they use regularly."

"How do you know they're giving orders?" Amber asked.

"That first night, the guy in the chop shop placed a call out to that location. From there, an alert went out to the other six locations. The first call hints at a subordinate either calling a superior or calling into a communal switchboard. The alert going out afterward could have either been an automated response or a person giving orders in response. The fact that there was almost a two-minute delay strongly hints at the latter. Someone had to figure out how they wanted to respond."

"Hints aren't facts," Amber said. "We need more than that."

"There's also last night's transmission," Dem said. "There was no incoming encoded transmission before the call to Club Karma. Comm logs show a single transmission through the CAP node into Karma."

Amber rubbed her chin as she thought. "So it's someone initiating orders, not passing them on."

"That's our take on it," Dem said. "Although, we all know that baby sis and I"—Acamas shot him an irritated look at the comment—"aren't the most reliable at interpreting facts sometimes. If there's a better way to view all this, we're open to correction."

Amber and her team looked at one another. No one seemed to have another take. "All right. So we're close. All we need is for another call to pass through your spiders?"

Dem nodded.

"Okay, anything more?"

"Changing the subject," Jordie said, "I've got contractors lined up to change the third floor into a gym, complete with showers and a locker room."

"Good. How soon?"

"The walk-through is tomorrow morning. Assuming they don't find any problems, the guy says he can get a crew on it next week."

"What about a Doc Box or two?"

Jordie shook her head. "They aren't licensed for medical installations. But I've got calls out to a couple of people I know. We should know something before the end of the week."

"And a few bunk rooms?"

Jordie looked confused. "Did you tell me about them?"

Amber sighed. "I honestly don't remember. Probably not. Can you take care of it, though?"

"Sure. The general contractor should be able to handle that. We just need to find room."

"If I could butt in here," Dem interrupted. "This neighborhood isn't really prime real estate."

Amber raised an eyebrow. "You interrupted to insult our location?"

"No. I interrupted to point out that there are several empty buildings in the immediate area that are very affordable. If PSC is going to be a legit security company, you might want to buy a few of them before the presence of a successful business drives the price up."

She considered. "That's not a bad idea, and I know you tell me not to worry about money. But you also mentioned yesterday that I would barely be able to afford incorporating us, so there evidently *is* an upper limit."

"If you'll recall, we were talking about more than three billion credits too. And I can give you the same answer now that I gave you then. By yourself, you could afford it, but only just. PSC, as a corporation with six fully invested partners, can do it without too much trouble. Even more so now that we aren't going to have to bribe several other companies to drop their past investigations."

"What?" Jordie turned a quizzical face to Amber.

"I'll tell you about it later," Amber said. She turned back to Dem. "So you're saying I—we—can buy another building without backing PSC into a financial corner?"

"More than that," Acamas said. "We discussed it, and we think you should purchase at least three more of the nearby buildings and enclose the area into a campus. Based on the organizational needs of some of the more successful security firms, you're eventually going to need a legal department, R and D labs, forensics, SAR, medical, accounting, holding cells, guards for the cells—"

"Wait a second!" Amber blinked. "I never intended us to get *that* big! I can't manage something like that and still work with the Fixers."

"You won't have to manage it," Dem said. "We will."

"We? We who?"

"Me and Acamas. We're already planning to handle your accounting and legal. We can even put together some advertising and take care of HR. The two of us can do anything that doesn't require an actual, on-site, physical presence. But you'll still need to hire reliable people to do the rest."

"But I don't have time to…" The idea was overwhelming.

Dem shook his head. "You aren't listening, Boss. You won't need to!"

"You won't," Acamas agreed. "It won't do to open PSC only to have it look stagnant. You have to keep it running, taking and solving cases. And not just when you happen to have some free time from the Fixers."

Amber looked at Richard and Jordie, who seemed as surprised at this proposal as she was. "You two didn't know about this?"

Both shook their heads.

"It's something Dem and I just came up with a few seconds ago," Acamas said as Jordie and Richard both shook their heads. "We've researched it, and it's a viable idea."

Dem became animated as he took over. "The truth of the matter is, even if you just want PSC for a front to cover your income, it needs to become a successful venture. You can't ignore cases and leave the building empty unless it suits you to work here. The company needs to run all the time, and it needs to be profitable. We can make that happen."

"And what about when Gibbs needs us on a Fixer case?"

"Then you work it. You don't have to be here all the time. Think about it. How often did you see any members of Securi-Tech's board of directors when you worked there?"

Amber sat back, stunned at the scope of their proposal. Yesterday, she was just beginning to realize that PSC needed to become a fully legitimate legal corporation. But at that point, all she was thinking about was getting the legal authority a LEO badge afforded. Now Dem and his sister had leapt ahead and worked out a plan to make it a full-blown working agency with multiple buildings and departments and presumably dozens—if not hundreds—of employees.

"But you're talking about hiring investigators, lab techs, management staff…"

"Yes, we are. But remember, Acamas and I will handle managing the day-to-day operations."

"Well, us and a few key personnel," Acamas said. "And I think one of the first people you should bring in is Chief Fischer."

"What?"

"We could buy out his contract and bring him in here at PSC. His insight in managing investigative teams would be invaluable. You could even offer him the opportunity to buy shares in the company."

"Stop!" Amber almost shouted it, and both AIs stopped and stared. "This is nuts! One second, we're talking about finding a way to get badges and the clout to handle a single case, and now there are buildings and employees, and we're buying Fischer's contract out from under Securi-Tech…"

"I think she means you guys are moving too fast for us to adjust to the idea," Jordie said. "We aren't AIs like you two. Give us some time to wrap our heads around it."

"Of course," Acamas said. All their tablets pinged at once. "I've sent a synopsis to your tablets so you can look it over when you have more time. Sorry. We didn't mean to overwhelm you."

Amber took a deep breath. "No, I'm sorry. I've spent the last few days reacting to one situation after another. This is just… I don't know what it is."

"How about this?" Richard said. "Let us clear this case. We can look at growing the company afterward."

"Sure." Dem managed to look contrite. "If it's okay with you, Acamas and I will move forward with planning, but we won't take any action on behalf of PSC until you're ready to sit down and talk about it."

"Thanks," Amber said. "Now, is there anything else? Anything related to the case, I mean?"

"One more thing."

She turned her attention to Richard, who suddenly looked uncomfortable. "What?"

He hesitated. His chest rose and fell once as he sighed heavily. "I took the liberty of calling Fem Warszawska this morning."

"Who?"

"Iza. Shamra's sister."

Amber felt her throat constrict. She'd managed not to think about her friend for several minutes. Having Richard bring her up put a tightness back in her chest. "Why?"

"To get details on the funeral arrangements. It's tomorrow morning. I'll send you the specifics."

Shen nodded. "Thanks."

"And if you don't mind, I'd like to go," he said.

"We all would," Jordie chimed in. "CC, Maestro, and Missy too."

Amber nodded again. "Sham would have appreciated that." She swallowed the lump in her throat. Then something occurred to her. "What about tomorrow's walk-through with the contractor?"

"Acamas and I can oversee it," Dem said. "Jordie's finished installing cams through most of the building and holo-projectors in the public areas. We can watch the contractor on the cams and meet with them in here."

Amber only needed to think about that one for a few seconds. "Meet them in one of the other conference rooms. When Missy gets back, she's going to want to fit up everyone's armor, and this is the closest thing we have to a workshop."

"Can do," Dem said.

"Good. Now, since we don't have immediate leads on another team of jackers..." She looked at Demophon. "We don't, do we?"

"Not yet."

"Then I want us to get to work on some of the chores around here that we've neglected. Jordie, make sure our security is up to date. Richard, help her with any grunt work."

"Gee, thanks."

"Dem and Acamas, see if you can find out how Stumpy Two and his partner got their information from Karma. See if it's anything we need to know about."

"And you?" Richard asked.

She lifted her tablet. "I'm going to read over the proposal Dem and Acamas sent and see just how big they expect PSC to get."

CHAPTER 33

For the first time in several days, Amber—and PSC in general—had a mostly uneventful afternoon. Nathan brought in another box of food—simple lettuce wraps this time. He didn't stay long, but his presence brought a smile to Amber's face. The fact that they'd finally put voice to their feelings for one another lifted her spirits more than she'd thought it would.

Missy got back shortly after Nathan left, having successfully tested her equipment designs. Scott and Maestro Harris weren't finished with their prisoner interviews, so she sent them a message, checked out a pod from the Fixer fleet, and brought several boxes of equipment back to PSC.

"What's taking them so long?" Amber asked.

Missy shrugged. "I don't know. I figured it was more important for me to get back here and start setting up our gear."

For the next few hours, they all followed Missy's instructions, affixing flexible mounting points on armor in strategic locations then attaching audio projectors and carbogen gas convertors.

Amber wasn't sure how long she'd been working when she heard Scott behind her.

"Hey, what's up?"

She turned to see him and Maestro Harris walk in. "Missy got creative. Everyone's armor is getting a makeover." She stood and wiped her brow. "Did you get anything from the Stumpys?"

"Nope. We didn't bother with Stumpy One, and Stumpy Two was

still pretty torqued over losing his hand. But the guy you were going to stomp was a little more cooperative."

The one who killed Shamra. It really was a good thing she hadn't gone with them. "What did you get?"

"Maestro got him to open his comm for us."

"You did?" Amber stood from where she'd been kneeling over her armor. "How?"

Harris shrugged. "The human body is having many places to cause pain without permanent damage. Someone with the proper knowledge of such places can be quite persuasive when asking questions."

"I'll say," Scott said. "I mean, I thought I knew all the major pressure points. But the maestro here would press someplace on the guy's neck then dig a knuckle into his thigh, and all of a sudden, the guy is screaming and crying like a baby."

Scott stepped over Amber's armor and laid the comm unit on the conference room table.

"Hecter," Acamas ordered. "Can you link to the comm unit?"

"I'm sorry, not without a direct connection. The unit appears to be shielded against wireless interfacing."

The AI didn't let that stop her. "Scott, is there a connectivity port on the comm?"

He picked the unit up and examined it. After a moment he frowned and sighed. "Nothing."

By this time, they had all gathered around, watching Scott as he turned the handheld unit over and over.

"Here," Jordie said. "Give it to me." She snatched the comm from her friend and pressed a tiny screwdriver she'd been using on her armor into a barely visible seam on the unit's casing. She'd pried off the face of the comm in seconds. "They put a custom case on it. It's completely sealed, waterproof, shockproof... but it looks like a standard comm board on the inside."

Jordie stepped over to where she'd been working on her armor, picked up a pair of magnifying glasses, and slipped them on. "They clipped the input connections. The only way they wanted anyone to be able to get into the thing was by dialing in."

"Which you can't do without the encryption key." Amber sighed. To have a major piece of the puzzle literally in the palm of their hands yet not be able to access it was impossibly frustrating. Then she saw the smile on Jordie's face. "Or can you?"

Jordie grabbed a small torch and some wiring and got to work. Less than a minute later, she had soldered the wires to various points on the comm's circuit board. When she was finished, she asked Acamas, "What kind of connector do you need?"

A short tech-speak conversation later, she had wired the comm into a connector that she then plugged into a port on the conference table. Seconds later, Acamas grinned. "Got it!"

Amber smiled. This might be their first major breakthrough. "What do we have?"

Acamas was silent for several seconds, her smile gradually fading. Holographic hands flew on her holographic tablet until, after several seconds, she looked up. "Not as much as I hoped. They have the unit programmed to wipe each conversation a few seconds after someone listens to it. There's a folder with a bunch of files in it, but the data in them doesn't seem to make any sense. It's just a bunch of random number matrices. Other than that, the unit's clean."

"Addresses?" Missy asked. "Coordinates?"

Acamas shook her head. "That's the first thing I checked. No, if there's a correlation between them, I can't figure it out."

"Show us one," Amber said.

A chart appeared on the wall. It was a file titled Boston. The content was nothing more than a chart ten cells wide by ten cells high, and within each cell was a single number.

"Show another one," Richard said.

The file disappeared, replaced by a similar matrix titled London.

"No," Richard said. "Show them side by side. As a matter of fact, put them all up. I need to compare them."

"There isn't enough room for all of them."

"How many are there?"

"Two hundred twenty."

"Then just show me half a dozen. I want to compare them."

"You see something the rest of us don't?" Amber asked him. She knew her partner liked to play with codes and ciphers. It made sense that he might recognize something the rest of them didn't.

"I'm not sure yet. Maybe."

Acamas projected six of the charts onto the wall, and Richard stepped closer to compare them. After a moment, he chuckled. "OTU keys."

"What are those?"

"If used correctly, they're impossible to decrypt," Demophon said. "That's what they are."

"Unless you know which key to use." Richard grinned. Before she could ask, he started to explain. "One-time-use keys. Imagine you need to get a message to a group of people, but you suspect someone else is listening in. You encrypt the conversation, right? But standard encryption depends on both parties having the same encryption key. Otherwise, the person receiving the message just gets a bunch of gibberish."

Amber nodded.

"Most people just get an encryption program, scramble their comms, and figure they're safe. The more complex the key, the harder it is to decrypt, right?"

For once, Jordie was less patient than Amber. "Are you going to get to the part where these charts make some kind of sense?"

Richard ignored her. "What if you're afraid your mystery listener's resources are better than yours? Maybe they have access to a huge intelligence department with the computer power to crunch your encryption and tap your comms. Every key can be cracked. At least in theory. You just dedicate enough time and computer power to it, and you'll eventually break it." He tapped the original matrix on the wall. "So you send an innocent message to your recipients. Maybe you tell them you're going to be out of town, visiting your cousin in Boston."

Amber looked at the Boston matrix again.

"Then you send your encrypted message," he continued. "Your recipients know to use the Boston key, decrypt the message, and get whatever information you were sending them."

She shrugged. "So? It's still just an encryption key. Like you said, eventually, someone will crack it."

"Which doesn't matter if you don't use the same key each time. One-time-use keys are just that. You use them once, then you destroy them."

"It's a mix of high tech and low tech," Acamas said. "An ever-changing, manually loaded encryption key. It's the low-tech equivalent of polymorphic encryption. Unless you know which key to use, you won't ever figure out more than one message at a time."

Demophon chimed in again. "Even then, it's likely to be after the information in the message is obsolete."

"But we have the keys right here!" Missy said. "That should make it easy to decrypt the messages now, shouldn't it?"

"It should," Acamas agreed. "But I've already uploaded these files into my decryption programs and tried to use them on the messages I captured last night. None of them work."

"What?" Richard looked surprised. "But…"

"And that's what I was afraid of," Demophon said. "It's common for people that paranoid to use layered encryption." He pointed at the projected charts. "There's another key in here somewhere. Either something these guys plug in manually or something the program does automatically without them knowing it."

"I am thinking you will find it is something automatically," Harris said.

"Why do you say that?"

"Because if it is something the jackers are plugging in, the owner of this unit"—he pointed to the comm—"would be telling me this."

"Maybe he held it back," Jordie said.

"I am not thinking so. I am much persuasive."

Amber brought the conversation back to the question at hand. "Assuming there's another layer, what could it be?" She stared at the matrices on the wall. To be so close yet still not have the final key was somehow even more frustrating than when they hadn't known how the encryption worked at all.

"I don't know. It could be a transposition cipher, a Playfair cipher, private key cryptography…" Dem frowned. "Sorry, Boss. We'll keep working on it. The key is bound to be here somewhere."

"I know you will." She checked her chrono and realized most of the day was gone. "Is it a bad thing that I'm surprised we made it through a day without anything bad happening?"

There were grunts and chuckles all around as the others checked the time.

"Let's call it a day," she told her people. "Everybody go home and get some rest. We have things to do tomorr…" Her voice trailed off as she remembered exactly *what* she had to do tomorrow. *Sham's funeral.*

Everyone else knew, too, and they hardly said a word as they darkened the windows and locked the conference room.

Her evening with Nathan was reserved. The joy at getting to spend a quiet evening beside the man with whom she had just that morning shared her innermost feelings, and who had confessed the same to her, was tempered by the knowledge that she was going to have to say her final goodbye to her closest friend in the morning. It made for a mélange of emotions that was difficult to reconcile.

In the end, they spent a few hours sitting in relative silence, watching the entertainment center. He usually ducked out when she wanted to watch what he normally called her *ancient insanity* vids, but that night, he shared her need to unplug from things. They watched for a few hours before exhaustion finally overcame her, and she finally settled into an anxious sleep.

DAY 07
MONDAY

CHAPTER 34

Amber and Nathan met with the rest of her team at the funeral home. She had often wondered at the misnomer. Home was a place for the living, not for the dead. The thought caught in her, distracting her from the service itself, and she knew it was a kind of self-defense—emotional self-defense that protected her from what hovered at the edge of her consciousness, waiting for her to look at it so it could leap to the forefront of her mind again, forcing her to admit once again that her friend was dead.

Shamra was gone, and it was Amber's fault. Her mind twisted back on itself, chastising her, arguing back and forth. *It's my fault. It isn't my fault. Is. Isn't.* And she welcomed the mental sparring match because it, too, distracted her from the overwhelming emotion. She feared that if she focused on the truth for too long, it would break her.

Her friend was gone. All the mourning and heartache—and all the tears in the world—wouldn't change the fact. But her new eyes didn't know that, and they tried to create a river across which the best friend she'd ever had might escape from the clutches of Death.

Eventually, the service ended. Amber saw Davy with his new family at the front of the room. Davy Boggs would one day become Davy Warszawska, and in time, his mother's last name would become nothing more than an old memory for him.

She hated the idea, but perhaps it was for the better. Maybe it was part of that incredible resilience for which children were known.

Amber didn't realize she'd been staring until Nathan leaned down to whisper in her ear, "Do you want to go up and talk to the family?"

She shook her head. "I would be a reminder." She sniffed and looked up at him. "They don't need that right now."

He nodded, and they left the funeral home, that *home of the dead*, as discreetly as they could. Richard, Scott, Jordie, and all the rest of her team followed suit, slipping out while others moved forward to pay their respects.

Nathan had reserved a private room at The Aquarium. It was one of the fancier restaurants in the city, where patrons sat in a building that housed more water than air and were surrounded by transparent walls housing ocean life of all shapes and sizes. His aunt was a world-class chef here, and she had personally prepared them a meal that, under other circumstances, would have inspired them all to awe. Today, however, they were too involved in their own emotions to fully enjoy it.

Amber knew she was stalling, avoiding having to immerse herself back into the grimy muck of the real world, if only for another hour or two. So they sat, eating and drinking—anything to avoid the memory that squeezed at her emotions.

Movement caught the corner of her eye, and she smiled when she turned her gaze toward it.

"What?" Nathan asked her.

She pointed. "It's Shylock."

It had been on their first date that she had seen the shark, and Nathan had made the terrible joke.

"That's Shylock," he had told her.

"Shylock?"

"Because he's the only shark in there."

"What?"

"He's a lone *shark."*

She had groaned, but the joke had endeared him to her, and they shared a smile over the recollection now. And while the memory served to lighten her mood a little, there was still the knowledge in the back of her mind. *Shamra's gone.*

Amber had lost people before. Her friends had pointed that out yesterday. Losing her partner Kevin had been a blow, as had losing T-bone. But they had been in law enforcement, and death was something everyone in the life knew was just around every corner, waiting for them to slip up so it could get its steely grasp on them.

And while their deaths had hurt Amber terribly, Shamra's somehow seemed weightier. She was an innocent, the epitome of what they were trying to protect, and her loss was a personal affront.

Amber held onto that thought. She took the ember of indignation and fanned it into outrage. Anger would serve her better than wallowing in grief. She whispered in Nathan's ear, and he waved to the waiter standing unobtrusively in the corner. The man approached, and Nathan quietly passed Amber's request on. When he returned several minutes later, he began placing glasses in front of each of them.

Jordie smiled at the sight, and Amber knew her eidetic memory would place the drink immediately.

Scott wasn't as familiar. He started to push the glass of frozen red and green swirls away. "Sorry, buddy. Froofy drinks aren't my thing. I'll take two fingers of bourbon, though, if we're having drinks."

"It's a frozen sangria swirl margarita." Amber stood and held her drink up. "It was Shamra's favorite drink."

Scott pulled the drink back as the waiter reached for it.

Amber continued. "I'd like you all to have a sip, at least, in memory of one of the finest people to ever walk the face of the earth." She raised her glass. "To Shamra Boggs. The world is a better place for having had her in it."

The others raised their glasses to a quiet chorus of "Shamra!" There was a moment of silence after they all drank, all of them waiting for someone else to speak.

Finally, Jordie put her glass down and stared at it contemplatively. "I only knew her for a few hours. She seemed like a wonderful person, and I respect the hells out of your friendship." Jordie looked up at Amber as she spoke. Then she pointed at the drink. "But that is the most sickeningly sweet glass of shyte I've ever tasted."

Everyone laughed, and some of the others nodded their agreement.

"Seriously," she said. "How could she drink that stuff?"

"I don't know." Scott took another sip. He smacked his lips before venturing, "I think I could grow to like it."

That brought another round of laughter, and the mood lightened considerably. But after a short while, Amber knew the moment had come.

"All right, boys and girls. It's time we did something more for Shamra. Let's go get the bastards responsible for her death."

Amber dropped Nathan off at home and changed clothes before heading back to PSC. They had lost the morning. Between the funeral, lunch afterward, and the quick trip home, it was after 13:00 hours when Amber got back to PSC. Scott and Jordie were both already there, putting the finishing touches on Richard's armor, but the others were still on the way.

Amber looked at the huge suit, nodding in appreciation at the result. "Good work. But how'd you get here so fast?"

"We keep extra clothes up on the second floor," Jordie said.

"Huh. That's a good idea. I should probably do the same." Amber looked around at the various suits of ballistic armor scattered around the conference room. "Hecter, open streams for Dem and Acamas."

When the two AIs appeared, Amber got straight to business. "Did you meet with the contractors?"

"We did," Dem said.

"What was the verdict?"

"They say they can do most of it. They're going to submit some floor plans tomorrow. But there isn't enough room up there for a gym, locker room, showers, and a bunk room. You're going to have to prioritize."

"Or," Acamas said, "let PSC buy some more property."

Amber had been reluctant when they'd first broached the idea the day before. But having had time to get used to the idea, she nodded. She looked at Scott and Jordie. "How do you guys feel about committing company resources to more property?"

Jordie lifted a shoulder. "I thought it was a good idea yesterday. But you were kind of overwhelmed with everything else going on. I just thought it would be better to let you think on it a while."

"Well, I have. I think it's a good idea too. But we're a partnership, and

I'm not going to commit PSC resources on something like this without everyone agreeing." She looked at Scott. "So what do you think?"

"I'm good with it."

She turned to Acamas and Demophon. "And based on your enthusiasm yesterday, I assume you two are in?"

They looked at one another, somehow managing to convey guilt in their completely artificial expressions.

"What did you do?"

"We already bought several of the buildings in this area."

"I thought we agreed you weren't to do that until we had time to think about it and discuss."

Dem looked somewhat contrite. "Not exactly. We agreed not to take any action on behalf of PSC."

"And we didn't," Acamas said. "We bought the properties on our own, as an investment. We figured you would eventually come to your senses and see the logic in our suggestion. And if you didn't—"

"Or if I thought of something an AI might miss as too creative?" Amber couldn't help but point out their shortcoming in that area.

"I'll grant you that as a possibility. But even then, we still owned the property through shell companies and could control who did or didn't gain access to them."

Amber felt her temper begin to raise its ugly head again but quickly shoved it back. She had no right to tell anyone, human or AI, what they could or couldn't do with their own finances. She didn't tell Jordie or Scott what gear they could buy. They knew better than she did. And she knew Demophon and Acamas were better suited to business decisions than she was. "All right. I trust you. If I didn't, I might as well start managing my own stocks and finances."

Jordie chuckled. "You mean the stocks and finances they set up for you in the first place?"

Amber smiled back. "Not just me. They set us all up."

"But Scott and I were already pretty well off. They just added to what we had."

Amber remembered when she and Richard had discovered the former thieves were already quite wealthy and owned multiple lucrative investments. It had come as a shock... and was a bit humbling. Now she was similarly humbled to realize that of her entire team, she was possibly the least qualified to handle finances.

She threw her hands in the air and laughed. "Okay, okay! I'm bad with money."

"Good thing you have so much of it," Scott said.

Amber looked at Acamas. "I'm sorry I doubted you. As far as I'm concerned, you can make any financial decision for the company that you deem appropriate."

"I appreciate that." Acamas inclined her head. "But we can't do anything on behalf of PSC without a vote. According to the contract we all signed, any financial transaction of more than five hundred thousand credits must pass by a quorum representing at least sixty-five percent of the total PSC shares."

"Does the vote have to be formal, or can you act based on the verbal approval we just gave?"

Acamas shrugged. "We didn't stipulate in the contract, so for now, at least, I think the discussion we just had should be good enough."

"Good enough for what?" Missy asked as she walked into the conference room.

Scott grinned. "I think PSC just bought some more property."

"Good for you!" She walked over to Richard's armor. "You know, if you guys are ever open to more investors, keep me in mind."

Amber tilted her head at Acamas and Demophon. "I think you'll have to speak to our finance department about that."

The tiny chemist nodded absently, inspecting the speakers and canisters attached to the various mounting points on Richard's armor and leaving Amber to mull over the offhand question. Acamas had suggested something similar when they had discussed the possibility of buying out Chief Fischer's contract, but Amber hadn't given it much thought until now. It seemed it might be something to discuss with the others though.

But that would have to happen later. For the moment, they had an organ jacker network to bring down. She turned her attention back to Acamas. "Do what you think best on the floor plans. If that means moving some of it into another building, then do it. Just send us copies of the proposed plans before construction begins."

Turning her attention to Jordie, Amber said, "I especially want you to look over any proposals with an eye toward what you'll need to set us up with a top-notch security system. Ductwork, reinforced walls, whatever you think we'll need. If we're going to do this, let's do it right."

Jordie grinned. "Sounds like fun!"

"Speaking of security systems... Dem, were you able to find anything with regard to someone hacking the security system at Club Karma?"

"Yes. Someone had inserted a dormant hack into the system's assistant. Anytime anyone accessed Karma's trouble files, it caused the cams in Staton's office to record the event. Ironically enough, the recordings were stored on a hidden share on the same security server. When the trouble file was closed, the trigger sent the recording of everyone in the room out on a burst transmission."

"Another encryption?" she asked.

"No. Just compressed and then sent through a series of satellites. They end up in a public library server, where anyone with a data chip can download them. I tried to access the library's security cams, but all of them are painted over."

Amber sighed. "So another dead end."

"I'm afraid so. I did file an anonymous request with the library to have them clean the security cams, but I don't expect anything to come of it. Gang tags are all over that area of the city."

Richard's arrival interrupted any further discussion, and they all got to work on the final adjustments of his armor before adding similar modifications to the rest of the team's suits as well.

Harris arrived in the middle of it all, carrying his armor too. Unlike Richard's rigid-plate suit, the maestro used a flexible carbon-nanotube woven armor with Wyvern-scale inserts, similar to Amber's. While flexible armor didn't offer as much protection, it did allow for faster movement and a greater range of motion. Amber nodded with approval. Not that he needed her approval, but she was glad to see his taste in protective gear ran comparable to her own.

Moments later, CC Miller entered the conference room, toting a large hardcase. He placed it on the table, where it took up a considerable amount of surface area, before unsnapping the latches that held it closed. Within the case, another helmet and plates of flat black ballistic armor even larger than Richard's waited to be assembled.

"Do we have enough toys to rig mine too?"

Amber grinned viciously. "If not, we'll order more."

CHAPTER 35

A COUPLE OF HOURS INTO THEIR work, Demophon interrupted. "Guys? One of my spiders just picked up another encrypted stream."

Acamas was already working her console, tapping away as she said, "I'm recording the stream."

"Can you tell what it says?" Amber asked.

"No. I'm almost certain there's a second key like we talked about. I just haven't figured out what it is."

"Well, where's the stream originating? You said you should be able to tell that."

"I got an address, all right," Dem confirmed. "But it's not the origin point. This time, it's someone calling in from outside." He tapped a few quick commands, and all their tablets chimed. "You have the address now."

Knowing better than to give the AIs too much to do in front of Harris, Miller, and Missy, Amber called out, "Hecter, show the address I just received on a wall map."

An instant later, a map of the city lit the wall. A single red dot pulsed on it. "Hecter, zoom in on the address and overlay with a satellite view."

The image zoomed and shifted as she had requested, showing a rooftop view. Scott groaned. Amber started to ask what was wrong when she noticed it too. In front of the building, dozens of pods filled a parking lot.

"Shyte. Hecter, show us a street view."

The view shifted, showing them the front of Lucienne's Cheery Reject Bar.

"They're using a public location to call from. There's no way to know who's making a call from there at any given time."

"But we can narrow it down," Dem said as he tapped. "The stream has already ended, but I can still get… there!" The display on the wall changed to a large grid of six video feeds. Each feed showed people sitting at a rustic old bar, a table, or a booth somewhere in the establishment. "This is a live feed from the security cams at Lucienne's. I'm recording the streams, and I'll run everyone through facial recognition."

Amber and her team moved closer to the wall, watching the people in Lucienne's as they milled about. They all knew that one of those people was the head of the organ jacker network.

"If he doesn't get a hit on facial," Missy said, "we still won't know who's making the calls."

"Maybe not," Amber said. "But he just narrowed our suspect list down from several million people anywhere in the city to whoever's sitting in that bar right now. That's one hell of an improvement." She started to have hope. "Dem, as soon as you run your facial rec, send us headshots of every person in there."

"You got it."

"Looks like my kind of place," Richard said. "You think maybe CC and I should head that way?"

Amber stared at the screens for a moment longer. It looked like the patrons of the place skewed disturbingly toward heavily augmented street bangers. If anyone could fit in, it would be Richard and CC. But she shook her head. "We don't know who or what we're looking for yet. All you would accomplish is letting whoever's there know we're homing in on them."

She turned away from the various views inside the bar, dropping her gaze to the armor scattered around the room. "Okay, so we can't do anything more to find the head of the snake. Dem, did you ever find any of the other jacker teams? We have all this new gear. We need a chance to test it."

"Sorry, Boss. Until I catch another comm stream, I can't narrow it down any closer. If it makes the pill any easier to swallow, though, now that we know the comms are coming from inside that bar, we have a decent chance of getting another team *and* the head of the snake, as you called it. All we have to do is watch the bar. Whenever we catch one of those encrypted streams, we can also check the bar and see who's on their comm at the same time. That should give us the sender and the recipient."

"There is something else though," Acamas said. "Yesterday, there were two hundred twenty OTU matrices. Now there are two hundred nineteen."

"And if they're using OTUs, that's the way it should be," Richard said. "They destroy the key when it's used."

"If they're using OTUs, then yes. But if that's the case, another one should have disappeared as soon as that last message went out. That's not what happened. There were two hundred twenty yesterday and two hundred nineteen this morning. Now, after sending that last message, there are still two hundred nineteen."

"Number of days in the year," Dem said, suddenly looking up from his tablet.

"Last time I checked, there are three hundred sixty-five days in a year," Richard said.

"It's closer to 365.2422. We just round it to three hundred sixty-five and throw in an extra day every four years for convenience." Dem finally stopped working on his console and looked up. "But since this isn't a leap year, we'll use three hundred sixty-five, like you said."

Richard cocked his head to the side in the same manner Amber had seen Odie do when he was confused. "Aren't you making my point for me?"

"Three sixty-five is their starting point. Yes, there are three hundred sixty-five days in the year. But today is May 27, the one hundred forty-seventh day of the year. That leaves two hundred nineteen days until the end of the year."

"I think your math's off," Scott chimed in. "One forty-seven from three hundred sixty-five is two *eighteen*, not nineteen."

But Demophon shook his head, grinning the whole time. "You have to include today too." He looked around at them all. "Don't you get it? The reason one didn't disappear after the message is because they aren't one-time-use keys at all. They're one-*day* use!" Turning to his sister, he continued. "Have you tried looking for a link between the number of days left in the year and the secondary key for the encryption keys?"

Her eyes widened, and she got back on her console. "I still have a copy of the file that disappeared yesterday. That tells us which key they used for the communication at Club Karma. I just need to find a correlation between that encryption key, the day of the year, and…" She stopped. "And what?"

"Some kind of shifting cipher?" Richard suggested. "Maybe something to do with the city names?"

Acamas nodded, tapping commands again. "Maybe the name of the file is converted into some kind of numerical value, and they use it in conjunction with the day of the year."

"Yeah," Richard said. "But there have to be thousands of ways to do that."

"Thousands?" Amber had begun getting excited when it seemed they were making progress. But thousands of possible permutations—thousands of possible keys just to find the correct encryption algorithm? That didn't seem like much in the way of progress. "So I take it you're not about to find it in the next few—"

"Got it!" Acamas shouted. "Richard was right. It was a simple shifting cipher. Convert the name of the file into a hexadecimal numerical value and subtract the number of days left in the year. That gives you the shifting value for the matrix, which then gives you the—"

"Acamas?" Amber interrupted.

"Yes. Sorry, Boss. We have it."

"You're sure?"

"We have the key to the one from last night. We also have the method to use on whatever they use in the future. The only thing I'm not sure of is how they determine which matrix to use on a given day. But honestly, that's pretty minor. We can run this method against all the remaining keys until we find the right one. I can automate it, and we'll have their messages decrypted within minutes of them sending them."

Amber grinned. "You got it."

Acamas nodded. "You want me to play the message from last night?"

Amber noticed everyone else had stopped working and had gathered around. "Yes. Play it, please."

There was a short pause before digitized voices crackled through the conference-room speakers.

Voice #1 - *Confirm target sighting.*

Voice #2 - *Confirmed.*

Voice #1 - *Instructions are to extract information and terminate. Protocol three, level covert. Confirm.*

Voice #2 - *Confirmed.*

The voices went silent, as did everyone in the room. Acamas broke the silence with an explanation. "The actual messages are text, not voice. Their comms convert speech to text, compress the text, encrypt it, and send it in these short bursts. I just converted back to speech on our end and put it through the speakers."

"And that's all you got?" Amber asked.

"I'm afraid so."

She had known, of course, but it still sent a shiver down Amber's spine to have it confirmed that they had planned to kill her no matter what she did.

Richard squeezed her shoulder. "You okay?"

She nodded. "What about the message a couple of minutes ago?"

"I'm running the program against the remaining two hundred nineteen matrices. It should only take a few minutes to find which one decrypts it."

Before Amber could ask more, Acamas cocked her head. "Or maybe less. Looks like they just use the keys in the order they were loaded." She shook her head. "These guys use a weird mix of high tech and low tech. But I have the decryption. You ready to hear it?"

Amber nodded. "Play it."

There was a quick chime, and the same digitized voices as before came through the speakers.

Voice #1 - *Operation status update?*

Voice #2 – *Protocol five, level extreme, pending threat evaluation and neutralization.*

Voice #1 - *Threat evaluations incoming. Primary target is Amber Payne, private investigator-slash-primary owner of Payne Security . Threat level, ini-*

tially low. Upgraded to high based on previous attempt to neutralize. Support team-slash-partners follow.

Richard Kayani, threat level high.
Jordan Dyer, threat level minimal.
Scott Pond, threat level high.
Demophon Delos, threat level unknown.
Acamas Delos, threat level unknown.

Three other associates. Identities unknown. One heavily augmented, threat level high. Others, threat level unknown.

Voice #2 - Instructions?

Voice #1 - Additional talent incoming. Rally point two. Coordinate your teams with specialists upon their arrival.

Voice #2 - Confirmed. ETA?

Voice #1 - Four hours.

Voice #2 - Four hours confirmed. Numbers?

Voice #1 - Five teams of specialists. Your people will serve as supplemental backup. Confirm.

Voice #2 - Confirmed. Twenty-five specialists. ETA four hours at rally point two. Local teams to supply backup.

There was a short silence as they each thought over the new information. Then Jordie cursed. "Those blue-fuggled asswipes! I only get a minimal threat rating?"

Amber chuckled, as did most of the others in the room. "Okay, enough joking. Let's sort this all out. CC, get your armor off the table. We need to see where this leaves us."

Richard helped the banger move the partially completed armor to the floor near everyone else's, and they joined the others at the table.

"So," Amber said, "I guess that saves us the trouble of trying to find them. They're coming after us."

"And they're bringing extra muscle," Jordie said.

"Four hours isn't a lot of time to get ready." Richard looked concerned.

"Well," Scott said, "just because they arrive in four hours doesn't mean they're coming after us right away. They'll need time to organize and plan. I think it's a safe bet we've got six hours at the very least. Probably more than that."

Amber checked her chrono. "It's 15:52—call it 16:00 hours. Six hours puts us at 22:00 hours. If they go longer, it will likely put them after midnight. I'd be willing to bet they'll wait until morning."

"Why do you say that?" Richard asked.

"If they're planning to get us all, then the only way to be reasonably assured of us all being together is to hit during the day… probably shortly after our posted office hours."

"They could come here tonight," Jordie said. "Try to get into the building to ambush us as we come in tomorrow."

"Or," Maestro Harris said, "they could to come for you in your homes."

Amber shook her head. "I don't think so. The only location they mention is the PSC building here. And that makes sense if they want to get all of us. They mentioned that you three"—she indicated Harris, CC, and Missy—"are unknowns. That means they wouldn't know where to find you at home."

"Unless this is part of the 'protocol five' they are to speaking of."

"I won't say it isn't possible," Amber conceded. "But I still think they'll try to get us here all at once. Probably tomorrow morning." She thought quickly. The maestro had a reasonable concern. "Dem, start listing possible scenarios as we talk them through. So far, we have a frontal attack in the morning, individual attacks at our homes, and a break-in tonight with an ambush as we get here in the morning."

A bullet-point list popped up on the wall a few seconds later.

"What else?" Amber asked.

"The fact that they refer to the new arrivals as specialists is a little worrisome," CC said. "Makes a person wonder what they specialize in. Is it just muscle, or are they bringing in explosive experts, snipers, or what?"

She'd already thought of snipers, but explosives were something she hadn't considered. As if they didn't already have enough to worry about.

"There's something no one has mentioned yet," Dem said. "Don't forget that the comm we decrypted didn't originate from Lucienne's. It came in from somewhere else."

Amber shrugged. "So?"

"The incoming stream is the one giving the orders. That means the person we thought was running things is taking orders from someone else."

"Which means this thing, this organization, is even bigger than we thought."

Everyone fell silent again, trying to see all the possible implications and realizing after only a few seconds that they couldn't possibly.

"So, what do we do?" Scott asked.

"I don't know if it helps or not," Acamas interrupted, "but I think I know who our person at Lucienne's is." She tapped her console and waved a hand at the wall, where a picture from one of the bar's security cam feeds showed once again.

Amber leaned in eagerly. "How do you know this is her?"

"Whoever was in there was the one receiving orders. During the conversation we decrypted, I labeled them as voice number two, and they spoke five times. So I hacked into the bar's security server and checked the recorded feeds that matched the time stamp on the encrypted comm streams. At the time those bursts went out, only one person spoke exactly five distinct times." She pointed. "Her."

Amber looked at the woman. She fit in with the clientele of Lucienne's, an obviously augmented street banger. The bulging plates of SDA covering all her vital organs went with the typical muscular augmentation of the average banger. Dark hair with slight purple highlights—unusual enough to be noticed but not so severe as to stand out too much. In short, while she might not fit in at a corporate board meeting, she blended perfectly with her fellow bangers at the bar. She definitely wasn't someone the average person would want to tangle with on the street.

"You have a name?"

"Sorry. Not yet. No hits on facial rec, no record at all to speak of. Either she's lived a squeaky-clean lifestyle—"

Scott snorted. "Not likely with those mods, in this crowd."

"Or she's had her records scrubbed from every known database. Neither possibility seems likely, but if I had to pick one over the other—"

Amber interrupted Acamas, "Then the scrub is the more likely of the two."

Acamas nodded. "And a scrub that good isn't cheap. It speaks to big money."

"Is she still at the bar?"

Acamas shook her head and tapped her console. The action on the recording sped up, and they watched as the woman finished her drink, slid a chit into the payment slot on the table, and walked out the door.

"How long ago was that?" Jordie asked. "Can you follow her on street cams?"

"It was just a few minutes ago, but street cams in the area are unreliable. The people in that neighborhood don't like leaving tracks, so they knock them out every chance they get."

"And city maintenance?"

"It's not cost-effective to keep changing them out every few weeks, so there's a regularly scheduled replacement circuit every six months. Most of them are down again within hours of being replaced, though."

"Which is probably why she uses Lucienne's as a point of contact," Richard said.

"So how do we play this?" Jordie asked. "We have a few different possible scenarios and limited resources."

Amber only thought for a few seconds before she began issuing orders. "First of all, if any of you have any friends or loved ones at your home, get them to leave until this is over. I still don't think they'll hit our homes, but there's no need to take any chances." She pointed to Acamas. "Those buildings you two bought… you said you bought them through shell companies, right?"

Acamas smiled. "Yes. There's no way to track ownership to any of us or to PSC."

"Then if you haven't already done it, get the keycodes so we can get into them. I have a feeling they might come in handy."

Acamas nodded. "Codes and corresponding addresses are on their way to all of you." Everyone's tablets chimed.

Amber picked up her tablet, and ignoring the message Acamas sent, she began a new one of her own. "Dem, I'm going to send you the names of a few Securi-Tech people. I want you to link them to a contract and file it with Securi-Tech. Pay enough to guarantee they take the contract. I want the people on my list here before sunrise."

"On it."

"As a matter of fact," Amber said, "add a twenty percent bonus if they get here by midnight."

"Calling in reinforcements?" Richard asked.

"We don't know what kind of specialists they'll be throwing at us. I want to even the playing field." She snapped her fingers and looked up as she remembered something Acamas had said earlier. "Acamas?"

"Yes?"

"I'll copy you on the message I send your brother. All the people I list by name, I want you to start researching how much it will cost to buy out their contracts."

Acamas gave a slight smile and nodded.

Amber kept typing until Richard interrupted. "What about the rest of us, Boss?"

"See what you can do to fortify this place. Make sure the security gates are working... security cams, floodlights, and whatever else you think we need." She looked up at Jordie. "You did install cams on the outside of the building, didn't you?"

Jordie nodded.

"Are they tied into our security system?"

"Yes. Proximity sensors—motion-activated telescopic lenses with low-light and infrared vision."

"Good. Set them up and lock us down. Nothing gets in or out without us knowing about it."

"You got it." Jordie pulled out her tablet and began typing commands.

"Everyone else," Amber said, "make whatever calls you need to make and then find someplace to crash. Get as much rest as you can. Tomorrow's going to be rough."

She followed her own advice, calling Nathan and convincing him to get Odie and spend the night in the panic room. It took a bit of persuading, but he finally accepted that she wasn't going to come with him.

"It's just a precaution," she told him. "I'm about ninety percent sure nothing's going to come of it. But if that ten percent were to happen, and I didn't do whatever I could to keep you safe, I'd never forgive myself."

When she disconnected with Nathan, Amber immediately called the next person on her to-do list.

"Payne? What's up?"

"Chief, you're going to receive a request for quote on a contract from PSC. Is there any way you can expedite it?"

"You want to hire Securi-Tech for a job?"

"I do. But I'm linking specific people into the contract, and I'm willing to pay a premium to get them—and to get them here right away."

From the corner of her eye, Amber saw Demophon signal her. She gave him a thumbs-up as she spoke. "My business manager just told me the contract should be in your inbox now."

There was a pause until Chief Fischer said, "I see it. Give me a second to look it over." After a moment, he whistled. "I know I don't have to tell you, but this is a pretty unusual way to file a contract."

"I'm aware. But I have a critical situation brewing here, and I'm on a deadline. I also have specific needs."

"So I see. Give me an hour to see if I can make this happen."

"Faster is better, Chief. We're in a real situation here."

"Is this related to the organ jacking thing I put you onto?"

"I'm afraid so. It grew into something big."

Fischer paused, and she could hear him typing in the background. A few seconds later, he grunted. "Okay. With the credit you're offering, I'm sure I can make this happen. You'll have the people and gear before sunrise."

"Any chance of making the bonus time at midnight?"

"I'll try, but I honestly don't know if I can pull it all together in time."

"I'll add personal bonuses of ten percent of their annual wage for everyone who gets here before midnight."

Fischer whistled. "I'll pass it on. I don't know if it'll get them there by then, but it'll make them try their best."

"Tell them the bonus drops by two percent for every hour after midnight. Like I said, we're in a fix. We'll take whatever help we can get. Thanks, Chief."

"You got it. Discomm."

"Discomm."

Amber had to admit it felt good to be working with Chief Fischer again. He wasn't her boss anymore, and the dynamic was different. But it was reassuring to have him backing her up again.

"Acamas?" she called out.

"Yes, fem?"

"Make sure Chief Fischer is on the list of contracts we want."

"Already done."

CHAPTER 36

Despite her earlier suggestion, Amber and the rest of her team were too anxious to sleep so early in the evening. They found other things to keep themselves busy. Jordie and Missy worked together, tweaking out the building's security, while Richard and Scott helped CC Miller and Maestro Harris finish the modifications on their body armor. Amber was the only one who didn't have much to do, so she took the elevator down to the parking garage and pulled out her flame blades.

The name was a misnomer of sorts. There were no flames involved. Not unless one counted any flammable substance exposed to them long enough to catch fire. They were made of a special cerami-steel alloy designed to withstand incredible temperature extremes without becoming so brittle that they would break. The manufacturing process was incredibly difficult, rarely successful, and quite expensive. But when it *was* successful, it allowed the material to get so hot that it glowed a bright white.

She worked over some of the newer techniques Maestro Harris had taught them over the last week. *Has it been only a week?* She was startled to realize it had actually been a little *less* than a week that he'd been training them.

Activating the heat elements on her blades, she slashed the air in front of her, going through the first twelve angles of attack Harris had taught them, first with her right hand then the left. Comfortable with the angles, she began shifting her weight, leaning into the strikes, adding additional range, and paying attention to her center line as she began shifting through the patterns, losing herself in the movement.

She'd worked up a light sweat when she heard the elevator door open to her left. She stopped moving and looked over as Scott and Maestro Harris stepped out.

"We saw you on the security cams," Scott said. "Figured we'd join you." He held up a couple of gear bags, and she recognized them as their training gear. Harris carried his case, in which she knew his custom training blades rested.

He put his case on the floor and stepped forward. "These are your blades?"

Surprised, Amber realized that he'd never seen her use anything other than her training blades. "Yes, Maestro."

Extending his hand, he asked, "May I?"

She released the dead man's switches on the hilts, and the glow faded from the blades almost instantly. The cooling systems dropped their temp from more than fifteen hundred degrees Celsius to room temperature in a matter of seconds. She pressed another button, and the blade retracted into the hilt with a sharp *snick*. She offered the short tube to him.

"To activate it, you just press—" She stopped as he thumbed the button to extend the blade then curled his fingers around the dead man's switch that activated the heating element. "Never mind."

She handed him the other one, which he activated just as quickly.

He moved them fairly slowly at first, and she recognized his movements as the same twelve angles she had started with. He followed them up with another series of movements, stepping forward, lunging, then retreating, speeding up with each sequence. Then he slipped into what must have been some sort of sword form he'd not yet shown them, and she watched in awe as he jumped and spun, thoroughly obliterating the imaginary attackers. Each movement was faster than the one before it until by the end of his warmup, the blades were little more than a blur—whirling, glowing, white-hot arcs of death.

Amber and Scott watched, mesmerized, as their instructor finished, stood, and deactivated the blades. He retracted them back into their hilts and turned back to Amber.

"These are most excellent weapons." He handed the nondescript oval tubes to Amber. "Thank you."

Amber slipped them into her thigh sheaths and nodded.

"Now," the maestro continued, "I are warmed up. Are you?"

She smiled at his phrasing and nodded. "I am."

"Am," he repeated, correcting himself. "I *am* warmed up. Are you wishing to spar?"

"Yes, but maybe without the stunners turned on? I have a feeling we may need to be at full strength in the morning."

She turned and signaled Scott, who tossed her bag to her. She pulled out her training blades and began the work of turning her light sweat into a dripping exertion.

The three of them stopped their workout a few hours later, and Amber finally felt like she might be able to sleep. The only thing that still bothered her by then was the rather odiferous reminder in the elevator that they still didn't have any showers. Instead, she had to settle for a whore's bath in the restroom before finally relaxing into her office couch for the night.

"Dem?" she called out.

"Here, Boss."

She looked around, expecting to see him before remembering that there weren't any holo-projectors in her office. Yet one more item for her to-do list.

"Anything I should know before I get some sleep?"

"I don't think so. CC and Maestro Harris have finished accessorizing their armor. Everyone now has carbogen pumps, gas grenades, and fear-frequency projectors mounted. Jordie and Missy added extra cams all around the building, and Acamas and I are using them to keep watch while you guys catch some sleep. You should be fine for a few hours of rest."

Amber stifled the yawn that tried to force its way out. "Thanks. Then I'm out for a while. Let me know if our reinforcements get here."

"Will do, Boss. Good night."

"G'night."

Amber finally allowed her eyes to close.

DAY 08
TUESDAY

CHAPTER 37

"Amber! Time to wake up, Boss!"

Her eyes snapped open. "Dem? What's going on?" She called up the chrono display in her eyes' HUD setting and saw that it was 01:32. She sat up in the darkened office with a slight groan. Automatically switching her eyes to low-light vision, she reached for the clothes she had dropped on the floor beside her couch. "Are our reinforcements here?"

"I don't think so," the disembodied voice said. "But there's definitely something brewing outside."

Heart quickening, Amber dropped her clothes and walked in her underwear to the display wall. "Put it on my screen."

The wall screen lit up with three different displays. Each showed a view from one of PSC's external security cams. On the first screen, five plain work vans made their way slowly down the road toward PSC.

"There's some sort of logo on those pods," she said. "What is it?"

"It's the company we contracted to renovate the third floor. But they're not scheduled to start until next week."

Amber kept silent, shifting her gaze to the second display. It was a simple view of a tall hedgerow at the edge of PSC's property. "What's this on screen two?"

The view abruptly shifted to infrared, and she cursed. The heat signatures of two more vans were clearly outlined behind the foliage, and people were exiting them, taking up positions at the edge of their property. "Wake everyone," she said. "No lights yet, but be ready with the external spotlights on my say-so."

"Already waking them," Acamas said. "And I have external windows set to blackout, so lighting won't be a problem. No one can see inside."

"Good. Keep lighting minimal, anyway. Emergency lights only, just to be safe. I want everyone geared up in two minutes." Following her own advice, she hurried to the closet in her office and pulled out her armor and undersuit. She slipped into the skinsuit as she continued talking. "Put us all on the same comm channel, and show any movement you deem important on every screen in the building. I don't want any of us caught with our pants down or off or whatever the saying is."

"Doing it now."

Amber's ears were immediately filled with the sounds of her people scrambling to get ready. "Listen up, people," she said. "Looks like I was wrong about them waiting until morning. We have three suspicious vans pulling up in front of the building now and more people holding back behind the hedges."

"How many?" CC asked.

"I don't know. Look at the nearest screen. Dem is streaming from our security cams on every display in the building." She slipped her armor over the skinsuit. "If you aren't already suited up, do it now. I imagine we can expect them to start breaching operations right away."

"What should we prepare for?" Missy asked.

"You know as much as I do. They said 'specialists.' Prepare for something special."

Scott snorted. Amber had heard the sound often enough to know it anywhere. "Something funny, Pondy?"

"Nope. Sorry, Boss. Just looking forward to the fun."

She rolled her eyes at that. "I have a feeling you're about to get about as much fun as you can handle."

"That's truer than you know," Dem said. "Look at the screen, Boss!"

She looked up to see several huge bangers exiting the vans out front. Each one of them had the obvious muscular augments and SDA plates of most street bangers. But the thing that chilled her to the bone was the sight of six of them kneeling together and assembling a giant metal cylinder. It was easily half a meter in diameter and had a pair of heavy handles on either side.

Amber wasn't the only one to realize what was happening. She heard CC curse. Then he proclaimed, "That's not possible! We stopped them! There weren't any of them left!"

"It looks like there were," Jordie said.

"What?" Scott said, but he immediately followed up with "Oh, fuggle me! Chosen Ones?"

"I guess that answers the question of who's behind the reorganization of the organ jackers." Richard's tone was dry and angry.

"They aren't chanting, though."

Amber looked closely and realized Jordie was right. The chanting that the previous Chosen Ones had used to trigger their nanite-enhanced strength and speed seemed to be unnecessary for these attackers. "They must have programmed that restriction out."

"Hey, guys?" Missy said when there was a gap in the conversation. "You mind letting the rest of us in on the big secret?"

"You see that giant battering ram?" Amber asked.

"Yeah."

"You're a chemist—good with weights and measures, right?"

"Uhhh…"

"Look at the length and diameter of that ram. Then run a quick estimate of how heavy it must be."

"I can't tell that without knowing what the material is."

"Let me save you the trouble," Demophon interrupted. "It's a battering ram, so the material has to be fairly dense. That's how they work. Even assuming it's a simple steel, you can estimate a metal density of about seven to eight grams per cubic centimeter. Giving it the benefit of the doubt, let's go with the lighter density of seven. I measured the cylinder, and it's about seventy centimeters in diameter by one hundred fifty long. Running those specs through a calculator gives us just a bit over four thousand kilograms. And that's assuming fairly mild steel. I would bet it's closer to five thousand kilos. The average person can lift less than an eighth of that."

They all watched as four of the men grabbed the handles on either side of the cylinder and lifted it. They didn't do so effortlessly, but four men lifted what should have taken at least twice as many street bangers, even with full augments.

"We don't have time to go through it all," Amber snapped. "The short of it is that these are almost definitely Chosen Ones." She slipped her helmet on and walked out of her office, speaking as she moved. "Everyone, double-check your carbogen pumps and your breathers. I have a feeling they might be our best chance of surviving this."

Missy seemed disinclined to move on, though. "What are Chosen Ones?"

"Enhanced speed, strength, and they don't seem to feel pain. Gibbs called them supersoldiers. They're the people who killed Zuzen Ybarra last year. They damn near killed me." CC's voice had a new tone to it—one Amber hadn't heard before. It was rage, with a tinge of uncertainty, perhaps even fear.

"Nearly killed me too," Amber said. "And I don't intend to let them finish the job."

"Want me to drop the security gates into place?" Jordie asked.

Amber thought quickly. "No. Our gates aren't anywhere near as good as what they had at the GMF, and those didn't stop that ram. Let them bust through the doors with the ram, then drop the gates behind them. Once the ram is inside, that might slow down the others in the parking lot and let us separate them into two groups."

"Sounds like a plan."

Missy wasn't convinced, though. "But what are—"

"Missy, put your damn breather on!" Amber snapped. "We don't have time to explain. Just trust us when we tell you that these guys are stronger and faster than anything you've ever come up against. As a matter of fact, I don't want you to get anywhere near them."

"What?"

"As good a chemist as you might be, those skills aren't going to help you here. I want you to stay on the third floor, overlooking the atrium. If you get a clean shot, take it. It might not stop them, but it should distract them enough for someone else to skewer them."

Amber's tone must have finally gotten through to Missy. Her only reply this time was "Yes, fem."

"Scott, hit your adrenaline pump and meet me downstairs. Maestro, you need to remember that there are several of these guys, and they're all going to be as fast as I am and stronger than Richard and CC."

"I am understanding this."

As she emerged from the hallway onto the walkway over the atrium, she told him, "Then we could really use you on the ground floor."

"I am already here."

Amber looked over the rail and saw him standing in the atrium below her. He held a long sword and a short one, similar to his training blades. But these had the matte-gray finish she'd seen on Scott's weapon. Scott had called it WBN—a wurtzite boron nitride coating—and it was the only thing she'd ever run into that could cut through her flame blades.

She jumped over the crosswalk rail to land on the floor beside him. "So I see."

"Show-off!" Scott emerged from the north stairwell. He was followed by Richard and CC. All of them wore full armor, including helmets, which Richard hardly ever wore. The built-in breathers made them necessary tonight though. Even Maestro Harris wore a half mask that covered his face from the nose down. She knew it also contained a breather, so they were all impervious to the carbogen.

"Hey, Amber?" Richard asked. "I just want to make sure… we're not trying to take them alive this time, are we?"

Amber was too tense to smile. She drew her blades and activated them.

He flexed his hands, and razors snicked from the tip of each digit. "I'll take that as a no."

As her blades began to glow, Amber called out, "Final gear check. Breathers?"

She was answered with a chorus of *check*s and *roger*s.

"Carbogen pumps?"

Another chorus.

"Ear baffles?"

But before her team could answer, Demophon shouted in their comms, "Here they come!"

His warning was immediately followed by a tremendous crash as the front doors flew across the atrium. One of them barely missed CC Miller, who was standing too close to the middle of the room. Immediately behind the flying doors, four roaring Chosen Ones carrying the battering ram ran across the threshold.

"Jordie!" Amber yelled. "Drop the gates! Acamas, full lights now!"

The heavy security gates were already falling as she spoke. Twenty centimeters thick and piston powered, an interlocking series of reinforced cerami-steel walls slammed into place, trapping the four Chosen Ones inside the building and keeping the others out... at least for the moment. Amber hoped that without their battering ram, the others would be stuck outside for long enough for her team to deal with the first four.

The lights inside flared to life as Missy reported, "Activating fear frequency."

Amber scrolled through the commands on her HUD and activated her shoulder-mounted speakers as well. She hoped Missy's upgrades had worked. Then she activated her vox unit and growled.

The four intruders dropped the massive cylinder and reached for the weapons strapped to their belts. Floor tiles shattered beneath the massive weight of the ram. She looked up at the nearest of the men, made sure her speakers were pointing directly at him, and screamed.

The man's eyes went wide as she leapt. He barely managed to dodge her strike and screamed back at her. His voice, though, was laced with fear rather than the vox-enhanced fear frequency. He drew a pistol and fired a stream of flechettes at her. Amber didn't bother trying to dodge. She knew the small-caliber weapon wouldn't even bruise through the multiple layers of her Fixer armor.

Seeing his pistol was useless, he threw it at her, and Amber batted the pistol aside with one of her blades. He reached for the blade at his waist but stopped as the tip of a sword sprouted from his throat, twisted, and withdrew, slicing through the left side of his neck on its way out. Blood fountained as Maestro Harris spun away to face the other three attackers.

Amber watched the man fall to the floor, and she felt somewhat cheated. She hadn't gotten in a single blow, and Maestro Harris was already toe to toe with his second opponent.

CC and Richard tag teamed the third one. As she watched, Richard grappled the man from behind, reached up, and raked razor-tipped fingers across the eyes of the man they were fighting, blinding him even as the man stabbed at CC with a large knife. The knife skittered across

CC's heavy plate armor as CC smashed his metal-gauntleted fist into the Chosen One's chest. CC flexed his arm, and the gauntlet sprouted a fifteen-centimeter spike that plunged into the man's heart.

Amber turned her attention to Scott.

CHAPTER 38

Scott was having more trouble with his attacker. As he had discovered last year when they'd fought Chosen Ones at the GMF, they were just as fast as he was and considerably stronger. The quicker he could finish the fight, the better off he would be. But he had some training with Maestro Harris behind him now. It wasn't a lot, but he had at least a few new tricks in his repertoire. With a new eye, he watched the kind of moves his attacker used. In his mind, he heard the maestro instructing him to ignore the specific movements and techniques his opponent used: "You should not to think of counter one to attack two. Observe instead the angles and ranges your opponent is to use."

He wasn't completely sure of himself and kept shifting between the two fighting styles, but at the very least, he was able to view his opponent's movements from a new vantage. That gave him options if he could only react quickly enough. For instance, it was immediately apparent that the giant slashing at him had very little formal combat training. He relied almost wholly on intimidation, rushing forward as he attempted to overwhelm his opponent with size, speed, and a ferocious attitude.

Scott, on the other hand, had years of training with various sword styles. He was a master of the blade in his own right. So much so that he had become complacent… until Maestro Harris had shown him he still had things to learn. Now he used all his knowledge, old and new, to counter the giant flailing away at him. The Chosen One had speed, strength, and reach. He wielded two long swords almost half again as long as Scott's single blade. To counter that, Scott had his own speed, equal to that of the other man by virtue of his adrenal pump, his superior skill, and a new eye to how the man moved. The bigger man rushed in again, a blade in either hand. His eyes were wide, his expression one of anger and fear. Scott assumed this was an indication that the carbogen and audio projectors were working, at least to some degree. But the atrium was open, allowing the carbogen to dissipate and minimizing its effect. So while the rising tightness and fear might be slowing the man somewhat, it was a far cry from turning him into a quivering mess of terrified bad guy.

Scott retreated before his attacker, letting him think he was forcing Scott back. At the last second, he evaded a wide slash, and rather than counter, he slipped past and ran a short distance away. He spun to watch as the Chosen One came after him. The man rushed forward once more, raising his right arm for a high downward attack. That was what Scott had been watching for. This time, rather than retreat, Scott tried something Amber had used on him. He powered forward as if to meet the man's attack. At the last second, he dropped to his knees and slid under the weapon. The combination of his adrenaline-enhanced speed and hardened armor kneepads allowed him to slide past his opponent on the smooth tile of the atrium, slashing beneath the other's blades as he skidded past.

The Chosen One spun to face Scott, who quickly jumped back to his feet and turned. Scott lowered his blade as the other tried to raise his own. The giant blinked a few times then staggered. He seemed puzzled as he looked down at the blood gushing freely from the expertly placed slice where Scott had managed to cut between the various protective plates of his subdermal armor. Then, blades falling from weakened hands, he dropped to the floor without another step. Scott watched as the life left his eyes.

Scott looked past the dead man to see the others watching Maestro Harris, who was engaged with the last standing Chosen One. Harris slapped his attacker's blade aside with his longsword, jumped inside the man's reach, and lunged forward to stab and withdraw his short parrying blade in a movement so fast it was hard to be sure he'd seen it. But the Chosen One dropped, instantly lifeless, and Scott realized that Harris had thrust through the front of the man's throat to sever his spinal cord with a single thrust. It was a move of incredible finesse and efficiency, and Scott doubted there was anyone in the room besides himself who would recognize the mastery needed to pull it off. Seldom had he ever seen such skill in combat, even in the combat events at the Glads.

As Maestro Harris turned to scan the room, Scott stood straight, moved his blade to his left hand, and offered Harris the formal salute of his style. Harris inclined his head in recognition as Amber spoke.

Amber looked around the atrium. She wasn't sure how the others felt, but she was stunned. The last time they had faced four Chosen Ones, they'd had more people, yet she and CC Miller had still nearly died. Another Fixer, Zuzen Ybarra, one of the twins who had fought alongside them, *had* died. This time, they appeared to have come through completely unscathed, and according to her chrono, it had taken less than three minutes. The new training and new armor from the Fixers had made all the difference.

"Dem," she called out, "Status on the ones outside!"

"They spent the last few minutes trying to raise the security gates. Looks like they're getting ready to try ramming one of the cargo vans into them now."

Amber walked over to one of the wall displays and watched as all five vans cleared a path in front of the main entrance. One of them backed across the parking lot and lined up with the gates where the front doors had been. "Will that work?"

"No," Jordie said. "I checked the stats on those walls when you asked me to help upgrade the place. Unless that van is full of explosives, all they'll end up doing is ruining a perfectly good cargo pod."

"And if it *is* full of explosives?"

Amber watched as the van began to accelerate toward the building.

Jordie cursed. "You guys might want to clear the atrium."

"Let's go!" Amber yelled, but it was unnecessary. Her people were already running to the various exits and corridors around the atrium. Amber watched to make sure they all made it to some kind of cover before taking one last glance at the display. The van was bouncing up the steps in front of the building. When it got to the end of the stairs and reached the covered plaza in front of the doors, she sprinted to a side corridor, thankful once again for her cybernetics. Seconds later, she heard a crash and felt the floor shake. But it was considerably less impressive than she'd feared.

"Looks like they didn't have explosives in it after all," Dem said.

Amber stood and looked down at the screen on the first-floor atrium wall. Switching her eyes to their telescopic setting, she watched several of the men reach the damaged van and begin pushing it back and away from the doors.

"Now what?" Amber wondered.

"The security gates don't go around the whole building," Jordie said. "They only cover areas with doors. If it was me, I'd start looking for another way in."

Amber stared at the screen, waiting to see what direction they would go. But instead of moving to one side or the other, they simply pulled back across the parking lot.

"What are they doing?" Richard said. "They can't be giving up already."

"They aren't." Acamas spoke for the first time that morning.

"Well, they don't seem to be looking for another way in."

The screen switched views as she replied, "That's because they're going to *make* one."

Acamas zoomed the camera in on the small group of men stepping forward from the shrubs. They didn't have the giant, obviously augmented physiques of the Chosen Ones. But they each raised a large rectangular tube to their shoulder. Each tube had half a dozen holes in the end, and it was obvious they were some sort of shoulder-mounted rockets.

"MXP units," Acamas said. "Multiple explosive projectiles. I suggest everyone vacate the first floor. *Now!*"

Amber nodded to her people. "Upstairs, people. Move it!" She waited as they all headed for the door to the stairs on the north wall. Once they were all away, she gathered her legs and jumped back up to the second floor.

She ran to the exit for the stairs and watched from the protection of the corner. The door behind her opened a few seconds later, and Richard sighed.

"Showing off again?" he said.

She turned and gave a slight grin to the giant blood-spattered black armor that housed her friend as he stepped up beside her. Scott, CC, and Maestro Harris were right behind him.

"That's what I said," Scott commented.

Their joking bravado was interrupted as the building shook and the security gates protecting the atrium disintegrated in a tornado of flying shrapnel. Then a horde of Chosen Ones poured into the building.

CHAPTER 39

"We can't take this many of them," Richard said. "There's no way."

Amber knew he was right. "Anyone have any other ideas?"

"I do," Jordie said. "Dem, give us full lights, inside and out. Aim the outside floods at those bungholes in the hedges out there. Blind those suckers."

"Can do," Demophon replied. Every light in the atrium flared to full power, and the outside of the building lit up like it was full noon on a sunny day. "Now what?"

"Now you guys take a break." Missy's voice crackled over the comms. "Let me and Jordie have a turn."

With that, the deafening staccato of a Fixer carbine erupted from the third-floor walkway above Amber. She had first heard the sound last year when Tinasha Gibbs and the Ybarra twins had fired on the Chosen Ones in the lobby of the GMF. Since then, she'd had the chance to become familiar with the custom carbines during her training at Fixer HQ, and the sound was unmistakable. The weapons themselves weren't all that special. But they were modified to fire hundreds of tiny explosive flechettes that did much more damage than standard ammunition.

The roar of the carbine was quickly joined by blasts from Jordie's custom shotgun. The shotgun didn't have the rate of fire that Missy's carbine had, but where Missy's weapon pelted the Chosen Ones with dozens of tiny hits before finally finding a chink in their SDA, each round from Jordie's shotgun dropped one in his tracks with a single hit. Amber recalled the special ammunition one of Richard's contacts in Dineh Village had made for Jordie. He called them sabot slugs and claimed they had nearly unparalleled stopping power. Judging by the carnage being inflicted below, Amber thought he just might be right.

In the atrium, Chosen Ones scrambled about, dodging as they ran for whatever cover they could find. A few managed to find shelter behind some decorative stone planters, others behind the unused receptionists' stations. In both cases, the cover was quickly disintegrating under the fusillade of miniexplosions.

Over the next fifteen seconds, Amber watched five of the invaders fall to Missy and Jordie's rain of death.

"And why didn't we do this with the first ones?" Scott asked.

"Because this ammo is highly controlled at Fixer HQ," Missy said into her comm. "I was only able to sneak two magazines out." Her carbine went silent. "And I'm loading the second one now."

The carbine sounded again, and another Chosen One dropped. The others had learned from their first losses, though, and didn't present much in the way of targets.

"They're going into the stairwells beneath you guys." Jordie leaned out from her place of cover and fired three more rounds, but her cursing let them all know she hadn't had any better luck than Missy.

Amber caught movement on the far wall, almost out of her range of vision beneath the walkway on Jordie's side. "They're going up the southern stairs too." She looked at the men behind her. "I need some of you to stop them."

Maestro Harris was closest to the door. He pulled it open and slipped through without a word.

"Right behind you," Scott called and followed their instructor through the door.

"Keep your pumps and speakers going," Demophon advised. "They should be more effective in the tight confines."

Amber hesitated then pointed at Richard and CC. "You two take the opposite stairwell." Richard nodded and tapped his friend on the chest. The two of them took off across the walkway. A few of the invaders took potshots at them as they ran, but Missy and Jordie kept most of them ducked behind what little cover they could find.

The sight of two armored behemoths running across the floor must have attracted attention from outside though. As Richard and CC skidded to a stop at the far end of the walkway, Demophon shouted into the comms, "Incoming!"

Despite the floodlights outside, Amber saw the flare of propellant against the early-morning darkness as four rockets streaked across the parking lot and into the building. Richard and CC made it through their door just before the first explosion.

Amber turned her head and ducked behind the corner just as the walkway exploded a few meters ahead of her. Flying debris showered her and the area around her, and she was thankful for her helmet as stone fragments pinged off it. When she turned back, most of the causeway before her was gone.

Scott followed Maestro Harris down the stairs. There wasn't a lot of room for them to move side by side in the narrow stairwell, but he wasn't about to let Harris take on multiple Chosen Ones by himself. Even someone as good as Harris would have trouble with those odds.

The stairwell was a short zigzag affair, with a small landing halfway down and lit only by the flashing red emergency lights. "Dem," Scott called into the comm, "can you turn on full lighting in the stairwells too?" There was no reply, but the lights flared to life just as a Chosen One rounded the corner of the landing.

Harris leapt, using his higher position on the stairs to his advantage. To Scott's amazement, the maestro landed with one foot on the Chosen One's shoulder and braced the other foot on the wall behind him. The man looked up, as surprised at the move as Scott was, and Harris plunged his longsword straight down. The blade entered the man's mouth, and Harris shoved half its length down his throat and into his chest before bracing himself and jumping up and back to land lithely on the stairs just below Scott.

"Fuggle me" was all Scott could think to say. The Chosen One was just beginning to realize he was dead and stumbled back against the wall behind him, grabbing at his throat.

The maestro flicked his blade to sling the blood off and told Scott, "There is being four more behind him."

Anything more he might have had to say was interrupted as Demophon yelled in their comms, "Incoming!"

A second later, the floor shook, and another explosion sounded through the walls.

Scott briefly wondered if the stairwell was going to come crumbling down around them. But he didn't have time to worry about it. Either the explosion would bury them, or it wouldn't. In the meantime, he had a job to do.

Scott jumped down to the landing just as the maestro's victim fell to his knees, and Scott shoved him into the next Chosen One on the stairs around the corner. The new attacker stumbled, and Scott swung his blade. It slid across one of the man's SDA plates, slicing skin but doing no real damage beyond that. Scott didn't care. He wasn't as interested in a quick kill as he was in gaining the level footing of the stairwell's landing. It was the only place where he and Harris could stand side by side and face their opponents.

As the man he'd sliced retreated a step, Scott kicked the maestro's victim farther down. Harris stepped casually down beside him. "This is good strategy."

The second Chosen One stepped over his dead companion, and it was Scott's turn to show off. He called on the extra speed his adrenal pump afforded him and lunged.

CHAPTER 40

"**H**OLY SHYTE!" JORDIE'S VOICE HELD a note of panic. "I could use some help here!"

Amber leaned forward just in time to see Jordie's shotgun tumble from the third floor to the atrium below. A pair of MXP rounds had taken out the second-floor walkway, but the other pair had caused just as much damage to the third floor. And dangling from the crumbling edge of that third floor, Jordie frantically scrabbled to hang on.

"Scott! Amber! Someone?" Jordie's legs and lower torso hung over the edge, and she was sliding backward, frantically grasping for something to hang on to. But the slick surface of her ballistic armor, combined with the smooth cerami-steel floor, made gaining any traction almost impossible.

"A little busy here," Scott said into the comm, and Amber heard shouts and fighting in the background.

"I got it covered," Amber said. "Jordie, when I tell you, I want you to let go."

"You want what?" the woman screeched.

"There's still a solid ledge in front of the stairwell across from me. You know what my legs can do. You drop—I'll jump across and catch you as I move to the other side. We'll land on the opposite side. It'll be easy."

"No offense, Amber, but that's a terrible idea! You might have super legs and all, but your arms are still flesh and bone, and you're hardly any bigger than I am."

"You have a better idea?"

Jordie slipped a little more. She kicked her legs up, trying to catch on the jagged edge of the walkway but only succeeded in sliding farther down. "Shyte, shyte, shyte! No, I don't!"

Amber estimated how far the jump was. "Okay, on the count of three, you let go. I'll jump across, and the impact will knock us over to the ledge where Richard and CC went into the south stairwell."

"You sure you can do this?" Jordie said. The panic in her voice was obvious.

"I'm sure," Amber lied. "On three." She took a couple of steps back and made sure she had a path clear of loose debris. "One." She took another look up at Jordie. "Two." With one last look at the ledge across from her, she ran forward. Just as she reached the end of her walkway, she shouted, "Three!"

She was already in the air when Jordie let go of her precarious purchase on the third floor. Amber called desperately for the battle brain that let her see things in slow motion, but it came too slowly. By her best estimate, she was on a direct collision course with her falling target, but she couldn't be sure.

She flew, and Jordie, twisting as she fell, met Amber's eyes with wide-eyed terror. A second later, Amber slammed into her, propelled by the full power of her cybernetic legs. Jordie uttered a loud "Oof" as the wind left her lungs, and the collision shifted their trajectory toward the southern stairwell.

Battle brain now fully engaged, Amber could see they weren't going to make it. It looked like they were going to be about a meter short. She shoved Jordie back, planted both feet in the woman's chest, and kicked out.

For every action, there is an equal and opposite reaction. Amber's kick slammed Jordie into the south wall less than a meter above the floor. It shoved Amber farther away, though, several meters from the ledge and closer to the middle of the atrium below. She saw Jordie fall to the remains of the walkway even as Amber tucked into a roll and managed to get her feet beneath her. A split second later, she landed on the atrium floor. Stumbling on the loose rubble of shattered security gates and walkways, Amber barely kept her footing. She scanned the area around her. Blood and bodies littered the floor, and the Chosen Ones who had taken cover watched her land. Two of them charged from behind a receptionist's kiosk. Missy dropped the leading man as soon as he left his cover. Blood sprouted from his neck to the accompaniment of a short cacophonous burst from her carbine.

While Missy kept them busy, Amber spotted Jordie's shotgun on the floor to her right and dove for it. She grabbed and aimed in one smooth motion, and the man running at her skidded to a stop. He winced as Amber pulled the trigger. His eyes went wide as he slapped a hand over his chest. He believed, as Amber did, that he was about to receive a hole in his torso, courtesy of the weapon that had been decimating his companions. Neither of them counted on Jordie having a biometric lock on the shotgun.

Amber started to throw the weapon at him, thought better of it, and threw it up to the ledge where she'd dropped Jordie. The giant before her started toward her once more, only to fall to another barrage from Missy before he'd taken another step. Amber scanned the room to see four more men leaving cover to rush her. Two of them had been with the first two, behind the heavy secretary's station. The others had taken cover behind heavy stone planters near the entrance.

She drew her flame blades and activated them. "Missy or Jordie, I need you to take out the two to my south." Amber struggled to keep her voice even on the comm as she ran toward the two near the entrance.

"I got it," Missy said. "But Jordie's out cold."

Amber remembered her friend slamming into the wall. Then Missy's weapon screamed. The first of the Chosen Ones to Amber's south dropped to the floor, blood streaming from his head. Amber had never known how good a shot Missy was and was once more reminded of how much she'd underestimated her team.

Missy cursed. "Get out of there, Amber. I'm out of ammo!"

But Amber was already running toward the two attackers near the entrance, with another one coming at her from behind. Everyone was moving much too fast for her to change direction.

If they had been ordinary street bangers, she would have jumped at the first attacker and taken him down with a kick, counting on her cybernetics to take care of the man. But these were Chosen Ones, their strength and reaction time markedly enhanced by the nanites coursing through their bodies. They moved almost as fast as she did and were several times stronger. If one of them got a hand on her, she was dead.

"Anyone else"—Amber jumped over their heads—"finished in the…" She hit the wall behind the Chosen Ones, feet first, a few meters above where the MXPs had knocked a hole in her building. She kicked back. "Stairs?" It was a move she'd practiced many times since she'd gotten her new legs, and she was as graceful as any gymnast as she executed a backflip over the men's heads again and landed in front of the single man who had been charging her from behind.

"Sorry, Boss," Richard panted. "Having a rough time on our own in here."

"Same here," Scott panted.

Amber knew the first two attackers would be charging her from behind, but at least she only had a single opponent for the moment. Her move surprised him, but he recovered quickly and slashed at her. Just a week before, she would have ducked or tried to parry in an attempt to evade the strike. But the maestro's training took over. She pivoted her hips and slid to her adversary's right. She caught his blade with her left one and spun clockwise, slashing with her right as she came behind him. The glowing blade parted head from neck with very little resistance, leaving Amber facing the other two attackers.

She toggled her vox on and screamed at them, hoping her proximity would allow the speakers on her shoulders to at least slow them somewhat. But there was no indication it did anything.

Then Acamas spoke. "Sorry to be the bearer of bad news, Boss. You have about thirty more people running in from across the parking lot."

Amber glanced past her opponents to see their backup entering the fray. That was all she had time to see before her attackers reached her. Then it was all she could do to try to keep the first attacker between her and his partner. For despite the efficiency with which she had dispatched the other Chosen One, she knew she had little chance of surviving a true fight with two of them at the same time. Her only chance was to keep one of them away until she killed the other. And she had to get past both of them before the backup troops made it inside.

She whirled her glowing blades at her opponent, shifting position to keep him in the way of his partner. She saw an opening, ducked past him, and slashed at his partner even as she kicked back to strike between the first man's posterior and anterior thigh plates, as she had seen Harris do to Richard during training. Her blade slashed a smoldering cut down the man's chest in front of her. He screamed in anger and pain, but her attack failed to incapacitate him.

The man behind her, on the other hand, fell to the floor, grabbing at his leg where she had kicked him. She jumped away from them both, retreating, to gain a few seconds and assess her situation. One man charged. A ragged smoking slash ran diagonally from his left collarbone to just below his nipple. It didn't bleed—her blades cauterized as they cut—but she was sure it hurt like hells above. His companion moved a little slower, but it was obvious that her kick was more of an inconvenience than an actual wound.

She looked past them and saw the first of the backup team had reached the steps out front and were running up to the covered plaza just outside the entrance. Then she cursed. "Well, shyte. I'm about to be overrun here, folks. That means your Chosen Ones in the stairwells are going to have backup in about thirty seconds."

Richard grunted with the exertion of whatever fight he was waging as he yelled, "Get out of there, Amber. We'll hold them back in the stairs."

"I wish I could." She looked up at the jagged ledge above her. She hadn't paid attention to where she was relative to that walkway and had jumped well past it into the area just in front of the first-floor conference room. The ceiling was lower here, and there was no room for her to jump high enough to clear the Chosen Ones coming at her. "Looks like I backed myself into a corner. I don't have any way out at this point."

Movement to her right caused her to turn, and she blinked. A similar flicker to her left made her spin that way. Before she knew what was happening, the room was filled with people who appeared out of nowhere.

And all of them were her.

CHAPTER 41

As soon as they ducked through the door, Richard realized that he and CC Miller being together in a narrow stairwell was a tactical error. The two of them made a good team when fighting Chosen Ones because they were big enough to overwhelm them. They didn't have the speed of the Chosen Ones, but when the two of them teamed up on one, they were able to attack on two fronts. There wasn't room for that in here.

Demophon's shout and the following explosion eliminated any thought of going back, though. Their situation was what they were going to have to work with.

Richard was only a few steps down the dark stairwell when he heard Scott on the comms, asking Dem to turn on the lights. Lights flared to life, illuminating the first of the Chosen Ones rounding the landing below them. There was only one thing Richard could think to do. He snicked the razors out from the tips of his fingers and jumped down the stairs. He slammed into the Chosen One, catching him by surprise and driving him back.

Richard felt the man's sword slide across his heavy ballistic armor and was thankful for the new material. Despite the Chosen One's enhanced speed and strength, Richard's armor offered little purchase for his blade. Richard drove the man back into his companions, their size presenting the same problem for them as Richard and CC faced. He alternated between slicing with his fingertips and shoving back with his sheer strength.

It was slow, but he was able to gain ground one stair at a time. They were only a few steps above the landing when Richard saw his opening.

He slammed into his opponent, shoving him into the wall at the back of the landing and driving his fingers into the man's throat. Holding tight to the bleeding man, Richard spun and shoved him back into CC's reach. A quick jab from CC propelled the spike in his gauntlet into the dying man's chest.

In a feat of raw strength, Miller lifted the lifeless body over his head, squeezed past Richard, and launched it down the stairs into the other Chosen Ones. That slowed them for the moment, and CC charged into them, his vox unit deafening as it echoed in the stairwell.

The man immediately in front of CC squinted as if he couldn't see, and Richard remembered Missy explaining how the subaudial frequency they were mixing into the deafening vox setup could cause a person's eyes to vibrate.

CC took advantage of the momentary distraction and drove his gauntlet into the hand the man held over his eyes. With a quick flex of his wrist, CC plunged his gauntlet's spike into the man's skull. He relaxed his wrist, and the spike snicked back into place, spring-loaded and ready for his next challenger. The lifeless Chosen One fell to the landing, and his companions paused as if finally realizing that the men before them were not the easy prey they had expected.

Over his comm, Richard heard Amber instructing Missy or Jordie to fire on someone in the atrium, but he couldn't afford to pay attention. In front of him, CC managed to latch onto the Chosen One in the lead. He took several powerful blows during the melee but yanked the man up the stairs. Once he saw an opening, Richard leaned in, grabbed the man, and dragged him away from CC. Fingers tipped with razors shredded the man's arm as Richard pulled him onto the landing, eliciting screams of fury.

The Chosen One stabbed over and over, but Richard's armor held. Then the man changed tactics and sliced back along Richard's arm. In the split second it took for Richard to realize what the man was doing, he had already lost two fingers off his right hand, and it was his turn to scream. But Richard's scream was backed by the vox unit and fear frequency. His opponent stepped back at the assault on his ears.

Seeing his chance, Richard pounced, ignoring the pain in his hand, jabbing over and over with right and left, raking razors at the dodging man's eyes and throat until he found the final opening. He jabbed the fingers of his left hand into the man's armpit and twisted, razors severing every tendon as well as the axillary artery. The Chosen One's right arm went limp, and the blade in that hand dropped to the floor.

Richard slashed again, this time connecting with his neck. Three razors severed the carotid on the same side of his neck as his useless arm. The man tried desperately to apply pressure to the right side of his neck with his left hand, but doing so left him completely defenseless. Richard knew the man's nanites would try to staunch the flow, but with a wound like that, he doubted they would be able to. He felt a moment of pity. Then the throbbing in his hand reminded him that he'd just lost at least two fingers.

Richard reached down with his left hand, snatched the man's short sword off the floor, and slammed the blade up at an angle between two plates of the man's SDA. He had seen it in past fights. There were limits to what the nanites could repair before the host died. A sword through the heart was beyond them. He turned to see how CC was doing.

Amber's voice called over their comms. "Anyone else…" There was a short pause. "Finished in the…" Another pause made Richard wonder what she was doing. "Stairs?"

"Sorry, Boss." Richard winced as he reached left-handed for the med kit strapped to the small of his back. "Having a rough time on our own in here."

He heard Scott answer similarly.

Seconds later, Acamas spoke. "Sorry to be the bearer of bad news, Boss. You have about thirty more people running in from across the parking lot."

Comms went quiet for several seconds as they all concentrated on their own battles. Then Amber spoke to them all again. "Well, shyte. I'm about to be overrun here, folks. That means your Chosen Ones in the stairwells are going to have backup in about thirty seconds."

That concerned him. He'd never heard Amber sound so… resigned. "Get out of there, Amber. We'll hold them back in the stairs."

"I wish I could. Looks like I backed myself into a corner. I don't have any way out at this point."

Dozens of lifelike Ambers charged the two Chosen Ones, screaming and drawing their flame blades as they moved. Amber stared, slack-jawed, at the chaos until Demophon spoke in her ear.

"I have you on a separate channel, Amber. Acamas and I can keep them distracted with holos, but you still have to take them out. And I suggest you move with the holos so you aren't the only one standing still."

Amber grinned savagely at the unexpected reprieve. She recalled how real the projectors at the Glads had been. Acamas and Dem's "father," T-bone, had been so lifelike that she'd thought for a moment he'd hijacked a body. That had been months ago, but she still remembered how disorienting it had been. Now that Jordie and Acamas had acquired and installed the same kind of system throughout the PSC building, there was no way for the Chosen Ones to know which of the rushing Ambers was real. She jumped to the side, removing herself from her original position and mixing with dozens of holograms.

The Chosen Ones swung wildly at any hologram that came near them, their blades passing harmlessly through empty air. As each target proved to be nothing more than photons and sound waves, they began to hesitate, unsure of themselves.

Amber continued to maneuver until she managed to get behind the rearmost opponent. As they had all learned, a strike to the chest, back, or abdomen was often an exercise in futility. Most bangers made sure to protect vital organs with the best SDA they could afford. But there was no way they could protect their necks and throats with that level of shielding. Not without losing the ability to swivel their heads. That made for a relatively small but quite vulnerable target.

She lunged from behind, plunging her weapon through her target before he even knew what was happening. Still facing away from Amber, his partner wouldn't even have known what was going on if not for the clatter of her victim's sword as it dropped from lifeless fingers.

The other man spun and lunged with all the speed at his nanite-enhanced disposal. Ignoring his dead comrade, he slammed a blade into Amber's with so much force that her blade sliced completely through the neck in which it was still embedded and flew across the room.

Amber's hand went numb with the force of the blow, and she whipped her left blade at the man. But unlike most of his companions, this man had skills beyond the speed and strength his nanites gave him. He also had training. Instead of stepping back, out of range of her blade, he jumped toward Amber and grabbed her by the wrist. Before she could shift her grip, he slung her into the wall behind her, knocking the wind from her lungs. She was stunned for only a second, but it was all the time he needed. Before she could recover, the Chosen One was on her. He stripped her remaining blade from her hand and lifted her by her throat, holding her out as far as his longer reach allowed as he squeezed her neck beneath the rim of her helmet.

She kicked as hard as she could, but in her position, her only target was the hardened SDA of the giant's chest, and all she succeeded in doing was kicking her lower body away from the man. His grip on her throat tightened, and she heard a crackling in her ears, accompanied by intense pain in her throat. She tried to cough but couldn't draw the breath to do so. Her vision began to narrow, darkening at the edges as consciousness receded. She couldn't hear anything over the blood pounding in her ears, and she clawed at the hand that held her aloft. The last thing she saw before her vision went completely black was the snarl on the Chosen One's face as he continued choking the life out of her.

Then he dropped her. Her head suddenly pounding with returning blood, Amber looked dizzily up at the man as he swayed. She still couldn't get a decent breath, and there was something very wrong with her vision still, because she could only see part of his head. Dem was shouting into her comm, and a loud but somehow distant explosive crack sounded at the same time. And all around, sounds of screaming and shouting got steadily louder.

"Get up, Amber! They're almost on you!" Dem sounded more panicked than she had ever heard him, and she started to look around just as the Chosen One, who had scant seconds before been choking the life out of her, fell to the floor beside her. She blinked at the sight, suddenly realizing that his head hadn't been an illusion. Most of the left side of it was missing. Blood, and worse, poured out as he hit the floor.

"Amber! Get up!"

The rest of the organ jackers, who were there as backup for the Chosen Ones—the so-called specialists—were just breaching PSC's shattered entrance. She staggered to her feet and looked up. If she could have, she might have sobbed with relief as she saw that the ledge of the northern walkway where she had started was within reach now. But she still couldn't draw in more than the tiniest sip of air. There was something terribly wrong with her throat. She was in no condition to fight any longer. In fact, she was pretty sure she was about to lose consciousness. Swaying only a little, Amber jumped before that happened.

CHAPTER 42

Scott heard Amber tell Richard that she was pinned in. Two Chosen Ones stood between him and his friend. He lunged and slashed with renewed energy, knowing her life might depend on how quickly he made it through these final opponents. He blinked his vox back to restricted comm and spoke to Harris beside him. "Be ready, Maestro. I'll go high to draw his guard."

"I am going low when I see opening."

Scott toggled back to his external speakers, maxed out his volume, and screamed as he swung at the Chosen One's head. The Chosen One raised his blade to block just as Harris slipped in from behind Scott and skewered the man through his left eye. He was dead as he began to drop.

Scott kicked him back, and the body thumped down the stairs toward their last opponent. To Scott's utter amazement, Maestro Harris jumped forward, landed on the chest of the falling banger, and rode him like a hoverboard. The final Chosen One did his best to overcome this unorthodox attack. He tried to sidestep, as much as the confines of the stairwell allowed, and used his enhanced speed, stepping back and slashing his blade in a flurry of wild attacks.

Even with his speed and strength, the man was no match for the maestro. Rather than even attempt to block the attacks, Harris dodged and shifted his position as he deflected and redirected the more powerful strikes—all while surfing down the stairs on the body of a dead man. Scott had never seen anything like it.

Seconds later, the last Chosen One was as dead as his companions.

Scott rushed down the stairs, avoiding the bodies as he hurried to catch up with the sword master standing at the bottom.

They burst out of the stairwell into chaos. Dozens of men and women rushed through the shattered front of the building, oblivious to the two swordsmen who stepped into their midst. It didn't last, of course. One of the jackers saw Scott and snarled.

Scott returned the snarl, his vox unit amplifying it, distorting it, and mixing the subaudial fear-inducing frequency that had worked so well in the confines of the stairwell. It didn't work as well in the open atrium, but it was still enough to wipe the expression from his opponent's face.

Scott slid to the side at an angle and slashed with his sword as he went past the man, leaving him dying before he knew what had happened. He ducked and lunged toward the next invader, who suffered a similar fate. A man fell to the floor to his right, and Scott whipped his head around to see the maestro drop another man. Looking back, Scott saw six bodies bleeding out. He had only dropped two of them.

Harris looked at him, grinned, and brought his blade up in a quick salute.

"Now, this is more like it!" Scott yelled above the bellowing. He turned to find two jackers running at him. It was almost too easy, though. They weren't Chosen Ones. Most of them weren't even street bangers. Scott easily felled the two and looked at the crowd around them.

Many of the jackers had some basic fighting mods—spikes, arm blades, and the like. Some even had specialized weapons. He saw one man whose arm ended with a spiked flail rather than a hand. But with his adrenal pump, none of them were any match for Scott. If not for their sheer numbers, he wouldn't have had the slightest concern. But there were so many of them, and as he and Maestro Harris drew more attention to themselves, the crowd shifted toward them.

He and Harris continued to drop one opponent after another, but even so, they quickly found themselves being backed to the wall. To make matters worse, Scott heard the beeping of his adrenal pump warning in his left ear. He had less than five minutes of speed left before he crashed.

"Maestro?" he called over the comm. "I hate to do this to you, but I'm afraid you're going to lose me in a few minutes. My pump is running dry."

There was a short pause as Harris dispatched another opponent. "Pump?" he asked. "This is the device giving you your speed?"

"Yep." Scott dodged and slashed another hapless opponent. "I'm getting a warning that it's running low."

"What I can do?"

"Nothing, I'm afraid. If it runs completely dry, my body will crash. I'll lose consciousness within seconds. And under these conditions…"

"We die."

"Well, I do."

"And without you to my back, I will follow."

"Shyte."

Scott risked a quick look behind himself, hoping to find the door to the stairwell. If they could get back to those restricted confines, they could limit the number of opponents they had to face at any one time. But he and Harris had come too far into the atrium, and there were too many jackers between them and the stairwell.

"This might have been a mistake, Maestro."

The maestro's wry chuckle came through his comm. "I am thinking you are correct." The two men turned back-to-back, covering one another and slicing at anyone who got within range. For the moment, the fight was almost a standoff, but the beeping in his ear told Scott it wouldn't last.

He felt Harris move away, heard him grunt as he launched another attack, and then he was back .

"Scott? Maestro Harris?" It was getting hard to hear above the shouting mass around them, and Scott had to blink the volume up on his helmet's internal speakers.

"Dem, is that you?"

"Yes. I need you to move farther into the atrium. I think we have some help if you can move closer to the center of the room."

"That might be a problem. I'm running out of—"

"I know. I heard. So you don't have time to argue. Get your asses to the middle of the room. Now!"

He'd never heard Demophon speak like that. "Aye, aye, Captain. Moving toward the middle of the room. You ready, Maestro?"

"I am always being ready."

He and Harris began a shifting, twisting dance, applying pressure on their opponents in the direction they wanted to go, allowing them to shift around to further separate them from the staircase. On one turn, Scott thought he could see the headlights of approaching vehicles, and he hoped that was the help Demophon had spoken of. If so, though, he feared they were too far away to do him any good. And if it was reinforcements for the organ jackers... well, he was dead either way.

The beeping in his ear sped up. Two-minute warning. In two minutes, his pump would run dry. His body would lose the pharmacologically sustained rush of adrenaline, and he would immediately begin to feel the worst case of the shakes and energy drain. Within seconds, he would lose consciousness, and the mob around them would rush in.

Well, at least I won't be awake when they kill me. It was scant consolation, but he would take what he could get.

"Stop there," Dem said. "Whatever you do, neither one of you step to your left or right."

"What?"

But the AI fell silent.

The beeping in Scott's ear didn't. It sped up to the final audio-warning level. He had one minute.

He continued to slice and dice, dropping opponents, driving others back, all while trying to maintain his position. But fighting this many people while confining himself to a single area of floor space was more difficult than one might imagine. A second later, he saw why it was so important, though.

He shifted the slightest bit to his right to face a large man rushing in from that direction. Scott pivoted and slashed... just as the man's head exploded into a mess of blood and tissue. Life strings cut, the body dropped.

Another man died similarly, and Scott heard the distant crack of a rifle. Two more fell before the jackers began to understand what was happening.

Then the door to the southern stairwell slammed open, and the gigantic armored form of CC Miller burst into the atrium. Richard followed right behind him. The two of them shouted and rushed at the jackers from behind.

Four Securi-Tech armored personnel carriers bounced up the stairs and into the plaza outside the shattered entrance. Armed men and women poured out of them before they had fully stopped.

The beeping in Scott's ear stopped. He reached into his pocket and grabbed the green popper he knew was there. Vision swimming, hand shaking, he slapped the popper against his neck as his knees went weak and he fell to the floor.

CC continued to wreak havoc on the remaining Chosen Ones on the stairs below and showed no sign of slowing down. Richard's concerns about them not being up to the task of taking on Chosen Ones in a one-on-one situation proved to be unfounded. The new Fixer armor compensated for the fact that they were slower and—in Richard's case—not quite as strong as the nanite-enhanced street bangers trying to force their way up the stairs.

Seeing that his partner had the fight under control for the moment, Richard fell back to treat his wound. He was pouring a coagulant powder over the bleeding mess where his fingers had been when Dem spoke in his ear.

"Richard, Amber's on a different channel. She's not moving, though, or answering comms. I don't have any way to tell how badly she's hurt, but it's safe to say that she's out of the fight for now. Scott and Harris just got into the atrium, but it's just the two of them against nearly forty organ jackers. I figure that leaves you running the show."

"Shyte." Richard slapped a medicated adhesive over his hand as he spoke. "What about Missy and Jordie? What's their status?"

"Missy's out of ammo, and Jordie's unconscious. Amber's stunt saved her, but it also threw her into the wall hard enough to knock her out. I can use the holos…"

Richard's comm went silent without warning. He reached up to tap his earbud, forgetting for a second about his helmet. "Damn it. Dem? What's going on?" Richard blinked through his menu, checking diagnostics on his comms. "CC, you good?"

The huge Fixer's reply was broken, accentuated by grunts of exertion. "Yeah. Just… a little… busy."

So his comms were working. That meant something had happened on Demophon's end. He was about to call out again when Dem spoke.

"The cavalry is on the way," he said. "Mikey's already in place in the building across the parking lot, and four APCs are rolling up the drive."

"Mikey? Who the hells is Mikey?"

"The Securi-Tech sniper that helped you guys out at Jolly's last year."

He vaguely remembered the young kid who'd picked off Amber's pursuers when she'd run the custom-made gauntlet in a junkyard, leading the Storm Bringers—an early version of the Chosen Ones—into a trap.

"Yeah, I remember him. Helluva shot."

"He is. Turns out he's the reason Amber is still with us. He just took out a Chosen One from the roof of the building across the campus."

Richard snorted. "Campus? We have a campus now?"

"We can argue semantics later. That last Chosen One was choking the life out of her. Mikey got a clean head shot from the roof of the next building over. It was a perfect shot from nearly four hundred meters."

Richard finished wrapping his hand and stood. "You're in communication with him?"

"Yes."

"Can you patch him in where I can talk to him?"

Richard peeked around the corner to check on CC. The man still appeared to have the situation under control, so Richard held back to talk to their backup.

A click and a short beep indicated a new connection. "Mikey? This is Richard Kayani. You remember me?"

"Yes, sir. You were the big banger running overwatch at the junkyard last year."

"That's me. My security guy tells me you have eyes on the situation in our building. I'm stuck in the south stairwell for the moment. Can you give me a quick report?"

"Yes, sir. I see a mob pushing in toward the north wall of your building. They're gathering around something I can't see from here."

"That," Dem interjected, "would be Scott and Maestro Harris. I'm watching through the security cams and monitoring their comms. Scott's getting a warning that his pump is about to go dry."

Richard recalled Scott telling him about that once. He didn't remember the specifics but knew it was bad. In their current situation, it was likely fatal.

"Mikey, can you help them out?"

"All I can do from here is pick off the people at the back of the crowd. If I'm really going to help them, I need them to get closer to the south wall."

Richard nodded. The south wall was also closer to him and CC. "Dem, tell them to move position."

"On it."

"Mikey, how far out are the rest of our reinforcements?"

"Pulling into your parking area now."

The new voice was more familiar. Richard had worked side by side with Charles Walker during that same Storm Bringer op. He was the head of Securi-Tech's search-and-rescue teams but also had a long background in the military. "Commander Walker? Is that you?"

"It is. We heard you guys were throwing another party."

"Yeah," Richard said, "and we've got crashers. Think you can help with that?"

"Just tell me where you want us."

"You see where the front door used to be? Just drive up the fuggled steps out front. I want every son-of-a-whore party crasher either dead or in custody right away."

"You got it."

"Dayum!" Mikey said.

"What is it?" Richard knew the kid was watching the crowd in the atrium. "Are my guys okay?"

"Sorry. Yeah. They're in position now. But I gotta say, those are two of the most badass bladesmen I've ever seen." His voice took on a more professional tone. "Is it safe to assume you want me to lend them a hand?"

"Do it. And, Mikey? Me and my buddy are going to be coming out of the south stairwell in a minute. Please don't shoot us."

Mikey chuckled. "Roger that. Now, let me go to work."

CHAPTER 43

From there, it was mostly a cleanup operation. Amber was seriously injured and unconscious on the second-floor landing near the north stairwell door, and Scott was barely alive on the atrium floor after running his pump completely dry. Jordie had a concussion, and an EMT was treating a serious knot on the back of her head where she had slammed into the wall.

With Amber, Scott, and Jordie all out of commission, Richard was left handling the final details, and some of them had to be acted on immediately. Unfortunately, there was an obstacle to his plans. Math.

He needed to act on behalf of PSC. Dem and Acamas each held five percent, while Richard and Scott each held twenty. That meant he only had fifty percent of PSC behind his actions until one of the others returned. He knew he couldn't wait, though.

He removed his helmet, looking around at the remains of the fight. There was rubble and debris everywhere. Bodies and worse were scattered as well. Walker and his men watched over what remained of the organ jackers. All the Chosen Ones were beyond needing help. None had survived.

He tapped the earbud. "Dem, Acamas, did either of you detect one of those encrypted comm signals going in or out of here?"

"No," Acamas replied. "I've been keeping watch over the whole area."

"So it's possible whoever is running the show doesn't know they lost."

"Possible, yes," Dem said. "But it's just as possible that there were instructions to call in once the job is done, and the lack of a call will let them know."

Richard nodded. "Then we have to move fast." He spent a few seconds giving the two AIs some rough instructions then located Commander Walker.

Walker looked up at his approach. "I heard Fem Payne was injured," he said by way of greeting.

"She and Scott both," Richard said. "That's part of why I wanted to talk to you. I… we need your help for a little longer."

Walker pursed his lips. "From what I understand, our contract tonight ends with the protection of this building and the apprehension of any attackers we might encounter."

"Yes, sir. And I'm asking if we can extend that contract somehow. I have a very time-sensitive situation, and with most of my team down, I could use some extra manpower."

Walker grinned. "Well, seeing how you already robbed us of most of the fun at this party before we got here, it seems only fair you should take us to another one." He pulled a nondescript comm unit from his pocket. "Let me call the chief."

"Is that a burner?"

Walker nodded. "Fischer said it might be best if we kept some of the details of tonight's operation off the books. Your boss lady has sort of a bad reputation with the higher-ups back at HQ."

"Yeah, all of us here at PSC do." He eyed Walker's burner. "So anything on that thing stays private?"

"Far as I know, yes."

"Come with me, then." Richard led Walker across the rubble to the main conference room. As they entered, Richard called out, "Hecter, connect Demophon and Acamas."

The AIs appeared almost immediately. "Dem, Acamas, meet Commander Charles Walker."

"It's a pleasure," Acamas said.

"Yeah, what she said." As usual, Dem was less formal. He looked at Richard. "What can we do for you?"

"I've asked Commander Walker to extend the terms of our contract far enough to lend us some manpower for a few more hours. He says he needs to confirm it with Chief Fischer, and he has a burner phone he wants to use. They're trying to keep any reference to Amber out of Securi-Tech records."

"Sounds smart," Acamas said. "What's it have to do with us?"

"First, can you use his comm to put us in a conference with Fischer?"

"Sure." Dem waved a hand at the table. "Use the contact port at the end of the table. Put the comm unit on it, and we can take it from there."

Richard held up his hand. "Before you do, did Amber ever commit to buying out those contracts we discussed?"

Acamas raised one holographic eyebrow. "She did, although the timing is still a little up in the air. You planning to discuss it now?"

Richard looked at Walker, weighing his options. "Commander Walker. If someone were to hypothetically offer to buy out your contract and give you the chance to work with a newly formed security firm with full benefits, a twenty percent bump in pay, and a chance to build your own teams from the ground up, would it be something you might be interested in?"

Walker grinned. "Hypothetically? I think I might be *very* interested."

"And Mikey?"

The older man thought for a second then nodded. "I think he might be interested as well. Hypothetically, that is."

Richard smiled. "Then let's contact Fischer."

Walker sobered. "That man is one of the few people there I would miss." He looked up at Richard. "If this hypothetical were to ever happen."

"Well, we couldn't have that, could we?" He put his hand out for the comm unit. "Let's give the chief a call to discuss things."

CHAPTER 44

RICHARD LEANED AGAINST THE WALL, dressed in old clothes. He'd left his armor behind to better blend in with the locals. The comm bud in his ear buzzed, and Demophon spoke. "This is Cyber One. We have an incoming encrypted stream. Intercepting now."

There was a short pause before Dem continued. "Got it. Decrypting. Message reads, '*Operation status update?*'"

"This is Street One," Richard said. "Let it through."

"Roger that."

"Cyber," Richard said. "Any hits on your spiders for that location?"

"Negative," Dem said. "Not yet. Narrowing it down, though."

A second later, Missy told them, "Peeper One here. Looks like she got it. She's typing a response." He knew Missy was tied into the security cams inside the bar. She would be watching their target and reporting everything she did.

"Stick to the plan," Richard said. "Do not let that message through."

"On it."

"Outgoing message intercepted," Dem said. "Decrypting. Message reads *Report is late. Assuming failure. Instructions?*"

Richard thought quickly. They had expected this and planned a few possible replies. "Send message one."

"Sending message one."

Acamas had already encrypted a few different messages. He'd instructed her to keep their current target from sending her report of failure. In its place, she sent a message—message one—that claimed they had overwhelmed their "target" with minimal casualties.

Three minutes went by. It was all Richard could do to keep himself from pacing back and forth in the street. Finally, Dem reported, "Incoming message intercepted. Decrypting." After a second, he cursed. "I think we blew it. The message wants a protocol number."

"Shyte!" Richard tried to think of what kind of reply they could send to keep the conversation going. Ideally, they wanted enough exchanges to let Dem's spiders trace the origin of the comm signal the same way he had done to find Lucienne's.

"Let me try," Acamas said. "It probably won't work, but it might buy us another exchange or two."

"Do what you want," Richard told her. "You can't make it worse than we already have. In the meantime, send the banger in Lucienne's instructions for our meeting."

"I'll do that," Dem said, "while Cyber Two tries to stretch the conversation with the big boss."

There was a short pause before Acamas replied. "Message away. I just manipulated their message from yesterday. I told them *Protocol five, level extreme.* Hopefully, it'll at least get a request for clarification. That'll be one more try for the spiders."

Richard sighed. He'd known the chances of everything going just right were slim. But he'd hoped to get a bit more on where to find the "big boss," as Dem had called them.

"She's receiving Cyber One's message," Missy reported. A few seconds later… "She's paying her bill. Everyone in position?"

Richard looked around, making sure no one was around to see or hear him. He tapped his earbud. "Street One is ready."

CC was next. "Street Two ready."

Walker's gruff voice spoke. "Detention is ready."

"Cyber Two is ready," Acamas said.

Then Mikey piped up. "Guys, I don't like my call sign. I want something cool… like Eagle Eye, or something like that."

"So noted," Dem replied. "Now, are you ready?"

"Yeah. Eagle Eye is ready."

Richard rolled his eyes.

"Well, now that that's established," Dem said, "Peeper One, is the target moving?"

"Just leaving her table now. Exiting the building in three... two... one..."

The door opened just as Richard reached for the handle. "Oh, sorry, fem." He held up his bandaged hand. "Guess I'm still a little clumsy. Can you believe the fuggled street doc messed me up so bad?"

The woman glanced at his hand, frowning at the blood soaking through the bandages. While she was concentrating on the mess of Richard's hand, CC Miller stepped up behind her and slapped a popper against her neck. She spun, quick as... well, quick as a Chosen One and slammed a fist into CC's face. He staggered half a step back before lunging back in. Richard hit her from behind, and the two of them struggled to hold on while Mikey shouted, "Hold her still, for Buddha's sake!"

For the longest three seconds of his life, Richard struggled to hold the woman still while the cocktail in the popper worked through her bloodstream. Now that she'd confirmed that she was nanite enhanced, he knew they were on a short timer. Within a minute or less, her nanites would break down the sedative that was trying to slow her down, and she would be back to full strength, speed, and health. On top of that, she would be pissed.

A dart appeared to spring from her neck, right in front of Richard's eyes. Mikey's handiwork. It was a macrodose of a stronger sedative—something that would hopefully slow even her down enough for Walker and his team to get more traditional restraints on her.

The combination of the popper, Mikey's dart, and the exertion of fighting against Richard and CC finally did the trick, and she slumped in CC's arms. Walker jumped out of the APC and ran forward, holding a mask. He strapped it over the woman's face and opened the nozzle on the attached tank.

"That should do it."

"Let's hope so." CC wiped his bleeding nose. "But I suggest you keep her out until we can deactivate her nanites."

Walker looked at the giant banger. "Believe me, I'm not taking chances with anyone who can give you two a run for your money."

Richard looked around. As long as the altercation might have seemed, he knew the entire thing had taken less than a minute. "Peeper One, anyone coming out?"

"Not yet. You're still clear."

Richard and CC hefted the heavily augmented woman into the back of the Securi-Tech APC. When they had her shackled in place with triple restraints, the two bangers stepped back out and closed the heavy door.

He turned to Walker. "You guys still have the old MRI in the basement?"

The older man shrugged. "Hells if I know."

"Then you'll want to contact Karen Allen in Forensics. She's the one who worked out the process for deactivating the nanites. Until you get that done"—he jerked a thumb, indicating the prisoner inside—"that woman in there is death on a stick."

"I'll comm the chief as soon as we're on the road."

"Got a pair of degenerates heading for the door," Missy reported. "You better get that carrier out of here."

Walker slapped Richard on the shoulder. "Gotta go. See you soon though."

Richard grinned. "Hypothetically."

The old man laughed and ran to the front of the carrier. He slapped the side as he climbed in, and the vehicle sped away into the barely lit predawn streets.

DAY 10
THURSDAY

CHAPTER 45

Amber awoke to the faint beeping of the diagnostics panel in a Doc Box. The last thing she could remember was having the life choked out of her by a Chosen One. She opened her eyes to see the green indicator on the panel above her. She didn't bother reading her report. She felt well enough, and the green light told her she was cleared to exit.

Physically, she felt fine. She felt better than fine. Her body was rested, and the Box had balanced any abnormalities in her blood chemistry and injected her with whatever vitamins or hormones it thought she was even the slightest bit low on. Even after all that, though, she was still emotionally drained.

She tapped the release button above her right hand, and the lid of the Box opened. Naked, she stepped out of the coffin-like chamber and saw a change of clothes on a bench in front of her. She recognized the room and knew someone had brought her to the med bay at Fixer HQ.

As she got dressed, she looked at the other Doc Boxes in the room. Two were in the reclined position, indicating they were still in use. She slipped her shirt on as she walked to the first one. The readout told her Scott Pond was inside. She thumbed the diagnostics button to see if she was authorized to see his status. As his team lead, she was. She read through the list of wounds he had sustained. Most of them were fairly minor lacerations. The only redline event on his chart was in the custom-mods column. He had run his pump completely dry. She knew this, in and of itself, wasn't a life-threatening event. But it must have happened during the middle of their fight, and *that* could easily have been fatal.

"He'll be fine." Jordie's voice from the doorway startled Amber. "It'll take him another day or so to replenish the tank, but he'll probably be out of the Doc Box in another few hours. He'll just be tired, cranky, and shaky while his adrenal gland works overtime."

Amber nodded. "Anyone else hurt?"

Jordie pointed to the second Doc Box. It was one of the larger units, so she wasn't surprised when Jordie told her, "Richard."

"How bad?"

"He lost some fingers. They found them in the stairwell, but we don't know if the Box will be able to reattach them or if he'll be able to use them if they can."

"Why not? Finger reattachment should be easy enough."

"Unless you wait too long to get into the Box. There were four or five hours between the time he lost them and when he finally slowed down enough for Gibbs to order him into Medical."

"Four hours?"

Jordie looked a little worried. "Yeah. A few things happened while you, me, and Scott were out."

"Wait a second. You too?"

"Yeah. Your stunt slammed me into the wall hard enough to knock me out. It wasn't all that bad, but the concussion earned me an hour or so in a Box."

"Shyte. I'm sorry."

Jordie shook her head. "Don't be. If you hadn't done it, I'd probably be dead. I figure I got off easy. At least I have all my limbs and digits." She held up her hands and wiggled her fingers as if to demonstrate. "And"—she dropped her hands, looking serious—"I didn't have to get trached in the back of a moving vehicle."

"Trached? Who had to…?" Amber trailed off at Jordie's meaningful stare. She remembered the agony when the Chosen One had squeezed her throat—the feeling of not being able to breathe even after he released her. Her hand slowly went to her own throat, and Jordie nodded.

Gibbs interrupted as she walked through the door. "Technically," she corrected, "it was a cricothyrotomy, not a tracheotomy. Either way, though, they had to cut your throat and shove a tube in it. And I have to admit, there've been a few times I've wanted to do that myself."

Amber blinked at the sudden appearance of Fem Gibbs. Suddenly self-conscious, she pulled her hand away from her throat and bit back the smart-assed reply that was her first reaction. This was her boss. Amber had accepted the Fixer contract. That was part of it. And like it or not, her relationship with Gibbs wasn't the same as what she'd had with Chief Fischer. It was new, and the two of them were still learning their boundaries with one another.

"Ah… hi, Boss. What can I do for you?"

"Assuming you're up for it, you can join me and the rest of your team for an informal debrief." And she turned without another word, leaving Amber and Jordie to catch up.

The three of them were silent as they walked the busy halls of Fixer HQ, and Amber couldn't help but notice the eyes that followed them. Those eyes told her that word of their case had made the rounds, but she couldn't tell if everyone was concerned for her safety or if they thought she had fuggled it all up.

She and Jordie followed Gibbs into a small conference room where Maestro Harris and CC Miller already waited. Harris stood and stepped to Amber. To her surprise, he kissed her on either cheek. "*Bom ver-te*, Fem Payne! *Tudo bem?*"

"She's fine," Gibbs snapped before Amber could even ask what he'd said. She walked around the conference table to take a seat opposite the rest of them.

Harris was unfazed, smiling as he nodded to Amber. "Good. It is nice to be seeing you once more on the feet."

"Thank you, Maestro."

"I said she's fine. Now, sit down, and let's go through all this."

There was a light knock, and Missy slipped in without a word. She moved quickly to sit beside Jordie.

Gibbs wasted no time, pulling out a tablet and tapping the screen. "Fem Payne, the preliminary reports I read tell me your operation nearly cost us the lives of some valuable agents and the best damn unarmed combat instructor we have."

Amber restrained herself once more and took a deep breath. *Still the boss*, she reminded herself. "I don't deny it, though to be fair, we had no way of knowing there were Chosen Ones involved in any of this."

Gibbs stared at her for several seconds. Clearly, she'd been expecting an argument, and Amber's words had defused the situation. Gibbs gave Amber a grudging nod. "No, you didn't." She sighed. "None of us did. And for what it's worth, I doubt any of my more experienced teams would have fared any better than your people did."

Amber knew that was true. She and her team were the only ones besides Gibbs herself and Danel Ybarra, the surviving twin from last year's GMF operation, who had ever faced Chosen Ones and survived to tell about it.

"So how are you feeling? I know you just got out of the Box, but this wasn't exactly a normal situation. Are you up for this debrief?"

Amber nodded slowly. "Though I'm curious to know how you knew I was out."

Gibbs snorted. "You think I wouldn't have alerts set on the Boxes in my own house? Now, give me a step-by-step on what happened, from your perspective."

Amber went through it, bringing as much detail into her verbal report as she could, while Gibbs read through the documents on her tablet. Amber knew from her experiences at Securi-Tech that she was comparing Amber's words to what she already had from other sources. Once Amber reached the point at which she jumped away from the fight and lost consciousness, Gibbs nodded. "I have reports from the rest of your team, except Mr. Pond, of course. I'll expect a written report from you before the day is out."

Amber nodded.

Gibbs turned to Missy. "For Fem Payne's sake, would you please give a quick summary of occurrences from where Fem Payne left off?"

Missy took only a second to gather her thoughts. "I saw Amber jump to the second floor. She was directly under me, so I couldn't see her once she got there, but I could see Jordie was unconscious on the second floor across from me. I had no way to get to her, but I knew I could get to Amber through the stairwell. I went down and found her unconscious. She had significant bruising and swelling on her neck, and she was struggling to breathe. I reported over comms to Demophon and Acamas, who passed the information on to the Securi-Tech med team.

"They sent a man up, and I helped him while he treated her. I heard him when he reported over their channel that…" Missy stopped and shot Amber a quick glance before continuing. "He reported that she had stopped breathing. Her trachea and esophagus were crushed, and her vitals were…" She stopped again then looked at Amber once more. "You almost died."

Missy trailed off. After a second, she took a deep breath. "They performed an emergency cricothyrotomy to open an airway. Once you were stable, Maestro Harris insisted they load you, Jordie, and Scott in the back of Scott's half-track."

She started to continue, but Gibbs raised her hand and turned to Harris. "Maestro, please take over from there."

Harris shrugged. "There is little for me to be telling. I am calling Fixers' emergency *médicos* to meet me in loading bay while I am driving here. Emergency crew meeting me in loading bay, and they move Amber, Scott, and Jordie to *os caixões*."

"Oosh cai… shoish?" Amber struggled to repeat the phrase.

"Coffins," Gibbs said. "It's what they call Doc Boxes in Novo Brasil."

Amber blinked in surprise. She accepted that Boxes did look a lot like coffins, but the similarity between the two structures wasn't something most people would appreciate. At least, not the people she associated with. Changing the subject, she asked, "Can I ask something here?" At Gibbs's nod, she continued. "Jordie already told me that Richard didn't get in the Box at the same time Scott and I did." She pointed to Harris as she directed her question to Gibbs. "And Maestro didn't make any mention of bringing him here either. Why didn't—"

Gibbs interrupted. "Which brings us to Mr. Miller. He worked with Mr. Kayani for the follow-up operation."

Chastised, Amber clapped her mouth shut and nodded. "Sorry."

Gibbs nodded to Miller, who started his account. "After the maestro left with the wounded, Richard worked a deal with some of the Securi-Tech team leaders. I don't know the details, but I got the impression there was some backroom-style dealing going on."

Amber pursed her lips, wondering what kind of arrangements her partner might have made. As soon as the thought crossed her mind, she shrugged mentally. It didn't matter. Whatever Richard had promised, it had gotten the job done. She trusted him.

Miller continued to describe how they went after the woman who had been organizing the organ jackers from Lucienne's bar, how Acamas and Demophon had intercepted incoming and outgoing messages, and how the team ultimately had captured the suspect without letting her get word to her superiors, whoever they were, and had managed to narrow down the location of said superiors.

This was the first time Amber had heard this part of the story, and she was impressed with how Richard had pulled it all off. It once more drove home the fact that she hadn't trusted her people enough. When Miller finished his account, Amber turned to Gibbs expectantly.

"And that brings us to now." Gibbs steepled her fingers as she leaned forward, elbows on her desk. "Fem Payne, I don't know if you're aware, but you spent two days in that Doc Box."

Amber blinked at that. "Two days?"

"Yes. You're lucky the Boxes we have here are more robust than the standard."

Jordie hesitantly raised her hand. "Fem Gibbs, could I get the specs and manufacturer for those Boxes? We're looking at upgrading the facility at PSC."

After a short glare from Gibbs, Jordie lowered her hand. "Maybe later," she muttered.

"However out of place that question might have been, it does bring me to a point I wanted to discuss with you." Gibbs turned her attention back to Amber. "I understand you've escalated moving Payne Security Consultants up from a PI firm to full LEO status. I think that's a smart move as long as you think you can handle the business side of it. PSC will make a great cover for your Fixer cases."

Gibbs tapped on her tablet screen. "Your second-in-command, Mr. Kayani, also did well in recognizing a window of opportunity and getting the local ringleader before she could get away. That was well done."

Amber kept silent, not wanting to point out that, according to Missy's report, they didn't actually have the woman and that she was currently cooling her heels in a Securi-Tech detention cell.

Gibbs continued. "I know there is still some cleanup you have to do on this. But overall, you and your team did a good job. I've escalated these reports to the Fixer case files so we can pursue it officially from here."

Amber opened her mouth to speak then hesitated.

But of course, Gibbs saw. "What is it?"

"I just thought this wasn't a Fixer-level case."

"It wasn't. Not until you found us the link we needed."

Amber immediately knew what that link was. "The Chosen Ones."

Gibbs nodded. "And have you had time to think about the implications of how many of them attacked your building?"

Amber furrowed her brow at the question, not quite following. "No, fem. I haven't."

"How many doses of the nanites did Conley have before her attempt to take the GMF last year?"

Amber struggled to recall but finally had to shrug. "I'd have to look back over the files."

"I don't," Jordie said. "When we took out the Storm Bringers, there were twenty-six doses unaccounted for. Fourteen Chosen Ones at the GMF brings it down to a maximum of twelve. And that assumes each one was successful and there were no losses due to experimentation."

Amber blew out a breath as she understood. "So if twenty-five of them attacked us, that means someone has either found another source, or they've figured out how to make them on their own."

"And *that*," Gibbs said, "rises to the level of a Fixer case."

Amber didn't know whether to be upset or relieved. She quickly decided she'd be happy with whatever circumstance got them more help. Especially if it meant clear access to Fixer resources.

"Now, unless anyone has anything else…?" Gibbs made it sound like a question, but they all recognized it as the dismissal it was. As they stood to leave the conference room, Gibbs raised a finger to get Amber's attention. "Fem Payne, I'd like a moment in private if you don't mind."

Again, it was one of those questions that really wasn't. Amber sat back in her chair as the others filed out. When the two of them were alone, Gibbs began without preamble. "I hope you don't mind, but I took the liberty of contacting Mr. Pedde while you were in the Box. I told him your case had taken a turn and that I'd sent you out of town to chase a lead. I didn't think you would want him knowing how close he came to collecting survivor's benefits."

"Thank you, fem." Amber was grateful Gibbs had taken care of that. At the same time, she was more than a little chagrinned to realize that this was the first time she'd thought about Nathan since getting out of the Doc Box.

Gibbs waved it off. "That being said, you should probably take a few minutes and give him a call."

"I will."

"Fem Payne..." Gibbs hesitated as if uncertain of how to continue.

After a moment of silence, Amber prodded her. "Something else?"

Gibbs placed her hands flat on the conference table as if bracing herself. "Working in law enforcement is tough enough on a relationship. But working in a secret organization where you can't tell your significant other anything about what you do—it's damn near impossible to keep a relationship like that going. The truth is, I've never seen one survive more than a few years."

She raised a hand to forestall any comment. "I only say this to warn you. I don't *want* your relationship to fail, but the odds aren't in your favor. That being said, I am happy to make calls like the one I made to Nathan or do whatever else you think might help keep him happy. I genuinely want your relationship to succeed."

Amber sighed. Gibbs was just putting voice to a concern she'd had ever since she and Nathan had gotten serious. So far, she'd managed to avoid examining the situation too closely. She'd been afraid to. Now Gibbs was forcing her to take a cold, hard look at it.

Amber's job was one that kept her from working normal hours and took her into the line of fire. Worst of all, it forced her to keep secrets from the man she loved. If she was honest with herself, she'd have to say she had her own doubts about having a successful relationship. But to have it spelled out like this... it forced her to think about what she was asking of Nathan and of herself.

She swallowed, nodding slowly. Then she looked at Gibbs and smiled. "A few years, huh?"

Gibbs nodded. Then to Amber's surprise, she smiled back. "Prove me wrong, Amber. You like doing that, don't you?"

"I'll do my best, fem."

"Good. Now, I'm giving you all a week off. I suggest you use it to solidify that relationship you want to flaunt in my face. Call your man. Go spend some quality time with him."

Amber shook her head. "I appreciate that, but even without the fact that we've officially taken this case to the next level, I still have too much to do. I have building repairs, prisoner extraditions from Securi-Tech, floor plans to app—"

"Stop." Gibbs held up a hand. "The time off isn't a suggestion. It's mandatory. Now, I understand you and Fem Dyer have been working on new floor plans for PSC. Send them to me, and I'll get our contractors on it. They're fully vetted and are hand chosen for their discretion. Plus I already have them cleaning up the damage to your building."

That last surprised Amber, but Gibbs didn't give her time to interrupt.

"I've also arranged for them to work with you on expediting a Fixer-sanctioned detention facility. Documentation is already filled out."

Amber raised an eyebrow. "And the Doc Boxes Jordie asked about...?"

"Don't let her know, but I ordered them yesterday."

Amber chuckled. "Thanks, Chie... er, Fem Gibbs."

The other woman cocked her head to the side. "Did you almost call me Chief?"

"Yes, fem. An old habit."

"I'm familiar with Chief Fischer." At Amber's startled look, Gibbs shook her head. "Only from reading his files."

"There are times when you remind me of him," Amber said.

"I'll take that as a compliment."

"You should."

Gibbs smiled and stood. "All right. Just give me a list of the tasks that you absolutely can't put off. I'll make sure they're handled."

"Thank you, fem."

"I want that list from you within the hour. After that, you're officially on leave." She walked to the door. "But first, call Nathan." She walked out and left Amber with the privacy to do just that.

CHAPTER 46

Amber thought she would have to hire a rental to take her to PSC so she could retrieve her pod from the parking garage. But when she started to make the call, she found a message waiting on her tablet. Gibbs had arranged for someone to bring her pod to HQ the day before. It was waiting for her in the Fixers' parking garage. She was beginning to understand why Gibbs was in charge. The woman seemed to think of everything.

She pulled out of the parking garage and had just set the navcomp for home when her dash comm pinged. She engaged the autopilot and pressed Accept. "Payne here."

"Hey, Boss." Dem's face popped up on the screen. "Glad to see you up and around again."

"Thanks. How did you know I—"

"We've been watching for your pod. You just passed a street cam."

"We?"

The screen split, and Acamas appeared beside her brother. "We were concerned. Jordie has tried to keep us up to date on how you were doing, but she has to be discreet while she's at HQ."

Amber nodded. "Well, as you can see, I'm fine. So what can I do for you? If it can wait, I'm heading home for a few days."

"Good," Dem said. "Most of what we need can wait. A lot of it has to do with rebuilding PSC."

"Oh, yeah," Amber said. "Gibbs is sending specialized contractors to take over reconstruction and enhancements to the new campus."

"They're already here. So far, it's just been cleanup, but she just sent forms for the construction work. That presents a problem, though."

"How so?"

"Because it means canceling the contract we already approved, and to do that requires a sixty-five percent shareholder sign-off."

Amber was starting to wonder if setting PSC up as a legitimate business was going to be more trouble than it was worth. She sighed as she ran through the math. "Okay, so you need me and Jordie to sign off, right?"

"Just you. Jordie thumbed her approval yesterday."

"Fine. Send it to me."

Her dash comm pinged. "That should do it," Dem said. "Next item on the agenda…"

"I did mention I was taking a few days off, right?"

"You did. That's why I'm not going to mention any of the two dozen noncritical items on your agenda."

"You keep using that word."

"What word?"

"Agenda. Since when do I have agendas?"

"Since you became the CEO and major shareholder of a business."

Yep. Definitely more trouble than it's worth. "Okay, I have about thirty minutes until I get home. At that point, I'm going to shut off my comm for at least twenty-four hours."

"Don't worry. We won't need that long." The dashboard *message waiting* icon began to flash again. "I just sent you a detainee transfer form. You need to authorize prisoner transfers from Securi-Tech to the Watervault Detention Facility. Did you know Securi-Tech charges an outrageous rate to hold prisoners for their clients?"

"No. But it doesn't surprise me." Amber scanned the document on her screen. "Watervault? Never heard of them."

"That's probably because they didn't exist until now. I couldn't very well list Fixer HQ as the destination, could I?"

"I guess not." She thumbed the screen. "I assume you're covering any inquiries?"

"We'll watch for them," Acamas said. "But considering the fact that

Fischer is still trying to keep the case low-key on his end, I doubt there will be any."

"Okay," Amber said. "Next?"

Her dash pinged again.

"This document amends PSC bylaws to allow a simple majority to make decisions on behalf of the corporation in instances where multiple shareholders are incapacitated and a sixty-five percent quorum is unavailable."

"Yeah," Dem said. "Like when you, Scott, and Jordie are all unconscious."

Again, Amber pressed her thumb to the agreement. After that, there were surprisingly few items that demanded her attention. After only a few minutes, Dem said, "Last item. Chief Fischer sent a message yesterday to PSC's corporate contact account."

"Still trying to keep my name out of things, I assume."

"That's what we figured too."

"So what did he want?"

"He's requested a meeting with the PSC agent of record. Since I made up a name for that on the paperwork, I replied that the agent was wounded in action and is currently unavailable. I also told him they would contact him at their earliest convenience."

"Got it. I'll get back to him right away."

"Not a good idea if he's trying to keep you off the record. Let me know when you want to talk to him, and I'll have him contact you on one of his burners. The man's gotten pretty competent when it comes to staying off Securi-Tech's recorders."

"Fine. Let him know the *agent of record* is available at his convenience."

"I'll do that. And with that, we're done."

"Finally!" Amber said it more enthusiastically than she'd intended, but neither Dem nor Acamas seemed to notice. "All right, then, I'm going to discomm before you think of anything else demanding my attention."

Dem chuckled. "Have a good evening, Boss. Call if you need anything."

"I will. And thank you. Both of you."

The two AIs gave a slight bow, Demophon's more flourished than his sister's, and their faces faded from her screen.

A few minutes later, her comm chimed again. There was no name associated with the UID, but she figured it was probably Chief Fischer. She punched the icon again. "Payne here."

Sure enough, Chief Fischer's voice came through the speakers, but there was no video feed. That confirmed he was speaking on his burner comm. "It's good to hear your voice, Fem Payne. I heard you were wounded on that op. Pretty severely, from what I was told."

"I'm fine, Chief. But I appreciate your concern."

There was a short pause. "It sounds like we're on speaker. Are you where we can speak privately?"

"I am. I'm in my pod, driving home for some well-earned downtime."

"That's too bad."

"What?"

"I think I have something you need to see. Some*one*, rather."

CHAPTER 47

Amber pulled into the empty parking lot in front of PSC. The damage to the front was impressive, in a *Godzilla destroyed my building* sort of way. But most of the debris and fallen facade had been cleaned up, and a construction crew was already working on repairs.

Gibbs wasn't messing around.

There was also a Securi-Tech armored personnel carrier parked in the middle of the parking lot. She pulled up beside it.

Chief Fischer stepped out of the passenger's side of the APC and met her as she stepped out. He smiled warmly and opened his arms for a hug.

Amber stepped in and embraced the man who had been a father figure to her for so many years. "Since when are you a hugger?" she asked as she stepped back.

He lifted a single shoulder. "Since I nearly lost one of my favorite people the other night. Besides, I thought I might as well get one in before I have to start addressing you as 'Boss.'"

She blinked. "How did you know about that?"

"Richard mentioned it when we were organizing your follow-up operation the other night."

"You know it's not set in stone, right? I mean, we don't even know if Securi-Tech will be willing to sell your contract."

"Maybe. But you and I both know that they're all about the bottom line. And from what Richard hinted, I suspect you can offer large enough numbers that they'll drop me in a heartbeat."

"And you'll be okay with that? Starting over with a small corporation?"

"Let's see… I leave a corporation led by a board of barely ethical businesspeople who are only in it for the credits, who proved to me last year that they don't care about their employees and view them only in terms of what they can wring out of them. Instead, I come to work with people who have repeatedly shown a moral fortitude that I personally think we're in short supply of, get in on the ground floor of a new LEO firm… and I get a bump in pay? I'd say that's a no-brainer."

"I second that," said a gruff voice from inside the APC.

Amber leaned over to look inside and saw Commander Walker smiling at her. "I sure hope I can deliver, then."

"Speaking of delivering…" Fischer pressed his palm on the biometric lock beside the APC cargo door, and it slid open.

Curious, Amber frowned and stepped forward. The man inside the carrier was shackled, hand and foot, to restraining bolts on the floor and the bench on which he sat. He was blindfolded, gagged, and had sound dampeners over his ears, so he couldn't see or hear her.

But she recognized him right away. The blindfold only covered part of that scar—the one she had seen in so many nightmares for the last fourteen years. Dewey Trev.

Part of her wanted to hide or scream in terror and fury. Another part of her wanted to draw her pistol, press it to his temple, and pull the trigger. Instead, she stepped inside the APC as calmly as she could manage. Fischer followed and closed the door behind them.

Amber reached out and removed the man's blindfold so he could see her. Then she pulled out the ball gag and lifted the earmuffs off his head. He stared at her for several seconds.

"You're Dewey Trev," she said.

He grunted. "I'm aware."

"Do you recognize me?"

His eyes narrowed as he studied her face. After a moment, he shrugged. "Sorry. You gonna tell me I'm your daddy or something?"

"I think I'd cut my own throat if that were the case. No. Fourteen years ago, you and Carl Hartzman hit me over the head, strapped me to a table, and took out my eyes."

He sighed. "If you expect me to remember you from that, you're in for a real disappointment. I meet all sorts of people in the strangest ways."

That took her aback. After all these years, all the nightmares and therapy, the man didn't even know who she was?

"Wait a second," he said. "Hartzman? Man. That *was* a long time ago."

She nodded. "It was just about the time the Reaper showed up."

Trev's smirk faded. "The Reaper? What do you know about him?"

Amber cocked her head to the side. "Him? What makes you think the Reaper was a him?"

The man swallowed nervously. "You sayin' you're the Reaper?"

"No. As a matter of fact, I am unequivocally telling you I'm *not* the Reaper." She leaned closer to him. "You believe me, don't you?"

Trev looked past Amber to Fischer. "You're my witness here. This woman's threatening me."

Fischer furrowed his brow to show his confusion. "What threat has she made?"

"If she's the Reaper, then he… she's responsible for the assault and death of a bunch of people I knew. She's a killer!"

Fisher shook his head. "But I very clearly heard her tell you that she's *not* the Reaper."

"Yeah, but she didn't mean… she said it in a way that…"

Drawing on her enhanced speed and reflexes, Amber shot her hand out and gripped Trev's chin. "What's the matter, baby? Don't you want to party?" Before he could say another word, Amber shoved the ball gag back into his mouth. She slid the earmuffs and blindfold into place and took a deep, shaky breath before turning to face Fischer. "Let's get out of this van. It reeks of Trev."

Out in the parking lot, she finally let go. Her legs were cybernetic, but the will to control them wasn't. She sat on the dirty plascrete and leaned back against her pod. Needing to move but lacking the coordination to do anything more, she wrapped her arms around her knees and began to rock back and forth. After a few seconds, she felt the tears begin.

Fischer knelt in front of her and, after a few awkward seconds, asked, "Since when can you cry?"

The non sequitur caught her off guard, and she stopped rocking. She wiped her nose on her sleeve. "It's the new eyes."

"What, they're defective?"

She chuckled. "It's an upgrade."

He let the declaration hang for a moment before replying, "If you say so."

He sat and leaned back beside her.

After a few minutes, she calmed down enough to talk about it. "He didn't even know me. He didn't know who I was. All these years, and I'm not even a blip on his screen."

"This is an evil man, Payne. Truly evil. And you were just one of hundreds of victims. Maybe thousands."

She nodded, hearing him, knowing he was right, yet still unable to fully fathom the fact that after all this time—all the years of searching—she had finally confronted the source of her nightmares.

And he hadn't even known who she was. The only thing that had gotten through to him was… she jerked her head to look at Fischer. "You knew I was the Reaper, didn't you?"

He nodded.

"But you never told anyone. As a matter of fact, from what you said back at the hospital last week, I get the distinct impression you covered for me."

Fischer said nothing, only stared at the hedgerow across the parking lot.

Amber wasn't willing to let it go, though. She turned to look at his face. "You did, didn't you? You hid the records of what I was doing, buried it."

"I did." His smile was far away. "It wasn't difficult. The last thing Securi-Tech wanted was a link between one of their detectives and some vigilante who was assaulting alleged criminals without a trial. It would have been bad for business."

She snorted.

"No," he said. "They were all too happy to rubber-stamp my investigation and move us on to the next case."

"But why did you do it?"

"You mean besides the fact that it was the right thing to do?" He sighed. "There were a lot of reasons. For one, you were single-handedly running organ jackers out of the city. And you *needed* to be able to take action. I've seen good people broken by less traumatic things than what those men did to you. I wasn't going to let that happen to you if I could help it. You needed to be able to strike back against the… the unspeakable horror that had been committed against you." Fischer looked fiercely at her. "Even back then, I knew you were one of the best and most determined LEOs I had ever known. It was my job to help you realize your potential, to have your back when things got bad. That was the main thing, I suppose. You were one of my people, and I needed to have your back."

He looked away and took a deep breath. "Besides, it's not like you ever killed anyone."

"Are you sure? What about Hartzman? Remember him? Showed up floating in a ditch?"

Fischer shook his head. "You didn't kill him."

"You can't know that. Maybe I did, and I just managed to hide any evidence."

"You didn't."

"But you don't…" Her voice trailed off as she stared at him. "How can you be so sure?"

Staring across the parking lot into nothing, Fischer said, "A few weeks after you lost your eyes, I saw a report in the night sheets. It was a low-priority report of a gang fight in one of the low-income districts. I knew Securi-Tech wouldn't be interested in it, but there was a picture from a street-cam vid attached."

He finally looked at her, though Amber was beginning to wish he wouldn't. She was pretty sure she knew where his story was leading, and she dreaded what it might mean.

"The still caught my eye, so I opened the report. The vid wasn't great. It was dark, and the angle wasn't good. But I saw enough that I was pretty sure I recognized the person in the middle of it all. I did a little research and found that the building where it had happened had been a suspected chop shop that everyone ignored because there weren't any paying clients involved. Everyone just reported it to the municipal LEOs, who were too overworked to bother with it."

Amber was pretty sure she knew which fight he was talking about. There was only one instance where she had been forced to fight in the streets. It was early in her campaign against the organ jacker community, before she had refined her technique—the second or third chop shop she had targeted, and the jackers caught her while she was trying to break in. She was lucky there had only been two of them.

She knew now that she'd been lucky in a lot of ways early on, and the lessons learned had taught her what gear and strategies she needed to be safer and stealthier.

"When I realized you were hunting organ jackers," Fischer continued, "I went back through the sheets, looking for similar reports. I only found a few, and I obviously knew when you had gotten out of the hospital, so I knew you'd only been at it for a week or two at most. I was worried you might kill someone, and I didn't want you to lose a promising career over something like that."

"That's when you started cleaning up after me?"

"More than that. I started following you at night."

"You what!" Amber forced her voice back to a lower volume and continued. "You followed me?"

"I did. I didn't think you knew what you were getting yourself into, and I wanted to make sure you didn't get hurt." He chuckled. "It only took a week for me to realize that you knew *exactly* what you were doing. I watched you refine your skills and technique. I felt like a proud father."

He shrugged. "I knew what you were doing and why. And I knew it was illegal. But I also knew even then that the law had long ago turned into something that the rich used to get what they wanted. So I followed you and watched your back from the shadows.

"Then one night, I was watching as you snuck into a building. I knew by then that once you set your sights on a building like that, it was almost definitely a chop shop. I watched you break in, and a few minutes later, I saw four men pull up outside. Three of them went around back, where you had gone, and the fourth drove off in their pod.

"I knew by then that you could handle yourself in a fight better than I could, but I was still worried. So I snuck closer and hid near the front entrance in case I needed to bust in."

"When was that?"

"The night a shooter tried to kill you."

Her mouth went dry. "You were there that night?"

"Why do you think he only took one shot?"

"What?"

"The three jackers had only been inside for a few minutes when the pod the fourth guy had left in came back in a hurry. He was talking to someone on his comm, running for the alley where you had gone. He was in such a hurry he never saw me hiding in the shrubs."

Amber remembered the silhouette ahead of her as someone jumped out from around the corner ahead of her… the window shattering over her head… the deafening boom of the hand cannon as she ducked and ran to hide in the back.

"He was right in front of me, and he never saw me," Fischer said. "I had a knife. He was distracted."

"That was Hartzman?"

Fischer nodded. "I put his body in the back of his pod and drove him across town. Dumped him in a ditch, dropped his pod off in another neighborhood known for pod thefts, and hired a rental to take me back to get my own pod. I don't know if you remember, but I showed up late the next day."

Amber shook her head. "I don't remember."

The two of them sat in silence for several seconds.

Amber didn't know how to react or what to say. Apparently, Fischer didn't want her to say anything. He stood abruptly. "We received authorization to pass Trev and the other prisoners over to some people from Watervault Detention. According to my paperwork, they're sending several transfer vehicles over this afternoon. I just thought you needed to see Trev before he disappeared into some prison somewhere."

She couldn't tell him that she was probably going to have access to Dewey Trev anytime she wanted for many years to come. The last few minutes had just shattered much of what she thought she knew about the man, and she needed time to sort through it all.

She stood. "Thanks, Chief. I appreciate it."

He nodded and stepped close. Lowering his voice, he said, "I understand if what I said changes your mind about wanting to bring me on board here. There's no obligation and no hard feelings. But I wanted you to know what I'm willing to do for those I care about. And I figure it's better you know before you buy my contract, than after."

Amber realized that once she got past the shock, what he told her was the same thing the Fixers stood for. She recalled Maestro Harris's words.

We are Fixers. We step in when the law is inadequate.

"It doesn't change a thing," she reassured him. "But I have to ask. Why? Why did you risk so much to keep me out of trouble?"

After several seconds, the man blew out his cheeks before repeating what he'd said earlier. "You were one of mine. It was my job to have your back." Then Chief Fischer surprised her, reaching up and grabbing her by the shoulder. His gaze was fierce as he stared into her eyes. "I will *always* have your back, Amber. Remember that."

He turned, walked back to the APC, and climbed in without another word.

Amber watched the carrier drive away, thinking about what Fischer had told her. After a moment, she climbed into her own pod. She recalled Fischer's comment when he'd seen her team gathered around her in the garage beneath Silver Crest Hospital. He'd smiled at them and said, "I see you kept the band together." She knew now that he'd been wrong. The band wouldn't be complete until she was working beside the man who had looked after her for years—even when she hadn't known it.

She tapped an icon on her dash console, and Acamas appeared on her screen.

"Yes, fem?"

"Has Securi-Tech responded to our queries on buying out those contracts?"

"They accepted the bid on Walker, but they're pushing back on Fischer and Mikey."

"Do whatever it takes to get Fischer. I don't care what it costs, just get him for us."

There was a slight pause before Acamas replied. "You realize that might get expensive."

"I do. But he's exactly the kind of person we want running things."

Acamas nodded. "I'll take care of it. Anything else?"

"That's it for now."

"Then I'll get back to work. In the meantime, didn't you say you were taking some time off?"

Amber smiled at the thought. "As a matter of fact, I am. Thanks, Acamas. I'll talk to you later."

"No problem. Discomm, Boss."

"Discomm."

A mandatory week off. Her smile broadened as she opened the navcomp and tapped the HOME icon. She could think of worse things than a week off with the man she loved. Amber engaged the pod's autopilot and began the short drive home.

THE END

If you liked this book, there is a bonus preview of the next Amber Payne novel just past the *Acknowledgements* and the *About the Author* pages.

FROM THE AUTHOR

Thanks for reading *Payne of the Past*, the fourth novel in the Amber Payne series. The story will continue in the fifth (presently untitled) Amber Payne novel. There is a bonus preview at the end of this book.

INTERESTED IN A FREE, SIGNED COPY of *Payne of the Past*? On the first of each month for the first year after the novel is published, I will hold a monthly drawing for an autographed copy of this, or one of my other books. You can enter in one of three ways.

1. Join my mailing list (https://sendfox.com/jlbrackett). Each new signup will become eligible for the monthly drawing, OR...
2. Leave an honest review of the book on Amazon, then email me a copy of your review at jlb.author@gmail.com, OR...
3. Become a patron on my new Patreon page! Every patron will be eligible for the drawings AND will get to see first drafts of my works *as I write them.* (https://www.patreon.com/jlbrackett)

On the first of each month, for twelve months after the publication date, I will draw one name (or perhaps more) at random and email the winner(s) to get shipping information.

The offer ends twelve months after publication date.

AUTHOR'S NOTE

Those of you familiar with the Amber Payne books will probably recognize the name of Shamra Boggs. In earlier books, Shamra was little Davy's mother, who lived in the apartment next door to Amber's. She was always there for a meal, a cup of tea, or just a bit of advice whenever it was needed. I based that character on the real-life Sham, and that was how she really was.

Sham and her husband, Kevin, have been family to me and my wife, often driving up from Houston to stay with us for a few days, just to visit and relax. We would spend evenings playing chicken foot dominoes, enjoying a fire in the fireplace (one of Shamra's favorites), or going out to eat.

In October of 2021, she came to visit for the last time. She wasn't feeling well but thought it was simply a bout of diverticulitis, an ailment she had battled a few times in the past. The day after they returned home, she took a turn for the worse and had to go to the ER. X-rays and various scans later, doctors diagnosed her with late-stage pancreatic cancer.

We went to see her and Kevin just before Thanksgiving, and she was still her cheerful self – or as much so as could be expected. She was weak but had come to terms with things. Doctors told her that with the right treatments, they might be able to give her six months. A few weeks before Christmas, she took another turn, and they revised their prognosis. The cancer was more aggressive than they had anticipated, and they gave her weeks rather than months. There was no longer any need for treatments outside of pain management, no more hope.

We drove down to see her again on Christmas Eve. The cancer had taken a huge toll on her body, but her smile was still there. She was so weak that it was difficult for her to even talk, but we were able to stay with her for a few hours, speaking between bouts of strength and weakness. It was bittersweet with all of us knowing it would be the last time we would see her. During our conversation, my wife, Meloney, asked Sham what she thought I should do with the Shamra character in my books. With a wicked grin, she said she wanted her to go out in a blaze of glory, on the dance floor, saving Amber Payne.

Kevin told us later that she faded quickly after that visit. She passed away peacefully on December 28th around 4AM. And while I'm not a religious person, Shamra was deeply devout, and had an abiding love for her Lord. She had a sunny disposition, an ever-present smile, and an optimistic outlook that stayed with her to the very end. The world has a Shamra-sized hole in it now, and those of us who knew her will never be the same.

I know, pretty heavy stuff, right? But I'm a writer, and this is what I do. I conjure emotions from words. And you all deserve to know what a wonderful person Shamra was.

We'll miss you, Sham.

ALSO BY JEFF BRACKETT

THE HALF PAST MIDNIGHT SERIES

BOOK 1 – HALF PAST MIDNIGHT

Half Past Midnight is a post-apocalyptic thriller – the story of Leeland Dawcett and his family, in the first days and years after the Doomsday War. It's the story of how one man learns that survival sometimes just isn't enough, and of friends who help each other through thick and thin while facing the enemies who make life after Doomsday a living hell.

BOOK 2 – THE ROAD TO REJAS: A HALF PAST MIDNIGHT NOVELLA

In the post-apocalyptic world of Half Past Midnight, Mark Roesch was the quiet guy - the gentle giant. The people of Rejas learned to count on him during the hard times after D-day. But every survivor had a story from before... and most of those stories dealt with the deaths of friends and loved ones.

BOOK 3 – YEAR 12: A HALF PAST MIDNIGHT NOVEL

Zachary Dawcett was eight years old on D-day, barely old enough to remember what life was like in the Old Days. He's a young man now. He's learned to live in this new world—learned to hunt and fight, and survive in the ruins of old East Texas. He, along with everyone else who survived the Doomsday War, have adapted to a new way of life. They have learned to accept that computers, electric lighting, automobiles, or any of the other conveniences they once took for granted are all things of the past.

Then, one night, Zachary spots a satellite in the sky - the first indication in twelve years that anyone is rebuilding. As events unfold, he is forced to question everything he thought he knew, and the decisions he makes will help determine the shape of a reemerging world.

THE AMBER PAYNE SERIES

BOOK 1 – STREETS OF PAYNE

When Alta Corp contracts Amber and her partner, Kevin Glass, to solve a case of high-stakes data theft, they will need every bit of their skill, experience, and determination to succeed. For the more they investigate, the more it becomes evident that this case is much more than it appears, and its resolution may forever alter the world in which they live.

BOOK 2 – THE PAYNE BEFORE THE STORM

When their supposedly secure, off-net research facility is hacked, Micronics Corporation hires Securi-Tech LEOs Amber Payne and Richard Kayani to find those responsible. The case quickly leads them down a rabbit hole of twists and turns they could never have anticipated. With the body count rising quickly, the only link seems to be a mysterious thunderbird tattoo.

BOOK 3 – PAYNE AND SACRIFICE

Taking down the nanite-enhanced Storm Bringers was only the beginning. Detective Amber Payne and her team of "strays" still have to find and capture the woman who created the super soldiers – former Securi-Tech board member, Carol Conley. And while Conley may be at the top of Securi-Tech's most wanted list, for Amber, the case is more personal. For Conley was responsible for the death of Amber's former partner, and she's determined to bring the homicidal maniac to justice

OTHER NOVELS BY THE AUTHOR

CHUCKLERS, VOLUME 1: LAUGHTER IS CONTAGIOUS

It begins as a system of beautiful, bioluminescent patches floating along ocean currents. But its beauty brings laughter. And the laughter brings madness.

A schizophrenic narcissist on an ocean cruise, a college student called home to settle her uncle's estate, and the head of a Houston survivalist group find themselves caught up in the outbreak of the disease known as Kampala Syndrome. Will any of them survive the heart-pounding battle for survival in a world gone insane?

PANGAEA EXILES

Tried and convicted for his crimes, Sean Barrow is sent into temporal exile—banished to a time so far before recorded history that there is no chance that he, or any other criminal sent back, has any chance of altering history.

Now Sean must find a way to survive more than 200 million years in the past, in a world populated by monstrous creatures that would rend him limb from limb if they got the chance. And that's just his fellow prisoners.

The dinosaurs are almost as bad.

SHORT STORIES BY THE AUTHOR

APEX (IN THE PREHISTORIC ANTHOLOGY VOL.1)

A team of operatives is sent to assess and neutralize a suspected biological terrorist threat deep in the jungles of Bolivia. What they find is far beyond anything they've been trained for. Yet, the fate of the world hinges on how they respond.

THE BURNING LAND

The kapin and crew of a primitive sailing ship on a world with green skies and red seas seeks a land of legend. A 400-year-old generation ship crosses the vast emptiness of space. Two vastly different expeditions, pushing the boundaries of possibility. See how they intertwine in "The Burning Land".

GHOST STORY

An abandoned hunting lodge is rumored to be haunted. When Sima and her team investigate, what they discover is more terrifying and dangerous than anything they ever imagined.

The most recent information on Jeff's publications can be found on his Amazon Author Page.

For advance information on new releases, sign up for his mailing list at https://sendfox.com/jlbrackett. Or to read his works *as they are being written*, you can support him on Patreon at: https://www.patreon.com/jlbrackett.

ACKNOWLEDGEMENTS

Here's to all you folks who helped get me through this one. So many people offered advice and the occasional commiserative shoulder. But there are those of you who deserve special recognition… who volunteered your names, your time, and in the case of my Patreon patrons, actual money.

This is the section in which I give recognition where it's due.

Amber Brackett - The inspiration for Amber Payne. We love you, daughter.

Jordan Dyer - Our "adopted" daughter whom we seldom get to see anymore.

Scott Pond - Whose character started as a redshirt, but refused to die.

Shamra Boggs - We miss you, Sham.

And to the other friends and acquaintances who helped in a million different ways: Anthony Staton, Brent A. Harris, Carl Hartzman, Cassie Robertson, Curtis "CC" Miller, Izabela "Iza" Ewa Warszawska, Joani Loveless, Kevin Boggs, Missy Eaton Hutson, Nathan Pedde, Stefanie Spangler Buswell, Tinasha Gibbs, Tracy Pierce Malloy, and any others I might have missed.

My heartfelt thanks to each and every one of you!

ABOUT THE AUTHOR

Jeff Brackett is the author of the "Half Past Midnight" series, the "Amber Payne" series, "Chucklers, Volume 1…" and other novels, short stories and novellas published in magazines and anthologies. After having lived almost his entire life in and around Houston, 2014 presented several life changes that brought him and his wife to Claremore, Oklahoma. There, they found a nice little house with a much larger yard, and are adjusting to the new lifestyle quite well. Jeff has even begun learning to garden.

His writing has won Honorable Mention in the action / adventure category of the "Golden Triangle Unpublished Writer's Contest", first place in the novel category of the "Bay Area Writers League Manuscript Competition", and was a finalist in the science-fiction/fantasy/horror category of the "Houston Writer's Conference" manuscript contest.

His proudest achievement, though, is in having fooled his wife into marrying him more than thirty years ago, and helping her to raise three wonderful children. He is now a grandfather five times over.

And his gardening? Well, let's just say he still has a bit to learn in that area.

You can follow Jeff's blog and sign up for notification of his latest publications at http://jlbrackett.com

BONUS PREVIEW

AN EXCERPT FROM BOOK 5 OF THE AMBER PAYNE SERIES

Amber arrived at the scene just before sunrise. There were no people there, no bodies, no witnesses. There was nothing but the temporary barricade marking the road before her as unsafe.

That was fine though. She wouldn't be interviewing witnesses or persons of interest this morning. This was nothing more than fact-finding, and it was better done without anyone's knowledge outside her organization.

The Fixers didn't work the way she had been trained at Securi-Tech. In a manner of speaking, they worked outside the law. During her training with them, one of the things they had stressed was that the Fixers worked outside the law in order to protect the law.

That wasn't to say they didn't have their own rules and regulations. To an outsider, they might appear to be a rogue element, but the truth was that they were very strict about their internal policies and procedures.

And if a Fixer were to break one of their internal regulations, the punishments were also outside the law. Rumor had it that some of the more egregiously rogue agents had sometimes simply disappeared. Not just killed, but their existence had been erased. By the time the Fixers were done, it was as if the rogue had never existed. Fixers did whatever needed to be done, in order to preserve society.

She got out of her pod and approached the safety barrier. It was a standard holo-barrier, designed to block the view of onlookers and record anyone passing through. She also knew from past experience that passing the barrier was supposed to trigger an alert to whatever company was currently investigating the incident. She'd worked behind many such blockades during her time with Securi-Tech.

In this case, though, she doubted the barrier was linked to any LEO firm. There currently wasn't any indication an actual crime was involved. According to her files, this was nothing more than a simple structural failure, albeit a major one. This was a major feeder that allowed vehicle traffic to merge onto one of the giant, cross-country highways. It was a giant spiraling corkscrew of a road… a six-tiered cloverleaf design that allowed a vehicle to move from ground level, all the way to the Intercontinental Highway, nearly a hundred meters above.

And while the on-ramp to the highway was huge, Amber still didn't understand why the Fixers were interested in a case involving simple materials failure. She had read through the files three times last night and didn't see how such a thing rated as the kind of case to attract their attention. Did they perhaps use such cases on trainees, in order to test them, somehow? Or was there more to the case than was immediately apparent?

Her reverie was interrupted by the approaching whine of another vehicle. She reached into her vest to reassure herself that she had her Federal Investigator badge. She did. The badge was fake, of course. But it would stand up to any scrutiny, up to and including a call to Federal Investigation Unit headquarters. The Fixers were so tightly woven into the bureaucratic underbelly of society that, any such ID they created was backed by a digital backstory and history that was indistinguishable from the real thing. It was, for all intents and purposes, a completely real identity.

But the badge proved unnecessary, for the moment. As she switched her eyes to telescopic, she recognized the vehicle approaching as Richard's single-wheeled uni. She waited as he pulled up beside her pod.

"Hey boss," the gigantic street banger said by way of greeting. He dropped the forward kickstand and swung his leg off the physics-defying vehicle as the gyro and fans powered down. "Cracked the case yet?"

She chuckled. "Thought I'd wait for you guys first. I can't do all the work, you know."

He grinned and walked toward the barrier. "You seen the damage?"

"Nope. I was just about to go in."

"Don't."

The single word came from the comm unit hanging on her belt. She unclipped the comm. "Dem? Is that you?"

"Of course. And I don't think you should cross that barrier just yet."

"Why is that?"

"If you guys would climb into your pod, I can show you on your dash screen."

Amber raised an eyebrow at Richard, who simply shrugged and waved a hand at her pod in an "after you" motion. She went to the far side, climbed in and waited while the much larger man struggled himself into the other seat. It occurred to her as she watched him that she really should get a larger pod… something large enough to accommodate her colleagues. After all, she could afford it now.

The thought still caused her to shake her head.

After several seconds, Richard settled into the passenger's seat beside her. At least she'd had the foresight to have the seats customized where he could slide them back to fit his herculean frame, though barely. "Comfy?" she asked.

"As comfy as it gets in here."

"Okay Dem," she said. "What do you have?"

The dash screen lit up with the face of a young man with glowing purple hair. "Hey guys. First, you might want to know that this isn't the only road failure like this in the area. There have been two others in the last three days."

Amber thought about it briefly before shrugging. "So what do you think? A bad batch of material?"

"Possibly. I'm waiting on reports from the foundries," he said. "But the real problem isn't the bridges. As of this morning, several people who have come into contact with these three bridges have fallen ill."

"With what?"

"No one seems to know. The symptoms vary from person to person. Some are fairly mild, some pretty severe. The only commonality is that they all got sick within hours of coming into contact with the bridges."

Amber fell silent, thinking. "How many people?"

"Twelve, so far. There may be more with symptoms so minor that they aren't seeking medical aid yet."

"What kind of symptoms? I know you said they vary, but give me some examples."

"Would you like me to wait until Fem Dyer and Mr. Pond join you? They're pulling up to the maintenance road now."

Amber turned to see lights pulling around the corner. "Are they in Scott's van?"

"They are."

"Good. Ask them to pull up beside us here and open the side door." She looked over at Richard. "I'm sure the big guy here would appreciate a roomier vehicle."

"Yes, he would," Richard said.

A minute later, they were climbing into Scott's armored half-track cargo van. The side door slid closed behind them as Amber followed Richard into the spacious interior.

"Thanks for hosting the party," Amber said.

"Sure. Dem has been catching us up."

"Dem, are we all up to the same point?"

"Mostly." A holographic figure popped into being in the cargo area. After working with T-bone last year, Scott and Jordie had installed holo-projectors to allow easier interactions with Demophon and Acamas, T-bone's digital offspring. Dem was wearing a white cloth wrapped around himself. A toga, he called it. He also had a little wreath of leaves on top of his head. It was his latest affectation. He claimed to be embracing the ancient myth of Theseus and Demophon after which T-bone had named his children. He didn't always wear the same thing, but she had noted that it seemed to be his garb of choice whenever he was in lecture mode.

Sure enough, he started his presentation. "You already know there were three road failures, not just this one. The first was a week ago… a bridge that crosses over the runoff from the Washburn Sanitation facility. The second was the next day. A small, hundred-meter bridge over Tapio Creek."

Amber interrupted. "Can you show the locations on a map?"

"Sure." A map popped up on the wall. Two red dots flashed at the locations of the two bridge failures.

"Add this ramp to the map."

A third red dot flashed and they all studied the map.

"Anybody see a pattern?" she asked. "Because I sure don't."

The dots were in different parts of the city. One was a small bridge over a waste management facility, the second over a natural creek, and this one, the largest, was a major traffic overpass.

No one had any ideas.

"Tell us about the on-ramp here."

A satellite view of the on-ramp took the place of the map on the wall. "The MacDonald on-ramp to the 874 Intercontinental is one of the larger ramps in the city. Since I-874 is a raised roadway, and the MacDonald ramp starts from one of the lower levels of town, it rises over a hundred meters above ground level, on a spiral on-ramp."

The picture changed to a still shot of the section of the spiral that had failed. "Three days ago, there was a catastrophic failure, approximately halfway up the ramp. A fully loaded, cross country hauler fell completely through the third tier of the spiral, and hit the tier beneath, which caused that section to partially collapse. The hauler went over the side, where it fell the remaining thirty meters to the ground below. The driver died on impact."

A picture of the wreckage showed the smoking ruins of the mangled hauler on the ground beneath the ramp.

Amber winced at the sight. "How does that lead to these illnesses? Could it have been whatever he was hauling?"

"Not likely," Dem said. "The hauler was loaded with home electronics. Inspectors have already gone over it."

The picture changed again. This time it showed a headshot of a middle-aged man with non-descript, short, brown hair. "This is Jeff Lawrence. He's an inspector with the Federal Transportation Infrastructure Board.

When the first bridge failure was reported, he was dispatched to find out what happened. His report was inconclusive, and requested follow-up inspections with the foundry where the material was manufactured, as well as with the fabrication facility where the beams were printed."

"What were his findings?"

"He never made it to the appointments. He reported feeling bad the day after he inspected the bridge, and called in sick. Last night, his wife called for medical assistance, reporting her husband was unresponsive and having seizures."

The picture changed to a video of a man on a hospital bed. It was the same face, but this man jerked repeatedly, obviously in the throes of a seizure.

"Any idea as to the cause?" Jordie asked from the driver's seat.

"Not yet," Dem said. "So far, the doctors seem to be at a loss."

The picture changed again. "This is Jonetta Miller. She's a heavy equipment operator who was called in on the Tapio Creek failure. She worked for two days on the bridge repair. She led her crew and got the bridge repaired. The next day, she called in sick. She went into an emergency care center with severe stomach cramps, nausea, and vomiting. Doctors can't find the cause."

Demophon put several other pictures up on the wall in a grid. "More than a dozen people who came into contact with these bridges are now in various hospitals or clinics. There's no discernable pattern or symptomology... just people who came into contact with these three bridges and got sick."

"Any other bridge failures? For that matter, any other structural failures at all... buildings, public transport... anything?"

Demophon shook his head. "Nothing in more than four months. And before you ask, I've checked the construction records for all three bridges. They all used materials that were printed at different locations, by different companies. And none of those companies got their raw materials from the same location. From what I can tell, there's no common factor here." He shrugged. "I can tell you this, though. I wouldn't suggest you get any closer to the damage site than that barrier outside. There's just too many unknowns."

Made in the USA
Columbia, SC
24 July 2022